INIQUITOUS LIVES

by

Richard Gardner

Grosvenor House
Publishing Limited

This book is published by
Grosvenor House Publishing Ltd
28-30 High Street, Guildford, Surrey, GU1 3EL.
www.grosvenorhousepublishing.co.uk

A CIP record for this book
is available from the British Library

ISBN 978-1-78148-221-6

Other novel by Richard Gardner

'Righteous Release'

CHAPTER ONE

"And who is that?" asked Joy Adamson.

Hilary Chambers gazed down sadly at the photograph.

"That is David, my youngest son," she replied, with an unmistakable fondness in her voice. "Good-looking young man," smiled Joy approvingly. "Hope I will have an opportunity to meet him while I'm here in England."

Hilary seemed slightly uncomfortable.

"I'm afraid that is highly unlikely. You see, we haven't spoken to David for eight years. Not since he rejected the word of the Lord."

"Oh, how dreadful for you," gasped Joy. "Do you find it difficult to talk about?"

"Yes, I do," answered Hilary, closing the photograph album and gently pushing it to one side.

"Even after all this time, the memories are still painful."

Joy had flown in from New York the previous day. A single American lady, it was her first visit to Britain for many years, having been invited to spend a fortnight as a guest of the Chambers family. Like her, they were devout followers of an extreme Evangelical sect.

The Eternal Fellowship believed in separation from the rest of the human race. Followers were forbidden from enjoying pleasures that most of us would regard as essential in order to remain sane in a stressful world. TV, the cinema, reading newspapers and enjoying a pint down at the pub were just a few of the pastimes that were not permitted.

The spiritual leadership expected their followers to marry other believers. However, having fallen in love with somebody from outside the faith, David had avoided religious meetings in order to be with the woman of his dreams. Such a course of action inevitably led to his expulsion from the Fellowship and his banishment by both family and friends.

"Does David have a family?" enquired Joy, eagerly selecting a chocolate éclair from amongst a plateful of cream delicacies that Hilary presented to her.

"He has a stepdaughter and two of his own," replied Hilary, as her hand was about to swoop down on a bun with a generous topping of jam and cream. "From time to time, David sends us letters whenever anything eventful happens in his life."

For a while, the two women sat in silence. Conversation would have been difficult while their mouths bulged with the sumptuous delights that they were busily consuming. Such moments of total bliss are meant to be savoured.

"You know, the Fellowship are less strict than they used to be," said Joy, having finally stopped eating. "I'm sure that nobody would object if you were to make contact with your son."

Hilary shook her head.

"John would never agree to it, unless David were to return to the Fellowship. I'm afraid my husband is a very stubborn man."

"But what about your other children?" asked Joy thoughtfully. "Wouldn't they like to see their brother and his family?"

Hilary wiped a tear from the corner of her eye.

"I know they all would. None of them want to get in touch, though. They are all frightened of upsetting their father."

"Such a shame," sighed Joy.

Anxious to change the subject, Hilary offered her guest another mouth-watering cake. Hardly a day went by when she didn't weep for her long-lost son. She often prayed that David and John could be reconciled once more. Sadly, even after eight years, her prayers had yet to be answered.

* * *

The door was wide open. From where he was standing on the landing, David could see clothes scattered on the floor, drawers half open and a tangled up duvet on the bed. He was already in a bad mood, and the chaos made him feel a whole lot worse.

David began descending purposefully down the stairs. His stepdaughter was now eleven, and he decided it was time she learnt to keep her room tidy. If her mother wasn't prepared to say something to her, then he would.

Amanda was sitting in an armchair watching TV when David burst into the lounge. The blonde-haired little girl was alone, as the rest of the family were elsewhere in the house. The only living being present was a white hamster scurrying around in its cage on the sideboard.

"Will you tidy up your bedroom, please?" barked David. "I've never seen such a mess in all my life."

"Later on," replied Amanda sulkily. "I want to watch this programme first."

"Do it at once!" ordered David, even more angry now that his authority was being challenged. "Leave me alone!" shrieked the girl. "You're not my real dad!"

"Don't answer me back!" replied David, raising his voice even more.

Sobbing violently Amanda rushed out of the room. Looking for sympathy, she headed straight for the kitchen, where Alison was preparing the evening meal. Her mother could always be relied upon to support her against the big, nasty bully. Mum had never been known to disappoint.

After switching off the TV, David lowered himself into an armchair. He could just about hear his stepdaughter, who, between short, sharp sniffs, was repeating the harsh words that had just been said to her. More audible were Alison's responses as she was made aware of the injustice that had just taken place under her roof. Soon she was pounding down the hall with a look of menace scrawled all over her face.

"Why must you keep bullying Amanda?" she demanded, as she pushed open the lounge door. "Because she needs to keep her bedroom tidy," protested David.

"But Amanda is only eleven years old, for goodness sake," snapped Alison, with her hands placed defiantly on her hips. "However, as it seems to bother you so much, I'll go upstairs right now and straighten up her room."

"You spoil that girl," said David scornfully.

"That is my business, not yours," replied Alison bitterly. "If you don't like the way I bring up my daughter, then go and live elsewhere."

The heated confrontation rather fizzled out after that. However, once Alison had stormed out of the lounge, David sat back and began to brood about his life in general. Amanda wasn't the only young person who was creating problems for him. There were many much more disruptive ones that he had to face in the classroom each day.

The following evening, he joined several colleagues down at the pub. Along with three fellow stressed out teachers, he clustered around a table at the far end of the bar. Having spent his working day surrounded by teenagers, it was a relief to be able to settle down with some adult company at last.

As chance would have it, David was sitting opposite Sophie Duncan. Having started at the beginning of term, she was the newest member of the teaching staff at Brookway Manor Secondary School. In her mid-twenties, she was pretty, intelligent, and as far as anyone could establish, appeared to have no male attachments.

Sophie taught English to the lower age group classes. Although academically gifted, she was experiencing difficulty in maintaining control of the pupils during her lessons. Unable to stamp her authority, she tried initially to solve the problem by reporting the main offenders to the headmaster. However, this measure proved to be ineffective, as the man at the top was incapable of keeping order himself.

"I just don't think I'm cut out for teaching," she sighed despondently.

"I know the feeling," said Ken Truman, a small, studious-looking man in his fifties, who taught science. "I get bullied by my students all the time."

There were nods of agreement from around the table. Each one present understood the frustration of trying to educate young people who had no interest in learning. Many pupils, they all believed, seemed to regard school as little more than a social club – a place where they could meet up with friends for a laugh and chat each day.

As the evening wore on, though, the gloom lifted. With the long summer holidays only weeks away, they forgot all their problems in the classroom and turned their thoughts to foreign travel. As all four teachers had plans to visit a different part of the globe during the extensive break ahead, the little group had much to talk about.

Soon after nine, Ken prepared himself to leave. Having gulped down the remaining three inches of beer in his glass, he stood up and put on his jacket. With the assistance of a moderate quantity of alcohol and some pleasant conversation with like-minded people, he was looking considerably more relaxed than the science teacher who had walked out of the school gates earlier that evening.

"Are you ready to leave?" he smiled.

Laura Nixon, the fourth member of the group, reluctantly climbed to her feet. A music teacher who could play a variety of instruments, she was plump and always applied a generous amount of make-up to her round face. Now over fifty, she longed to retire on a good pension and a stress-free life.

"My car is off the road this week and Ken is my acting chauffeur," she explained with a laugh. David was about to announce his departure, too, but quickly changed his mind. At that moment, Sophie was showing no inclination to leave, so he decided to keep her company for a little longer. It also meant he would have time to finish his beer at leisure, rather than having to gulp it down.

"Won't your wife wonder where you are?" asked Sophie, once Ken and Laura had left the pub. David shook his head.

"I phoned Alison earlier to say I would be late. She allows me off the leash sometimes if I am lucky."

Sophie looked down thoughtfully into her half-empty wine glass. "Do you get on well with your wife?"

For a split second, David hesitated. His marriage to Alison had always been a happy one, although recently there had been a few niggles. Their argument over Amanda's untidy bedroom the previous evening was just one example.

"We have our ups and downs," he smiled. "No relationship can be perfect all the time." "Marriage has never really appealed to me," said Sophie. "I enjoy my independence too much."

At that moment a young bar attendant arrived at the table to remove the empty glasses. As he went about his task, he exchanged a warm smile with Sophie. It was only when he had loaded up his silver tray and wandered away, that the two teachers continued their conversation.

"Any boyfriends in your life?" asked David with a sly grin.

"They come and go," replied Sophie, as she ran her slender fingers up and down the stem of her wine glass.

David realized that he was beginning to feel attracted to the young woman. It intrigued him that she should wish to avoid any lasting relationships in her life. There was one question, though, that interested him even more. What type of people, he wondered, were these boyfriends who simply came and went?

He might have discovered more, but at that point, the conversation was cut short. Having answered a sudden call on her mobile phone, a guilty expression immediately appeared on the English teacher's face. Standing up to leave, she smiled apologetically at her drinking companion.

"It completely slipped my mind," she said. "A friend invited me round to her place for a meal and I'm already half an hour late."

Having been left on his own, David decided it might be a good time to leave, as well. However, while driving home, he couldn't help thinking about Sophie and wondering about her social life. In his experience, it was rare for an attractive woman not to be in a permanent relationship.

The following evening David had a visitor. From time to time, Simon would drop in and update him with news of family and friends with whom he had lost contact. People, in fact, who had abandoned him for disregarding the beliefs of the religion in which he had been brought up.

At the age of twenty-three, David's life had dramatically changed. For a while, he had been contemplating breaking off his engagement to Ruth, a rather assertive young woman he was beginning to dislike intensely. That in itself would have been a bold move, as his fiancée was a committed follower of the sect. Any termination of this arrangement would have been met with strong disapproval by the church hierarchy.

However, what David did next was unforgiveable in the eyes of the Eternal Fellowship. He struck up a relationship with Alison, somebody he had been at school with and a non-believer. Then, when it was discovered that he was going out delivering political leaflets with her, instead of attending religious meetings, there was outrage. He was immediately expelled from the sect.

It was a traumatic experience for the young man. Having been living with his parents, he was suddenly forced to leave the creature comforts of home and look for alternative accommodation. Then, to make matters even worse, his employers, who were also followers of the Fellowship, dismissed him from the only job he had ever known. Suddenly he was cut adrift in the real world, which held many mysteries for him.

However, very soon, he began to appreciate some of the pleasures that had always been denied to him. Having rented a room in a hotel as a temporary arrangement, he had access to a television set for the first time in his life. It was an exciting experience, and very soon he was hooked on the rich variety of entertainment that this little box had to offer. Suddenly, a whole new world was opening up to him, as he was introduced to parties, dancing, cinema and many other pleasures.

Politics, too, was to play a major part in his new existence. Alison was an enthusiastic Labour Party activist, so David had also decided to become a member, in order to further his relationship with her. Not only did the ploy work, but he was also able to make friends and join forces with people who spent their time canvassing voters and poking leaflets through their letter boxes.

At first, everything seemed perfect. However, David soon experienced problems adjusting to his new way of life. He had been taught by his parents to avoid much that went on in the outside world, where the Devil ruled supreme. Now, though, he was forced to become very much a part of it.

At times, David felt like an outsider. Knowing so little about a lifestyle that most people regarded as normal, he was laughed at by work colleagues and looked upon as a bit of an oddball. In fact, the situation depressed him so much that he actually asked to be taken back into the Fellowship – a request that was, incidentally, rejected, after he refused to accept one of the conditions that would be imposed upon him were he to return.

The Fellowship had appointed a committee to decide on whether David should be invited back.

Finally, an agreement was reached, whereby he would be permitted to return to the fold, providing he married a believer with a strong Christian faith. However, on learning that the wife they had in mind for him was Ruth, he was horrified. With unpleasant memories of the woman he had once been engaged to, he stayed in the real world and eventually ended up marrying Alison.

Now eight years on, David still had practically no contact with anyone within the sect. However, two followers who had remained loyal to him were Simon and Rebecca, the Broadbent twins. Having formed a close bond with him throughout their childhood, they couldn't bring themselves to sever those ties. At senior school, they had been in the same class and had suffered abuse and ridicule from other students. Having been persecuted for obeying their parents and trying to remain separate from non-believers inevitably brought the threesome even closer together.

Today, Simon had arrived on his own. Rebecca, who had moved away after her marriage some years before, wasn't so frequent a visitor. Now, with a young family of her own, it was often difficult to get away for any length of time. Nevertheless, she was always keen for her brother to report back to her with any news he had about David whenever the two men met up.

"Martha is pregnant again," smiled Simon, as he sat back in his armchair.

David beamed with delight. This would be his youngest sister's fourth child, yet he had never set eyes on the three already born. He would have enjoyed being a good uncle to them, but that was never likely to happen under the circumstances.

"When is the baby due?" he enquired.

"About September or October I believe," replied Simon, who was always vague about such details.

"I hope she will be able to cope with so many children," said David, as he lifted up his mug from beside his foot on the carpet and took a sip of tea.

Simon grinned.

"She seems to manage perfectly well at the moment. I'm certain that another one won't make any difference."

"I'm sure she is a wonderful mother," smiled David proudly.

A sudden shriek prompted Simon to stand up and gaze out of the window. Looking out on to a large garden, he watched as three children chased each other on the lawn. There were two girls and one boy.

"They look bigger every time I come to visit," he muttered, as he resumed his seat again. "We must feed them too much," joked David. "Anyway, when do you become a dad?"

"The baby is due in about four months," replied Simon with a glowing smile. "At the moment, I'm finding it hard to take in."

"It's always the same with the first one," said David. "It will only register with you when a screaming little bundle is placed in your arms."

"There speaks a man of experience," laughed Simon.

At that moment, they heard a woman's raised voice. As both men stood up to gaze out of the window, on this occasion they could see Alison, who was in the process of taking washing off the clothes line, giving the two youngest children a threatening glare at the same time. The playful shouting that had been almost continuous for some while suddenly came to an abrupt halt.

"So do you have any more news from the world of the Fellowship?" asked David when he finally turned away from the window. "It must be a few weeks since we last met up."

Simon began to fidget uncomfortably in his armchair. The smile on his face had now given way to a look of sadness.

"I'm afraid your grandfather Chambers has had a stroke."

Immediately, David's jaw dropped. For about thirty seconds, he was speechless as the news gradually began to sink in. During this brief pause in the conversation, he simply sat gazing into space with a bemused look on his face.

"Has the stroke effected him badly?" he asked finally.

"I'm afraid so," answered Simon with a gentle nod. "According to your grandmother, he keeps saying that he wants to be with the Lord."

"Of course, there must be a chance that he will recover," said David, still trying to gather his thoughts. "Grandpa has always been so robust. In fact, I've never known anyone with so much energy."

Simon shook his head sadly.

"You are remembering him as he was eight years ago. Even before the stroke, your grandfather had become so frail that somebody needed to support him whenever he walked. These days he is just a shadow of his old self."

"What made him change so quickly?" asked David in disbelief.

Simon shrugged.

"Lots of people remain active until late in life, then suddenly go downhill very rapidly."

David was suddenly filled with remorse. Memories began flooding back to him of his childhood and happy times spent with his grandfather, like the occasion when they had rowed down the Thames together on a boat hired at Windsor. So absorbed were the pair of them in spotting wildlife on the riverbank, that neither of them realized that they were drifting far away from the original starting point. When they finally returned, a rather irate attendant, who was on the point of sending out a search party, demanded an extra fee for being nearly two hours late.

Until his departure from the Fellowship, David had always been close to his grandfather. Even in his late teens, he had often confided in him in a way that seemed difficult with his parents. Unlike some of the other followers within the sect, Bill Chambers could always be relied upon to provide a sympathetic ear without being judgmental.

"Could you please arrange for me to see him?" pleaded David.

"I'll see what I can do", Simon promised, as he stood up in preparation for leaving. "However, your father is likely to stop it from happening. He has never forgiven you for having forsaken the word of the Lord."

"You are probably right," sighed David wearily. "I would still appreciate any help you can give me in arranging something."

Simon immediately gave his friend a warning look.

"In the unlikely event that you get your wish, promise me one thing. Just say that we met accidentally in the street when I told you about your grandfather's stroke. Don't mention that we have remained friends over the past eight years. I was supposed to have cut you off like everyone else in the Fellowship."

David nodded reassuringly.

"Trust me."

CHAPTER TWO

Brookway Manor was a mixed secondary school. The pupils who attended were predominantly from the poorest area of Brockleby and examination results were well below the national average. Many seemed to regard the education process as a punishment, rather than a gift that could provide them with lifelong benefits.

History was David's specialist subject. Like most of his colleagues, he tried to make his lessons entertaining, as well as informative, but too often, it felt like a losing battle. Many of the young people that he was paid to teach were simply not interested. They just shut down their minds until the next break, or when it was finally time to go home.

David had a free period. Deciding to spend the time profitably, he headed straight for the staff room to mark a pile of essays. The papers that he had just collected up from Year Ten were on the causes of the French Revolution, and he was anxious to get down to work. He didn't want to spend the best part of the weekend sitting at home making numerous corrections in red pen.

Of course, in order to be most productive, David needed peace and quiet. It would be difficult to achieve much if a colleague insisted on unburdening him or herself with problems they were experiencing in the classroom. So his heart sank when he opened the door and spotted a white shoulder bag resting on the table.

Sophie Duncan was alone. Relaxing in a comfortable, but somewhat threadbare armchair that had seen better days, she was intently studying a newspaper. It was a few moments before she glanced up to see who had just arrived on the scene.

"Aren't you running a little late?" asked David, glancing down at his watch. "I thought you were supposed to be taking Year Eight for English."

Sophie immediately burst into tears.

"I just can't stand up in front of that class anymore," she sobbed. "Those kids just seem to spend the whole lesson taunting me."

As a fellow teacher, David was able to empathize. Earlier in his career, he had suffered panic attacks, moments before having to confront a roomful of difficult young people. Somehow, though, he had always managed to overcome his fears.

"Please don't upset yourself," he said gently.

Sophie dabbed her eyes with the small white handkerchief she had been holding.

"I need to find a job outside teaching," she confided, suddenly sounding a little more composed.

"When you walked into the room a few moments ago, I was just scanning through the local paper to see if there was something that might suit me."

Still standing, David looked down fondly on the pretty young English teacher. Following the progress of a teardrop that was gradually trickling down her cheek, he suddenly felt very protective. Soft skinned, slender and with her fair hair tied up at the back with a bow, Sophie looked so vulnerable, like a small girl who had lost her mother.

"But you've only just qualified as a teacher," said David. "You have to give it more time before deciding to waste all that training."

"It's all very well for you", said Sophie resentfully. "The kids at this school seem to respect you, whereas they just laugh at me."

David quickly glanced down at his watch once again.

"Look, you're only ten minutes late for your lesson. Follow me and I will show you one way to keep those kids in order. Trust me, they won't give you any trouble today."

Reluctantly, Sophie got to her feet.

"Wait while I go and check my appearance in the ladies' loo," she said, managing a half smile. "It wouldn't do for that lot to see that I've been crying."

Very soon, the two teachers were standing outside the classroom. Sophie's spirits sank even lower as she listened to the shouts and laughter from within. Having already decided that she had chosen the wrong profession, she doubted whether all the help in the world could improve matters.

A look of grim determination suddenly appeared on David's face. Then, having glanced briefly at Sophie, he threw his hand forward to indicate that she was to follow him. In a split second, he pushed open the door and marched purposefully into the classroom, before coming to an abrupt halt beside a curly-haired youth, who just happened to be occupying the teacher's chair.

"Get back to your place, Radley, and be sharp about it," barked David, as he glared sternly at the thirteen-year-old (the average age of the class.)

Radley seemed to consider the situation briefly, before finally rising to his feet. Then, with a broad grin, he returned to his desk at the back of the class to join a clique of friends, who had obviously enjoyed his display of bravado. Several girls closer to the front turned around to give the hero a look of admiration.

"I'm glad that you enjoyed being entertained by Radley," said David, as his eyes wandered around the room. "Perhaps you would like a repeat performance tomorrow afternoon, when the rest of the school will be outside playing football and netball."

Howls of protest instantly rang out from around the class.

"But we have an important match with Calderwood," came a voice from the back row.

David turned his gaze towards a dark-haired youth sitting at a desk across the aisle from Radley.

Larkins was probably the most talented footballer in the class, although he excelled at practically nothing else. However, his parents, who could hardly be described as academically gifted, believed that their son was destined for a glittering career in the field of engineering.

"Then somebody from another class will have to take all your places in the team," replied David, before glancing briefly at Sophie, who was standing by the door.

"But Sir, the school team can't afford to play the match without some of us," said Larkins anxiously. "I am top scorer in the side and Radley is a brilliant goalkeeper."

"And what about Webb over there?" piped up Radley, who seemed to have lost his earlier swagger. "No forward can get past him at centre back."

"And what about the netball team?" called out Tracy Butcher, always the most outspoken female. "Who is going to stand in for some of us? Most girls in the school just aren't interested in playing outdoor games."

Immediately, other pupils were adding their voices to the discussion. Without exception, all were of the opinion that the sporting reputation of Brookway Manor would be greatly diminished were various pupils of Year Eight prevented from representing the school. In one quarter of the room, an argument actually broke out as to which footballer would be the greater loss to the school team.

Of course, David was bluffing. He had no wish either to spend the following afternoon in the classroom, when there was an opportunity to get out in the fresh air. Also, as a football enthusiast himself, he had been looking forward to the occasion almost as much as the boys who would be playing. He was as keen as anyone to see Calderwood take a good hiding.

"Be quiet, all of you," he shouted, before giving a glare in turn to all those pupils he knew to be the most disruptive. "Now I'm going to give you all one final chance. However, if I hear of just one single person causing trouble, the whole class will be sitting in here tomorrow for a lesson on good manners."

There was a brief silence as Year Eight reflected on the situation. The ringleaders, like Radley, hated the idea of yielding to authority in the presence of their friends. However, the very idea of being kept in of an afternoon instead of playing sports was far worse.

Suddenly turning her head around, Tracy Butcher provided Radley and his close neighbours with a threatening scowl.

"Just shut up for once will you," she snapped angrily. "You lot back there are always trying to spoil it for the rest of us."

"You can do your share of talking in class," retorted Radley scornfully.

"Right, well let's stop arguing and get down to work then," said David, before raising a warning finger. "However, I shall be speaking with Miss Duncan after her English lesson with you, just to make certain that everybody's behaviour has been impeccable."

"I shall give you a full report, Mr Chambers," answered Sophie in a loud voice, as David was about to leave the classroom.

Five minutes later, David was back in the staffroom, sipping tea. A nagging voice inside his head was instructing him to mark those essays on the French Revolution. But he was too concerned about Sophie to be able to switch his thoughts to more learned matters.

Later that afternoon, the two teachers met in the school car park. Having finished for the day, David was just about to drive away when he saw Sophie hurrying towards him. Immediately switching off his engine, he climbed out of his Ford Focus and closed the door with a gentle shove.

"How did it go?" he asked, with a mild look of concern. Sophie beamed with delight.

"Hardly a murmur from them. The only time that anybody opened their mouth throughout the lesson was when I asked a question."

"Sometimes it's just a matter of understanding these kids and the way their minds work," said David, who was feeling rather proud of himself for having brought about such a successful outcome.

"There is so much that I need to learn about teaching. I'll never be as good as you," said Sophie, with a look of admiration.

"It's all down to experience, really," said David, as he waved to the headmaster, who was just driving away. "Perhaps we could sit down together some time and I could give you a few tips."

Immediately, Sophie's eyes lit up. Then, having unfastened the catch on her shoulder bag, she started to rummage through the contents. Finally, she produced a small notebook, with a picture of a young girl on horseback displayed on the cover.

"Let me consult my diary," she muttered, while flicking through the pages.

"I suppose we could meet up in the pub one evening next week," suggested David.

"Better still, you could call round at my flat," replied Sophie, having finally arrived at the page she had been searching for. "It will be easier to talk if there is nobody else around to distract us."

"Perhaps you're right," replied David, just a trifle too eagerly. "Pubs do have a tendency to get noisy".

"Monday night is badminton and Tuesday I have my yoga class," said Sophie, as she studied her diary. "Look, how are you fixed for Wednesday evening?"

Unlike Sophie, David didn't have a diary to refer to. Although not so well organized in that respect, he generally managed to memorize his social engagements without difficulty. Therefore, without having to think too hard, he was able to provide a prompt reply.

"I'm free," he replied. "What time should I call round?" Sophie started to scribble her address on a scrap of paper.

"Make it just after seven. That will give me plenty of time to get changed and make the flat look a little more presentable."

Throughout their marriage, David had rarely kept secrets from Alison. But while driving home, he decided that it might be a good idea to make an exception on this occasion. Admitting that he intended to spend an evening alone with a young female teacher might just provoke a few very awkward questions.

It was several days before David received a telephone call from Simon. He could tell immediately from his friend's downcast voice that he was in for a big disappointment.

"Your grandmother says she appreciates your concern, but is trying to restrict the number of visitors coming to the house," said Simon. "Apparently, she is only allowing certain people to come and see your grandfather."

"Presumably she means those who have remained loyal to the Fellowship," said David acidly. "I think you can be pretty sure of that," replied Simon.

"Anyway, how is my grandfather?" asked David, having decided that venting his anger served very little purpose.

"Going downhill fast, I'm told," answered Simon. "Apparently, he is so weak that somebody has to feed him now. It is quite a strain on your grandmother but fortunately, the district nurse comes in every day to help."

It was nearly ten by the time all three children were in bed. Exhausted after a particularly stressful day, David was at last able to sink down into his favourite armchair and aim the remote control at the TV set. Deep down he was still brooding about the way the Fellowship continued to shun him. It was so sickening that even when an elderly relative lay dying, he was still refused permission to see them.

As he sat watching the news, he could hear Alison speaking on the telephone. Standing in the hall, she was engaged in one of those prolonged female-to-female conversations that would be beyond the stamina of most men. Finally, having concluded the mammoth dialogue with the person on the other end of the line, she came to join her husband in the lounge.

"Carol has just been saying that there is to be a meeting next Wednesday evening," began Alison, once she was comfortably seated. "It has been arranged to discuss the council by-election."

"I can't go," said David, immediately remembering that he had agreed to see Sophie the same evening. "I'm going out with several of the other teachers for a drink."

"Can't you put it off?" pleaded Alison. "Carol says it's very important that everyone attends."

David briefly considered the matter. Labour were keen to capture the seat, which was in the Sefton ward. In recent years, it had been held by a Conservative, until he had died of a heart attack several weeks earlier. The residents in this particular district of Brockleby were a cross-section of people. Hopeful of getting their candidate elected, all three major parties were starting to stage a very strong campaign.

"Look, they won't miss me this once," said David, who felt that party meetings were often little more than talking shops. "But I'm happy though to go out delivering leaflets."

"But you know that we all value your opinion," said Alison. "Surely your colleagues won't mind if you say that you have another engagement."

"Sorry, but I've promised to go down the pub and that's the end of the matter," said David firmly, as he turned the volume up on the TV in order to drown out his wife's voice.

Alison went off into one of her huffs. Wishing to demonstrate the extent of her annoyance, she stormed out of the room and slammed the door behind her.

On Saturday afternoon, David went for a short drive. Less than twenty minutes after leaving home, he pulled up outside a large detached house on the other side of Brockleby. The front garden, with its rockery and neat flowerbeds, was on a very steep slope, while the walls were spotlessly clean, as though freshly painted.

It was the first time in over eight years that David had come to visit the house. As a child, it had always given him a thrill to climb those twenty or so concrete steps to the top. He and his youngest sister would race to see who could arrive at the front door first to ring the bell. Being that much older than Martha, he was invariably the winner.

In the past, he could always be sure of a warm welcome. Those were the days, of course, before, in the eyes of the Eternal Fellowship, he had rejected the word of the Lord in order to serve the Devil. Now, as somebody who supposedly embraced the wicked ways of the world, he thought it more likely that he would be greeted with a certain coldness.

Having unfastened the metal catch on the gate, David began to make his ascent. Slightly out of breath from his steep climb, he was soon standing outside the light blue door that had been so familiar to him as a child. Then with a feeling of apprehension, he slowly lifted his hand up and rang the bell.

After a while he heard the voice of an elderly woman somewhere within the house. Then, after a brief silence, there followed a shuffling sound, which gradually grew louder. Finally, with the security chain in place to prevent intruders from forcing their way in, the door suddenly opened about six inches.

"Hello Grandma", said David cheerfully. "I heard that Grandpa was seriously ill, so I just stopped off to find out how he was."

"I'm afraid there has been no improvement in his condition," replied the old lady mournfully. "We are all praying that the Good Lord will take him soon".

"Could I just pop in for a few minutes to see him?" pleaded David, reasonably confident that he might never get the opportunity again to see his grandfather alive.

The old lady hesitated for a moment or so, still refusing to remove the security chain from the door. David was only able to see part of his grandmother's face through the small gap. However, clearly visible was the top of her snow-white hair, adorned with a bright blue bow.

"I'm afraid I can't let you in," came the sad, apologetic reply. "Oh, just for two minutes," pleaded David.

"No, I mustn't," answered the old lady, before finally closing the front door.

David swore under his breath. As he descended back down the concrete steps, he swung his foot angrily at a large stone and succeeded in kicking it over the front fence below and into the road.

As fortune would have it, the missile narrowly avoided a passing car by no more than a few feet.

꧁ ꧂

It was one of those sultry days in early May. With the windows open, mother and son were sitting sipping cool drinks, while relaxing in front of the TV at two o'clock in the afternoon. The programme they were watching was one of those mildly amusing repeated comedies. It had first been seen by viewers over a decade ago.

"I bumped into a friend in the high street this morning," said Joan Wright, when there was a break in the programme for adverts.

"Great," answered Mark, trying to sound more impressed than he really was.

"She was telling me that her granddaughter goes to ballet classes," continued Joan, as she created a slight breeze by fanning herself with a magazine.

"Very nice," replied Mark, with more than just an inkling as to how the conversation was about to progress.

"I wish I could talk to people about my granddaughter," said Joan, with a hint of resentment in her voice. "But unfortunately I haven't had any contact with her for eight years".

Suddenly, Mark, too, felt the pain of having lost touch with Amanda. Rising up from his armchair, he wandered over to the mantelpiece and lifted up her photograph. The pretty little three-year-old was kneeling on the lawn in the back garden, cradling a doll in her arms. It had been a warm summer day, and the child's blonde hair gleamed in the sun.

"Don't you think I miss her as much as you do?" said Mark miserably.

"Then why don't you insist that Alison allows you to see Amanda?" suggested Joan. "She is your daughter, after all."

Mark shook his head firmly.

"Alison would never allow it. I keep telling you that she detests me."

"That's hardly surprising, after the way you treated her," replied Joan, glaring accusingly at her son. "You were too lazy to get a job, so you used to borrow money from Alison just to waste with your mates down the pub. I don't know what she used to see in you, to be quite truthful."

Mark was in no mood to be lectured. Gently replacing the beloved photograph back on the mantelpiece, he walked out of the room and headed for the stairs. Due to his financial difficulties, he was left with no alternative but to live at home with his mother at the age of thirty-one. Because of their constant arguments, and with no money to go out and enjoy himself, he now spent most of his life in his bedroom playing music. It had been that way for a very long time.

CHAPTER THREE

Sophie Duncan rented a one-bedroom flat in Musselworth. It was situated on the top floor of a three-storied house that had once served as home to a succession of wealthy families. In the late sixties, a successful businessman had bought the large semi-detached property and converted it into several self-contained apartments.

Being high up, Sophie could enjoy a panoramic view over the rolling Kent countryside. Often, after a stressful day in the classroom, she would relax in an armchair by the window and gaze down on the landscape below. Listening to a Mozart or Beethoven CD, she would sip red wine, while attempting to shut out all thoughts of the unruly kids who made her life a misery.

Tonight, though, would be different. Instead of eating a ready-made meal straight from the microwave, she was busy in the kitchen peeling and chopping up vegetables, while carefully following instructions from a recipe book. It had been a while since Sophie had cooked for two and her guest, she decided, was a little bit special.

David had been advised not to eat before his arrival. Therefore, he was feeling ravenous by the time a tempting lamb dish with spices and mixed vegetables was served at eight o'clock. By then, he had provided his hostess with several tips on how to control a class of misbehaving kids.

"Confidence is key," he said as they sat down to dinner. "Never let the little buggers think that you are frightened of them."

"I'll never be able to control a class like you do," said Sophie as she sprinkled salt on her meal. "Just give it more time," replied David, with an encouraging smile. "At the beginning, I thought that I would never be able to cope with a crowd of rowdy teenagers – but the more experienced I became, the easier it got."

David took a sip of red wine. He had bought a bottle of Beaujolais on the way, as his contribution towards the meal. After that, there was a pause in the conversation as the pair of them got down to the serious business of eating.

"Does your wife know that you are spending the evening with another woman?" asked Sophie, finally breaking the silence.

It was a question that caught David off guard. For a split second, he was undecided as to whether he should tell the truth or not. Then some inner instinct prompted him to be honest. It seemed wise to let Sophie in on his little deception. After all, it was always possible that Alison might find him out, should the two women meet up at any time in the future.

"No," David confessed, feeling embarrassed at having to own up to his lack of integrity. "I told her that I was going out drinking with some of the other teachers."

"Would Alison be worried if she knew where you were right at this moment?" asked Sophie, with a mischievous smile.

"I'm not sure," answered David, having given the question a little thought. "Anyway, I decided to tell a fib in order to be on the safe side."

Picking up a little white jug, Sophie poured more gravy over her potatoes.

"Whether Alison worries or not depends on how much she trusts you," she said, having laid down the jug and resumed eating again. "Although in my experience, no man can be trusted."

Suddenly, the conversation came to an abrupt halt. After a quick apology to her guest, Sophie hurried into the hall to answer the telephone. It turned out to be a lengthy call, and by the time she returned to the table, David had eaten his meal, while hers had almost gone cold.

"Just a friend that I hadn't seen for a while," explained Sophie, as she lifted up her knife and fork once more.

"Right," said David, wondering why his hostess hadn't offered to ring the friend back once she had finished her dinner.

He was pleased to see that the main course was followed by a dessert. Then, when they had both finally finished eating, David helped Sophie stack up the dirty crockery in the kitchen. His offer of help with the washing up, though, was flatly refused.

"It can wait," said Sophie, as she opened a drawer on the sideboard and took out a pile of CDs. "Take a seat on the settee, while I try and find something soothing to play."

"I'm intrigued to find out about these men who come and go in your life," said David, once he had settled down where he had been invited to sit.

"They are guys who are looking for the same thing as me," explained Sophie, with a sweet smile. "A casual relationship without any strings attached."

"But supposing one of these gentlemen suddenly decides he wants something more serious?" asked David. "How would you shake him off?"

He didn't get an immediate reply. Having selected music that she felt would be suitable for the occasion, Sophie took the disk out of the red plastic case and placed it inside a shiny silver CD player. Then, having listened to the first few notes of a piano recording, she turned the sound down slightly, before settling down on the settee alongside her guest.

"In answer to your question," she smiled, "I just send them back to their wives."

"Are they always married men, then?" enquired David, who was beginning to feel aroused by the closeness of this very alluring woman.

"Nearly always," replied Sophie, who was sitting with her eyes closed and her head resting against the settee. "I find them more attractive than single men."

David recognized that a battle was raging inside of him. His loyalty to Alison was being tested to the full as he gazed down on his hostess, who was only inches away. Feeling reasonably confident that any tentative advances he made wouldn't be met with rejection, he decided it was time to act.

Turning slightly, he leaned over and kissed the silky white cheek closest to him. Without opening her eyes, a knowing smile appeared on Sophie's face as she raised herself up. Then, wrapping her arms around David's neck, she forced her lips against his.

Soon passions were reaching a peak. Quickly discovering that the settee hardly provided them with either the width or comfort for the physical activities in which they were desperate to engage, Sophie hurriedly led the way to the bedroom. Then, in a matter of a few moments, clothes were being removed with some urgency and thrown to the floor.

In the sexual frenzy that followed, David gave little thought to Alison. It was only when he had reached a climax and lay on his back staring up at the ceiling that he was finally troubled by feelings of guilt. This was the first time in his marriage that he had been unfaithful to his wife.

"I can't understand why you try to avoid being in a permanent relationship," he said, having joined Sophie under the duvet in order to cover up his naked body.

"Because romance begins to grow stale when you've been with one person for too long," explained Sophie with a sigh.

"But don't you want to have children?" asked David, taken rather aback by her somewhat negative response.

Sophie shuddered.

"Not if they are going to end up like the kids in Year Eight."

David quickly checked his watch. As all his clothes lay scattered on the floor, it was the only thing that he was wearing.

"Better be going," he announced as he pushed back the duvet. "Alison will start wondering where I've got to."

"Aren't you the lucky one?" laughed Sophie. "Out of one woman's bed and into another." As soon as he left the flat, David rang home. While apologizing to Alison for being late, he knew only too well, that he had far more to be sorry about. He had cheated on his wife and would have to live with the guilt.

As he was about to drive off, he received a call on his mobile. Tony, Carol's husband, was eager to know whether he was free to go out canvassing the following evening. As many people as possible, it seemed, were desperately required to go out door knocking in the Sefton ward.

Tony was the organizer for the Brockleby Labour Party. He had held the post for many years, as well as being a borough councillor. Unlike many who had signed up as members and then left, after having become disillusioned with politics, his commitment had always remained solid.

"I'll be there," replied David. "Then perhaps afterwards you can debrief me on what was discussed at the meeting tonight."

"Great," answered Tony, like a small boy who had just been told that his pocket money was about to be doubled. "I'll put your name down, then."

David sighed as soon as the party organizer had rung off. Like many political activists, he had never really enjoyed canvassing. He just did it out of loyalty to the party he believed in.

The next evening, the canvassers returned to party headquarters feeling rather downcast. They had called on some of the most expensive homes in the Sefton ward and the response from these affluent voters was far from encouraging. Hardly anyone had discovered a Labour Party supporter.

"Snooty lot," said David scornfully.

All those sitting at his table in the bar made similar disparaging remarks. The morale of the group had hardly been helped by the weather – the consensus being that they had been tramping the streets on a hot clammy night for a lost cause.

"I think that canvassing around that area is a complete waste of time," commented Kenny Simpson, a man with whom David had shared a house before he got married.

"That lot up there are rock-solid Tories and will never be persuaded to vote for anyone else."

"We need to target an area where the residents are more likely to be undecided," said Carol, the only woman in the group.

Tony, who was in charge of the by-election campaign, nodded at his wife's suggestion. "Next time, we'll try our luck in more promising territory."

"What do you think our chances are of winning this seat?" asked David, after he had taken another large gulp of bitter.

Thirsty because of his evening's exertions in the heat, he was quickly getting through his second pint. Fortunately, Carol had agreed to drive him home, so that he wouldn't get into difficulties with the local constabulary.

"On a knife edge at the moment," said Alec Stokes, having just managed to squeeze himself in at the end of the table.

Alec, a man in his fifties, was the Labour candidate for the by-election. Naturally, having been selected to represent the party, he was expected to do more of the canvassing than anyone else. As an enthusiastic activist for several years, and desperate to win, he could hardly be accused of failing in his duties. When not at work, every spare minute he would be out knocking on doors and speaking to householders.

"I have managed to find out something about the Tory candidate," announced Tony with one of his sly grins.

The others on the table looked towards him expectantly.

"Go on", said Alec eagerly, hopeful that his main opponent in the by-election had done some foul deed that might upset the voters.

"Well, in the literature that they are putting out, the Tories simply claim that Gavin Blake works for a large financial institution. Anyway, I have now discovered that he is actually an overseas investment manager for an American bank," said Tony with a self-satisfied grin.

The rest of the group looked rather unimpressed. Hopeful that Gavin Blake had been involved in a lurid sex scandal or photographed in the tabloids dressed as a Nazi in high heels, they found Tony's revelation something of an anti-climax. Not for the first time, it seemed, the election organizer was getting excited about nothing.

"So what if he does work for a bank? He's hardly committing the crime of the century," said David, with a look of amusement.

"But you must agree that bankers are hardly the most popular people on the planet," replied Tony, stroking his beard, which was laced with a few stray white hairs amongst the darker ones in the thick growth. "Having got themselves into a financial mess, some have expected the taxpayers to stump up huge sums of money to rescue their businesses. Then, to add insult to injury, the bastards at the top go and reward themselves with fat bonuses."

"Corporate greed," said Kenny in disgust. "It's about time the Government stepped in and nationalized these failing banks."

The suggestion was greeted with enthusiastic nods from all around the table.

"It annoys me when I hear Government ministers almost begging banks to lend more money in order to regenerate the economy," said Tony, getting on to his favourite hobby horse of the moment. "Why don't they just take control of these greedy institutions and make them work for the benefit of everyone?"

"So getting back to the original point," said Alec, eager to return to matters directly relating to the forthcoming by-election. "When is our next leaflet going to be produced?"

"At the weekend," answered Tony.

"Then why don't you include an article explaining exactly what Mr Gavin Blake does for a living?" suggested Alec.

Tony smiled as he was about to swallow the last drop of lager in his glass. "I already have."

Harvey Lucas was studying the racing pages. With a smouldering cigarette between his thick lips, he was sitting with a newspaper spread out over the steering wheel. Such was his concentration that he barely flinched when Mark Wright climbed into the passenger seat beside him.

There was no need for Mark to fasten his seat belt. The silver Porsche Cayenne would remain parked by the side of the road for as long as he remained seated in its luxurious interior. After all, this was no social occasion.

It was six o'clock in the evening. Harvey was there in his usual spot, where he liked to do business with clients.

INIQUITOUS LIVES

At times, these meetings could turn very violent and he had no wish to attract spectators. So a quiet little lane that bordered a cemetery on one side and Brockleby Woods on the other suited him perfectly.

"Last week you agreed to pay me two hundred quid off your outstanding debt," said Harvey, without looking up from his newspaper.

"I don't have it," answered Mark, attempting to sound bolder than he was actually feeling inside. "Then how much have you got?" asked Harvey, as he took the pencil from behind his ear, before placing a tick beside the name of a horse.

Mark could feel his heart thumping. At that precise moment, his entire worldly wealth consisted of three five-pound notes and a handful of loose change. However, he had no intention of parting with any of it.

"Look, I'm skint," he confessed, while fidgeting nervously in the passenger seat. "Just give me one more week and I swear you'll get the money."

Harvey threw his cigarette butt forcefully out of the window before turning to face the young man next to him.

"That's exactly what you told me *last* week," he snapped. "My patience is starting to wear a little thin."

Of course, the moneylender was quite correct. Mark had promised faithfully to pay two hundred pounds off his outstanding debt the previous week. As usual, though, he had no source of income from which to come up with the money.

Mark could best be described as an occasional worker – somebody who moved from job to job, but took long breaks between each one. In the past, he had managed to survive on state benefits, which by now had been stopped, and the financial support he received at home. Then his widowed mother finally made a stand and announced that she would no longer be providing her son with money. In future, he would either have to get a job and stick to it or go short, she warned.

The threat prompted Mark into action. With help from the job centre, he was hired the following week to serve behind the counter in an electrical shop. The pay wasn't excessive, but at least he would be able to afford the necessities of life and the occasional luxury.

By the end of the first month, the manager had become very impressed with his new assistant.

Each morning, Mark arrived at the shop on time, worked hard throughout the day and was courteous to the customers. He seemed like a man transformed.

Sadly, things went downhill after that. Having seen his first pay slip, he became excited at having received so much money and celebrated with a heavy drinking session down at the pub.

Then, after waking up the following morning with a splitting headache, he decided to take the whole day off without even bothering to ring in sick. On that occasion, he escaped with a mild warning, but when the same thing happened twice the very next week, he was told to leave.

As usual, Mark put his dismissal down to bad luck. He sought both sympathy and a loan to tide him over from his mother, once his money had run out, but he was given neither. Out of the goodness of her heart, she agreed to provide him with food and shelter, but nothing else.

Friends, too, refused to take pity. Many had helped him out financially in the past, but had never been repaid. In fact, over time, he had acquired the reputation of being something of a scrounger.

In desperation, Mark had turned to a moneylender – someone he had heard about who was unconcerned about the applicant's credit rating. There was no need to fill out lengthy forms or to own assets that could be used as collateral were the debtor to default on repayments. One could walk away with a wad of bank notes up to the value of a thousand pounds. It was only necessary to provide a signature and proof of address.

The business, which Harvey operated with a partner, was kept secret from the Inland Revenue.

Interest on loans was charged at an exorbitant rate of thirty per cent, the heavy cost of which often created substantially more financial difficulties for clients in the long term. However, with little sympathy for those desperately trying to make ends meet, each outstanding debt was ruthlessly pursued.

Harvey had served time in prison for violent assault, as had his business partner. Leo MacDonald, a Scotsman known to many as 'Mad Dog', was a giant of a man who had once been an amateur boxer. He was not only powerfully built, but also possessed a menacing look in his eyes. They warned of the danger that one was likely to face were they to upset him.

"Look, I will definitely pay you next week," said Mark anxiously, fearful of being thumped at any moment. "I'm starting a job on Monday and I shall ask for an advance on my wages."

Of course, it wasn't true. There was no job, but at least a lie might keep 'the heavies' at bay for a little longer. Hopefully, in seven days, he might devise a master plan that could just save his skin.

For a moment, Harvey was deep in thought. In his position, he couldn't afford to let anyone think that he was turning soft. Clients needed to be aware that he was a man without mercy. The success of his little business enterprise depended on it. With this in mind, grabbing Mark by the T-shirt, he wrenched him forwards until their faces were only inches apart.

"I want three hundred pounds by this time next week – otherwise, you are dead meat, my son," he snarled.

"I thought we agreed on two hundred," stammered Mark.

"I've raised it a hundred because you let me down today," replied Harvey, with a threatening glare. "Now get out of my car."

Mark was only too happy to obey. He was relieved at having emerged from the Porsche in one piece. Were he to be so lucky next week was another matter entirely. Somehow, three hundred pounds had to be found. The question was whether the sum was going to be raised by begging, stealing, borrowing or working for it. It was a problem faced by most of Harvey Lucas's clients sooner or later.

CHAPTER FOUR

It was twenty past three on Friday afternoon. The sound of shouts and laughter filled the air, as a horde of pupils in blue uniforms streamed out of the school gates. Some hurried, while others chose to stroll sedately. Teachers had another exit route. Behind the science lab, there was a car park for their use only. A long driveway provided access to the main road.

David was eager to catch Sophie before she left the premises. He hadn't had an opportunity to speak with her since their evening together almost forty-eight hours ago. Once they had briefly passed one another in the corridor between lessons, but had merely exchanged smiles. With pupils about, neither wished to give the impression that their relationship was anything other than professional.

The car park was almost empty by the time David arrived. He had been briefly delayed by one of his more promising students, who had raised a question about the Hundred Years War, after the rest of the class had sprinted out of the door. Generally, he would have welcomed the young man's curiosity, but not on this particular occasion.

Sophie was just about to drive away when she spotted David's energetic wave out of the corner of her eye. With a broad smile, she rolled down the window.

"Are you free anytime over the weekend?" enquired David, having looked carefully around to make sure that nobody else was in hearing distance.

The English teacher looked thoughtful.

"Sunday is out," she replied after a few moments. "I've arranged to travel down to Portsmouth to visit my parents. Then tomorrow, I'm catching up with the housework in the morning and meeting friends in the evening."

"How about the afternoon?" asked David, noting that there was a gap in her social engagements.

"OK," answered Sophie brightly, having briefly considered the matter. "Come round about two o'clock if that fits in with you."

"Suits me fine," answered David cheerfully.

In fact, the arrangement fitted in with his plans perfectly. As a Crystal Palace season ticket holder, he had fully intended to go and watch the match the following day. The matter had already been mentioned to Alison earlier in the week. However, for once, he could skip football and drive over to Musselworth instead.

The next morning he had set aside for marking homework. Year Ten's essays on 'The causes of the French Revolution', were now stacked up in one large bundle on the dining room table. Closing the door in an attempt to discourage any intrusion from the children, he settled down to the task.

To begin with, David was allowed to work in peace. The two younger children were sitting quietly in the lounge glued to the TV, while Alison was busy in the kitchen. Then, suddenly, a cacophony of what could arguably be described as music, blasted out from overhead.

Unfortunately, by now, David was already in a bad mood. Class Ten's grasp of the subject matter that he had tried so hard to teach them was disappointing to say the very least. Immediately, he slammed down his red pen and stormed out of the room.

"Turn that racket down!" he bawled from the bottom of the stairs. "I'm trying to do some work down here."

For a few minutes, David waited. However, when there was still no reduction in the sound, he became even more infuriated. Then, hurrying up to the landing, he hammered on Amanda's door before bursting into her bedroom.

Once he was inside, the music was deafening. The eleven-year-old was dancing in front of her dressing table mirror, while pretending to strum a non-existent guitar. It therefore came as a shock to her to turn around and see that she had an audience.

"Didn't you hear me shouting to you?" asked David, taking one step towards the CD player and turning the volume down. "I'm trying to mark some homework downstairs and it's impossible with that noise blaring out."

"Leave me alone," shrieked Amanda, as she rushed down the stairs to seek the protection of her mother. "I hate you."

Already Alison had emerged from the kitchen. Soon mother and daughter were standing in the hall with their arms wrapped around each other. Between loud sobs, the little girl was giving a slightly biased account of what had just happened.

"Don't worry," said Alison, in a soothing, motherly voice. "Everything will be all right." Almost immediately, they were joined by the wicked stepfather. Knowing that

Alison always supported her daughter in these heated confrontations, David was anxious to defend himself.

"Look, I'm trying to do some work," he began, in a voice intended to appeal to reason. "So how do you expect me to concentrate with that unholy din pounding out overhead?"

"Instead of losing your temper, you merely had to go and ask Amanda to turn the sound down," responded Alison angrily. "You're not in the classroom now."

"If you shout at me again, I shall run away," sobbed Amanda, suddenly reassured by her mother's backing. "I'll go and find my real dad and go and live with him."

Alison was always more wounded by a remark like this than her husband. Mark, Amanda's real father, had done very little for his daughter since the day she was born. All too readily, he had agreed never to make contact with the child, on condition that nobody would try and claim maintenance from him.

"Look, just give me a few hours of peace and quiet," pleaded David in a more conciliatory voice.

"This afternoon, I'll be out watching Crystal Palace, so everyone will be able to make as much noise as they want."

By the time he was ready to leave, the atmosphere had become more convivial. Having lied to Alison about where he intended to spend the afternoon, David had taken the precaution of wearing his supporter's scarf; a precious garment that he always took when watching Palace play.

"Who are they playing today?" asked Alison casually.

"Cardiff," replied David, as he slipped his shoes on at the door.

"Are they a good team?"

"Near the top of the table."

The conversation was a familiar one. Every Saturday, as David was about to set off for a match, Alison would ask the same two questions. However, the answers she received probably just went in one ear and out of the other. She understood little about football and cared even less about the game.

On his way over to Musselworth, David got caught up in traffic. Earlier, there had been an accident and looking ahead, he could see a long line of vehicles at a standstill. Fearful that he was going to arrive about two hours late, he cursed himself for not having taken down Sophie's mobile number.

It was twenty to three by the time he finally walked down the garden path. Sophie was standing at the front door with an amused expression on her face. Having been keeping a lookout from her top floor flat, she had spotted her guest's car draw up outside.

"Thought you weren't coming," she laughed, while leading the way into her sitting room. "Sorry, but I got delayed by a traffic accident," explained David, before going on to provide her with the full details, in the way that road users are prone to do.

"Poor you," whispered Sophie seductively, before throwing her arms around David's neck and squeezing her body against his. "Would you like a cup of tea, or shall we just skip the preliminaries?"

"Let's go for the second option," answered David, as he felt her soft fine hair against his cheek. "I'm not particularly thirsty right now."

Swiftly, they headed for the bedroom. Moments later, passions were aroused to the full as two intertwined people writhed and thrusted on top of Sophie's soft springy mattress. Then all too soon, the storm died down as they settled into each other's arms.

"So do you think that Alison suspects anything yet about your infidelities?" asked Sophie, as she rested her head on David's chest.

David scowled.

"I wonder if she would really care. This morning we had an almighty row." "Oh dear, what happened?" asked Sophie.

"It was over Amanda again," explained David, with more than a hint of irritation in his voice. "I was busy marking homework when suddenly, she decided to deafen everyone with her music."

Briefly, Sophie was silent as she reflected on her new lover's problem. As a woman who had been in affairs with a few married men, she was quite used to listening about their less than perfect lives at home. She even prided herself on the quality of advice she was able to give them.

"Your stepdaughter seems to be driving a wedge between you and your wife," she said, having given the matter some consideration. "But you should try and be more tolerant with her, as she is still very young. Otherwise, sooner or later, your marriage is likely to break down."

"That might be a good thing," answered David scornfully. "I need a wife who appreciates the pressures that I am under in the classroom. Perhaps another teacher, such as you."

Sophie playfully scolded him.

"What we have together is beautiful and mustn't be allowed to turn sour. When we eventually go our separate ways, you and I will have some precious memories that will last with us forever."

A look of bewilderment appeared on David's face.

"Why must it be inevitable that our relationship won't last?"

"Let's not discuss it now," replied Sophie, as she disentangled herself from the other naked body in the bed. "I'll go and make us both a nice cup of tea."

⁂

Time was slowly running out. It was Saturday afternoon, and Mark was still no closer to solving his problem. Although three hundred pounds hardly seemed a vast amount of money, the means by which he could raise it by Thursday evening simply eluded him.

He realized it was futile asking friends for a loan. Either he had borrowed money from them in the past and hadn't repaid it or, they were just aware of his reputation. Even his closest relations were unlikely to throw him a lifeline. His mother wasn't the only one to have reached the conclusion that providing him with financial assistance was hardly in his best interest. It just discouraged him from finding a regular job.

Mark decided to stroll down Brockleby High Street. With weekend shoppers out in their droves, he was hoping to catch sight of a familiar face who might just provide the answer to a prayer – perhaps an old school acquaintance that he had lost contact with. It was a long shot, but certainly worth a try.

After a while, Mark began to think that he was wasting his time. Surrounded by a sea of strangers on a hot, sticky afternoon, he was about to give up and go home, when he spotted a stocky young woman heading towards him. Smiling brightly and stopping in her tracks, she was obviously setting the stage for a conversation.

Tina Bailey's family had lived in the same street as Mark for many years. As a child, she had been seriously unattractive and time certainly hadn't improved her overall appearance. In fact, the kindest thing to say about her was that she was plain, and just leave it at that.

Now in her late twenties, Tina was still single. She was not unpopular, however, and had a wide circle of friends, nearly all of whom were of her own sex. Having once brought the subject up, neither Mark nor his mother could ever remember seeing her out with what might possibly have been a boyfriend.

"Out shopping?" enquired Mark cheerfully.

"Just out buying a few odds and ends," replied Tina, raising up a blue shiny carrier bag slightly, as if to prove it.

Already, Mark's scheming brain was busy at work. In front of him was no longer a particularly unattractive female, but rather a possible angel of mercy – somebody who might be persuaded to lift a heavy burden off his shoulders and provide him with the odd luxury as well.

"Fancy a coffee?" he smiled, while reaching into the side pocket of his jeans and pulling out a handful of loose change. "I think I may just about have enough money to buy you one."

For a moment, Tina watched on as Mark counted out a few coins in his hands. However, it soon became apparent that he was well short of what was required. Seventy-three pence wasn't going to purchase a great deal at current prices.

"If you don't have enough, I'll pay," Tina volunteered eagerly.

"Oh, I couldn't possibly allow you to do that," answered Mark, putting on his best manners.

"Don't be silly," laughed Tina. "You can buy the coffees next time."

"OK then," smiled Mark, "if you really don't mind."

Brockleby High Street wasn't short of catering establishments. Having eaten in most of them, Tina was something of an expert as to which ones offered value for money, so Mark was only too happy to allow her to choose where they should go for their refreshments.

Tina led the way up a flight of stairs and into a spacious cafeteria. It was packed, but having been served at the counter, she happened to spot a table for two that had just been vacated by an elderly couple. Followed by Mark, who was carrying a brown plastic tray, she quickly hurried over and pulled out a chair before somebody else could stake their claim.

"I haven't seen you around lately," commented Mark, before sinking his teeth into a current bun, bought for him in addition to the coffee. "Are you still living at home?"

Tina shook her head.

"I moved out over three months ago," she replied, while spreading butter on a toasted teacake.

"My friend and I are now renting a flat together."

"Boyfriend?" asked Mark.

Tina giggled.

"No, it's just a girl that I work with."

Mark pretended to look surprised.

"Surely there must be a man in your life."

Tina blushed like a shy schoolgirl.

"Not at the moment. Are you going out with anybody?"

Mark stared down sadly at his partly eaten bun.

"Afraid not. It seems as though we are two lonely people together."

At that moment, there was a slight pause in the conversation. A young woman in a bright red uniform arrived at the table to collect the cups and saucers that the previous customers had left. There was a bored expression on her face as she placed the dirty crockery on a tray.

"Are you working at the moment?" enquired Tina, as soon as the assistant had sauntered away to perform her joyless duties elsewhere.

"Yes," replied Mark proudly, wishing to present himself as an eligible bachelor. "I've got a very good job in an office".

"Oh that's nice," smiled Tina as she sipped her coffee. "A while ago, your mum was telling me that you were unemployed and couldn't find a job."

"Not these days," answered Mark, keen to distance himself from the past. "I'm doing very well for myself".

"I'm in the insurance business," said Tina, looking pleased with herself. "At the beginning of the year, they promoted me, and now I'm on a very good salary. That's when I decided to leave home and become independent."

Mark smiled approvingly. As somebody who had accomplished little in his own life, he generally disliked being told about the achievements of others. This though, happened to be an exception to the rule.

He was now deciding upon a plan of action. Somehow it seemed inappropriate to ask for a loan of three hundred pounds at that precise moment. Had he got the money, he would have asked Tina out for a romantic evening and then made his request. However, because of the dismal state of his finances, the idea was out of the question.

"What kind of music do you like?" he asked, casually changing the subject. Tina shrugged.

"Anything, except classical or jazz."

"Look, are you free on Monday evening?" asked Mark hopefully.

"Yes," answered Tina, immediately deciding that a prior engagement to meet an old school friend would have to be cancelled.

"Great," answered Mark, with the widest smile he could manage. "We can sit down together and listen to some of my CDs. Mum will be out playing bingo, so we will have the house to ourselves."

"What time?" asked Tina, trying hard to disguise her excitement. Could romance be finally knocking on her door, she wondered.

"Make it seven-thirty", answered Mark, after briefly considering the question. "Mum will have gone by that time."

Shortly after, they left the cafeteria and went their separate ways. While Tina disappeared into the crowds to continue her shopping, Mark decided to make his way home. Having found a possible saviour who might rescue him from suffering at the hands of Harvey Lucas, he was beginning to feel more optimistic about his future.

When Mark was less than a hundred metres from home, he got stopped by Mrs Fisher. A lady in her eighties who lived alone, she would often be seen leaning over her garden gate waiting for somebody to talk to. Having lived in the road for many years, she knew most of the neighbours and practically all of their life histories.

"Still out of work?" she called.

Mark nodded gloomily.

"No jobs around at the moment".

"It's all the fault of these bloody banks," said Mrs Fisher with venom. "They are to blame for the country being in such a mess."

"You're right there," replied Mark, ready as always to blame anyone other than himself for being unemployed.

"I hate banks myself," continued Mrs Fisher, pleased to have found an audience to listen to her. "Don't trust them and have never held an account."

"Where do you keep your money, then?" asked Mark, who was suddenly reminded that he needed to get home in order to answer a call of nature.

Mrs Fisher beckoned him to come closer, as though fearful of being overheard by a Russian spy.

"Under the bed," she whispered, before bursting out laughing.

That evening Mark thought long and hard about Mrs Fisher's savings. It was certainly true that those greedy bankers weren't likely to lay their hands on her money, but others might. It was even possible, he decided, that he might not need a loan from Tina Bailey. However, she could still come in useful to him.

CHAPTER FIVE

Alison spent the best part of Sunday afternoon in the kitchen. Carol and Tony had been invited around for the evening and she was busy trying to prepare an exotic dish, while following the instructions provided in a newly acquired recipe book. The task was hardly made easier by the two youngest children constantly seeking her attention.

Finally, she lost patience. With a determined look in her eye, she strutted into the lounge in order to track down her husband. Much to her annoyance, he was laid out on the settee, watching an old black and white film on TV.

"Look, can you take Joshua and Abigail out for an hour or so?" she said, in a manner which seemed more like a command than a request.

"Very well," sighed David. "Give me five minutes."

Both children possessed an abundance of energy. Joshua, a four-year-old, was forever kicking a ball about, while Abigail, who was two years older, had a preference for skipping with a rope or performing somersaults on the lawn. The hard part was always keeping them both happy at the same time.

David drove the children down to the park. Armed with a rubber ball and a bag of bread for the ducks, he hoped to keep them amused for a while. He had also ensured that he had enough change in his pocket to buy ice creams, should all else fail.

It was yet another hot day. Like David, many others had decided to spend their afternoon in the park. Some were exposing ample portions of flesh as they sunbathed on the grass. Then there were those who sat shoulder to shoulder on wooden benches, just watching the world go by.

On their arrival, both Joshua and Abigail hurried off in the same direction; the attraction being the playground inside an enclosure, fenced in by green iron vertical bars. Throngs of children swung on swings, slid down a slide and clambered up climbing frames, while their parents looked on.

David stayed outside the enclosure. Then, while keeping a watchful eye on his two children, he made a call on his mobile phone. It was a number he had taken down only the previous day.

"Hi David," answered Sophie, having seen his name appear on her phone.

"Just wondered how you are," said David, before waving to Abigail, who was stood waiting for a swing to become available.

"I'm relaxing in my parents' garden and enjoying a glass of wine," replied Sophie, with a laugh. "Tea will be served on the lawn at four o'clock, so I've been told."

"Look, are you free one evening this week?" asked David hopefully. "I was thinking that perhaps we could go out to a restaurant."

"I'm doing nothing on Wednesday," replied Sophie. "But we had better go somewhere not too close to your home. Just in case somebody you know sees us together and reports back to Alison."

Suddenly David's attention was distracted by an incident in the children's playground. A dispute had broken out between Joshua and a boy of a similar age, over the possession of a swing.

As they stood eye to eye, each attempting to pull the wooden seat away from the other's grasp, it seemed likely that a fight could break out at any second. However, before David could set off to act as mediator, the other boy's mother intervened. Probably unjustly, she decided that Joshua had a greater claim to the swing and hauled her son away from the scene to howls of protest.

"How about London?" suggested David, continuing the telephone conversation as though nothing had happened. "I know a nice little restaurant in Soho."

"In that case, let's meet at Charing Cross station at seven-thirty," said Sophie, who was used to planning secret encounters with her married boyfriends.

Tony and Carol arrived just after eight that evening. The children had eaten earlier and the two younger ones were already tucked up in bed. Amanda, who was that much older, chose to stay in her room watching TV, rather than sitting downstairs with the adults.

"Jacqui Dunn has put her name forward for the by-election up in Cumbria," announced Tony, as soon as he passed through the front door.

"I understand that it is a very safe seat for Labour," said David thoughtfully. "The MP who has just died had one of the biggest majorities in the country."

"Do you think Jacqui has a good chance of being selected as the party candidate?" asked Alison, as she guided her guests into the lounge.

"Central Office are keen to get her back into Parliament," replied Carol. "Jacqui was an excellent junior minister at the Foreign Office when Labour were in Government."

"Also, it will help increase the number of women Labour MPs," added Tony. "This is quite a sensitive issue with all parties at the moment."

Jacqui Dunn had been a popular councillor in Brockleby for a number of years. Her hard work finally rewarded when she was selected as a parliamentary candidate for the Labour Party. The seat had always been held by the Tories and was considered to be one of their strongholds. However, when boundary changes were introduced, the constituency looked as though it could become a marginal seat.

In 2003, the sitting MP was murdered. Discovering that Charles Dawkins had finished with her, his mistress stabbed him to death one night in his own front garden. After an acrimonious political campaign, Jacqui won the seat in the ensuing by-election and held on to it for another seven years.

The Tories finally regained Brockleby in 2010, when the Labour Government got turned out of office.

"Dinner will be served in ten minutes. Would anyone like an aperitif?" enquired Alison, waving her arm in the direction of the cocktail cabinet.

Having noted everyone's order, including his wife's, David accepted the role of drinks waiter. "So if Jacqui ends up as MP for this Cumbrian constituency," he began thoughtfully, while filling a glass with a generous quantity of whiskey for Tony, "then the Brockleby Labour Party will have to find a new candidate for the next General Election."

Tony nodded.

"And should that be the case," he said, "I could be putting my name forward".

"Why not?" said Alison enthusiastically. "You've been a councillor for many years. Perhaps it's time to advance your political career."

"Of course, you don't want to build up your hopes too much," warned David. "Jacqui might not get selected to fight the Cumbrian seat."

At that moment, the little group were disturbed by a small voice overhead. Abigail, who always had difficulty in getting to sleep, was calling for a glass of orange juice. Concerned that she might wake her younger brother, David was soon hurrying upstairs with the drink, before putting his daughter back to bed again.

Tony and Carol were a childless couple. David often wondered how the pair of them would have coped with meeting the demands of a young family. They seemed to devote their whole lives to the world of politics. It was highly unlikely that the Labour Party had a more dedicated supporter amongst the membership than either of these two.

The subject of the Brockleby Labour Party candidacy surfaced again over dinner. While Alison had been trying to tell her guests about a psychology course she was thinking of taking at evening classes, Tony's attention was clearly elsewhere. Having stopped eating, he was staring into space with a glazed expression on his face.

"Jacqui won't be standing again in Brockleby," he announced suddenly, having cut Alison off in mid-sentence. "She is determined to find a safer seat by the next General Election."

"How can you be so sure?" asked David, who, like the others at the table, was taken a little by surprise at this unexpected interruption.

"I just have a feeling," replied Tony.

"What Tony is trying to say," began Carol, intervening on her husband's behalf, "is would you both be supporting him, were he to put his name forward as a candidate?"

"Of course," replied Alison immediately.

David, though, was hesitant. While appreciating that Tony worked hard for the party, he wondered whether the councillor was really cut out to be an MP. Doubts were beginning to mount up in his head as he considered the matter.

Few would have called Tony a smart dresser. A T-shirt and jeans were his normal attire, with a scruffy, well-worn jumper appearing during the colder weather. If he possessed a tie at all, the garment probably hadn't seen the light of day since it was purchased.

Tony was an idealist, rather than a lover of the human race. In the council chamber, he would speak up passionately for the poor and disadvantaged, yet appeared to care little for them as individuals. When knocking on doors during an election campaign, his only concern was obtaining votes, rather than listening to the problems of the people that he spoke to.

"Let me think about it," said David finally, before receiving a painful blow on the ankle.

Alison glared at her husband from across the table. Quite obviously, the sharp kick she had just given him was delivered in anger, rather than an accidental swing of the foot.

"I'm sure David will support you," she said reassuringly, turning to face Tony, who was sitting next to her.

David smiled, but made no comment. Attempting to avoid any bad feeling, Alison quickly changed the subject. However, later that evening, having waved the guests off at the door, she confronted her husband over the matter.

"Surely, you must back Tony to be the candidate," she said, setting to work on the washing up. "He and Carol are two of our closest friends."

"I just want to see who else puts their name forward," explained David, who stood holding a tea-towel, in preparation for the mountain of crockery about to come his way. "After all, we are supposed to be selecting somebody who might one day be a Member of Parliament. Not some dude to read out quiz questions in one of our fund-raising events."

Alison made no reply. Instead, she deliberately nudged her husband aside as she lifted up a pile of dirty plates and placed them in the sink. From then on, the washing up continued in a stony silence.

Tina Bailey was punctual. At seven-thirty, she arrived at Mark's house carrying a bottle of white wine. She was hopeful that a few glasses of alcohol might help further a budding romance. Her host, on the other hand, had no such amorous intentions for the evening. He barely noticed the crimson dress she had rushed out to buy in her lunch hour.

"Take a seat," smiled Mark, while settling himself into an armchair.

"Thanks," replied Tina, disappointed that they wouldn't be sitting side by side on the settee together. "Like the music, by the way."

"It's Queen," answered Mark, "one of my favourite groups". "Mine, too," beamed Tina, eager to please her host.

The CD player was usually kept in Mark's room. Whenever he had argued with his mother, he would shut himself away and play music. With frequent heated disputes and practically no money to go out and enjoy himself, this was how he now spent much of his life.

"Of course, it's quite expensive buying CDs," said Mark, keen to discuss money, before going on to the business of trying to borrow some.

"I know," replied Tina gloomily. "It's the same with everything these days, and the cost of living seems to go on rising all the time."

"I suppose it isn't so bad when you have a good job like yours," said Mark, anxious to probe into the state of Tina's finances.

The expression that immediately appeared on the young woman's face, suggested to him that perhaps she didn't possess great riches after all.

"Before leaving home, I was quite well off," she explained. "Now, though, the landlord takes a large share of my salary. Then to make matters worse, my flat mate told me tonight that she is moving out at the weekend to go and live with her boyfriend."

"Does that mean that your rent will be doubled?" asked Mark. Tina nodded.

"I'm afraid so. You see, the lease is in my name." "But don't you have savings?" asked Mark.

The look that Tina gave him suggested that the question was quite absurd.

"All I've got is credit card debts, and that's about it."

Mark could feel his heart sink. It now seemed unlikely that he could borrow his way out of trouble and more extreme measures would have to be considered. Picking up the wine bottle that Tina had brought, he wandered into the kitchen in search of a corkscrew.

"Perhaps I could move in with you," he suggested, having returned to the lounge a few minutes later, holding a glass of wine in each hand.

Tina immediately perked up.

"Could you afford your share of the rent?" Mark gave her a reassuring smile.

"Of course. Remember that I've got a good job now."

Eagerly, Tina picked up her shoulder bag from the floor. Then, after rummaging around inside for a few minutes, finally withdrew a brightly-coloured note pad and a black pen.

"Look, you need to know where I live, then," she smiled. "When would you like to come over and take a look at the flat?"

Mark shrugged.

"When are you free to show me around?"

"Wednesday evening would suit me," answered Tina, as she scribbled down the address. "Come any time after seven."

Tina's visit turned out to be a short and disappointing one, from her point of view. It was true, of course, that she had managed to find somebody who seemed interested in sharing the flat with her. On the other hand, nothing had materialized on the romantic front. Her host had spent the best part of an hour talking football, a subject that she knew nothing about – then suddenly announced that he would have to retire to bed early, as the wine had given him a severe headache.

The following morning, Mark kept watch from his bedroom window. Because the day was bright and sunny, he confidently expected to see Mrs Fisher standing at her garden gate before too long, ready as ever to waylay just about anybody who happened to be passing by.

Sure enough, the old lady appeared just after nine-thirty. Dressed in a white cardigan and a floral skirt, her head turned from side to side at regular intervals in search of another human being to talk to; rather like a bird of prey keeping a watchful eye out for the next meal.

Slipping on his shoes, Mark was ready to take a walk. He was anxious to get to his neighbour before she decided to go inside.

"Good morning," he said cheerily, when he was within ten metres of Mrs Fisher's front gate. "Good morning," replied the old lady with a warm smile. "Going anywhere nice?"

Mark shook his head.

"Just thought I'd take a stroll down the high street. It's too nice to be sitting around indoors." "It certainly is a beautiful day," agreed Mrs Fisher.

"Do you get out very much these days?" asked Mark casually.

"Not with my bad leg," replied the old lady regretfully. "I can't get around like I used to."

Mark was anxious to steer his elderly neighbour away from the subject of her ailments. He hadn't the patience to stand and listen while Mrs Fisher described in precise detail the problems that affected various parts of her anatomy. There were far more urgent things on his mind.

"You must get out sometime," he insisted.

"Not often", replied Mrs Fisher. "Having said that, though, I do go along every Friday to a coffee morning at the church. Somebody comes and picks me up in their car."

Perfect, thought Mark. Now he just needed one further small detail.

"What time does your car arrive?" he enquired, with a casualness that might easily have been mistaken for disinterest.

Mrs Fisher hesitated briefly, while putting her failing memory to the test. "Usually about a quarter to ten," she answered at last.

Mark had heard all he needed to hear, although, out of courtesy, he pretended to listen sympathetically as his elderly neighbour went on to complain about the council, who had failed to collect her rubbish the previous week. His thoughts, though, were elsewhere as the voice droned on and on.

✎﹏✎

Joy Adamson slipped into the passenger seat. As the car gradually moved down the drive, she smiled and gave Hilary, who was standing at the front door, a final wave. She had enjoyed her two-week stay with the Chambers, but it was now time to return to New York – get back to all her friends and, of course, the two cats she treated like children.

John Chambers sat quietly at the wheel. Being self-employed allowed him to drive his guest to Heathrow on a Monday afternoon without having to consult anyone else. Also, as an aircraft enthusiast, he would have the thrill of watching low flying planes as they lifted off and came in to land.

"Do you miss your son?" asked Joy suddenly, as they drove along a country lane, bordered by hedgerows on either side.

"Presumably, you are talking about David," replied John, as he glanced at his passenger. "Yes", answered Joy. "Hilary was telling me that she thinks about him all the time."

"And so do I," admitted John. "However, he ceased to be a member of my family when he rejected the word of the Lord."

Joy had expected such a response. During her stay she had formed an entirely different impression of her two hosts. While Hilary was kindly and gentle, John was a pompous man who always expected others to agree with his opinion.

This American lady, though, had a mind of her own. Unmarried and living with just two cats for company, she wasn't used to having somebody around the home making decisions on her behalf. Nor did she approve of bullies imposing their will on others.

"I think you are being very unfair," she began boldly. "Hilary should be allowed to visit David if she wants to. After all, he is her son as well as yours."

John was taken aback. He was a senior member of the Brockleby Eternal Fellowship and not used to having his authority challenged – at least, not by another follower, and a woman at that.

"But we are told by St Paul in the First Book of Corinthians that we must remove the wicked one from amongst us," explained John, with just a hint of annoyance in his voice.

"I also remember that Jesus talked of forgiveness, even when he was nailed to the cross by his torturers," retorted Joy. "Can't you at least allow David to see his grandfather before the old man dies?"

John didn't reply. The journey continued in total silence until they saw Heathrow Airport coming into view over half an hour later. Concerned that she had upset her host after all his generosity over the past two weeks, Joy was beginning to feel quite ashamed of herself.

Finally, John spoke.

"Perhaps you are right," he said wearily. "I know that Dad would like to see his grandson. Hilary has got David's address, so I will write him a letter the moment I get home."

"Thank you, John," smiled Joy. "And perhaps you'll allow Hilary to see David, as well?" "I will need to pray for guidance before agreeing to that," replied John coldly.

CHAPTER SIX

When David arrived home, he had a letter waiting for him. Without having to prise open the envelope, he had no doubts as to whom it was from. The spidery handwriting was unmistakably that of his father. A smile crept across his face as he read the contents.

"Dad has agreed to allow me to see Grandpa," he called out to Alison, who was in the kitchen. "That is very generous of him," came the sarcastic reply. "Perhaps the miserable sod is starting to mellow."

"Possibly," said David thoughtfully. "Anyway, I will have to ring him when I get a minute and arrange a time and day for my visit."

"Good gracious," said Alison, suddenly joining her husband in the lounge. "When was the last time that the pair of you spoke?"

"Eight years ago," replied David. "When, according to him, I rejected the word of the Lord in order to follow the Devil."

Alison smiled.

"And although we have never met, your father probably still regards me as a servant of the Devil – a woman who has deliberately led his son into wicked ways".

"How about a modern-day Jezebel?" laughed David.

"What about a blood-sucking vampire?" replied Alison with a toothy grin, before heading back to the kitchen to check on the dinner.

David, of course, wouldn't be eating with the rest of the family. It was Wednesday evening and in less than two hours, he planned to catch a train to London. Not wishing to keep a lady waiting, he had stopped off at Brockleby Station on the way home, just to make certain that there wouldn't be any delays on the line.

Very soon, he was under the shower. As the warm water cascaded over his body, he sang aloud to himself. He was beginning to feel like a starry-eyed teenager, rather than a responsible thirty-one year-old schoolteacher.

David took his time in deciding what to wear. Over the past week or so, he had suddenly become more conscious of his overall appearance. As in his more youthful days, he was gazing at himself in the mirror, at every available opportunity.

"You're looking smart," commented Alison approvingly, when her husband eventually appeared in the hall. "Going anywhere nice?"

"Just going out for a meal with a few of the other teachers," replied David casually. "Somebody suggested that we should go to a posh restaurant in the West End."

"Partners not invited, then?" enquired Alison, with more than a hint of resentment in her voice. "Not on this occasion," answered David. "Perhaps next time, though".

Alison gave him a disgruntled glare.

"Forget it," she snapped. "I shall go out one evening with my friends to a posh restaurant, and leave you to look after the kids."

Charing Cross Station was crowded when David arrived. Many commuters were standing on the concourse, staring up at the electronically controlled departure board, waiting for information about their train. Others who had reached their destination were streaming through the platform ticket barriers in their droves.

After a while David began to get restless. It was a quarter to eight, and Sophie had still to appear.

He was just about to send her a text message when he spotted the lady in question amongst a sea of faces.

"Sorry I'm late," said Sophie, tucking her return ticket into a red leather purse. "I should have caught an earlier train."

"Not to worry," smiled David, relieved that she had shown up at all. "We had better hurry, though. I've booked us a table for eight o'clock."

"Which restaurant are you taking me to?" enquired Sophie eagerly, as they left the station. "One of the best in Chinatown," beamed David. "I remember you were saying that you like Chinese food."

Soon they were walking briskly along Charing Cross Road. David would have loved to stop off at one of the many fascinating second hand and antiquarian bookshops on the way, but there wasn't time. He didn't want to risk losing their table to another customer.

At times, David and Sophie were forced to walk in the road. As usual, the West End had attracted scores of visitors, who mostly ambled along the pavement as though they had all the time in the world. Also blocking the way were long queues of people waiting to be admitted to theatres and cinemas.

The two teachers were ten minutes late, although it hardly seemed to matter. The restaurant wasn't at its busiest and there were a number of empty tables to choose from. A smiling waitress who suddenly appeared directed her latest customers, to one by the window.

"So how was Portsmouth?" asked David, after having ordered a bottle of Burgundy. "Very relaxing," replied Sophie, with a broad grin. "All my meals were cooked for me and I didn't see a single teenager during my stay."

"How are you coping in the classroom now?" asked David, as the smiling waitress returned to lay a basket of prawn crackers on the table.

Sophie shook her head sadly.

"Not very well. In fact, I'm thinking about living in Portsmouth with my parents for a while. I just need time and space to decide what I want to do with my life".

David was taken aback by the news. Of course, he was acutely aware that their relationship would probably have to finish at some point. However, he hoped that the end would come deep into the future, perhaps when they were starting to tire of each other.

"So what about me?" he asked, helping himself to a prawn cracker. "Brockleby and Portsmouth are some distance apart."

"But you've got your wife and kids," answered Sophie. "I never had any intention of coming between you and your family."

At that moment, they were interrupted. The smiling waitress had arrived at the table with the wine. Then, having poured a small quantity into David's glass, she stood back and waited for his approval.

"That's perfect," said David, having drunk the sample in one gulp.

"Look, I'm sorry if I've put a damper on your evening," said Sophie, once the waitress had gone. "We can keep in touch if you like."

"Yes, I would like that," replied David, although hardly consoled by the idea of just remaining in contact. "When do you think that you will be making this move?"

Sophie shrugged.

"I haven't exactly made up my mind as yet. It probably won't be too far into the future, though." Over the meal, Sophie talked a lot about herself. She had studied at Southampton University, before deciding to train as a teacher. At the time, it had seemed like a noble calling, but her recent experiences in the job had changed her earlier perception.

Until a year ago, she had been living at home. Then her parents, who had recently retired, decided to go and live by the sea. Sophie was invited to move with them, but instead, she opted to rent a flat and have her own independence.

She had always been attracted to married men – and having signed up for a car maintenance course at evening classes, she had little difficulty in becoming acquainted with a few. Now, with her own flat, she would invite the occasional one back for coffee and things would rapidly take off from there.

"And then when you get bored with these guys, you simply send them back to their wives," said David, when Sophie had paused to take a sip of wine.

"No," replied Sophie, rather wounded by this assessment of her behaviour. "I end the relationship before things start getting serious. I'm not a marriage breaker."

"More like a heart breaker," replied David, as the smiling waitress suddenly appeared to remove the dirty dishes.

"Don't say that," answered Sophie, as she stretched her arm across the table to touch David on the hand. "You'll soon forget me."

⚜ ⚜

"And this is the kitchen", announced Tina, having almost completed her guided tour of the flat. "As you see, it has all the essential amenities."

Mark cast his eyes around the room. At home, this was not a place in which he spent much time. He would wander in at various intervals during the day to prepare himself a drink or quick snack, but that was about it. Cooking in general was his mother's job, as far as he was concerned.

"Looks fine", he answered, having spotted a micro-wave, his favourite kitchen appliance, standing alongside the bread bin.

"Do you want to share the cooking with me?" asked Tina hopefully. "At the moment, Lisa, my flat mate, organizes the meal one evening and I do it the next."

"I'm not much of a chef," confessed Mark. "I'll probably just get by on takeaways and using the microwave."

"OK, then," said Tina, resigning herself to the fact that from now on, she would need to spend every evening in the kitchen, rather than alternate ones. Because of the expense, living on fast food was not an option, as far as she was concerned. "So the next thing we need to decide is how to share the housework between us."

Alarm bells began to go off in Mark's head. Cleaning and tidying up were further tasks that he was happy to leave to his mother. Then it dawned on him that he would also be responsible for washing and ironing his clothes. All of a sudden, the idea of independence was beginning to seem less appealing by the minute.

"This housework," he began apprehensively. "How long does it normally take you each week?" Tina looked thoughtful.

"Only a couple of hours or so," she answered, rather dismissively. "I usually do a bit in the evening and then have a good session on Saturday morning. It isn't so bad once you get into the routine."

"So how do you suggest that we divide the chores up, then?" enquired Mark, hopeful that he might be able to negotiate some of the less arduous duties for himself.

He was immediately invited to go on yet another guided tour of the flat. This time, though, it was to point out what was expected of him, in order to keep his new home looking clean and tidy. For somebody who was both work-shy and untrained domestically through choice, such phrases as 'you need to scrub this floor', 'polish that table', 'vacuum the hall carpet' and 'clean inside the toilet', weren't very well received.

"So that's it, really", said Tina, having finally listed out the new tenant's chores. "Now, would you fancy a glass of white wine?"

"Sounds good," replied Mark, feeling quite exhausted at just the thought of such hard labour.

"Are you happy to move in then?" asked Tina, once they were both seated in the lounge with drinks.

"Perfectly", smiled Mark.

He was now feeling more content with life. The solution that would rescue him from the miseries of housework was perfectly simple, he had decided. If he avoided doing his share, Tina would be forced to do the lot or allow the flat to become a filthy tip. Either way, being a messy slob himself, he didn't really care which option she chose.

Tina had been hopeful of a little romance. Sadly for her, though, Mark had other ideas, as he took it upon himself to switch on the TV without bothering to ask for permission. He already appeared to regard the flat as his new home, even though he had yet to contribute a penny towards the rent.

For the whole evening, he took charge of the remote control. While showing no interest in socializing with his hostess, he sat and watched whichever programmes that suited him. For her part, Tina felt obliged to tolerate this selfish behaviour in silence. She had no wish to discourage a possible tenant from moving in with her – particularly a man who, she hoped, might just become a future lover.

"I'll be going to bed soon," she announced, when it had just gone eleven. "I need to be up early in the morning for work."

At first, Mark seemed not to have taken the hint that it was time for him to leave. Having no such commitment to a job himself, he had little empathy for those who were employed. However, when Tina arrived in the lounge in her dressing gown, the message finally managed to sink in.

"See you on Saturday morning, then," he said, wearily lifting himself out of the armchair that he had occupied all evening.

"Don't forget, I need a week's rent from you," said Tina. "The landlord expects to be paid in advance".

"No problem," answered Mark, confident that his finances were about to take a dramatic change for the better.

"Goodnight," said Tina, as she waved her future flat mate off at the front door. Having hoped for a departing kiss, she went to bed sadly disappointed.

The following afternoon, Mark went on a long walk. Having just had another argument with his mother, he needed to get away from the house for a while. In addition to that, he wanted to be alone in order to think. The next twenty-four hours would be crucial if he was to turn his life around.

Just after five, he was almost back home – but having just turned the corner into his road, Mark's heart sank. There, parked outside his house, was a car that he recognized only too well. He had often sat in the front passenger seat of the Porsche, without ever being taken for a ride.

For a split second, he considered heading off in the opposite direction. Harvey Lucas had never called at his house before and suddenly, he was beginning to feel even more threatened. Worse still, it meant that his mother, who knew nothing about his outstanding debt to the loan shark, would probably be dragged into the situation as well.

Mark gritted his teeth as he fumbled around in his pocket for the key. Of course, he still wasn't in a position to pay Harvey Lucas the three hundred pounds that had been agreed upon at their last meeting, exactly a week ago to the day. Telling an unsympathetic creditor that he would need to be patient for just a few more hours wasn't going to be easy.

The atmosphere seemed cordial enough as Mark entered the lounge. Three pairs of smiling eyes followed him as he made his way to a vacant armchair. His mother and the two visitors were all sitting holding a china teacup in one hand and a matching saucer in the other.

"We were just passing, so I thought it would be a good idea to pop in and introduce you to Leo MacDonald," said Harvey genially. "He was very keen to meet you."

"That's right," confirmed Leo in a broad Scottish accent. "I understand that we might be seeing quite a lot of each other in the future."

Mark felt a shiver running down his spine. Having heard much about 'Mad Dog MacDonald', he didn't relish the prospect of having an ongoing association with him. The former amateur heavyweight boxer had a reputation for acting like a wild animal with anyone who upset him.

"Nice to meet you," said Mark, managing a half-smile.

"Look, I'll leave you gentlemen in peace," said Mark's mother. "I have some ironing to finish off." Once the lady of the house had left the room, the mood quickly changed. No longer smiling, Leo stood up and quietly shut door. It was time to talk business, and he didn't want any inferring middle-aged women to stick their noses in.

The Scot was well over six feet. As always, he wore a tight fitting T-shirt in order to highlight his broad shoulders and expose his muscular arms. Then, to appear even more menacing, his head was shaven and he had a swastika tattooed on the side of his neck.

"Where's our money?" he growled threateningly.

"I need just one more day," replied Mark anxiously. "This time tomorrow, I'll be in a position to pay my loan off in full."

A suspicious look appeared on Harvey's face.

"I seem to remember that at our last meeting, you were talking about starting a new job this week. However, your mum has just been telling us that you are still unemployed. That seems rather strange to me."

"The company rang me up the following day to say, that they didn't need anyone after all," answered Mark, managing to come up with this explanation on the spur of the moment.

"Without a job, then, I'd like to know how you are going to come up with our money tomorrow," said Harvey, before glancing at his partner and giving him a knowing wink.

In present company, Mark might have been safe in telling the truth. After all, his two visitors were no strangers to crime themselves, having served time in prison for violent assault. However, it seemed wise not to advertise the fact, that he was planning a robbery.

"My uncle agreed to give me a loan," he explained, hopeful that there wouldn't be any further awkward questions to answer.

"In that case, you had better tell your uncle to provide you with bank notes," said Harvey. "I don't want any dodgy cheques to bounce on me."

"Don't worry, I will definitely be paying you in cash," replied Mark, sounding and feeling more confident this time.

Leo who was still standing, moved his towering body one step forward. In his opinion, verbal threats were all very well, but sometimes, there were those clients who needed that little bit extra, to get the message home to them. Having swung his right arm back, he landed the palm of his hand on the side of Mark's face, with as much force as he could manage.

Immediately, Mark was rocked back in his armchair. Suddenly, he was in a daze as bright lights began flashing in front of his eyes. It took a few moments before he became aware of the sharp stabbing pain to his left cheek.

"If we don't get paid tomorrow, that is just a little taster of what is to come," warned Leo, with a menacing glare.

"We'll be here at four o'clock," added Harvey, as he scribbled the appointment down in a large black diary. "Just make certain you're at home when we arrive."

The two bullies nodded to one another. Then Harvey stood up and followed his business partner out of the room, leaving Mark alone. With plenty of clients to call on, they were anxious to be on their way.

It was after midnight when Mark sneaked out of the house. Carrying a large paper carrier bag, he headed for the woods, which were only a short walk away. Feeling both nervous and excited, he went over the plans once more in his head. His whole future seemed to depend on success in the morning. Failure was just too horrible to even think about.

CHAPTER SEVEN

It seemed strange hearing his father's voice again. The two men hadn't spoken for eight years, although they had exchanged the occasional letter. From time to time, David would send his parents photographs of their grandchildren, whom they had never seen in the flesh and in return, would receive an almost business-like reply, usually accompanied by a cheque.

Strangely, it wasn't distance but religion that had driven them apart. After the rift, both David and his parents had continued to live in Brockleby, but on opposite sides of the town. Still, it was surprising that their paths hadn't crossed at one time or another.

"So when do you want to come round, then?" asked John Chambers, in a brusque voice that suggested he was in a hurry and had more serious matters to attend to.

"Tomorrow evening, if that is all right with you", answered David.

"All right, but I can't allow you to stay for long," warned John. "Your grandfather is very sick and visitors tire him out very quickly."

"I understand," answered David respectfully.

"Just as long as that is understood," said John, before ringing off.

David had to smile to himself. He had just called his father on a mobile phone, which struck him as amusing.

Until recently, the Eternal Fellowship had condemned these devices, along with computers, fax machines and the internet, believing them to be tools of the Devil, designed to corrupt mankind. Then, one day, the spiritual leadership must have had a change of heart. Suddenly, given the green light, the common foot soldiers were racing down to the shops to buy as much of this equipment as they could load into their cars.

After school, David drove down to his grandparents' house. Then, having rung the front door bell, he soon came face to face with his father. Concerned that his youngest son might outstay his welcome, John Chambers decided that he had better supervise the visit, rather than David's grandmother, who had been advised to remain in the kitchen.

"I told him you were coming," said John, as he led the way up the stairs. "You may find that your grandfather's mind wanders at times."

David felt strange at being in the large detached house again. Even after eight years, just the very sight of the hall and stairs brought childhood memories flooding back to him. He only wished he could have been permitted to stay for much longer, and be free to make a tour of all the rooms. Sadly, though, he knew that as a lapsed follower of the Fellowship, such an opportunity would not be allowed.

Once on the landing, John Chambers came to an abrupt halt. Then, turning to face David, he put a warning forefinger up to his lips.

"He is probably awake, but I will just creep in and make certain," he whispered.

David watched as his father gently pushed open a door that had been slightly ajar. Even after all this time, he remembered that this was the entrance to his grandparents' bedroom. He could still picture the wallpaper, with the multi-coloured floral pattern, even before coming face to face with it once again.

"David is here to see you, Pop," said John, in a raised voice. "David who?" came a feeble, rather mournful reply.

"Your grandson, of course," answered John. "I mentioned last night that he was coming to visit you today."

David was standing motionless at the end of the landing as he listened to this conversation. Although well aware that his grandfather was not long for this world, he was nonetheless shocked to hear him speak. The man he remembered would speak at Fellowship meetings in a strong confident voice that could be heard clearly throughout the church.

Suddenly, John appeared on the landing again and beckoned to his son. "You can come in for just a few minutes, but no more," he called out.

The bedroom was very much as David remembered it. The floral wallpaper had not been replaced, although it had now started to fade. Bill Chambers was never the most enthusiastic decorator in the world, and he hated getting someone in to do it. The pinkish curtains and the thick, red, well-worn carpet were also familiar.

Like his surroundings, Bill Chambers had clearly aged. His face and willowy right arm, which rested limply on top of the duvet, were both emaciated and sallow. There was a distant look in his watery eyes as he stared up at the ceiling.

"Hello Grandpa," said David, with a warm smile. "How are you feeling?" The old man slowly turned his head.

"Not too well," he sighed wearily. "I expect the Good Lord will be calling me home very soon now."

"I'm sure you'll get better before long," said David reassuringly.

"No," replied the old man with a little shake of the head. "The time has nearly come for me to leave this sinful world and go on to a better one."

At that moment, David wondered whether his grandfather actually recognized him. He had appeared to show no surprise at having come face to face with somebody he had last seen eight years ago. Perhaps the old man had become so tired of life, he hardly cared who came to visit him.

"Do you remember the day we went to Windsor and took out a rowing boat on the Thames?" asked David, with a wide grin.

"Lovely little place, is Windsor", replied the old man as his eyelids began to close. "Lovely little place."

"You must go now," said John, who was stood at the foot of the bed. "Your grandfather needs to rest."

David gently touched the old man's arm before following his father towards the door. At the very last moment, he turned to take one last look at his grandfather. He knew, beyond a shadow of doubt, that he would never see him again. All that he would be left with were fond memories.

David didn't expect his father to invite him to tea. Because of their religion, the Fellowship neither ate or drank with non-believers. As far as possible, they tried to remain separate from the rest of humanity.

"It's very sad to see Grandpa like that," said David, as he was about to step out of the front door. "He always used to be so robust and full of vitality".

John smiled.

"On the contrary, we should all feel happy for him, as he will soon be going to a better place." "But of course, he will be badly missed once he dies, though," said David.

"We will only be parted for a short time," answered John, reassuringly. "Then all those with faith will be reunited in Heaven."

David knew it was pointless to argue. From past experience, he had learnt that all the reasoning in the world would never shift his father's deeply-held convictions. John Chambers believed that those who spent their time praying for their souls would get preferential treatment in the next life over those that didn't. The good work that people did on the Earth apparently counted for little with the Almighty.

"You and Mum are always welcome to visit us," said David, as he shook his father's hand. "My wife and children would like to meet you."

John nodded his appreciation, but said nothing. After all these years, he was still angry with his son for having abandoned the Eternal Fellowship. Much of the blame he attached to Alison, an ungodly woman, in his opinion, who had led David into the arms of Satan. He had no wish to be introduced to his daughter-in-law or her offspring.

Later that evening, David was sitting in front of the TV, but found it difficult to concentrate on any programme. His thoughts kept returning to his grandfather and the transformation that had taken place in him. He was alone, as the three children were now in bed, while Alison was in the middle of a lengthy telephone conversation with one of her friends.

In his mind, David began to skip a generation. It was no longer his grandfather who lay dying, but his father and then his mother. Could it be, he wondered, that the next time he would be allowed to see his parents would be on their deathbeds?

Suddenly, these morbid ideas were interrupted. Having finally put down the phone, Alison strolled into the lounge wearing a big smile.

"Jacqui Dunn has been chosen as the Labour Party candidate for the by-election in Cumbria," she announced excitedly.

"Brilliant!" exclaimed David. "Hopefully she will soon be back in Parliament, then."

"Carol says that Tony is over the moon," said Alison, as she dropped into an armchair. "He believes he should be favourite to become the Brockleby Labour Party candidate at the next General Election".

"Perhaps he shouldn't be too confident," warned David. "Others might well be putting their names forward, too."

"Well, whoever they are, I intend to support Tony," replied Alison, determinedly. "How about you?"

"As I said before, I want to see who is standing before making a decision," answered David. "The branch members should be looking for the best candidate to take on the Tories."

Alison looked disgruntled as she grabbed a magazine off the coffee table.

"I just think that Tony should be rewarded for all the hard work he has put in for the party over the years," she said irritably.

"Can we drop the subject?" said David wearily, as he attempted to switch his faltering attention back to the TV set. "I'm not in the mood for arguing tonight."

Friday morning was bright and sunny. By half past nine, Mark was standing anxiously peering out of his bedroom window. Fully dressed, he was ready to set off the instant Mrs Fisher had been driven away to her coffee morning.

At twenty minutes to ten, the old lady arrived at her front gate. Looking smarter than usual, she was wearing a blue jacket with a matching skirt, while her wispy grey hair, which usually hung down over her cheeks, was tied up neatly in a bun. She had obviously made an effort with her appearance, being that it was her biggest, if not her only social engagement of the week.

Soon a car pulled up alongside Mrs Fisher's front gate. After a few moments, a large, rather overweight gentleman climbed out and gallantly opened the back door for the old lady. Mark could just make out two other passengers who were already inside.

Finally, the coast was clear. The car had turned the corner at the end of the road and it was time to be on his way. Although Mrs Fisher's house was likely to be unattended for some time, he was desperate to get the whole thing over and done with.

Soon he was in the woods. Much to his relief, the large paper carrier bag was exactly where he had left it the night before. Well covered by bracken, it had probably escaped the attention of any morning strollers who just happened to be passing by.

The contents of the bag had been lying in the loft for several years. The dark blue overalls, matching peaked cap and heavy-duty boots had once been Mark's father's work clothes. After his death, it was decided to store them away, as they might come in useful one day. Clearly, that day had now come.

Colin Wright had been about the same height as his son, although much stockier. Mark had squeezed two thick jumpers into the bag, so that the overalls wouldn't hang too loosely on him. The boots were unfortunately on the small side and pinched his toes when he walked. However, he was prepared to tolerate the pain for just the short period that he would be wearing them.

In addition to the clothes, he had one piece of equipment. It was a twenty-ounce claw hammer that he had taken from the shed. The tool was handily concealed once he had placed it inside the deep pocket of his overalls.

Having left his shoes in the carrier bag, he set off. As he was about to leave the woods, Mark put on a pair of dark glasses to complete his disguise. His heart was pounding hard as he pulled the peaked cap down even further over his forehead.

Soon he was back in his own road again. Much to his relief, there was no sign of anybody who might be likely to accost him at any moment. Of course, he couldn't be certain that a neighbour or two wasn't keeping a watchful eye on him from behind net curtains.

Mrs Fisher, like Mark, lived in a semi-detached property. The layout was the same, with a large kitchen window at the side of the house. Being about five feet above ground level meant that a stepladder was required in order to clean it.

Mark appreciated that any hesitancy would invite suspicion, so boldly pushing open the gate; he confidently strode down the garden path before making his way around the side of the house.

Facing the kitchen window was a six-foot high wooden fence. He felt reasonably certain, that the next-door neighbours were unlikely to disturb him. On both sides lived childless couples who were normally out all day at work.

Mark found two black dustbins in the back garden. Needing something to stand on, he took one and placed it below the window. Then balancing himself on top, he took out his claw hammer and pounded it hard against the centre of the glass, which immediately shattered, leaving a large gaping hole.

For a split second, Mark froze. He felt that the whole neighbourhood must have heard the sound of shattering glass. Most fragments had landed into the kitchen sink before dropping to the floor. A few, though, had dropped on to the gravel path outside.

He quickly regained his composure. With the hammer, he proceeded to knock out the jagged edges of glass that were now all that remained of the window pane. He was anxious to avoid cutting himself and thereby, leaving traces of blood either in the house or the road outside.

Once inside the kitchen, he hurried upstairs. Looking first into the front bedroom, he noted a dressing table and a woman's skirt hanging up in the far corner. With a feeling that this was where Mrs Fisher kept her savings, he fell to his knees and looked under the bed. There, much to his excitement, was a white shoebox.

Mark put his dark glasses to one side. After breaking in, he had removed this part of his disguise in order to see properly and had been holding them in his right hand. To avoid leaving fingerprints, he had taken the precaution of wearing some old rubber gloves.

With his heart in his mouth, Mark gingerly lifted off the shoebox lid. Suddenly he felt like jumping for joy, when he saw the little treasure trove that was stored inside. Bound up in elastic bands were wads of five, ten and twenty-pound notes – more money than he could remember seeing in his whole life.

Mark tried to calm himself down. When planning the robbery, he wondered whether the container storing the money might be too bulky to carry away, which now proved to be the case. He had brought a white plastic bag with a supermarket logo printed on the side. Soon he was rapidly filling it up with the loot.

In five minutes Mark had left the house and was making his way down the road. In his haste though, he had forgotten to pick up his dark glasses. It was a costly mistake as he was about to find out.

Just ahead, on his left, he suddenly saw a front door swing open. A middle aged woman then emerged and scurried down the garden path in her carpet slippers. It was Mrs Bailey, Tina's mother.

"Hello Mark", she called out. "I saw somebody coming out of Mrs Fisher's house and I was wondering who it was. As a matter of fact, I was thinking of calling the police".

Mark gave her a watery smile. Under his breath he cursed himself, suddenly aware that he had left his shades behind. They had meant to be an essential feature of his disguise.

He felt like a cornered rat. News of the burglary would spread like wildfire once Mrs Fisher returned from her coffee morning and Mrs Bailey would doubtless, provide her with the likely culprit. Tina's mother had a reputation for being the biggest gossip in the road.

"Just doing a bit of electrical work", explained Mark, trying his best to appear casual.

"I didn't know you were any good at that type of thing", said Mrs Bailey, with a look of admiration. "Tina will be pleased to know you are so handy. You will be able to make yourself useful when you move into her flat".

"Yes", answered Mark with a nervous smile. "Look I must be going. They are expecting me back at the office in fifteen minutes".

"Yes, Tina was telling me that you had a good job in an office. I must say, it is very generous of them to allow you time off to go and help a neighbour out", said Mrs Bailey, hopeful of prolonging the conversation as much as possible. She was eager to find out a little more about her daughter's future flat mate.

"I have a very friendly boss", replied Mark, as he gradually edged away. "Anyway, must be going now. Duty calls".

Having turned the corner he quickly removed his overalls. Deciding to abandon his shoes in the woods, he quickly walked around the block in order to arrive home from the other end of the road. He had no wish to arouse Mrs Bailey's suspicions anymore, by passing her house for a second time.

Once inside, Mark was on the phone. It was time to get in touch with an old friend that he hadn't seen for a while – somebody that he had been trying to avoid for a very good reason.

"Hello Ross, it's Mark Wright," he said, having recognized the voice on the other end of the line. "Where's my money?" answered Ross gruffly. "You owe me four hundred quid".

"You can have it today, plus another four hundred if you'll put me up for a few days," said Mark. "I've just had a bust up with mum and I need to get away for a break."

"You won the lottery or something?" asked Ross, sounding a little surprised.

"Never do the lottery," laughed Mark. "No, it's just that an uncle of mine died a while ago and I've just received a nice little legacy from his estate."

"Very well, then," answered Ross. "I'm sure mum won't mind you taking a little holiday with us. We can put you in the spare bedroom. What time will you be arriving?"

"Two hours at least," said Mark. "It takes ages to get to your place on the bus." "Remember to bring my money, though," warned Ross.

Having put down the phone, Mark hurried upstairs to pack his suitcase. He wanted to sit down and count the money he had stolen, but that little job would have to wait. It was also annoying that he hadn't the time to hang around for his four o'clock appointment with the two loan sharks. Although he wanted to clear his debt in order to get the bullies off his back, it meant taking a huge risk. The police would probably have arrested him by the time Harvey and Leo arrived.

❧ ⚕ ☙

It was mid-afternoon when Joan Wright received an unexpected visit from the police. Although shocked to discover that the two men in blue wanted to speak to her son about a burglary that had taken place in the road, she couldn't advise them of his whereabouts. Having been out for most of the morning, she had arrived home just after twelve to find that Mark had gone out.

At four o'clock, Joan received two more visitors who had come to see her son. She had met these gentlemen once before, but on that occasion, they had seemed much friendlier. Unlike the police though, they hadn't come to discuss Mrs Fisher's missing savings. Instead, it was to collect an outstanding debt that they were owed.

"I'm afraid I can't help you", said Joan. "Mark isn't here and I can't tell you where he is at the moment."

"Perhaps you could settle up with us then," suggested Harvey, with a steely look in his eyes. "I want three hundred quid now or your son will wish that he had never been born".

"Well I certainly can't afford to pay the money.", insisted Joan. "You will need to speak to Mark about it".

For a moment Harvey considered forcing his way passed Joan, grabbing her arm and pulling her into the living room. Once inside the house he and Leo would then terrorize the poor woman into handing them any money she had. As the man next door was cutting the lawn and seemed to be keeping one eye on what was going on at his neighbour's house though, the loan shark quickly dismissed the idea.

"Make no mistake, we'll soon track your son down," snarled Harvey. "We have our methods." "Rest assured, Mrs Wright," added Leo, clenching his enormous fists. "Rest assured."

CHAPTER EIGHT

It was the day after the burglary. Still in a state of shock, Joan Wright was sitting in an armchair staring blankly out of the back window. As it was warm and sunny, she would normally have been found pottering about in the garden, pulling up the odd weed or tending to the flowerbeds. But at present, she dreaded venturing outside and coming face to face with one of the neighbours.

There must have been a mistake, she kept telling herself. She was convinced that somebody else had stolen Mrs Fisher's money. As his mother, she knew better than anyone that Mark was incapable of carrying out such a callous act.

In the middle of the afternoon, Joan had a visitor. Wishing that she could completely cut herself off from the rest of the world, the sudden sharp ring of the doorbell made her shudder. However, concerned that it might be the police dropping in on her again, she didn't feel comfortable remaining still and pretending to be out.

The woman who stood on the doorstep was a stranger. In her late forties, she was dressed smartly in a grey trouser suit and carried a shiny black briefcase. Wearing a beaming smile, she had the appearance of a door-to-door double-glazing sales representative.

"Good afternoon," she said cheerily. "My name is Maureen and I wonder if I might come in for a few moments to talk about your son. I think I may be able to help him."

"Come in," replied Joan, concerned that her visitor didn't remain on the doorstep. She didn't want the neighbours to overhear anything that could cause their tongues to wag.

"Right," said Maureen, once she was seated with a notepad on her lap. "I want you to help me track down Mark before the police do. If your son has stolen the money, I may be able to persuade him to return it to the old lady. In that case, he would likely be given a lighter punishment."

"But the robbery only took place yesterday", answered Joan in surprise. "I thought only the police and a few neighbours knew about it. How did you find out so soon?"

"By word of mouth," smiled Maureen. "I represent a little group in Brockleby who try to help victims of crime. I was tipped off about the robbery by somebody who lives in this road".

"All right, then," said Joan still looking perplexed. "But I don't understand why you should be so concerned about my son. Why should it matter to you what punishment he receives?"

Suddenly, Maureen's smile gave way to a look of sympathy.

"My little group aren't just concerned about your son," she replied. "We would like to see poor Mrs Fisher recover her life savings."

"And is your organisation publicly funded?" asked Joan, who was still on her guard. *Watchdog* programmes on the TV had taught her to be wary of smooth-talking strangers in suits, turning up on the doorstep.

"We are a charity that depends on private donations", explained Maureen, after a moment's hesitation.

"Right then, so how can I help you?" asked Joan, having decided to put her trust in the stranger.

She could see how everybody's best interests could be served by being co-operative.

Maureen tried to hide her relief as she prepared to take notes.

"Right, well I would like to start by asking whether you have any idea where Mark may be at this very moment."

"As I told the police yesterday, when they came to the house. I don't have a clue", answered Joan, with a firm shake of the head.

"Then is it possible to give me the names, addresses and telephone numbers of any friends or relatives who may know where he is?" asked Maureen, suddenly sounding very business-like.

Having fetched an address book from the next room, Joan began flicking through the pages.

Because they were her own family as well as Mark's, she had no difficulty in supplying the relatives' details. When it came to her son's friends, however, this posed more of a problem. She knew some by their first names, but had no idea where they lived, let alone their telephone numbers.

"He has a good mate called Paul Chapple who lives in St. George's Street. I don't know the house number, though," said Joan apologetically.

"Not to worry," answered Maureen, eagerly writing this information down in her note pad. "I can get the number from the electoral register."

The two women sat together for nearly an hour. Maureen was pleased with the help she was getting from her hostess. The fact that Joan wasn't able to provide more details about her son's friends could be overcome, she told herself. Often people had a close network of acquaintances, and it was only necessary to contact one in order to discover the whereabouts of the others.

"By the way," said Joan, as her visitor was about to step outside the front door. "Mark was supposed to have been moving into a flat today, with a lady called Tina Bailey. I completely forgot to mention it earlier."

"Do you know where Tina lives?" asked Maureen, as she was about to delve into her briefcase once more for the note pad.

"No but you could always go and ask her mother," suggested Joan. "She happens to live down the road at number seventy-one. Mrs Bailey was the witness who said she saw Mark coming out of Mrs Fisher's house yesterday morning."

"I'll drop in on her now," smiled Maureen gratefully, as she set off down the garden path.

"I just want to say," called Joan, for the ears of the next-door neighbours as well as those of her departing visitor. "I am quite certain that my son is innocent."

Maureen turned back and nodded.

"I'm sure you are right."

❧ ❧

Maureen arrived home at seven o'clock that evening. After yet another lengthy meeting, she had left Tina Bailey's flat with more names in her note pad. Feeling both hungry and exhausted, she just wanted to eat and spend an hour or two relaxing in front of the TV.

"How did you get on?" asked Harvey Lucas, as he wandered into the kitchen. Maureen shrugged, before putting a ready-made meal into the microwave.

"I've been given plenty of contacts to follow up on. Let's hope that one of them knows where this guy has disappeared to."

"We need to track him down before the police do," said Harvey.

"And before he spends the sixty-five grand," added Maureen, glancing around at her husband. "We need to get hold of the money that he owes us."

"And the interest, of course," said Harvey, with a mean look in his eyes. "Believe me, after absconding like that, there will be plenty of interest for him to pay. When I catch up with him, I'll break every bone in his body and leave him with just a little bit of loose change in his pocket – just enough for him to find his way to the nearest hospital."

◦◦◦

The weather had changed for the worse over the previous few days. The recent hot spell seemed like a distant memory as light drizzle drifted down at frequent intervals below blankets of grey clouds. On the streets, people no longer strolled around in shirtsleeves and summer dresses, but instead hurried along in raincoats while supporting brollies over their heads.

The depressing conditions had hardly affected David's mood. On his journey home from school, he began to sing to himself in the car. He was feeling lighthearted because earlier in the day, Sophie had invited him over for an evening meal. In order to be discreet, she had sent him a text message during the lunch break.

"Guess what?" gasped Alison, before her husband had even a chance to hang up his coat. "The police want to interview Mark Wright in connection with a burglary that took place last Friday."

For a moment, David had to stop to think. Alison rarely mentioned the man she had once been engaged to. He was somebody that she tried hard to forget.

"Do you mean Amanda's father?" he asked finally.

"That's right," answered Alison, while thrusting a newspaper at her husband. "It's here on the front page."

The *Brockleby Times* had printed the bold headlines 'Pensioner robbed of her life savings'. The report that followed revealed that a thief had broken into a Mrs Fisher's home and had stolen sixty-five thousand pounds, which was all the money she had in the world.

A Mrs Bailey also featured in the newspaper's account. She was the witness who had seen a neighbour leaving the old lady's house at the time of the robbery and then accosted him. Although suspicious, she had accepted Mr Wright's explanation that he had been inside the property to undertake some electrical work. Mrs Joan Wright, the mother who lived at the same address as the suspect, had told the news reporter that she had no knowledge of her son's whereabouts. The police were, therefore, requesting information from the public that might assist them to apprehend Mr Wright.

Alongside the report was a passport-size photograph of the suspect. David had met him once, when Mark had called at the house to see his daughter about seven years earlier. It had been on that occasion when he had reached an agreement with Alison to stay well away from Amanda. If Mark complied, a promise was made that he would never be pursued for maintenance.

"Unbelievable," said David, when he had handed back the newspaper to Alison. "How could anyone stoop so low?"

"I just wonder where he could be hiding out," replied Alison thoughtfully. "With his picture in the local paper, I don't think he would be stupid enough to remain in Brockleby."

"With sixty-five grand to play around with, he could travel an awful long way," commented David. "Even leave the country, if he wished."

Alison shook her head.

"Unless he has changed, I doubt it very much. Mark was always too much of a little Englander to go and live abroad."

"As far as you know, did he have connections in any other part of the country?" asked David, as he finally got around to hanging up his coat.

Alison shrugged.

"Not when I knew him, but that was a long time ago, of course. What surprises me, though, is that Mark should resort to housebreaking. Whatever his faults, he was never a thief."

"Desperation, perhaps?" suggested David.

At that very moment their conversation was interrupted by the telephone. As usual, David allowed Alison the privilege of hurrying down the hall to answer it. Very soon after their marriage, he had reached the conclusion that the bulk of the incoming calls were likely to be for his wife.

David wasn't due to arrive at Sophie's flat for almost three hours. To kill a little time, he joined the two younger children in the lounge to watch a cartoon on TV. A pulsating beat overhead sent out a clear message that Amanda was in her bedroom enjoying a noisier form of entertainment.

"That was Carol on the phone," said Alison, suddenly bursting into the room. "We've arranged to meet up at the station in half an hour. Can you make certain that Joshua and Abigail are both in bed by eight?"

David turned to her in alarm.

"But I've arranged to go out, too," he gasped.

"Listen, you promised at the weekend to stay in with the kids tonight, while Carol and I went up to London," said Alison, standing with her hands on hips and glaring threateningly at her husband. "You can't change your mind now."

Immediately, David panicked as he recalled the conversation. The matter had been discussed over Sunday breakfast, while he had been trying to study the football results in the newspaper. For some reason, though, he had completely forgotten about the agreement.

"Look, I've promised a few of the teachers that I'll be meeting them in the pub tonight. Can't you ask your mum to come over and look after the kids?" pleaded David.

"Don't you ever listen?" answered Alison, staring up at the ceiling in exasperation. "My mum is on holiday this week in the Lake District. I must have mentioned it to you at least a dozen times."

"Isn't there somebody else who could help us out this evening?" asked David in desperation. "Not at the last moment," answered Alison. "Anyway, it won't hurt you to bath and put the kids to bed for once."

David knew he was beaten. He was now left with the task of ringing Sophie and telling her that she would probably be spending the evening alone. It concerned him to think that after letting her down, he might never get another invite. Worse still, she might even bring their affair to a close.

Once Alison had gone out, he left the two children watching TV and wandered into the kitchen.

Then, having quietly shut the door behind him, he reluctantly called Sophie on his mobile phone. He only hoped he could convey his overwhelming disappointment at having to cancel.

"Look, I'm sorry about this," began David, as soon as he heard Sophie's voice. "But I'm afraid I've got a problem."

"What sort of problem?" asked Sophie, sounding a little surprised.

"Alison has gone out tonight and I've been left to look after the kids," explained David, sounding like a small boy caught stealing toffees from a sweet shop. "As much as I'd love to, I'm afraid I won't be able to come round this evening. I'm really disappointed."

"Oh for goodness sake," protested Sophie, indignantly. "After making a special effort to prepare a nice meal, you tell me at the last minute that I've got to sit and eat it by myself."

"Perhaps you could save it until tomorrow night," suggested David. "I'm free if you are." "Forget it," snapped Sophie. "I've arranged to go out with friends."

Once the call was over, David cursed out loud. Then, to vent his feelings to the full, he gave the plastic rubbish bin an almighty kick. Immediately, he regretted his reckless behaviour. Not only was the kitchen floor covered by an assortment of unsavoury-looking debris, but soggy tea bags were slowly sliding down the wall, leaving a trail of wet stains.

David feared that his adulterous relationship was over. Sophie had talked about how she always returned her married lovers back home to their wives once she had finished with them. Now he wondered whether it was his turn to get the elbow.

Soon the music overhead suddenly became a few decibels louder. David had just managed to persuade the two younger children that it was time to switch off the TV and get themselves ready for bed. It was quite obvious that they wouldn't be getting any sleep unless the CD player was turned down.

David was in no mood to be conciliatory. Although he had calmed down somewhat, after having taken his frustration out on the rubbish bin, he was far from happy. Not only had his entire evening been spoilt, but he had managed to convince himself that the carnal relationship which had brightened up his life was now a thing of the past.

After storming up the stairs, he hammered on Amanda's door. Meanwhile, Joshua and Abigail, who had followed in his footsteps, watched on with fascination. They always enjoyed the frequent confrontations between their father and half-sister.

"Turn that racket down", bellowed David.

Within seconds his command was obeyed. Appreciating that her mother wasn't around to defend her, Amanda decided to be compliant. However, she wasn't prepared to be entirely submissive.

"Leave me alone", she answered back. "You're not me real dad".

David ignored the remark as he retreated down the stairs. He managed to restrain himself from replying that unlike Mark Wright, he wasn't a thief. He had agreed with Alison not to tell Amanda what her real father had done for fear of upsetting her.

The following evening David volunteered to go out canvassing. It was Thursday and in exactly a week, residents in the Sefton ward would have an opportunity to vote for a new councillor. Both Labour and the Tories were pulling out all the stops to win the seat.

Earlier in the day it had been raining. However, much to everyone's relief, by seven o'clock the black clouds had drifted away, leaving large patches of blue sky. The Brockleby Labour Party headquarters were packed with supporters willing to lend a hand. Apart from local members, a number of enthusiastic activists had arrived from outside the constituency.

Canvassing wasn't exactly David's favourite pastime. On this occasion though, he welcomed the opportunity to call on residents and discuss political matters with them. For a couple of hours it allowed him to forget all his other troubles.

It was just after nine when he returned to headquarters. Having bought a pint of beer at the bar, he took his place amongst some of the local activists. As usual, they were gathered around two tables which had been joined together at the ends.

"How did it go this evening?", asked Tony, casting his eyes around the group.

"So-so", replied Kenny, "Some people said they were voting for us, but there were others who are still undecided about which party to support".

"What do you think?", asked Tony, turning to face Alec Stokes. "As the Labour candidate in this election, are you finding that many voters have yet to make up their minds?".

"I fear that many of the people I have been speaking to won't be bothering to vote at all. They seem to have lost trust in all the major parties. They blame Labour for causing the economic crisis in the first place, and the Coalition government for making the cuts," replied Alec despondently.

All those present nodded in agreement. As experienced political activists, they knew only too well that council elections were often decided on national, rather than local issues. If a candidate happened to represent an unpopular party, then voters would rarely take into account that person's suitability to serve the local community.

"If people on the doorstep insist on talking about national issues, let's give it to them straight," said Tony, who was anxious that everybody should remain upbeat. "Tell them that the cuts are unnecessary and Labour will reduce the deficit by increasing taxes on the very rich."

"Perhaps Britain's finances would be in better shape if we stopped invading countries like Iraq and Afghanistan," suggested Kenny, with a look of scorn.

"Very good point," agreed Tony. "The problem is, though, that we seem to have too many warmongers in our own party to be able to capitalize on that."

"Changing the subject," said Alec, thoughtfully, "how many people so far have put their names forward to be the next parliamentary Labour Party candidate for Brockleby?"

Suddenly a smile appeared on Tony's face as he gazed down at his beer mug.

"Nobody," he replied after a few seconds. "Carol gave me the news today that she is pregnant. As a father-to-be, I will no longer be in contention."

Immediately, everyone brightened up. Carol, the only woman in the group, had largely been ignored until that moment. Now, suddenly, she became the centre of attention. Even fanatical party activists, it seemed, could at times be diverted from discussing politics.

"When is the baby due?" asked David, eager to be the first to get a question in. "Early January," replied Carol proudly.

Not wishing to be outdone, Kenny was next.

"Do you want a boy or a girl?" he enquired, remembering it was a question his aunt always asked.

"Providing the baby is healthy, I don't really mind," smiled Carol.

"Will you breast feed or give the baby a bottle?" asked Alec, before receiving strange looks from some of the other men.

"Breast feed," replied the expectant mother. "Mother's milk helps babies fight off infections." Tony was beginning to feel distinctly uncomfortable. In his opinion, matters such as this were better discussed in prenatal classes, rather than a group of men drinking pints of beer. It was time, he decided, to get back to the original subject.

"As I'm not standing for the position of parliamentary candidate, perhaps somebody here might consider going for it," he said, looking in turn at all those around the two tables. "We don't want somebody who lives outside the constituency being imposed on us centrally by the National Executive Committee."

For a few moments, there was complete silence. Then, with the exception of two members of the group, everyone began shaking their heads. The two who remained perfectly still had once been housemates before one of them got married.

"I need time to consider it," said Kenny finally.

"Me too," said David. "I will need to discuss it with Alison before I make a decision."

CHAPTER NINE

Mark Wright and Ross Young were old school friends. As pupils of Lavington Park Secondary, neither had managed to impress any member of the teaching staff with their academic abilities, yet both were highly respected for their footballing prowess. They were undoubtedly the two best players in the first eleven.

After leaving school, Mark and Ross had remained in touch. Both were regulars at The White Horse, and together they had been persuaded to join the pub's Sunday league football team. Much to the landlord's delight, with the addition of a prolific goal scorer and a hard tackling centre back, the side were quickly promoted to the top division.

For several years, Ross, like Mark, had been in and out of work. Having taken a number of low paid jobs with few prospects, he had noticed an advertisement in the local paper that had started his pulse racing. The very next day, he arrived at the Army recruitment centre in the high street to make enquiries.

Ross was feeling nervous when he first entered the showroom. He was soon put at his ease when given the opportunity to test out a battlefield simulator to replicate a conflict situation. Then, after a lengthy conversation with a soldier – somebody who had served both in Northern Ireland and Iraq – he was invited to fill in an application form.

With care and precision, he began putting down answers to the numerous questions. For the first time ever, he knew what he wanted to do with his life. He longed to carry a rifle and put on a smart uniform, rather than lug a tool kit around, while wearing greasy overalls in a factory. It was now a matter of convincing those in charge that he was the right material for a military career.

Finally, Ross completed the form and handed it in at the desk. Knowing that the Army were eager to recruit, he expected to hear back from them reasonably quickly. However, he was made to wait for a while as references were taken up and security checks were carried out. Then one day he returned home to find an official letter waiting for him on the mantelpiece. It was a request that he should attend an assessment day.

Ross was overjoyed. Unfortunately, the date of the assessment wasn't until the autumn, which meant that he would have to remain in his soul-destroying job for another six months. With so many bills to pay, he couldn't afford to be unemployed.

Everyone was keeping their fingers crossed for him. Then one evening he marched into The White Horse with a big grin on his face. Waving a letter triumphantly in the air, he announced to his friends that the Army had enrolled him on a training course and he had just given in his notice at work. To celebrate the good news, he went up to the bar to order a round of drinks.

Mark had been in the pub that evening. Like everyone else, he was delighted for Ross, but appreciated that he would be seeing far less of his friend in the future. As a member of the armed forces, he would doubtless be sent out to any one of the trouble spots around the world.

Almost two years later, the good news suddenly turned sour. According to the *Brockleby Times*, Private Ross Young had been seriously injured in Afghanistan. He was the victim of a roadside bomb while on foot patrol in Helmand Province. The report concluded by stating that the soldier had been treated at the field hospital at Camp Bastion, before being flown home to the UK.

It was a few weeks before Mark discovered the extent of his friend's injuries. He had wanted to travel up to Birmingham, where Ross had been placed in a military hospital, but as usual, he couldn't afford the train fare, so he had to wait for others to undertake the journey and then report back to him with the details.

Mark was stunned when at last he was given a first-hand account. It seemed that Ross had completely lost the use of his legs after the explosion. The injuries were so bad that the doctors treating him didn't believe he would ever walk again. Sadly, the war hero was likely to be confined to a wheelchair for the rest of his life.

During the period that Ross had been in Afghanistan, his parents had moved. Having sold their three-bedroom house in Brockleby, they had gone to live in a small village some nine or ten miles away. Alterations on their new bungalow, paid for by the Army, had since been carried out to accommodate the needs of a paralysed person in a wheelchair.

Like Mark, Ross had never married. Women had come and gone in his life, but there had never been any lasting relationships. The thought of being responsible for a family, with a long-term mortgage to pay off, had never really appealed to him. He liked to be free to go out drinking with his friends whenever he pleased – and then afterwards, to return to a doting mother, who could always be relied upon to take care of all his domestic requirements.

Having been severely incapacitated by his injuries, Ross's social life was to change forever. Once he had been released from hospital, it became awkward to go down the pub regularly. Now he depended on friends to drop in for a chat, while knocking back cans of beer at the same time. At first, there were plenty of people who were keen to come to his home and pay tribute to the war hero. After a few weeks, though, the numbers rapidly dwindled.

Mark had visited Ross only once. It was on that occasion when he had borrowed four hundred pounds. Dropping in on him a second time then became a problem, as he hadn't the money to repay the loan. That is of course, until he had robbed Mrs Fisher of her life savings.

❧ ☙

At a leisurely speed, the bus travelled along a succession of winding lanes with hedgerows on either side. From the top deck, Mark gazed down upon fields coloured in various shades of green and bright yellow. Bathed in the early afternoon sunshine, it seemed as though a magnificent patchwork quilt had been laid out over the rolling Kent countryside.

On another day, Mark might have sat back and admired the glorious scenery. However, at present he had more pressing matters to consider as he made the long journey from Brockleby to Craneyford. Haunted by a nagging fear of being captured by the police, Harvey Lucas or possibly both, it was often difficult to think straight. But gradually, he began to put a plan together that he hoped would keep him out of arm's reach of his pursuers.

Finally, the bus arrived at Craneyford. Mark was relieved to be able to stretch his long legs, after having being seated for so long. It was almost a mile from the high street to Ross's bungalow, but he was grateful for the walk, even if it did mean wheeling a squeaky suitcase in front of him.

The guidebook stated that in the 2001 census, Craneyford had a population of three thousand five hundred. Most of those of working age commuted to London on a daily basis. Only a few shops, four independent pubs and several farms offered any form of local employment.

Mark remembered the way from his first visit to see Ross. He recognized the Norman church to his left, built in stone and surrounded by yew trees, which cast lengthy shadows over the ancient gravestones beneath. Very much at the heart of the village, it was always well attended by worshippers at both morning and evening services on a Sunday.

Ross lived on an estate. It seemed to be one of those quiet, respectable neighbourhoods, where people kept their gardens neat and tidy and didn't have the type of children who committed acts of vandalism. At last, he came to a stop outside the bungalow he had been looking for and pushed open the gate.

Ross's mother looked solemn as she greeted her guest at the front door. "It's nice to see you again, but I'm terribly sorry to hear about your uncle."

For a split second, Mark went blank. Then he suddenly remembered that he had lied to Ross about a non-existent uncle who had died, leaving him a nice little legacy. Under the circumstances, he could hardly have said that his newly acquired wealth had been stolen from a shoebox, hidden under an old lady's bed.

"Thank you, Mrs Young," replied Mark politely.

"Was he very old?" asked Mrs Young.

"Ninety-three," answered Mark, simply clutching a figure from out of the air. Mrs Young looked at him in amazement.

"You have an uncle of ninety-three?" she gasped.

Immediately, Mark spotted his error. It made him appreciate even more, that he would have to be extremely careful in the future before telling lies. Mrs Young was familiar with his mother and had met his father on several occasions before his death. It was no wonder that she had been shocked to learn that either of his parents, would have been old enough to have such an elderly brother.

"Actually, he was a great-uncle," said Mark, finally correcting himself.

"Oh well, that seems to make more sense," replied Mrs Young, as she ushered her visitor into the lounge.

Ross glanced away from the TV as Mark entered the room. Sitting upright in his wheelchair, he had been in the middle of watching yet another repeat of one of those half-hour comedy programmes. It had first been shown years ago, and the actors on the screen had either long since retired or gone to a better place in the sky.

"Good to see you again," said Mark with a warm smile.

"And you," answered Ross, as he swivelled his wheelchair around in order to face his friend. "My sister was only talking about you last night, as it happens."

"And how is Jessica, by the way?" asked Mark.

"Keeping active as ever," replied Ross proudly. "Anyway, it seems that her daughter Amy, is in the same class at school as your daughter."

Mark's ears immediately pricked up. Ever since he had agreed not to make contact with Amanda seven years earlier, he had never received a word about her until now. He was only too well aware, of course, that he and Alison moved in completely different social circles.

"Did Jessica have any news about Amanda?" Mark enquired eagerly.

"Only that she doesn't get on very well with her stepfather," answered Ross. "Apparently the two of them are always arguing."

"Amanda actually told Amy, that she was going to find her real dad and then run away with him," chipped in Mrs Young, who had seated herself in an armchair.

"Bless her," answered Mark, gazing forlornly down at the carpet. Suddenly a cunning smile appeared on Mrs Young's face.

"I have an idea," she said enthusiastically. "I know that you are not allowed to see your daughter. Supposing Jessica were to invite Amanda around to have tea with Amy, and you just accidentally dropped in at the same time?"

A few days earlier, Mark would have immediately agreed to the plan. However, what had just occurred that morning had put an entirely different complexion on everything. Once news got around that he was a thief who robbed vulnerable old ladies, not even his own daughter would want to know him.

"Let me think about it," he smiled.

"By the way, I'll make you a cup of tea," said Mrs Young, springing to her feet. "You must be exhausted after your journey."

It was a while before Mark finally got around to unpacking. However, before putting his clothes away, he emptied out the wads of notes from the white plastic bag. Then with his heart beating like a pile driver, he began counting out the proceeds from the robbery.

"Just over sixty-five grand," he muttered breathlessly, as he laid down the last fiver. "The silly old fool should have had the sense to put it in the bank."

Ross was pleased to be presented with the four hundred pounds that he had lent to his friend.

Mrs Young, though, refused to take any money off Mark for his food and lodgings during his stay. He was good company for her son and was welcome to come any time, she assured him.

"How long do you intend to stay for?" Ross enquired.

It was a tricky question for Mark to answer. He needed to make certain arrangements before moving on. On the other hand, he couldn't afford to stay with the family for too long. As Ross was known to be a close friend, one of his pursuers might well be knocking on the front door in the very near future.

"I shall go on Sunday morning, if that is OK," he replied, after considering the matter for a few moments. "Hopefully by then, the air will have cleared a bit at home and mum will be in a better mood".

Tea was on the table at six-thirty. That allowed Mr Young, who had just arrived home from work, a few minutes to wash his hands before sitting down to eat. He was just one of the hordes of commuters who had deserted the City of London for the weekend.

Later, the four gathered around the TV in the lounge. Mrs Young was an ardent *EastEnders* fan, so the three men felt obliged to sit in silence while the programme was on. As somebody who disliked soap operas, Mark used the half hour to give a little more thought to his future plans.

Once the evening's episode had come to an end, everyone felt free to speak again. Mrs Young would have to wait until the following Monday to discover whether a bald-headed character was actually going to walk out on his girlfriend. Probably nobody else in the room cared two hoots whether he did or not.

"Is there a library close by?" asked Mark, now that he was able to catch everyone's attention. "There is one in Chandlersgate," answered Mrs Young. "That's where I borrow my books from." "I hope you won't think me rude, but I would like to pop over there in the morning, then," said Mark. "It's just that I need to check something out in the reference section."

"As it happens, I am going over there myself tomorrow to buy a few odds and ends," said Mrs Young. "I could drop you off at the library at the same time."

At eleven o'clock next morning, Mark was left standing outside a red brick building. He waved Mrs Young before she drove away to do her shopping at Sainsbury's, which was further down the high street. His hostess for the weekend had agreed to pick him up in an hour and a half. This, he assured her, was more than enough time to find the information he was seeking.

Like most Saturday mornings, the library was more crowded than normal. However, he was still able to find a table on which to rest the yellow soft-covered book that he had removed from the shelf. Soon he was busy scribbling down names, addresses and telephone numbers. Then, having recorded the details of ten guest-houses, he neatly folded up the sheet of A4 paper and tucked it into the back pocket of his jeans.

Perhaps the recent spell of hot weather had helped him to make up his mind. He had decided to live by the sea, but not in a resort with a shingly beach. In his opinion, there was something magical about bright yellow sand that felt soft under the feet and was perfect to sunbathe on. As a child, he had loved to build a castle from those fine particles of decomposed rock; then sit and wait for the flimsy construction to be swept away by the advancing tide.

Choosing a new hometown for himself, hadn't been difficult. As a small boy, he had often been taken there by his parents during the summer holidays. Usually it was just for the day, but occasionally, the family had stayed for a week. Although not exactly a million miles from Brockleby, at least it was well away from his pursuers.

Mark left the library and went into the nearest sweet-shop. Then, having given the assistant a twenty-pound note for a chocolate bar, he asked for his change in coins. Once he was back on the street, he spotted a telephone kiosk just outside the post office. Grateful that nobody was currently using the facility, he briskly crossed the road and pulled open the door, before anyone else had an opportunity to stake their claim.

After making several calls, he began to panic. Every guesthouse that he had rung so far was fully booked up for weeks ahead. More than one person that he had spoken to advised him, that during the summer months, it was practically impossible to get in at the last moment.

The coins that he started with were being swallowed up quickly. He was beginning to consider changing his plans as he dialled the next number. This time he was made to wait for a while, before somebody finally picked up the receiver at the other end.

"The Friendly Welcome Guest House," announced a female voice. "Sorry to keep you waiting." "I would like to book a single room for a week, starting from tomorrow," said Mark, with his fingers tightly crossed.

"How lucky are you?" said the voice cheerfully. "Only ten minutes ago, somebody called to cancel their reservation for a single room. The poor lady had been looking forward to a week by the sea, but was suddenly taken ill late last night."

Had he not have been in a tightly enclosed telephone box, Mark would have punched the air in delight.

"I'll take it then, please," he replied, without hesitation.

"In that case, I shall need a deposit of twenty-five pounds from you," said the voice.

Mark immediately realized he faced a new problem. Two years earlier, he had built up a credit card debt of one thousand eight hundred pounds. Having been broke at the time, he had begged his mother to come to the rescue. After some persuasion, she agreed to clear the balance in full, provided that he shredded the little piece of plastic in his wallet. Since then, he had made all his payments in cash.

"Unfortunately, I've had my credit card stolen," explained Mark nervously. "Can I pay you tomorrow?"

"Sorry, but I can't hold the room for that long without a deposit," replied the voice apologetically.

"Is the room vacant now?" asked Mark.

"Yes," replied the voice. "My last guest moved out over an hour ago."

"Suppose I were to bring forward my holiday," said Mark thoughtfully. "If you could just hold the room for two hours, that would give me enough time to get down there on the train."

"Very well," replied the voice, with a friendly laugh. "I don't want to stop you having a nice relaxing week down at the seaside. I am Mrs Derbyshire, by the way. Could I take your name and address?"

This time, Mark was fully prepared. While in the library, he had scanned through a directory that listed the names, addresses and phone numbers of certain private residents in Craneyford and the surrounding area. At random, he had scribbled down the details of a Mr Paul Brown, which is what he now read out. No doubt the gentleman in question would be slightly bemused when he received a Christmas card from a certain Mrs Derbyshire later in the year.

Mark was slightly taken aback to learn that he would need to part with three hundred pounds. In return, he would receive the use of a single room with an en suite bathroom, while being served breakfast and evening meals for a week. It seemed very expensive, but then, he was hardly in a position to argue.

"Jack rang me while I was in the supermarket," announced Mrs Young, after she had picked Mark up in the high street. "He is organizing a barbeque, so we will be having lunch in the back garden."

"Great," replied Mark cheerfully.

In fact, he had no intention of joining the Youngs for a midday meal. As soon as they arrived back at the bungalow, he planned to pack his things and hopefully leave undetected. He had neither the time nor the patience to explain why he needed to make such a hasty departure. Of course, he knew that the whole family would think that he had been extremely rude, to sneak off without even saying goodbye. However, that was the least of his worries. After all, once Ross and his family discovered that he stole money from vulnerable old ladies, he realized only too well that their opinion of him would sink to rock bottom in any case.

"One thing which I meant to ask you," said Mark, as the car eventually pulled up in the drive. "Which school do Amanda and your granddaughter attend?"

"Collingwood Secondary," replied Mrs Young, without hesitation.

Mark decided to scribble down the name at the earliest opportunity. It was nice to discover one fact about his daughter. He only wished he knew a great deal more. That now seemed less likely to him than before, though. He felt reasonably confident that because of the robbery, Amanda, like many others, would never again want anything to do with him.

CHAPTER TEN

It was mid-afternoon by the time the train arrived at the station. With only a road name to assist him in locating his ultimate destination, Mark had to stop a stranger and ask for directions. Still pushing the squeaky suitcase by its extended handle, he eventually turned a corner and spotted a large board no more than a hundred metres away. On it, printed in bold black capitals on a blue background, were the words 'The Friendly Welcome Guest House.'

Mark opened the gate and strolled down the garden path. Ahead of him was a three-storied, semi-detached property with large bay windows at every level. On the lawn were a red and white striped parasol and several deck chairs, which at that very moment were unoccupied.

As he was about to ring the bell, the door swung open. Suddenly he came face to face with a large woman in a bright floral dress, which revealed her suntanned shoulders and arms.

"Mr Brown?" she enquired, with a warm smile.

"That's right", replied Mark, feeling a little strange at having answered to a false name. "I'm Mrs Derbyshire," said the woman. "My husband and I are the owners. I hope it isn't a problem, but I forgot to say on the phone that your room is on the top floor."

"Doesn't bother me," answered Mark, with a shrug of the shoulders.

"Oh that's good, then," said Mrs Derbyshire, with a look of relief. "If you follow me, I'll show you where it is."

After climbing several flights of stairs, Mark was eventually led into a small room. Having noticed that the ceiling slanted down sharply over the bed, he feared hitting his head when getting up in the morning. Much of the remainder of the floor space was covered by a double wardrobe and a chest of drawers. However, even though it was far from spacious, the room was clean and cheerful, while from the window, it was possible to see the sea between the two houses on the opposite side of the road.

Mark handed the landlady three hundred pounds for the week's board. In exchange, he received keys to both his room and the front door, before being given instructions on how to use the shower. Only when she felt confident that her new guest wouldn't be responsible for causing a flood did Mrs Derbyshire leave him alone to unpack.

After a quick wash in the en suite bathroom, he tipped the contents of his suitcase on to the bed.

Looking down upon the white plastic bag containing all those wads of bank notes reminded him that he faced yet another problem. It was a matter of deciding whether to take the money with him when he went out or risk leaving it in his room.

It wasn't just the fear of being robbed that concerned him. In his absence, the cleaner, whoever that might be, could decide to rummage around in the drawers and wardrobe. Should that be the case, anyone who discovered sixty-five grand lying around would naturally be suspicious. Why, they might wonder, would he require so much to spend on just a seven-day holiday at the seaside?

After giving the matter some thought, Mark decided to lock the money up in his suitcase for the time being. Having put all his clothes and other possessions away, he changed into his shorts and headed for the beach. He longed to relax in the sun and perhaps even dip his feet in the cool sea.

The dining room opened at seven o'clock. Most of the other guests were already seated and studying the menu by the time Mark wandered in. With her usual beaming smile, Mrs Derbyshire directed him towards a table for two, which was close to the wall. Then, having taken his order for both the first and second courses, she quickly breezed out of the door.

While waiting to be served, some of the other guests spoke in hushed whispers. Mark was just able to overhear a conversation between two elderly ladies who were sitting on the next table. As he had nothing to do other than to read the wine list, he found that their dialogue provided him with some mildly amusing entertainment.

"I do hope that my neighbour remembers to feed Suzie," said one in a hoarse whisper. "Does your pussy pine for you when you're not there?" enquired her companion quietly. "I know that mine does."

The first one gave a firm nod.

"You should see her scamper towards me when I return from one of my holidays."

The two ladies suddenly fell silent. Mrs Derbyshire had returned from the kitchen carrying a large silver tray and stopped beside their table. Then, with the beaming smile that rarely left her face, she presented her elderly guests with bowls of soup. After this brief intervention, the subject moved on from pining felines. In fact, by the time the second course arrived, the ladies had already discussed the vicar's posh new car, the increase in the cost of a first-class stamp and somebody in the news who had won the lottery.

The following morning, it was a lot noisier in the dining room. Some of the bolder guests, who had introduced themselves to people on other tables, had managed to create a more relaxed atmosphere. Those hushed, almost self-conscious whispers had given way to normal conversation and even some laughter. Mark may have been one of the few who would have preferred to eat his breakfast in peace.

"I'm Paula, by the way," said the proud owner of Suzie the cat. "This is my friend Dorothy".

Mark acknowledged the two elderly ladies on the next table with a half-smile.

"Paul Brown," he replied, remembering just in time to introduce himself by his newly adopted name.

"We're here for a week," said Paula. "How long are you staying for?"

"Just a week, like you," answered Mark.

"And where do you live?" asked Dorothy, who seemed keen to play her part in the interrogation.

"Craneyford," replied Mark, ensuring that his answer was consistent with the information he had already given to Mrs Derbyshire.

"And what do you do for a living?" asked Paula.

"I'm a vivisectionist," replied Mark, managing to keep a straight face. "I cut up animals in a laboratory for medical research".

Paula's face seemed to drop as she glanced across the table at her companion. Cutting up furry little creatures was not something that she liked to think about at the breakfast table. However, now that the subject had been raised, curiosity was beginning to get the better of her.

"What type of animals do you dissect?" she enquired, with a look of concern. Mark shrugged.

"All sorts. Mice, rats, cats ...."

"You cut up poor little pussy cats?" asked Dorothy, with a look of horror.

"All the time," replied Mark, who was beginning to enjoy himself. "Cats are very good animals to experiment on. It's very easy to tell how much they are suffering when you are carrying out a trial."

At that moment Mrs Derbyshire arrived with her silver tray. Wearing her usual fixed smile, she placed a large plate before each of the two elderly ladies. Then, before scurrying back to the kitchen, she stopped at another table to enquire, whether a middle-aged couple were ready to order their breakfast.

"Doesn't it upset you to see a poor little cat in distress?" asked Paula, suddenly remembering her sweet little Suzie back home.

Mark shook his head.

"I'm used to it. As it happens, I don't really like cats that much. Give me a dog any day."

The conversation had almost put Paula off her food. She could hardly bear to look down on those two curled up rashers of bacon lying side by side on her plate. A poor little piggy had been sliced up, she told herself, just so that the guests in the dining room could sit down and enjoy a good hearty, full English breakfast.

The two elderly ladies left Mark alone after that – not just for the meal, but for the rest of the holiday. It was the view of both Paula and Dorothy that any person who was unable to sympathize with a poor defenceless animal being tortured was not somebody worth speaking to.

The truth was that Mark was quite squeamish. He had always hated the sight of blood and would have found it almost impossible to dissect any creature without being violently sick. Although not exactly an animal lover, he had no objection to them in principle.

After breakfast, he headed for the beach once again. Dressed only in shorts and trainers, he was determined to make the most of the hot weather while it lasted. During breakfast, he had overheard somebody say that the next few days were going to be wet and windy.

There was little more than a scattering of people on the beach when Mark arrived. Several small boys were gathered around a rock pool, searching for crabs or anything else brought up on the last tide. A few adults had ventured into the sea for a swim, while others, close to the shore, splashed amongst the waves with young children.

Mark was soon soaking up the sun. Spread out on a white bath towel, borrowed from the guesthouse, he lay with his eyes shut. It was so peaceful, and the only sound to disturb his thoughts, were the cries of seagulls as they circled around overhead.

In several hours, the beach was packed with holiday-makers. It was now hotter still, and at one point, he ventured into the sea for a swim. When he just happened to turn his head to the shore, he spotted Paula and Dorothy reclining in deck chairs and both reading a Sunday newspaper. He made certain not to look in their direction when finally stepping out of the water to dry off.

In spite of applying sun cream lotion to himself at regular intervals, Mark still got burnt. Much of his body felt as stiff as a board when he returned to the guest house later in the day. However, he was happy to suffer the agony, knowing that his bright red skin would turn brown in a few days.

The following morning the sun had disappeared behind grey skies. While the temperature had dropped significantly, there was drizzle in the air and the beach was practically deserted. A few holidaymakers were wandering around the shops, but most had decided to remain in their hotels, guest houses and self-catering apartments.

Mark wasn't too unhappy that the weather had changed for the worst. He now felt more motivated to tackle his most pressing problem. The room at the guesthouse had been booked for one week only, after which another holiday maker would be moving in. He needed to find somewhere permanent to live before finally handing back the keys to Mrs Derbyshire on Saturday morning.

His first thought was to search through the advertisements in a local newspaper. However, as Mark made his way down the high street, he happened to pass one of the many restaurants that competed for business in the resort. Outside was a glass frame and underneath were a dozen or more postcards. Each one was advertising either services of some description, goods to sell or accommodation to rent.

His attention was instantly drawn to the words 'bedsit'. Noting that the room had cooking facilities and the weekly rent seemed reasonable, Mark scribbled down the contact number. Concerned that others might also be interested, he decided to ring up straight away. As it happened, there was a telephone box only fifty metres away.

"Yes, the room is still available", answered a rather high-pitched female voice. "Great," answered Mark enthusiastically. "When can I come round to see it?"

"I'm in most of the day, as it happens. Give me a time and I'll make certain I'm in," said the voice.

Mark quickly checked his watch.

"Let's say eleven o'clock, then," he replied, keen to get the matter sorted out as quickly as possible. "Could you give me your address?"

"Fifty-one Buckbridge Road," replied the voice. "If you're walking up the high street with your back to the sea, it's the first turning on the left after Boots. My name is Mrs Garfield by the way".

"Fine," said Mark cheerfully, "I'm Paul Brown, by the way. I'll see you at eleven o'clock".

"There is one thing I must mention," said Mrs Garfield. "I like to take up references before I am prepared to take in my lodgers. Can you provide me with the contact details of your GP or somebody like that?"

Mark put down the receiver without even bothering to reply. Being on the run from the police, he certainly had no intention of contacting his doctor for a reference. Immediately returning to the restaurant with the post-cards pinned up outside, he scribbled down the phone numbers of two more bedsits.

"Sorry, but the room was taken a week ago," said a deep male voice. "I must remember to go down to the high street and take the card out of the window."

Slightly dispirited, Mark rang the second number. This time there was no reply, so at this point he decided to revert to plan A. Having bought a local paper, he wandered into a nearby cafe for a coffee and a chance to study the 'rooms to let' advertisements.

Mark managed to get a table to himself, but he hadn't been seated for more than two minutes before a young man, roughly about his own age, came over to join him. He was tall, had a mop of untidy fair hair and his face was bright red, almost certainly the result of spending too much time in the sun during the recent hot weather.

The two men greeted each other with a cursory nod. Mark was just about to unfold his paper and turn to the advertisement pages, before suddenly changing his mind. It occurred to him that it might be very useful to acquire some local knowledge.

"Do you live around here?" he asked casually. The stranger nodded.

"I've got a room just around the corner. Used to live in London, but I decided to come down here a few years ago to be by the sea."

"Exactly what I'm hoping to do," replied Mark. "It's just a matter of finding somewhere to rent." The stranger looked thoughtful for a moment.

"My landlord owns a number of properties in the area," he said finally. "In the house that I live, he lets out five rooms and one just happens to be vacant, if you're interested."

"Does he require references?" asked Mark, thinking of his earlier telephone conversation. "None of that rubbish," grinned the stranger. "Providing they pay their rent, Roland couldn't care less who his lodgers are or what they get up to. It doesn't matter to him whether you bring a woman back or smoke cannabis."

"Can you give me Roland's number?" asked Mark, sensing that this could be the answer to a prayer.

The stranger took out his mobile phone and began to push several buttons. Then after only a few seconds, he read out an eleven-digit number that Mark eagerly scribbled down.

"I'm Gary, by the way," said the stranger. "When you ring Roland, tell him that you are interested in the room at seventeen Blakestone Street. That's where I live."

Mark introduced himself to Gary by his real name, rather than as Paul Brown. He just had the feeling that there wasn't the need to use an alias. His newfound friend didn't seem the type to start prying into his affairs.

"You could ring Roland right now," said Gary helpfully. "He's always happy to discuss business". "As soon as I get outside, I'll use the telephone box down the road," answered Mark.

Gary smiled as he took out his mobile once more. Then having pressed a few more buttons, he sat back in his chair and took a sip of coffee.

"Hi Roland," he said after a slight pause. "It's Gary Kelly. Got a guy here who is interested in renting the vacant room next door to mine. I'll just put you over to him."

After a brief exchange of words, Mark agreed to meet Roland at the house in twenty minutes' time. Having finished their coffee, Gary walked with his new friend to the front gate before heading off to work. As a porter in an old people's care home, he explained that his shift began at midday.

No sooner had Gary disappeared than Roland drove up in a white van. Thick-set and probably in his early fifties, he was one of those people who did everything at a leisurely pace. Having produced a large set of keys from his coat pocket, he slowly led the way through the front door of a semi-detached house and up a flight of stairs.

"This is the room," he said, inviting Mark to follow him through an open door at the end of the landing.

Once inside, Mark was less than impressed. Casting his eye around, he noted the drab black and grey curtains, the threadbare carpet and the door, which looked in desperate need of a lick of paint. The room was no more than ten by twelve foot and much of the floor space was taken up by a single bed, a rickety-looking wardrobe and a badly chipped chest of drawers.

"It's very cosy in here during the winter," smiled Roland, as he pointed almost proudly to a small electric fire in the corner. "That little heater over there will keep you as warm as toast."

Mark was far from convinced, but nodded all the same.

"And this is the electricity meter over here," continued Roland, pointing in the direction of a silvery grey metal box attached to the wall. "I always remind my tenants to keep a good supply of coins handy."

"Good idea," mumbled Mark.

"Now let me show you the bathroom and kitchen," said Rowland, as he ambled towards the door. "You'll be sharing these facilities with four other tenants, so it will be a matter of trying to fit in with everyone else."

Mark made no comment about the bathroom, but felt confident that his mother would have been horrified had she been present. It looked as though nobody had ever made a serious attempt at removing the black and brown stains in either the bath or toilet. The floor, too, needed to be scrubbed vigorously with boiling hot water and disinfectant.

Disappointed with what he had seen already, Mark was feeling downcast as he was led into the kitchen. What he witnessed next depressed him even more. Not only was the gas stove smeared in fat that had been left to turn solid, but one of the tenants, or perhaps even two, had left a pile of washing up in the sink.

"Over here there's a fridge and a microwave," said Roland, appearing to turn a blind eye to the state of the kitchen. "And you can store all your food in that cupboard."

"That's very useful," answered Mark, while wondering how he was expected to keep his groceries separate from those of his fellow lodgers.

Having completed his guided tour, Roland turned to face Mark. "Well, do you want to move in then?" he asked.

Mark would have liked to have declined. However, he realized that in doing so, he would be taking an enormous risk. If every landlord and landlady of superior bed-sits were to insist on a doctor's reference, he could well end up sleeping on the beach.

"I'll take it," he replied, just managing to raise a half-smile. "Excellent," beamed Roland. "When would you like to move in, then?" "This coming Saturday," answered Mark.

"In that case, in order to hold the room for you, I'll need to take a deposit of two hundred pounds", said Roland. "You must understand that bedsits like this one are in great demand around here. Before next Saturday, I am absolutely certain that there will be plenty of other people making enquiries about it."

Mark suspected that Roland was being highly optimistic, but paid the deposit just the same.

While walking back to the high street, he knew he would appreciate the rest of his stay at the Friendly Welcome Guest House even more – to enjoy the luxury of returning to a neat and tidy room, after a day on the beach, and finding freshly laundered sheets on the bed and clean towels hanging up in the bathroom, then to be served with two meals a day in the dining room, even if it did mean having to listen to inane references to Suzie the cat and other such nonsense.

CHAPTER ELEVEN

It was twenty minutes past ten on Saturday morning. Having waved goodbye to Mrs Derbyshire, Mark Wright was about to move into a rather depressing bedsit. At the same time, some forty miles away, the Chambers family had just finished breakfast. As David and Alison were about to start the washing up, they were interrupted by the doorbell.

"Can somebody see who that is," shouted Alison, meaning any one of the three children. "It's a lady to see you, Mum," called back Amanda after a few minutes.

Quickly removing her apron, Alison left David to continue the washing up by himself. She would have liked to stand in front of a mirror briefly, to check her appearance. Having got up so late, meant that she hadn't had the opportunity to brush her hair or apply make-up.

She was to feel even worse when she arrived at the front door. Her visitor was dolled up as though she was about to be presented to the Queen. Dressed immaculately in a grey trouser suit, she was carrying a black shiny briefcase.

"I'm Maureen," announced the woman with a warm smile. "I'm trying to find Mark Wright. I'm from a local charity that tries to help victims of crime. Would it be convenient if I came in for five minutes or so?"

Alison was somewhat taken aback.

"Come in by all means, although I won't be able to help you very much. The last time I saw Mark was seven years ago."

Alison guided her visitor into the lounge. Having tidied up the evening before, she was annoyed to see the room looking as though it had been struck by a bomb. The two younger children had been playing in there earlier, before abandoning their toys on the floor and heading off into the back garden.

"Sorry about the mess," said Alison.

"Don't worry about it," answered Maureen, with a sympathetic smile. "I haven't come here to do an inspection of your home. The purpose of my visit is to try and gather information that might help me to track down Mark Wright. As you may know, he has been accused of stealing a pensioner's savings just over a week ago and I want to see that as much of that money as possible is returned to her."

"Isn't that police work?", asked Alison suspiciously.

"It is really, but they are quite happy for me to do a little bit of investigation work. You know how over-stretched the police are these days", answered Maureen.

"I hope you are successful," replied Alison, as she removed an assortment of toys from an armchair before sitting down. "Unfortunately, you would be wasting your time by talking to me, though. I haven't a clue where Mark is."

"I wouldn't expect you to", replied Maureen, having managed to find an armchair that was free of the children's playthings. "The reason I called was to speak to you about Amanda. It is just possible that your daughter may be able to help us find Mark."

"How could she do that?" asked Alison in surprise.

"Because as Mark is her father, he may just decide to get in touch with his daughter," explained Maureen.

"He wouldn't dare show his face around here", answered Alison adamantly. "I'd be on the phone to the police in a flash."

"I agree, it is highly unlikely that he would be hanging around your home," said Maureen. "He could well be waiting for Amanda outside the school gates, though."

Alison shook her head.

"I would be surprised if Mark even knows where Amanda goes to school."

"Actually, I happen to know that he does," answered Maureen. "Yesterday I went to visit Ross Young, one of Mark's closest friends."

"I remember reading about him in the local press," said Alison. "He was that soldier who was badly injured in Afghanistan and ended up in a wheelchair."

Maureen nodded.

"Anyway, it seems that Ross's niece and Amanda are classmates at Collingwood Secondary; a piece of information that Ross's mother just happened to pass on to Mark."

At that precise moment, the two younger children poked their head around the door. They had been hoping to sit and watch one of their favourite TV programmes, but the glare on their mother's face was a warning signal that the lounge was currently out of bounds to them. Clearly disgruntled, Joshua poked his tongue out at Alison before storming up to his bedroom.

"As far as I am aware, Mark has made no attempt to contact Amanda over the last seven years," said Alison, having ignored Joshua's outburst. "Had it bothered him so much, surely he would have found out long ago which school Amanda went to without much difficulty."

"You are probably right," conceded Maureen. "Nevertheless, please let me know if you hear of anything that might help me to locate Mark. I am absolutely determined that poor Mrs Fisher gets at least some of her money before the whole lot is spent."

"Have you managed to contact many of Mark's friends and relatives?" asked Alison. Maureen smiled as she held up a large note pad. During their short meeting, it had been resting on her lap and from time to time, she had used the pages to scribble something down as Alison had spoken.

"In here are the names and addresses of at least twenty," she answered. "During the last week, I have gone to visit each one of them."

"And have any of these people been able to assist you very much?" asked Alison.

"Not as much as I would have liked," admitted Maureen, as she began to jot down something on a scrap of paper. "But I am confident that were one of them to come up with any information, they will be in touch with me straight away. After all, even most friends and relatives are unlikely to have much sympathy with those who steal off poor old ladies."

Alison glanced down at her watch. It was now a quarter to eleven and she had a hundred and one jobs to do around the house. She was therefore relieved to see that her visitor appeared to be preparing to leave.

"Just in case I hear something, you had better give me your telephone number," she said. Maureen, who had just got to her feet, handed Alison the scrap of paper she had just been writing on.

"There you are," she smiled. "Just ring me on my mobile any time of the day or night. I would appreciate any little detail that could assist me in my enquiries."

"I hope you are successful in your search," said Alison, as she shook hands with her visitor at the front door.

"Oh, we will catch up with him all right. Make no mistake about that," replied Maureen with a look of determination. "I just need it to be sooner rather than later."

❧ ☙

David cursed himself for the thousandth time. Why, he kept asking himself, hadn't he remembered that he had agreed to stay in with the children three nights ago? Because of his crass stupidity, he had allowed Sophie to prepare a meal for them both and then had to cancel at the very last moment. He could hardly blame her for being annoyed with him.

David was desperate to make amends. He realized that prompt action was required, just in case Sophie was considering breaking off their relationship for good. Having finally washed up the breakfast things, he slipped out to the car. Alison was still in conversation with her visitor, while the three children were all up in their bedrooms.

Once inside the car, David took out his mobile phone. For a few moments, he sat motionless in the driver's seat, deciding exactly what to say. Feeling anxious, he took a deep breath in order to calm himself down, before finally making the all-important call.

"Hello David," answered Sophie, obviously having seen the name appear on the screen of her mobile phone.

"Look, I've rung to apologize about Wednesday evening," said David, as he fidgeted around in his seat. "I completely forgot that I'd promised to look after the kids, while Alison went out with her friend."

There was a brief silence at the other end of the phone, while Sophie no doubt, was considering her response.

"I was really so mad with you," she said at last. "On my way home from school, I especially called in at the supermarket to buy the shopping for our meal. Then you just casually ring up and tell me that you aren't coming over."

"I'm really sorry," replied David sheepishly. "I promise it will never happen again."

"You and I are finished if it does," said Sophie sharply.

"Look, could we meet up this afternoon?" pleaded David, with his fingers tightly crossed. "I'm really missing you."

"All right, then," replied Sophie, almost grudgingly. "I've got plenty of housework to catch up on, so be here any time after two."

Once he was back indoors, David punched the air in delight. For a little while longer, he could go on experiencing the excitement of a starry-eyed teenager who was dating the first love of his life: always slyly checking his reflection in shop windows as he wandered along the high street. Forever concerned that his hair looked just right, while the clothes that he wore were both fashionable and made him look sexy.

After her visitor had gone, Alison debriefed David on her meeting. Having read the front page of the local newspaper, the couple had talked a great deal about the robbery. In spite of all his faults, neither of them could quite believe that Mark was capable of carrying out such a callous act, particularly as the *Brockleby Times* had reported that he was a man without previous convictions.

"I suppose Amanda wouldn't recognize her father after all this time," said David thoughtfully. "That's right. She was only four when she last saw Mark," replied Alison. "I will tell her to keep an eye out for strangers just in case Mark does try to contact her."

"Changing the subject," said David casually. "I am going to the Oval this afternoon with two of the other teachers to watch a bit of cricket. One of them managed to get some free tickets."

As the football season was finally over, he now needed another excuse for going out on a Saturday afternoon. Although she wasn't a fan, Alison was still aware that Crystal Palace had played their last game for a few months. So, having given the matter some thought, David decided that the game of cricket could come to the rescue. The fact that he knew practically nothing about the game was neither here nor there.

"Don't you see enough of your colleagues in the week?" asked Alison irritably. "I was hoping that we could take the kids out this afternoon – possibly go out into the country and take a picnic."

"We could always go tomorrow," suggested David.

"It's out of the question," snapped Alison. "I'm taking Joshua and Abigail to a party in the afternoon. Then, as I told you before, Mum is coming over in the evening for a meal."

"Perhaps next weekend, then," said David.

Without replying, Alison stormed into the kitchen and slammed the door. Over the years, she had learnt that the most effective way to triumph over her husband was to make him feel guilty. On this occasion, though, the ploy was doomed to fail. David was determined to visit Sophie, and nothing was going to deter him.

For the rest of the morning, David busied himself with marking essays. While Alison had shut herself in the kitchen, he was sat at the dining table, surrounded by sheets of A4 paper and holding a red pen. There was tension in the air that even the youngest children could sense. Both Joshua and Abigail were unusually quiet, while trying hard not to upset either parent in any way.

The two adults had still not spoken by the time that David had left the house after lunch. Until the last few weeks, he would have gone to Alison and tried to make it up with her – perhaps buy her flowers or agree to cook the evening meal. Now, though, was different. All that mattered to him was being with Sophie.

It was just after two when David came to a halt outside Sophie's flat. After looking into the rear mirror to check that his hair was in place, he took a long, deep breath. It was only when he was perfectly composed that he emerged from the car.

Sophie was standing at the front door as David made his way down the garden path. For the last ten minutes, she had been looking out for him from her top-floor flat. As soon as her guest was in touching distance, she threw her arms around his neck.

"I've missed you," she whispered in his ear.

David was taken aback. In his wildest dreams, he had never expected to be greeted like that. In fact, he was half suspecting that Sophie was growing cold towards him and was about to send him back to his wife.

"I've missed you, too," he murmured back.

Once inside the flat, they got down to business. Having hastily shed their clothes between the lounge and the bedroom, they buried themselves under the duvet. With sighs and whispered words of affection, their bodies clung together as they made love.

Then, suddenly, the storm subsided.

"I cried on Wednesday evening after you rang and said you weren't coming," admitted Sophie, as she rested her head on David's chest. "I was beginning to think that you had got tired of me."

"Far from it," replied David, gently stroking her soft hair. "The truth is, I am growing more serious about you all the time."

"Would you be prepared to leave your wife for me?", asked Sophie.

David was so surprised by the question, that he was unable to give an immediate response. It wasn't that the idea didn't appeal to him, because it certainly did. However, he recognized that there were many factors that had to be taken into consideration before making such a bold move.

"Rather than asking me to leave me wife, I thought that you were planning to send me back to her," he laughed.

"Because you are different from all the other men that I have ever known, I am having second thoughts about our relationship," replied Sophie, as she lifted her head in order to look directly into David's face. "But I'm not prepared to share you with anyone else."

"Couldn't we just go on as we are for the time being?" pleaded David. "You must appreciate that I will need time to think things out."

"Of course – I understand that abandoning a family and home is not a step to be taken lightly," replied Sophie, as she pulled the duvet over her silky white shoulders. "On the other hand, I am not prepared to wait indefinitely for you to make up your mind."

"Are you still thinking of moving down to Portsmouth?" asked David. "You were talking about spending time with your parents while trying to decide what to do with your life."

"What I do in the future will depend on you," said Sophie. "If you decide to leave your wife, we could share this flat together, while looking for something bigger."

For a time they lay peacefully in each other's arms. Having been given much to ponder over, David felt as though he had reached another of those crossroads in his life. It was very much like the decision he had been forced to make eight years earlier. On that occasion, too, the choice had been far from simple. He recalled all the soul searching he had done at the time, trying to decide whether to abandon the Eternal Fellowship and being shunned for the rest of his life by family and friends; knowing that to take such a course of action would inevitably mean being evicted from his home and losing the only job he had ever known. He had been aware that once he had made the move, he would then be part of a strange world from which he had always been shielded: a place where people enjoyed hedonistic pleasures such as watching TV, listening to the radio, dancing, and reading newspapers.

Looking back, he knew he had come to the right decision. Nonetheless, leaving the Fellowship behind had left scars on him. He still missed his parents, brothers, sisters and many of the kind, gentle folk who had once been his friends. The experience made him appreciate only too well that breaking up with Alison and having to make do with seeing the children just once a week would be no less agonizing.

Having extricated herself from David's arms, Sophie emerged from under the duvet. Then, having climbed out of bed, she covered her naked body with a red woollen dressing gown. Without a word, she slipped out of the bedroom and returned five minutes later carrying two cups of tea.

"By the way, I'm thinking of standing for Parliament," announced David casually, as he sat up in bed and reached out for his cup.

Sophie looked suitably impressed.

"That sounds exciting," she replied, before taking a sip of tea. "I remember you once said that you were involved in politics."

"That's right," said David. "Anyway, the Brockleby Labour Party is searching for a candidate to stand at the next general election. So I thought I would throw my hat in the ring."

"I should imagine that you will face plenty of competition," answered Sophie thoughtfully. "There must be lots of people who would like to become an MP."

"Of course," said David. "And Brockleby is a very winnable seat for Labour. With all the cuts that the Government are making, the Coalition is going to be very unpopular come the next general election."

"If my memory serves me right, Labour have won the seat in the past," said Sophie, as she sat down on the edge of the bed.

"That's correct", said David proudly. "Jacqui Dunn was our MP until last year. Unfortunately, she got beaten by the Tories at the general election."

Sophie shed her dressing gown and joined David under the duvet once more. "Just think," she smiled, "they might make you the Education Secretary."

"I'd make a few changes if I were put in that position," answered David, feeling the anger swelling up inside him. "For a start, I'd put an end to tuition fees. If the country has the money to send troops to war, it can afford to give our young people a good education."

That afternoon the time seemed to pass very quickly. Had he received an invitation, David would have readily agreed to spend the night in the flat. As Alison had ignored him for most of the morning, he felt confident that his absence would hardly trouble her. However, as Sophie was meeting up with friends later that evening, he seemed left with little choice but to make his way home.

"I love you," whispered David, after a final passionate kiss on the doorstep.

"I love you, too," replied Sophie softly. "But just remember that I don't share. You will have to make a choice between your wife and me."

Those words were still ringing in David's ears as he parked the car in the drive. Hardly expecting a warm welcome at home, he was rather surprised to find Alison waiting to greet him in the hall. She didn't seem in the least morose, but instead, there was a look of remorse in her eyes.

"David, I'm afraid your grandfather has died," she said, while throwing her arms around her husband's waist. "Your dad rang with the news about half an hour ago."

David tried to hold back the tears. Of course, he understood that his grandfather hadn't long to live, but that didn't make his death any easier to bear. Once again, he regretted those eight lost years when they could have spent so much time together. Sadly, they had been driven apart by the dogmatic beliefs of the Eternal Fellowship.

"When I have a few moments, I had better go and knock on my parents' door and offer my condolences," said David, managing to keep his voice steady and free of the slightest sob. "Not that they will let a heathen like me in the house, of course."

Alison squeezed him gently against her body.

"I'm sorry I wasn't very nice to you this morning," she whispered.

A tear slowly trickled down David's cheek.

"It was entirely my fault," he answered, speaking directly from the heart.

CHAPTER TWELVE

David pressed the bell. It felt strange to be standing outside that large, detached property again.

Until eight years ago, the house had been his home. Then one day, his life had changed forever. Having been banished by the Eternal Fellowship for having forsaken the Lord, he had shut the front door behind him for the last time, carrying a large suitcase.

It was Monday afternoon and David had stopped off on his way home from school. After learning of his grandfather's death, he had considered phoning or writing to his parents to offer his condolences. Finally though, he decided that a face-to-face visit would be more appropriate.

When there was no response to his first ring, he tried a second time. While waiting, he tried to listen out for signs of movement inside the house, but could hear nothing. He was on the point of leaving when out of the corner of his eye, he saw the blue curtains at the downstairs window draw back very slightly.

David decided to ring the bell one last time. If on this occasion nobody answered the door, then that would be a clear indication to him that his presence wasn't welcome. It would also mean that it was pointless calling again. He might as well climb into his car, drive away and never bother to come back. If the family choose to ignore him at a time like this, then it was obvious that he wouldn't be welcome on future occasions.

Then suddenly he heard a shuffling sound in the house. As the noise got steadily louder, he realized that somebody was making their way down the hall. After stopping for a moment to release the catch, the mystery person then swung open the front door.

"Hello Mum," said David, feeling a lump in his throat as he spoke. "I just called to say how sorry I was to hear about Grandpa."

Hilary Chambers smiled serenely.

"There is no reason for anybody to be unhappy. Death is something to celebrate, not mourn." David noticed the change in his mother since he had last seen her eight years ago. Her hair, which hung loosely to her waist, as worn by all Fellowship women, was now streaked with grey; while the lines that stretched across her forehead had now become more pronounced. She had put on a little weight, as well, but the clear blue eyes still sparkled with the vitality of youth.

"But you are bound to miss him, though," replied David, who rejected the idea of rejoicing in the passing away of such a kind and gentle human being.

"We will only be separated for a short while," answered Hilary. "One day very soon, all those who walk in the ways of the Lord will be together again in Heaven."

David didn't feel inclined to have a theological debate on the matter. In any case, he knew it would be futile to argue with his mother. Like most followers of the Eternal Fellowship, she had a set of beliefs, and all the reasoning in the world, was never going to persuade her to abandon them.

"How are all the family?" he asked, having decided that it was pointless to pour out more sympathy.

Hilary suddenly looked uncomfortable.

"I wish I could invite you in and give you all the news, but unfortunately, I can't."

"I know how it is," smiled David. "Dad thinks that a sinner like me might corrupt the rest of the family."

"Like me, he is praying for your soul," answered Hilary, as ever, coming to the defence of her husband. "We hope that you will see the light one day and return to the Lord. Perhaps even persuade your wife and children to join you."

"We'll see," said David, having already dismissed the idea out of hand. "Anyway, give me all the gossip about the family. I really don't mind standing here on the doorstep for a while."

Hilary glanced down anxiously at her watch.

"Sorry, but I don't have the time," she replied with a shake of the head. "Your father will be home very shortly for his tea and you know how he hates to be kept waiting."

David knew only too well. Like some eastern potentate, John Chambers seemed to regard his wife as little more than a slave girl – a downtrodden lackey who had a duty to obey him and take care of all his creature comforts. Included in that role was to ensure that the master was served with a meal as soon as he returned home of an evening.

The door closed before David had an opportunity to reply. The fact that he had been slighted neither surprised nor upset him. Had his mother been caught talking to him, he knew for certain that she would have been in trouble with his father. Hilary Chambers had a gentle temperament that was unsuited to standing up to tyrants.

By offering his condolences, at least David was able to go away feeling he had done his duty. He would have liked to have attended his grandfather's funeral, but knew that his presence would not be welcomed by the Eternal Fellowship. The last thing he wanted to do was create any acrimony at the graveside. In a few days, he would send a wreath to his parents address and just leave it at that. There were, after all, more pressing problems on his mind, such as Sophie Duncan.

⚜ ⚜

The following day, David rang Simon Broadbent. He needed someone who he could talk to about his complicated love life. He had little doubt that his friend would advise him to remain faithful to Alison. Nevertheless, that didn't concern him at all. Rather than seeking advice, he was looking for the opportunity to unburden himself.

"Thought I would ring up to find out how you were," said David, only partly telling the truth.

"Any news from your end?"

"Funny you should ask that," replied Simon, who happened to be seated at his desk in the office.

"I've just found out that your brother Peter has been banned from driving for twelve months."

"Had he been drinking?" asked David, knowing that alcohol was one worldly vice that the Fellowship didn't condemn.

"Not half," laughed Simon. "He was well over the limit when the police breathalysed him."

"What an idiot," said David scornfully. "It is typical of the Fellowship. Most followers claim to hold the moral high ground over everyone else and then go and break the law."

"I suppose it could happen to anybody,", answered Simon, coming to the defence of the sect, of which he was still a member.

"Not me,", said David, suddenly feeling very self-righteous. "As somebody who values human life, I never drink and drive."

"Anyway," said Simon, wishing to avoid an argument. "As Peter is a salesman, losing the use of his car is causing a headache for his company. They are going to have to employ a chauffeur, just to drive him around to visit his customers."

Simon continued by passing on other snippets of Fellowship gossip to his friend. He revealed that Miss Percy had been given a nasty shock after receiving a pile of pornographic photographs through the post. Apparently, she had promptly returned them to the sender, enclosing a strongly worded letter of complaint.

Another amusing story related to old Mr Dunlop. After putting some gardening tools away, he had accidentally locked a neighbour's cat in the shed. Needless to say, when he finally opened the door five days later, he was given a nasty scare. He was set upon by a frenzied animal, which hadn't been fed for the best part of a week.

"I would have enjoyed seeing old Dunlop's face when he opened the door," laughed David. "Apparently he needed a stiff whiskey or two to settle his nerves," replied Simon.

Strange as it may seem, the consumption of alcohol is the one vice that the spiritual leadership permit their followers to indulge in. It was decided years ago that anyone in the Fellowship who had been acting sinfully might reveal all after a few stiff drinks.

"Are you free to come over on Saturday afternoon for a chat?" asked David. "I'll be on my own as Alison is taking the kids to the zoo".

"Sounds good," answered Simon eagerly. "I'll bring Rebecca with me. She just happens to be coming up from Broadstairs for the weekend."

David was delighted that Simon would be accompanied by his twin sister. To be given an intelligent woman's opinion on the problem he was facing would be invaluable – even if she did conclude that he would be well advised to stay with Alison.

That evening, David agreed to go out canvassing in the Sefton ward. With only two days remaining before the council by-election, both Tory and Labour activists were stepping up their efforts to try and win the seat. Everybody, including the local newspapers, were predicting a close result between the two parties.

By nine-thirty, most activists had returned to the Brockleby Labour Party headquarters, exhausted after their evening's work. Carrying a pint mug of beer, David joined a group of seven comrades gathered around two tables placed end to end. Most attention seemed to centre on Alec Stokes, the by-election candidate.

"Feeling confident?" asked Carol. Alec shrugged.

"I feel the result could go either way. We'll just have to wait and see".

"Have you decided yet whether to put your name forward to become the next parliamentary candidate?" asked Carol, the only female in the group.

All eyes turned towards Kenny, the person that Carol had been addressing. As a local councillor for a number of years, most people in the association suspected that he had much greater political ambitions. Now in his early thirties, the time seemed right for him to set his sights on the House of Commons.

"Yes, I intend to throw my hat in the ring," answered the councillor with a sly smile. "It could be a long time before an opportunity to represent Brockleby comes up again."

The announcement was greeted enthusiastically around the two joined-up tables – not that everybody intended to support him in his attempt to become the candidate. It was just that they appreciated his dedication to the party.

"And what about you, David?" asked Carol. "I remember that you were trying to make up your mind whether to put your name forward."

"I still haven't decided,", replied David. "I need to discuss it with Alison before giving you an answer".

"Shouldn't you be asking all our members whether they are interested in standing Tony?" asked George, the oldest member of the group and now a retired councillor.

"I'm sending out a newsletter to everyone over the weekend", answered Tony, looking slightly embarrassed. "I haven't done it sooner because the council by-election has been keeping me busy."

David wondered who else in the association, other than Kenny, might provide some rivalry.

Glancing around the bar at all the drinkers, he doubted whether any of them might be tempted to put their names forward. There were, of course, all those people who regularly attended meetings and had plenty to say for themselves. Yet when it came to doing any work for the party, they were nowhere to be seen.

"By the way," said Carol. "You will all be surprised to learn that I will be a contender."

The announcement was greeted with quizzical looks. Nobody spoke, though, in case she was winding them up, and they didn't want to swallow the bait. It wasn't that they thought Carol was incapable of being an MP, because both her intelligence and political experience were widely respected within the association. However, with the slight bulge that was clearly visible under her red jumper, it seemed likely that she might have more pressing matters to focus on in the months ahead.

"I need female candidates to keep the National Executive Committee happy," explained Tony. "My intention is to get an equal number of men and women on my final shortlist."

"Please don't vote for me, though," warned Carol with a grin. "I don't want to bring my baby up in the House of Commons."

The following evening, David joined up with the canvassing team again. With only a few hours to go before the polls opened, he felt more motivated than usual to go out knocking on doors and speaking with householders. Before leaving home, he managed to drag Alison's attention away from the children for about ten minutes.

"How would you feel about me becoming an MP?" he began. Alison looked mildly surprised.

"But I thought you were happy being a teacher?"

"To be honest, I'm frustrated by all the changes that are being made," explained David with a scowl. "What is the point of helping kids to get qualifications, if there aren't any jobs for them when they leave school?"

"I know how you must feel," replied Alison sympathetically. "Until recently, pupils might have studied hard in order to get into university. Now, many of those from poorer families will be put off from going into higher education because of tuition fees. The prospect of starting their working life in debt hardly acts as a great incentive to work for a degree."

"Precisely", said David bitterly. "Hopefully by becoming an MP, I could make a difference in some way. Instead of yet another barrister in the House of Commons, there could be an experienced teacher in Parliament, speaking out for young people."

Alison's eyes shone with pride as she flung her arms around her husband. She was suddenly reminded about why she had agreed to marry him. Like her, he resented social injustice and wanted to change the world for the better. He was a man who believed in principles, rather than one who just strived for worldly gain.

In fact, Alison had been responsible for bringing her husband into politics. As David admitted later to her, he had only joined the Labour Party in an attempt to start a relationship with her. At the time, he cared little about who governed the country and the way it was run. As it happened, coming from a strict evangelical family, he had been brought up to believe that what happened in this world hardly mattered much. Far more important was getting to Heaven in the next one.

"So now I understand why you were hesitating about supporting Tony when he was thinking of standing," laughed Alison, as her head rested against David's chest. "The truth was that you wanted to be the candidate yourself."

"That's right," admitted David.

Alison lifted her head and kissed her husband passionately on the lips.

"Go for it," she whispered. "I rather fancy being married to a government minister. Even if it means that all those stupid right-wing tabloids will start criticizing my dress sense."

The following day, David didn't go into school. As agreed with the headmaster, he had taken the time off to help get Labour Party supporters down to various polling stations. Apart from being an unpaid taxi driver, the job involved trying to persuade a number of apathetic people to go and use their vote.

All the political parties seemed to have numerous helpers. As it was a council by-election in a marginal seat, many activists within the Brockleby constituency and beyond were keen to lend a hand. There were tellers at every polling station taking down the details of those residents who had voted, while at regular intervals, cars with loudspeakers boomed out the name of one of the candidates who was standing.

Tony and Carol's lounge was being used as one of the election rooms. As transport co-ordinator, Carol mainly took calls from people needing a lift to go and cast their vote, before passing their details on to drivers such as David. Her other duty was to provide tea and coffee to anybody who just happened to drop in.

For those like David who were constantly on the go, the time passed quickly. Finally, at ten o'clock in the evening the polling stations shut their doors. Those big black boxes that contained the all-important voting slips were placed on a lorry and quickly transported to the town hall.

The count was well underway by a quarter to eleven. David was one of the Labour Party activists who had been invited along to watch proceedings. Not surprisingly, as the result was far from certain, the atmosphere in the main hall was tense. For the two candidates who had the greatest chance of winning the seat, it was a particularly anxious time.

The people employed to count the votes worked in silence. They were seated at tables placed end to end to form three parallel rows in the hall. Their endeavours were being watched closely by party supporters keen to ensure that no mistakes were being made. A candidate could possibly be cheated of victory should a few of those white slips of paper happen to end up in the wrong pile.

It had been a long day for the party workers. Other than witnessing their favoured candidate being defeated, what they dreaded most was a recount. The agony of having to stay up until the early hours of the morning, watching on as those endless votes were being counted all over again.

By eleven thirty, David's mind began to wander. Sick to death of those endless white sheets of paper, he began to dwell on a matter so important to his future. It was a problem that had haunted him since the weekend. Before too long, he would need to choose between staying with his wife and children or whether to leave them for Sophie. Of course, he still wanted to listen to what both Simon and Rebecca had to say on the subject, but ultimately the decision was down to him.

Breaking up his marriage seemed to be a drastic move to make. Deserting his family was something he might live to regret. It occurred to him that if things didn't go well with Sophie, he might well end up in rented rooms and having to obey the house rules of some tyrannical landlord. Certainly, paying two mortgages on his meager salary was hardly an option.

Finishing with Sophie seemed the easy way out. It would be painful at first, but time was a great healer, or so he had been told. He expected that it might be a bit like giving up smoking. You were desperate for a cigarette to begin with, but after a few weeks, the craving went away.

"I think that the result will be announced soon," said Tony, interrupting David's thoughts.

He was right. In five minutes, the returning officer requested that all the candidates should join him on the stage. Immediately six people, from different directions, emerged from the crowd. All wore colours that clearly identified their political allegiance.

During the next few minutes, most eyes in the hall were focused on two men. Alec Stokes and Gavin Blake, the Tory candidate, were the only likely winners on the night. The remaining four, who had their names on the ballot papers, were mainly concerned with the number of votes that they received.

Some of those watching had their hearts in their mouths. Those more experienced political supporters knew that the returning officer would give the candidates the result in advance and then ask whether any of them wanted a recount. Once given the news, the expression on one of the contenders' faces might provide a clear indication as to whether they had won or lost. Just a flicker of a smile or a shake of the head was all that was required. On this occasion though, both Alec and Gavin

Blake stood with their hands behind their backs looking totally impassive.

"Do you think we've won?" asked Kenny anxiously.

"Don't have a clue," confessed Tony. "I tried waving at Alec, but I can't get his attention." After the usual preamble, the returning officer blew hard into his microphone.

"I will now announce the result of the election in alphabetical order according to the candidate's name," he boomed.

For a few seconds, there was total silence. In that large hall, which was often used for lavish functions, it would have been possible to hear the proverbial pin drop.

"Blake .... One thousand, six hundred and fifty-one votes", he shouted to large cheers from the Tory group.

The Labour contingent received the announcement with some concern. It was certainly a good result for their opponents, although not exactly unbeatable. For the next few minutes, they had an agonizing wait while the smaller votes tally of three of the other candidates was read out.

"Stokes ...." roared the returning officer, before putting on his spectacles to check the figure on his sheet of paper. "One thousand, eight hundred and twenty-three votes."

There were whoops of joy from the Labour camp. Tony punched the air with delight, while Kenny did a little jig with Carol. From the stage, a broad smile appeared on Alec's face as he waved to those supporters who had worked so hard to get him elected.

Having been officially declared the new councillor for the Sefton ward, Alec took the microphone from the returning officer. Uncertain as to which way the result would go, he had prepared both a winning and losing speech. Much to his satisfaction, he was able to leave the second one in his jacket pocket.

"Tonight the people of the Sefton ward have said no to the Coalition cuts," he shouted, with his eyes blazing. "Before too long the whole nation will be repeating the same message in a General Election. Make no mistake. The days of the Tory and Lib Dem posh boys are numbered."

David left the town hall feeling pleased with life. However, as he drove home he began to think of Sophie once more. Of course it made perfect sense to give her up, he thought, but it would be far from easy. He had allowed himself to fall in love with her, and that had been a terrible mistake.

CHAPTER THIRTEEN

It was almost midday. Having just finished marking a pile of essays, David was relaxing in the back garden reading a newspaper. Lying well back in a deck chair with a coffee table close to his elbow, he occasionally took a sip of cold lager from a straight pint-sized glass.

The blue sky was cloudless. As it was now early June, the sun was almost overhead. Occasionally a cool breeze gently rustled the pages of his *Guardian*. But for the intermittent sound of a distant lawn mower, everything was quiet.

A fox suddenly appeared from behind the shed. Seemingly unconcerned that a human was close by; it circled the rhododendron bush in the centre of the lawn. The animal then vanished through a gap in the fence to pay a visit to the next-door neighbour.

David followed the creature's progress with casual interest. With light brown mangy fur, the intruder was hardly the most attractive specimen of the species that he had ever seen. He wondered whether it had been responsible for attacking a black bin bag full of rubbish a few nights ago – an incident that had caused him to spend ten minutes gathering up an assortment of items he had hoped to see the last of.

David was at home by himself. Having been informed that Alison was taking the kids to Regent's Park Zoo, he had declined the invitation to accompany them. He had said that he was trying to reduce the overall cost of admission by not going. In truth, the reason that he wasn't joining the rest of the family had more to do with the need to take a break from being in the presence of squabbling young people. As a teacher, he had to put up with enough of that in the classroom.

Once the fox had disappeared, he turned his attention back to the *Guardian*. As usual, there was very little good news to celebrate – only reports of phone hacking by the tabloids, a civil war raging in Libya, a European single currency that was threatening the world economy and bankers still pocketing large bonuses after almost making the nation insolvent.

There was little of interest on the sports pages. The football season was now over, and in the summer of 2011, there were no Euros or a World Cup to look forward to. Even the transfer market had gone very quiet.

David put down the newspaper and shut his eyes. Immediately, a picture of Sophie appeared in his mind's eye. He hadn't spoken to her since his last visit to the flat the previous Saturday. They had exchanged polite smiles while passing in the school corridor, but that had been the only contact between them. Neither one had telephoned the other or sent a text message.

By keeping his distance from Sophie, David was putting himself to the test. He was trying to get some idea of how much he would miss her were they to break up. If it didn't feel too bad, then perhaps he would finish the relationship once and for all. Over the last few days, though, he had started to feel depressed. He was feeling like a small child who had been forbidden to go out and play.

Suddenly, his thoughts were disrupted by a rather tinny version of Mozart's fortieth symphony.

After digging deep into the pocket of his jeans, he wrenched out a mobile phone. Having quickly glanced at the miniature screen, his pulse quickened as he noted the caller's name.

"Are you coming over today?" asked Sophie. "I know you are usually free on a Saturday afternoon."

"Sorry, not today", answered David, feeling annoyed with himself for having to refuse. "Two friends are coming around for a cup of tea."

"Not trying to avoid me, are you?" asked Sophie suspiciously.

David hesitated for a split second. He was tempted to tell her that it was all over between them.

There was no reason in the world to feel guilty about it, he reminded himself. After all, hadn't she asked him to choose between her and his family? All he needed to say was that he had finally made that choice.

Strangely enough, when he spoke, none of these words came out. Instead, he heard himself say something entirely different. Like the weak-willed gambler trying to quit, he felt himself falling at the first hurdle.

"No, of course I'm not trying to avoid you," he laughed. "It's just that I'm so busy at the moment, you wouldn't believe it."

"So busy, you hadn't even got time to send me a text I suppose," replied Sophie disconsolately.

"Listen, I was on the point of ringing", said David, deciding that dishonesty was the best policy on this particular occasion. "I wanted to know whether you were free one night next week."

"Are you sure you can spare the time?" answered Sophie sarcastically. "I know what a busy little bee you are."

"Look, I promise to make myself available whenever it suits you," said David, anxious to make amends.

"How about Wednesday, then?" asked Sophie.

"Great," replied David brightly. "I've heard there is a quiet little restaurant just outside Musselworth that serves exquisite food. I'll pick you up at eight."

"OK," said Sophie, almost grudgingly. "But don't you dare cancel at the last moment. Otherwise I shall never speak to you again."

Having finished the call, David sat gazing into space for a while. Rather than his mind being blank, he was desperately trying to think up a solution to his problem. Quite clearly, things couldn't continue as they were. If he couldn't decide between giving up his family or his mistress, then circumstances would surely make that choice for him.

David took another sip of lager. The glass was now almost empty, but under the coffee table, shaded from the sun to keep it cool, was another can waiting to be opened. As he wouldn't be called upon to drive that day, he felt at liberty to indulge himself in an ample quantity of alcohol.

After a bite to eat at lunchtime, David sat in the lounge waiting for his guests to arrive. Still no nearer to reaching a conclusion to his problem, he hoped that Simon and Rebecca might be able to come up with a suggestion or two – not that he would necessarily be taking their advice, but at least it would be interesting to hear their views.

The Broadbent twins arrived just after two. David and Simon shook hands warmly in the hall, while Rebecca took a few seconds to remove her silky blue headscarf – a garment worn by all Fellowship women whenever they were outdoors.

As both lived in Brockleby, David often met up with Simon for a chat. He saw far less of Rebecca, though, who had moved down to Broadstairs after her first marriage to Malcolm. She had remained in the seaside town even after the death of her husband. It was a terrible tragedy, as the young man had been killed by a hit and run driver.

As they were former classmates, David had developed a strong bond with the twins. As the only Eternal Fellowship pupils in the school, the three of them had been instructed to remain separate from the other pupils. Stay clear of all those young people who had not been brought up in the ways of the Lord, was the message. Consequently, having been coerced into isolation from their peers, they had naturally clung together for companionship.

"Sorry to hear about your grandfather," said Rebecca. "I know you two were very close at one time."

"Luckily I was able to see him before he died," answered David, as he sat down in an armchair.

"He looked so frail, I could hardly recognize him."

"Did he know who you were?" asked Rebecca. "I heard that his memory was getting quite bad at the end."

David shook his head.

"That was the most upsetting part."

"How are your children?" asked Rebecca, deciding to move on to a more cheerful subject. "They must be getting quite big now."

"The kids are fine," answered David proudly. "How about your family?" "Quite a handful," she laughed. "I'll let you see them for yourself." Immediately, she bent down and put her hand inside a white plastic carrier bag.

"I've brought some photographs for you to see," she said, as she pulled out a brown leather binder. "You probably won't recognize some people, so if you sit alongside me on the settee, I'll point out who everybody is."

Dutifully, David did as he was asked. Soon, he was watching on as Rebecca slowly turned over the thick, heavy pages, with several photographs affixed to each one. In fact, many of the faces that stared up at him were familiar. They were, however, now looking slightly older, and their bodies, in certain cases, somewhat more portly in appearance.

Rebecca proudly pointed out her four children. There were two of each sex. They were smiling angelically at the camera, as though butter wouldn't melt in their mouths. The oldest girl, with long dark hair flowing down to her waist and pale, delicate features, had a striking resemblance to her mother.

Once there had been doubts whether Rebecca would ever have children at all, let alone a quartet. Having been unable to conceive with her first husband, she had automatically assumed that she was infertile. After Malcolm's death, though, she had later married Graham and very soon her dreams of motherhood became a reality. Within a few months of her second wedding, much to her delight, she became pregnant.

"So what have you been up to then?" she asked, having finally come to the last page of the album and being reminded that it was still blank.

David hesitated for a few moments. Although he had known the twins all his life, he had no idea how either would react to his latest revelation. After all, these were people who had been sheltered from the wicked world and all its vices, very much like he had before parting company with the Fellowship.

"I'm having an affair," he announced, rather self-consciously.

The twins gaped at him in amazement. Clearly, they were lost for words as this startling news was given time to sink in. It was rather as though their friend had just owned up to a murder, or pleaded guilty to blowing up Buckingham Palace with the Queen in residence.

"Poor Alison," groaned Rebecca, finally coming out of shock. "Does she know yet?" "Not as far as I am aware," answered David. "I've tried my best to keep it a secret."

"I don't believe it," said Simon. "I thought you and Alison were devoted to each other."

"It doesn't make sense to me, either," said David, with a shake of the head. "I still love her and the kids, yet I'm crazy about this woman as well."

Rebecca's female curiosity was now at breaking point. Soon she was peppering David with a multitude of questions. Who was this woman? What did she do for a living? Where had he met her? and so on and so on.

"If the school find out that two teachers are having an affair, won't you both get the sack?" asked Simon, when his sister's questions had finally dried up.

"I couldn't be sure, but it is more than likely," replied David.

"You must give her up," said Rebecca firmly. "Otherwise this woman will ruin your life. You could end up losing everything."

David didn't need to be told about the risks that were involved. It had been uppermost in his mind for a while. Already, he was regretting taking the twins into his confidence. How on earth, he wondered, could two people who knew so little about the big bad world, possibly offer him any sound advice?

Simon seemed to know what David was thinking. Having never had an affair himself, it wasn't easy to put himself in his friend's position. That didn't mean, of course, that he wasn't prepared to try.

"Can't you just go on as you are and pray that Alison doesn't find out?" he asked.

"Simon!" exclaimed Rebecca in horror. "How could you even suggest such a thing?" "Because Sophie says she isn't prepared to share me. Put bluntly, I have to choose between breaking up my marriage or losing her," explained David, completely ignoring Rebecca's intervention.

"Then call her bluff," said Simon. "Tell her that you love her, but you can't possibly abandon your three poor children. Explain that they are at a difficult age and need two parents, not one."

David gazed thoughtfully at his friend. Certainly putting the ball in Sophie's court made perfect sense. If she really loved him, then she might reluctantly agree to allow things to carry on as they were – just meeting once or twice a week in secret, and making love at every available opportunity.

Of course, by taking up Simon's suggestion he risked losing Sophie. Heartbreaking as that might be, though, at least it would be an indication of how much she cared for him. If she were content to finish their relationship, then why, for goodness sake should he even consider sacrificing so much for her?

"Thanks for that," smiled David gratefully. "I am going to follow your advice. If the affair comes to an end, it will probably be for the best."

Rebecca gave her brother a look of disgust.

"I just don't believe it. You men are all as devious as each other."

These were the last words said on the matter. Seeing the indignation on Rebecca's face, the two men quickly changed the subject. David regretted seeking an intelligent woman's opinion on his problem. It was always likely that she would come out on the side of members of her own sex – or at least, empathize with those who didn't meddle around with other people's husbands.

Having talked for another hour or so, the guests got up to leave. David had never got into the habit of kissing Rebecca on the cheek as he often did with other female friends. Because of her strict religious upbringing, he feared that such behaviour would be poorly received. So as usual, he made do with a warm handshake.

"You must come with Simon to visit me in Broadstairs," smiled Rebecca. "It seems ages since you last came down."

"Sounds good," replied David.

"Then how about eight weeks today?" she said, having quickly referred to a diary that she had just removed from her bag.

The two men were less organized and said they would need to check with their wives. Although neither of them could remember being told of anything that had been arranged on the day, they weren't absolutely certain. Both agreed to get back to Rebecca in the near future to confirm that they were free.

From the computer, Maureen printed out a list of debtors. They were all individuals who had got into financial difficulties and in desperation, had gone to Harvey Lucas for a loan. It was a move that many lived to regret. Charged exorbitant rates of interest, they soon owed far in excess of what they had originally borrowed.

Since the economic downturn in 2008, business had been good for Harvey. The banks had become more cautious about lending and were shutting their doors to many of those looking for credit, so people in dire circumstances were increasingly turning to loan sharks to come to their rescue. These were, in the main, back-street gangsters, who used bullying tactics to get the money they claimed was due to them.

Looking down the list, Maureen drew a red ring around the name of Mark Wright. It wasn't unknown for clients to disappear in order to avoid paying off their debts. Because a lot of them were destitute, though, it was hardly worth the expense and effort of trying to track them down. This young man, however, was entirely different. He was hiding out there somewhere, in possession of a small fortune.

Maureen had spent a lot of time on the case. She had spoken to dozens of Mark's relatives, friends and neighbours in an attempt to discover if anyone had a clue as to where he may have gone – just some little detail that could point her in the right direction. Much to her frustration, though, after more than two weeks of hard graft, she was still no closer to solving the mystery.

Also enlisted to help were an agency that specialized in tracing missing debtors. The owner was a personal friend of Harvey's and was happy to be paid in cash for his services. Having dealt with them in the past, Maureen had always been impressed with the firm's success rate. However, on this occasion, she wasn't expecting rapid results from them. They were a back-up to her investigations and no more than that.

Maureen passed the list of debtors across the table to her husband. He had just arrived home after spending the morning with clients. In other words, he had been sitting next to them in his Porsche, either collecting money from those who could afford to pay or threatening those who were penniless.

"Any news on Mark Wright yet?" asked Harvey, as his eyes were drawn to the red circle.

"Absolutely nothing," replied Maureen wearily.

"Have you spoken to all his old neighbours?" asked Harvey, concerned that his wife may have been missing a trick.

"I've been to every house in the road," answered Maureen. "Nobody can remember seeing him since the robbery. I even carried his photograph, just in case there were people who couldn't remember exactly what he looked like."

"I reckon that somebody must know where he is but is keeping quiet," said Harvey.

"I'm not so sure," said Maureen, as she lit a cigarette. "People that I speak to are disgusted at what he did to that poor elderly woman. I've heard that the old girl is suffering from chronic depression and may even have to go into a home."

Harvey, who had almost smoked a cigarette down to the butt, jabbed the smouldering end into a blue ashtray. Around the edge of it was the logo of a well-known brewer, suggesting that it might have been pilfered one evening from a local pub.

"Fancy stealing from a dear old lady like that," said Harvey, with self-righteous indignation. "It just goes to show what a heartless bastard he is."

Maureen smiled to herself but said nothing. Never in her life had she met anyone who was so devoid of compassion as her husband. Harvey seemed to derive the greatest of pleasure from terrorizing his clients and had no compunction from taking their very last penny from them. What gave him even more job satisfaction was roughing up those who continually got behind with their repayments.

"I wonder whether there is a flaw in our plans," said Maureen, deciding it was time to voice her concerns. "It is all very well catching up with this guy and grabbing what remains of Mrs Fisher's savings. But we are in trouble if he ends up getting himself arrested. The cops will decide that the old girl should get her money back and then they will come looking for us."

Harvey gave her a sly grin.

"Mark Wright isn't going to get arrested. He is a missing person and will remain so for evermore. Just leave it to me."

"Bloody hell!" exclaimed Maureen. "Are we talking murder here?"

"I prefer to think of it as manslaughter," said Harvey, who was in the process of lighting up another cigarette, having just put out the last one. "I shall organize a nasty little accident for our Mr Wright."

Maureen fidgeted a little uncomfortably in her chair. "And what did you have in mind for him?"

Harvey ignored the question. Instead, he rubbed his hand over his scalp, which he liked to keep as smooth as a baby's bum. A shaven head, he believed, made him look hard and was therefore vital for anyone in his line of business.

"I've got a job for you to do," he said, standing up and checking his appearance in a mirror on the wall. "It's starting to get a bit prickly on top."

CHAPTER FOURTEEN

Finally, hunger got the better of him. Drawing back the duvet, Mark swung his legs over the edge of the bed before crossing over to the window. It was in those few seconds that he said a silent prayer for sunshine. Rain would be a drag. Until the weather improved, it would mean traipsing around the shops or remaining cooped up in the bedsit.

Having parted the curtains no more than six inches, he heaved a sigh of relief. In a blue, cloudless sky, the sun peered in at him in all its glory. It looked perfect for another of those days lazing around on the beach. As it was Saturday, though, he was prepared for more company than usual. After a week toiling away at work, the crowds were likely to be arriving in their droves.

Once he was washed and dressed, Mark was ready to go out. Because of the mess left by other lodgers, Mark always avoided cooking himself anything in the kitchen. Instead, he chose to eat in any of the many cafes and restaurants in the town. As money was no longer a problem, he had no reason to be put off by the cost.

It was exactly a week since he had moved into the bedsit. Already, the Friendly Welcome Guest House seemed like a distant memory. Gradually the idea of being on a permanent holiday was losing its appeal. Life was just starting to get repetitive. Be they male or female, he needed someone to brighten things up a bit. Sunbathing on the beach every day would have been perfect were there someone lying beside him to talk to.

He had all but written off his fellow lodgers as possible companions. Gary, who had introduced him to the bedsit, was hardly ever around. When he wasn't at work, he was spending time with his girlfriend. The others were much older and barely spoke when he passed them on the stairs or in the hall.

The evenings seemed the loneliest time. It was a choice between staying in his cheerless room, sitting in a pub amongst strangers or going for a walk. With so much money to spend, he couldn't believe that his options were so limited. He wanted some nightlife, but didn't know where to find it. The town seemed to cater for families, rather than young people looking to enjoy themselves.

Having no transport was at the root of his problem. He knew of places that provided the sort of entertainment that he was looking for, but they were too far away. A car seemed to be the only solution – getting his own motor and going wherever he wanted to. Perhaps driving a woman home after a night out and seeing what that might lead to.

Of course, Mark knew it would be taking a risk to get his own vehicle. As an owner, his address would be registered with the DVLA, and before long, others were likely to gain access to that information. In fact, he might as well advertise his whereabouts on commercial television. In no time at all, his pursuers were sure to start moving in.

Fortified by a full English breakfast, Mark strolled down to the sea. The day trippers had yet to arrive, and there were just a scattering of people on the beach. After spreading a bath towel over the sand – an item purloined from the Friendly Welcome Guest House – he sat down and began to read a newspaper that he had bought in the high street. It was one of those tabloids that specializes in pin-ups, gossip columns and astrology predictions.

It didn't take long before he had read his newspaper from cover to cover. Putting on earphones, he switched on his iPod and stretched out fully on the towel. After two weeks of sunbathing, he was beginning to become as brown as a berry. He only wished there were some attractive women around that he could impress with his tan. Looking around him, all he could see were elderly couples and families.

Mark began to reflect on his life again, trying to think up ways to improve it. Then all of a sudden, the idea came to him in a flash. Of course, shouted an excited voice somewhere inside his head. The best way to meet local people was to join a club. You were always good at football, it was saying, so go and sign up for a Sunday league team.

To celebrate this moment of inspiration, he slapped the palm of his hand against his thigh. It was such an obvious solution to the problem, he couldn't believe that it hadn't occurred to him sooner. Then almost immediately, much of the enthusiasm began to drain away. He remembered that it was only early June and the new season was still weeks away. He needed to make friends now, today, not when the summer was drawing to a close.

In a while, he sat up and looked around. Many of the day trippers had arrived and taken their places on the beach. He had become encircled by clusters of semi-naked bodies of all shapes and sizes. Most were sat back relaxing in brightly coloured deck chairs or lying flat out on sun-loungers.

Mark checked his watch. It was almost eleven thirty so he decided to go for a quick swim before taking an early lunch. It occurred to him that were he to eat later, every catering establishment in the town would be packed with holiday makers.

There was no need for him to change. Having removed his shorts, he displayed to anyone who was facing his direction, a pair of blue tight fitting Speedos. Then he began wading through the mounds of sand towards the water edge. As he looked ahead he could see the heads of swimmers as they appeared to bob about amongst the gentle waves. Meanwhile, others who were mainly accompanying toddlers, paddled closer to the shore.

The beach was in a bay, shaped like a horseshoe. There was a small harbour pier where fisherman stood for hours waiting to make a catch, while there were boats that were moored alongside. When the tide receded, rock pools would appear, attracting young children who were looking to get a glimpse of crabs or other sea creatures that had been separated from the sea.

After his swim, Mark felt invigorated by the exercise. Having slipped on his shorts again over his wet Speedos, he climbed up the stone steps from the beach and on to the promenade. Hunger was beginning to get the better of him, so he went in search of somewhere to eat that didn't appear to be too busy. Although he had nothing to rush for these days, it still annoyed him when he was forced to join the end of a long queue.

Mark strolled past the window of a cafe and stopped immediately in his tracks. It wasn't so much the two empty tables that attracted his attention. Of far greater interest was the pretty young waitress in a skimpy skirt and a pink low cut blouse. Without even bothering to check what was on the menu, he wandered inside and took a seat.

Like all customers who came through the door, his eyes were immediately drawn to a large mural on the wall. It depicted a jolly-faced, rather plump gentleman in a brown cloak with a hood that covered the top of his head. The painting was there to explain why the proprietor had decided to call his cafe 'The Friar Tuck-In Kitchen'. It wasn't a name that exactly rolled off the tongue.

This establishment could best be described as rough and ready. No fresh vegetables were available for those who had a preference for healthy eating. As advertised on the menu fixed on the wall behind the counter, all meals were served with chips. Then when the customers had departed, the Formica table tops were given a quick once over with a damp cloth.

Mark laid his bath towel on the vacant chair beside him. Although proud of his tan, he had slipped on the white T-shirt that he had worn down to the beach. For some reason, he didn't feel entirely comfortable eating lunch amongst strangers while exposing his bare chest. Dressing appropriately in public was something that had been drummed into him as a child. His mother was one of those women who believed in maintaining certain standards, even when she and her family were on holiday.

After a few moments, the pretty waitress wandered over to his table. There was a bored expression on her face as she held up a pencil in one hand and a small note pad in the other.

"What would you like then?" she asked, in a weary voice suggesting that she hadn't been sleeping too well of late.

"I'll have two eggs, a sausage and chips, please," smiled Mark, hopeful that his order wouldn't create too much inconvenience for her.

"What would you like to drink?" she enquired, while still scribbling in her note pad. "Make it an orange juice with ice, please," replied Mark with a smile.

"Right, then," said the waitress, when she had finished writing and was about to walk away. "Have you worked here long?" asked Mark.

The waitress shook her head.

"Just a few weeks," she replied, before putting her hand over her mouth while she yawned. "I only work in here on Saturdays, just to earn a bit of money for myself."

Mark was pleased that she seemed happy to talk. However, he was anxious not to spoil everything by getting the girl into trouble with the cafe owner. Having glanced around, he had noticed a middle-aged gentleman with a swarthy complexion watching them from behind the counter. It was probable that he didn't approve of members of his staff wasting time chatting when there was work to be done.

"What do you do for the rest of the week?" asked Mark, hopeful that the cafe owner's patience remained intact for just a few precious moments longer.

"Sitting in a classroom," laughed the waitress. "I'm still at school."

Mark was completely taken by surprise. He couldn't believe that he had been on the point of asking her out. He realized that it could have led to an unpleasant encounter with an angry father. It also embarrassed him to think that at thirty-one, he was starting to chat up school kids. The girl wasn't exactly young enough to be his daughter, but she wasn't that far off.

"Make that a large orange juice, by the way," he said, having removed the smile from his face. After lunch, he returned to the beach. He had briefly considered taking a walk for a change, but had dismissed the idea on account of the weather. It was just too hot to do anything other than lie out in the sun, he decided.

By six o'clock, many of the deckchairs had been abandoned, as holidaymakers began to make their way home. The sea had lost some of its attraction once the tide had gone out. Some of the ice cream stalls had shut up shop, while the elderly gentleman who was in charge of the children's merry-go-round was packing up for the night.

Mark decided to go back to the bedsit. He was keen to have a wash and get out of his Speedos before setting off for his evening meal. Standing up, he brushed the sand off himself, unaware that he was being closely watched. Neither did it remotely occur to him that he was being followed as he slowly headed for home.

Mark had just finished in the bathroom when the door-bell rang. As he was making his way along the landing to his room he heard voices from below. Then much to his surprise, one of his fellow lodgers called out his name. Carrying his towel over his arm he quickly descended the stairs to investigate. Then his heart almost stood still when he saw the face that was staring up at him.

"Hello Tina," he said, trying hard to steady his nerves. Tina Bailey beamed at him.

"Lovely to see you again. You've got a great tan there."

"Have you come here alone?" asked Mark, anxious that a fleet of police cars might be parked outside on the road.

"Don't worry," smiled Tina reassuringly. "Nobody knows that I'm here."

"Look, we'll talk in my room," said Mark, concerned that others might be listening. Apart from possessing a key to the front door, he had also been provided with one to his room.

It gave him peace of mind to know that anyone else living in the house couldn't just walk in and start snooping about. Had anyone of them found so much money hidden under the mattress, they would have thought that all their Christmases had come at once.

Of course, he appreciated that a locked door wouldn't prevent a thief from breaking in. But the person who worried him most was the landlord. With a key of his own, he had no need to use force to gain access. Nevertheless, he had little choice but to leave the cash exactly where it was. He couldn't risk carrying a great stack of notes around with him and accidentally losing the lot on the beach. Neither was he prepared to open up a bank account and end up advertising his whereabouts to the world and his wife.

Tina frowned the moment she set eyes on the bedsit. Her expression then turned to one of disbelief as she examined the dilapidated furniture in closer detail. None of it met her approval any more than the musty smell in the air. Quickly crossing the room, she pushed the open window back as far as it would go.

"How did you know where to find me?" asked Mark.

Tina gave a long hard look at a wicker chair in the corner. Then wondering whether it had ever been cleaned during its entire lifetime, she opted to sit on the edge of the bed. In spite of her disapproval of the surroundings, she suddenly managed a half smile.

"I happened to come down here today to visit a great aunt who has just gone into a care home," she began, while attempting to scratch a small black mark off the pillowcase with her fingernail.

"Anyway, I left about four and came down to the beach to sunbathe. Then, after I had been lying there for a while, I happened to look up and much to my amazement, there you were in the sea with water up to your waist. I sat up and waited for you to finish your swim and watched as you went back to your clothes. After that, I kept a close eye on you and when you finally stood up and started making your way across the sand, I began to follow you."

As he listened, Mark felt his stomach churning over. Now that one person knew where he was living, it was likely that others would soon be told. Somehow he would have to persuade Tina to keep quiet or quickly find alternative accommodation. If he couldn't manage to do either, then the consequences were simply too dreadful to even think about.

"So are you going to let anyone know where I am?" he asked.

"If I did, you would end up in prison", said Tina, as she looked disapprovingly at the faded wallpaper. "I know about the robbery."

"So it looks as though I am at your mercy, then," said Mark.

"Doesn't it just," smiled Tina, who seemed to be enjoying the moment. "What I can't understand is why you moved into a dump like this with all that money."

Mark was trying his best to remain calm. He was beginning to feel like a cornered mouse that was being toyed with by a cat. If Tina intended to shout her mouth off to the police, he wanted her to come out and say so.

"To rent anywhere nice, I would need to apply for references," explained Mark. "For somebody who is on the run from the police, that would be a pretty dumb thing to do."

"So have you spent much of the money yet, then?" asked Tina. Mark shook his head.

"Hardly any of it. There was the train fare down here, I paid to stay in a guesthouse for a week, then there is the rent on this place. Apart from meals, toiletries and a few clothes, that's about it."

"But why aren't you enjoying a life of luxury, then?" asked Tina in amazement. "I would have expected you to have bought a great flashy sports car by now."

"Because I can't," snapped Mark irritably. "You can't buy anything of real value without filling out a bloody form. Everybody seems to want to know who you are and where you live. Then, before you know it, your address is being circulated around the whole world."

Tina looked at him thoughtfully. He was one of the most attractive men she had ever met – even more so, with his deep tan. It seemed such a shame, she felt, that somebody so desirable should be locked up in a prison cell for any length of time.

"Tell you what," she grinned. "Buy me a meal and I promise not to tell anyone where you are hiding out."

Mark could hardly believe his luck. Appreciating that he had an excellent deal, he readily agreed to go ahead with it. He knew of a little Italian restaurant in the high street, which in his opinion had a touch of class. It was a place with gleaming white cloths on the table, with serviettes to match and where smartly attired waiters addressed the customers as 'Sir' and 'Madam'.

"Look, I'm sorry I couldn't move in with you two weeks ago," he said, after ordering spaghetti bolognaise for two and a bottle of Burgundy.

Tina shrugged.

"Doesn't matter now. After you let me down, I had no choice but to give the landlord a month's notice. As I was broke, though, Dad is paying the rent for me until I get out in two weeks' time."

"Where will you move to?" asked Mark.

"I had intended to go back home to live with my parents for a while, but I have suddenly come up with a much better idea," said Tina, with a gleam in her eye.

At that moment she was interrupted by the waiter. He was tall, with dark wavy hair and possessed those Mediterranean good looks that are seductive to many women. Having shown Mark the label on the bottle, he proceeded to pour a small sample of wine into his glass. Then, when he had received a nod of approval from the customer, he filled both glasses on the table with a more substantial measure of the dark red liquid.

"What have you got in mind?" asked Mark, as soon as the waiter had disappeared.

"Look," said Tina, after taking a sip of wine. "You have the money and I would have no trouble in getting references. So why don't we combine these two assets?"

Mark gave her a quizzical look. "I don't quite follow you."

"Well, let's start with somewhere to live," began Tina, who was trying hard to contain her excitement. "I'll go and find a nice flat, sign an agreement with the landlord in my name only and then we move in together."

Mark was silent momentarily as he considered the proposal. The idea of leaving his dingy bedsit for more spacious and cheerful surroundings was certainly very appealing. However, he could see that there could be one or two snags.

"Suppose your mum turns up unexpectedly," he said thoughtfully, before glancing around to make certain that nobody was listening in to their conversation. "If she finds me living in the flat, I'm pretty certain she would be on to the police in a flash."

"I'm already ahead of you on that one," smiled Tina. "I'll get the landlord to put a spy hole in the front door. Then, when somebody knocks, at least we'll have a chance to decide what to do. In the case of my mum, you would probably need to hide somewhere in the flat for a while, until I could get her down to the beach or something".

Mark looked down thoughtfully at his wine glass. There were several other concerns that he had about the plan, but decided to keep them to himself. He was only too well aware, that if he didn't try to keep Tina happy, he might well end up regretting it.

"Shall we live down here by the sea, then?" he asked.

"OK by me," answered Tina. "You can't possibly live anywhere remotely close to Brockleby. Your photograph was plastered all over the front page of the local paper."

A horrified expression immediately appeared on Mark's face. Until that very moment, it hadn't occurred to him that he had actually made the headlines, and that possibly most of the people he had ever met would know that he was a criminal. It struck him like a hammer blow that he had become famous in his hometown for all the wrong reasons.

"I didn't realize that I had caused such a sensation," said Mark, staring blankly into space. "By the way," said Tina, as she placed a serviette on her lap. "Just in case any of your friends hadn't read about the robbery in the *Brockleby Times*, a lady called Maureen has kindly been spreading the word around. In fact, I had a visit from her earlier this week."

"Not her," replied Mark, burying his head in his hands. "Maureen is the wife of a loan shark I owe money to. If her husband and his partner ever get hold of me, I am likely to end up in a very serious condition."

Before Tina had an opportunity to respond, the waiter arrived with a tray. As the good-looking Italian laid a plate of spaghetti Bolognaise in front of her, they exchanged a warm smile. Then he turned to her male companion to serve him with his meal, but on this occasion there was no eye contact. Mark was just staring down at the table as though it was about to explode.

"Don't worry," said Tina, as she attempted to wrap a long coil of spaghetti around her fork. "As long as everything major you buy is in my name, they will never track you down."

"But you managed to find me today, so why shouldn't others?" answered Mark gloomily. "Look, you need to keep away from crowds," said Tina. "For a start, you should find a quiet little bay to bathe in – not one of the most popular beaches along the coastline. With so many people around, you could be spotted without even knowing it."

"You're right, I suppose," conceded Mark, before sucking a coil of spaghetti into his mouth. "OK, so that's sorted out," smiled Tina. "Now, let's celebrate our new partnership by getting drunk. Once we've finished this bottle of wine, you can order another one."

Soon Mark began to relax. The newly formed alliance talked excitedly about how they would spend the stolen money. The model of car they wanted was their top priority, but many other luxuries were also on the shopping list. They felt like billionaires who could have anything that took their fancy.

Mark had always thought that Tina was particularly ugly. As the wine began to take an effect on him, though, she was gradually becoming more attractive in his eyes. Suddenly, he could feel himself becoming aroused by the two large bulges that stuck out from beneath her tee shirt. It was when they were about to leave the restaurant, about half-past ten, that he decided to make his move.

"As it's getting late, why don't you spend the night at my place?" he suggested hopefully. "You could go back home tomorrow."

Tina looked surprised.

"But you've only got a single bed in your room."

"It's big enough for the both of us if we cuddle up close enough," he replied, putting his arm around her.

"OK, then," smiled Tina. "I suppose it is one way to cement our business arrangement." "Sleeping partners is the term they use, I believe," laughed Mark.

CHAPTER FIFTEEN

David had been looking forward to a quiet, relaxing day in the garden, lying back in a deck chair, drinking cold beer while dressed in shorts; enjoying the luxury of reading the *Observer* at leisure and making an attempt to solve the cryptic crossword puzzle, and then falling asleep after lunch, with no boisterous children around demanding attention.

The whole family had planned to spend Sunday in the country. When Alison's mum had pleaded to be included in the jaunt, though, it had created a bit of a problem with numbers. As only five passengers could be fitted into the car, it was obvious that somebody would have to miss out. All too willingly, David volunteered to stay at home.

But when he drew back the curtains that morning, his heart immediately sank. Fine rain was falling from the heavens and the dark, gloomy clouds overhead hardly suggested that better weather was on the way. All his plans for a lazy day were in ruins. Not only was sitting in the garden out of the question, the rest of the family were hardly likely to relish the prospect of getting a soaking while traipsing through the woods or sitting near a riverbank with a picnic.

"Would you mind picking mum up?" asked Alison, as soon as David came down to breakfast. "I've invited her over to lunch. We've decided to take our drive in the country another day."

David managed a half –smile, even though he felt more like scowling and stamping his foot. He was very fond of his mother-in-law, but preferred her company in small doses – perhaps an hour here and there, rather than being stuck with her for the whole day.

Mrs Johnson had a preference for small talk, rather than serious conversation. In an attempt to help herself and those around her to cope with life's little setbacks, she was forever repeating irritating catchphrases and proverbial sayings. Amongst her favourites were 'keep your chin up', 'no use in crying over spilt milk' and 'every cloud has a silver lining'. Nevertheless, she was a kind-hearted soul, and was always willing to look after her grandchildren whenever called upon.

"Are you ready then?" asked David, when his mother-in-law opened the front door.

"Hang on a moment," answered Mrs Johnson. "I'll just pop upstairs and get the Monopoly set. It's just the thing for a wet day." David groaned inwardly. The last thing in the world he wanted to do was play Monopoly, particularly the old-fashioned version that his mother-in-law owned, with London stations for sale at two hundred pounds and the Old Kent Road on offer at a measly sixty quid. Playing a game that seemed to go on for evermore while sitting behind a pile of fake bank notes was really not his idea of entertainment.

However, he had found a way of minimizing his agony. Not buying up any of the properties that he landed on while travelling around the board invariably led to early bankruptcy. Then, once all his money had been passed on to other players, he could relax in an armchair with a newspaper. The fact that the rest of the family regarded him as a pretty poor capitalist was a price he was happy to pay.

"Thank goodness that Alison had the sense to marry you and not that dreadful Mark Wright," said Mrs Johnson, as she slipped on to the passenger seat alongside David. "I can't believe that my daughter was once engaged to that man. Fancy stealing that poor old lady's life savings."

"It's terrible," said David.

"l'm surprised that someone isn't making an appeal on her behalf. If enough people contributed, she could even recover all the money that was stolen off her," said Mrs Johnson.

"That's not a bad idea," said David thoughtfully. "Perhaps I should speak to the *Brockleby Times* and ask them to put something in their paper."

"I should do it soon, while the robbery is still fresh in everybody's mind," advised Mrs Johnson. "I always say that he who hesitates has lost."

David managed to avoid wincing as he heard her repeat the proverb for the thousandth time. "I could be the first person to make a donation as well," he said enthusiastically. "Perhaps a cheque for five hundred pounds would look very impressive".

"Have you gone mad?" answered Mrs Johnson, clearly taken aback by such rashness. "I should think that a tenner would be generous enough."

"Not for somebody who has ambitions of becoming an MP," said David, with a crafty grin. "Didn't Alison tell you? I am putting myself forward to be the new Labour Parliamentary Candidate. So making a sizeable donation would buy me some valuable publicity in this town."

The subject was brought up again over lunch. While Mrs Johnson was still trying to persuade David not to part with half a grand, Alison sat quietly scheming. As an enthusiastic political activist, she knew that her husband was in with a real chance of winning the Brockleby seat for Labour. It was just a matter of convincing enough voters in the constituency that he was the right person for the job.

"Why don't you and I go and see Mrs Fisher this afternoon?" she suggested. "Mum can stay here and look after the children for an hour or so."

"Why?" asked David, giving his wife a surprised look.

"Because if we are going to get an appeal going for the old lady, it is only right that we should get her permission," explained Alison, a little impatiently.

"But why do you both need to go?" asked Mrs Johnson, looking as puzzled as her son-in-law. "Because I vaguely know Mrs Fisher," explained Alison, with a crafty smile. "Very often, she would be standing at her garden gate when I was on my way to visit Mark. Don't forget, they only lived several doors away. Anyway, occasionally I would stop for a while and have a chat with the old lady. She was really quite sweet."

David nodded. He was able to see the advantage of taking his wife with him. As Mrs Fisher had probably been traumatized by the robbery, then she might not feel inclined to open the door to a strange man.

The Chambers set off in the car, leaving Mrs Johnson to keep the children amused. The rain was continuing to fall and there was hardly anyone about as they drove down the high street. Most of the shops were shut, but those with the doors open for business were probably not doing much trade. It was just the sort of day that kept people at home in front of the TV.

Mrs Fisher lived on the other side of town. As Alison was more familiar with the area, she was able to direct the way without the need to use the SAT-NAV. Finally, she instructed David to pull up outside a rather shabby semi-detached house. The front garden was overgrown with weeds and all manner of shrubs. The net curtains looked more black than white, while the swinging gate seemed as though it might part company from its rusty hinges before very long.

Alison stepped forward and pressed the bell. She wanted to be the first person that the old lady came face to face with, rather than being confronted by a stranger. After a brief wait, she heard a shuffling sound from inside the house before the door opened by no more than a few inches.

"Hello Mrs Fisher," said Alison cheerfully. "I expect you remember me. We had many long chats when I used to pass your house."

The old lady stared blankly at her. Then deciding that her visitor didn't look too threatening, she opened the door a little wider. Suddenly conscious of her appearance, she pushed the long strands of wispy white hair out of her eyes.

"I can't say I remember you, dear," said the old lady with a shake of the head. "How long ago would it have been?"

"I suppose the last time we spoke must have been about eight years ago," said Alison. "I used to walk up and down this road quite frequently then."

"Yes, of course," smiled Mrs Fisher. "I knew I had seen you somewhere before. You were the lady that was engaged to Mark Wright."

"That's right," replied Alison, as she stepped aside so that the old lady could see David. "Look, could my husband and I come in for a few moments? We think we may be able to help you."

Mrs Fisher nodded as she beckoned them in. Alison and David were then led down the hall and through a door on the left. They found themselves in a drab sitting room in which the furniture looked even older than Mrs Fisher – good, solid tables and chairs that had been made to last, but probably not into the 21st century. Only the TV in the corner appeared to be a product of the modern age.

There was a strong musty smell in the room, as though the windows hadn't been opened in weeks. Alison wondered if they were jammed, or whether it was just that Mrs Fisher had a dislike of fresh air.

"We were sorry to hear about the robbery," said David, as he sunk down in an armchair amid high-pitched protests from the springs.

Mrs Fisher immediately burst into tears at the mention of the robbery.

"Rotten sod stole all my money," she sobbed. "He didn't even leave me a few pounds to get the window mended that he smashed. All I have to live on now is my pension."

Alison who had sat down alongside Mrs Fisher on the settee, put her arm around the old lady's shoulders.

"David and I want to get some of your money back for you," she said soothingly. "If you are happy about it, one of us will speak to the *Brockleby Times* and ask them to start an appeal for you. I'm sure there must be many local people who would be pleased to make a donation."

There was a brief silence while Mrs Fisher reflected on the proposal. Sitting on the opposite side of the room, David was beginning to feel uneasy. He was wondering how Alison was so confident that the local paper would be so willing to co-operate. The last thing he wanted was to give the poor old lady false hopes.

"Supposing they manage to recover my money," said Mrs Fisher after a few moments. "Apart from the police, there is a lady who is trying to track that thieving bastard down. She called around here the other day asking questions. She said she was from a local charity that tries to help victims of crime."

Alison nodded.

"I've had a visit from Maureen, as well. Mark and I have a daughter, and that woman wanted to know whether that thieving bastard, as you call him, has tried to get in touch with Amanda."

"Look, if you end up with more money than you had before the robbery, then give the extra bit back to charity," suggested David.

"In any case, it might take them a while to catch up with Mark, by which time the money could be spent," said Alison. "I can't imagine that he would be so stupid as to start advertising his whereabouts. He will probably be lying low for the time being."

"Very well, then," replied Mrs Fisher, managing a half smile. "I would appreciate your help."

"By the way," said Alison, with a warning glare, "as soon as you get some money, I will help you to set up a bank account. It's too risky to keep your savings under the bed."

"You're very kind," said Mrs Fisher, as she dried her eyes with a small white handkerchief. "Anyway, now we've sorted that out, you can make us all a nice cup of tea," said Alison, as she removed her arm from around the old lady's shoulders.

For the next hour or so, the three of them sat talking. In spite of her lack of money sense, David was surprised to discover that Mrs Fisher was a lot more intelligent than he had first thought. In her younger days, she had travelled a great deal and talked at length about the places she had visited. Her favourite destination was the USA. Enthusiastically, she described the beauty of New England in the fall and the fascinating Sonoran Desert in the southwestern states, with cactus plants that grew well beyond fifty feet.

"I hope you haven't raised Mrs Fisher's hopes too high," said David, as soon as he began to drive away. "What happens if the *Brockleby Times* won't help with the appeal? Without the publicity, we aren't likely to raise a great deal of money."

"They will," answered Alison, as she sat back in the passenger seat. "And I will see to it that you will be there when the photographer arrives at Mrs Fisher's house."

"Why are you so confident?" asked David.

"Because I am and you are going to make the first donation to the appeal," said Alison, with a self- satisfied expression on her face. "I want to see you on the front page of the *Brockleby Times* handing Mrs Fisher a cheque for five hundred pounds. It will do your election prospects the power of good."

The next evening, the Brockleby Labour Party held their regular monthly meeting at headquarters.

David and Alison were two of the thirty or so members who had turned out in the rain to attend. As usual, everyone was seated around the outside of a number of tables joined end to end to form a rectangle.

Once Bert Vine, the chairman, had opened proceedings, Harry Strong was invited to read out his treasurer's report. It was the part of the meeting that many members dreaded most. For about ten minutes, the money-man drawled on about the ever-deteriorating state of the finances. Having complained that revenue from fund-raising events was down and bar sales were falling, he then had a good moan about the rise in outgoings. Then, looking as though he might be about to burst into tears at any second, he summed up with a warning that something needed to be done rapidly in order to avert a liquidity crisis.

After that, it was Carol's turn. In her role as membership secretary, she was called upon to advise the gathering on how the latest recruitment drive was going. Like the treasurer, though, she had no positive news to report back on. With a gloomy expression on her face, she announced that not a single person had joined in the previous month. Even the Lib Dem, councillor who had for some time, been talking about defecting to Labour, had finally decided to join the Tories instead.

Once Carol had finished depressing everyone, the gathering turned its attention to her husband. The next item on the agenda was something that Tony was dealing with. Collecting the names of those wishing to become the next parliamentary candidate for the constituency was his job.

"How many people have put themselves forward so far?" asked Bert Vine.

"Only two," answered Tony. "My wife Carol and Kenny Simpson."

"Make that three," called out David. "I have decided to throw my hat in the ring as well." All eyes immediately turned to the latest candidate. As a hard-working party activist for the last eight years, he was generally well respected. Good looking and well mannered, he was particularly popular with the female membership.

"Three very strong candidates", smiled Bert approvingly. "However, I am surprised that more people aren't showing an interest".

"I'm afraid it's my fault," explained Tony, with a look of embarrassment. "Because of the council by-election, I have got a bit behind with other matters. I've only just sent out a letter to members asking whether they are interested in becoming the candidate."

Bert gave the party organizer a stern look. As chairman, he was a hard taskmaster and had little patience with lame excuses. The fact that Tony worked harder than anyone else in the association made no difference to him.

"Anyway, moving on," he said, turning his eyes away from the slouch who had failed to do his duty on time, "I had a phone call today from the National Executive Committee. It seems that they are very keen that Heather Marsh finds a winnable seat by the next General Election".

The room went perfectly silent. There was probably nobody at the meeting who needed to be reminded of Heather Marsh. They were aware that she had been a junior minister in the last Labour Government, before losing her seat to the Tories in 2010. Having shown great promise in her position, it was no secret that the party hierarchy were eager to see her back at Westminster as soon as possible.

"So can we take it that she has her eye on this seat then?", asked Alec Stokes, the newly elected councillor.

Bert nodded.

"And the NEC are insisting that there are an equal number of male and female candidates on our shortlist".

"But Brockleby should be represented by a local person who knows the town well. Not just anybody that the NEC decide to impose on it", protested Kenny angrily.

"If my memory serves me right, Heather Marsh is another of those bloody barristers", shouted one middle aged man scornfully. "There are enough of that lot in Parliament already. The only talent they have is an ability to avoid answering a direct question".

Immediately, others began shouting similar unflattering remarks, about both the former junior minister and her profession. In an attempt to bring calm to the proceedings, Bert lifted his hand up like a policeman trying to control traffic. Having presided over many acrimonious meetings in his time as chairman throughout the years, he had become experienced at restoring order.

"Look, it is we the members of the association who will ultimately decide who will be our candidate", he said, once the shouting had died down. "However, let me remind you, that we must choose the individual best qualified to serve the people of Brockleby and the party as a whole".

Having decided that he would have the last word on the subject, the chairman quickly moved on to the next item on the agenda. Rather belatedly in David's opinion, he congratulated Alec Stokes on his council election victory. A ploy that managed to turn the howls of dissent into loud cheers.

After the meeting David and Alison joined a few friends at the bar for drinks. Everybody it seemed, were still fuming that the NEC should be interfering in local matters. Kenny in particular, was getting hot under the collar.

"I reckon that Bert Vine wants Heather Marsh to be our candidate", he said bitterly. "He likes the fact that she has a high profile in the party".

"There are probably others in this association who feel the same", said Carol. "They just like the idea of being close to well-known people".

"On the other hand", said Alec Stokes, before stopping to take a sip of lager. "There are going to be members like me, who will be loyal to those who have worked hard in this constituency and deserve to be rewarded".

"The problem is that we will have several local candidates who end up on the short list and the loyalty vote will get divided", said Tony thoughtfully. "If Kenny and David are on that list, we can't vote for both of them. That could be the factor which gives victory to Heather Marsh".

The conversation continued for a while longer. Alison though, remained unusually quiet as she stood sipping red wine. While appreciating that Heather Marsh and Kenny Simpson would be strong contenders to become the candidate, she knew she could outsmart them both. In her mind's eye she saw her husband standing up in the House of Commons and making his maiden speech.

Finally the group at the bar gradually began to break up. As soon as Alison slipped into the car alongside David, she switched on her mobile phone and noted the text message that she had received. It was the one she had been waiting for.

"The Brockleby Times have agreed to help us make that appeal for Mrs Fisher", she said with a smile.

"Great stuff", answered David, as he got the car started.

"They are sending a photographer to her house on Saturday morning as I requested. So you had better take your best suit to the cleaners and don't forget to write that cheque out for five hundred pounds", said Alison.

"It may take a lot more than a little helpful publicity to beat Heather Marsh though. She will have a lot to impress the members with when she speaks at the selection meeting. Particularly when she reminds them what she managed to achieve as a junior minister in the last government", replied David.

"Let me do some research on this woman", said Alison, as she sat back in the passenger seat and shut her eyes. "I wonder whether she was one of those MPs who falsified their expenses. I'm sure that everybody would be interested to know".

CHAPTER SIXTEEN

Mark was woken up by strange noises. It was rather like the sound of a jet engine being switched on and off at regular intervals of about five seconds. After turning over in bed he discovered that the disturbance was unconnected to any mechanical device. It was just that the woman who lay under the duvet with him had a particularly loud snore.

Mark gave Tina a firm nudge. Hopeful that he had fixed the problem, he shut his eyes and tried to sleep. After the amount of wine he had drunk the evening before, he was now left with the mother of all hangovers. His head felt as though it was about to split in two.

After Mark had taken remedial action, the snoring came to an abrupt halt. But that didn't mean that he had managed to secure for himself a period of peace and quiet. Having been struck by an elbow, Tina had cried out and was now massaging her rib cage with some considerable vigour. The next minute she was sat on the edge of the bed and examining her injury with some concern. As she wore only bra and knickers, this exercise didn't require the removal of any clothing.

"Why can't you learn to keep still in bed", she complained irritably. "You almost half killed me just then".

"Sorry it was an accident", answered Mark, not wishing to admit to a deliberate assault.

The pain must have quickly eased off. Any thoughts of turning up at A & E and asking for the medical staff to check for broken bones were quickly dismissed. Tina was now gazing around as though she was searching for something.

"I'm surprised you haven't got a television in here yet", she said suddenly.

"It's a question of the license", explained Mark. "Get one and my address is advertised around the world. Go without and I end up getting nicked because the detector van just happens to have drawn up in the road outside".

"Not to worry", replied Tina. "Once we get our own place, we'll have a TV for every room".

Once the two of them were washed and dressed they set off for breakfast. There was a fine drizzle in the air as they walked the short distance to the high street. Tina, like Mark, was nursing a sore head after drinking excessively the evening before. She was hopeful that a cup of black coffee might help to revive her.

Mark wanted to eat in the cafe where he usually sat down to bacon and eggs in the morning. On this occasion, though, he found himself being overruled. Tina took one look through the window before turning her nose up in disgust. Then she led the way down the high street until she found a catering establishment that met her approval.

Actually, in Mark's opinion, there was little to choose between the two cafes. In fact, on balance he preferred his regular haunt, because the owner called him mate and always asked how he was doing, whereas in the establishment that Tina had selected, the staff were more reserved when serving customers.

"Why didn't we do it last night?" asked Tina suddenly, while slicing up her fried egg.

Mark looked at her as though she was speaking in a foreign tongue. The hangover was continuing to befuddle his brain, in spite of his stroll down the high street in the light rain. His mental processes at that moment were quite incapable of solving a conundrum.

"What didn't we do?" asked Mark, while squeezing a liberal amount of tomato sauce over his full English breakfast from a plastic bottle.

Tina glanced around to ensure that nobody was in earshot. Using a certain three-lettered word in a public place didn't seem entirely appropriate to her, particularly as it was so early in the day.

"Have sex," she whispered. "I thought that was the reason you invited me back to your room last night."

Mark had no wish to take part in an inquest on the matter. For a start, he could barely recollect anything that had taken place after leaving the Italian restaurant the previous evening. He had no memory of walking home, undressing himself or climbing into bed. All he could vaguely remember was that Tina kept talking while he was trying to fall asleep.

"Sorry, but I was too drunk to do anything last night," he replied, with slight embarrassment. "Perhaps things will be different when we get our own flat together," said Tina hopefully. "Just think. We can make love whenever we want to. I'll make sure that the landlord provides us with a double bed with a nice soft comfortable mattress."

Mark almost choked on his fried bread. The very thought of having a sexual relationship with the woman on the opposite side of the table appalled him. In his opinion, she was seriously ugly, and he had never quite decided which was her least attractive feature. It seemed to be a close run thing between the wide nose and the thick unshapely lips.

The previous evening, it had all seemed so different. While he had been knocking back glass after glass of red wine, Tina had seemed rather desirable. It was rather as though the frog had miraculously changed into a fairy princess. The problem was that in his drunken state he had made certain overtures to her, which he was now regretting. At some point in the future, he would have to explain to her that he had a preference for sleeping alone.

"Pity it's raining," remarked Mark, anxious to change the subject. "We could have gone down to the beach".

"What on earth do you do with yourself when the weather is like this?" asked Tina. "You don't even have a TV to watch."

Mark laughed.

"I kneel down and pray for sunshine."

Tina gazed thoughtfully at the tomato sauce bottle. Her jaws had stopped champing up and down like some battery-controlled toy that had suddenly run out of power.

"If the weather is bad, you could always travel up to London," she said, with the elated look of somebody who has just fathomed the answer to the last clue of a cryptic crossword puzzle. "From the station down here, you can catch a train which goes directly to Victoria."

Mark reflected on the idea before commenting. Even though his brain was malfunctioning, he was still able to see that the suggestion presented him with some very interesting possibilities. There were the numerous West End cinemas, for a start.

He was beginning to appreciate how much Tina could become a major asset to him. What she lacked in beauty, she more than made up for in other ways. Less than twenty four hours ago, he had been down in the dumps, but now he was beginning to feel more positive about his future. Most importantly, he had found somebody he could trust. After all, if this woman was desperate to sleep with him, she was hardly likely to get him carted off by the boys in blue.

"I think you've hit on something," he said, while nodding approvingly at the wise one. "If it's raining to-morrow, I shall definitely be heading for the great metropolis."

"And how about today?" asked Tina, with a teasing grin. "Anything planned, other than going back to bed to recover from your hangover?"

Mark shook his head.

"I have nothing in mind. In my present state, I don't feel like going up to London. A two-hour train journey is the last thing I need right now."

"It's just that I was thinking of popping in on my great aunt again before going home," said Tina. "Do you fancy joining me?"

Normally, Mark would have rejected the invitation out of hand. Sitting in a care home, surrounded by a gathering of old people, was not exactly his idea of fun. But as he turned to face the window and saw that the drizzle was continuing to fall, he felt that the other options available to him were hardly more appealing.

"OK. Let's go and visit your great aunt, then," he replied, managing to sound more enthusiastic than he was actually feeling.

The Amblemoor Residential Care Home had been purpose-built in the 1990s. It was two-storied, with sixty six single rooms and five double rooms, all with en-suite facilities. It was privately owned by a large group, who had appointed a manager and a team of staff who prided themselves on providing their charges with a wealth of entertainment. With bingo, quizzes, singsongs and dances to amuse them, there was never a dull moment in the place – according to the glossy brochure, anyway.

Mark and Tina were greeted at the door by a member of staff in a blue uniform. Having signed the visitors' book, they were guided into a large communal lounge. Placed in various directions were about thirty armchairs upholstered in exactly the same grey fabric, about half of which were occupied by elderly people. Affixed to the wall was a large flat TV screen. Although the set was on, nobody seemed to be paying the slightest attention to Sky News. The residents appeared to be unmoved by reports that Tripoli was being bombed or that the financial markets might be about to collapse. In fact, some were fast asleep, while others stared blankly into space. Only one woman who sat reading a magazine looked fully awake.

"Hello Auntie Angela," said Tina, addressing one of those residents who was in a trancelike state. The elderly lady slowly lifted her head up. For a moment, she looked rather mystified and then a smile gradually crept over her thin wrinkled face. Staring down at Auntie Angela, Mark noticed that her bright red hair had long silver roots.

"Hello," she said, in a croaky voice. "I was just wondering when you were coming in to see me."
"Actually, I came to see you yesterday," laughed Tina. "Don't you remember?"

Auntie Angela looked surprised.

"Are you sure?"

"Absolutely," answered Tina. "I was here for most of the afternoon."

The expression on Auntie Angela's face suggested that she was far from convinced. Her memory had been deteriorating for a long time, but recently, it had got a whole lot worse. It was a problem made even more serious by the fact that as she had been living alone, there had been nobody to keep an eye on her.

One morning, the old lady had gone out shopping and hadn't been able to find her way home. For several hours, she had wandered around in a confused state before finally being spotted by a neighbour. After the incident, it was quickly decided that she needed constant supervision. After having been driven around a few of the local residential care homes by a lady from social services, Auntie Angela decided that Amblemoor was probably marginally better than the rest.

Tina and Mark gathered up armchairs and sat facing Auntie Angela. From their position, they were able to look out over the well-tended landscaped grounds belonging to the home. Had the weather been better, many of the residents would have been seated on the lawn. Today, though, with the light rain still falling, the scenery would have to be enjoyed from the window.

"Did you stay here overnight then?" asked Auntie Angela.

Tina paused for a moment. Although thirty and single, she was still rather hesitant about admitting that she had shared a bed with a member of the opposite sex. Not wishing to upset an old lady in a residential care home she decided to conceal the truth.

"Yes, I booked into a guest house," she smiled.

"Is this your young man?" enquired Auntie Angela, nodding her head in Mark's direction. "Mark is a friend that I brought along to meet you," answered Tina casually, while trying to ignore the old lady's mischievous smile.

"And do you live in Brockleby as well?" asked Auntie Angela, addressing Mark for the first time.

Mark didn't have a chance to answer. At that moment, a member of staff arrived with refreshments. On her trolley were two large urns, cups, saucers and a large red tin of biscuits.

"Tea or coffee luv?" enquired the tea lady in a broad Lancashire accent.

"Tea please, Pat," replied Auntie Angela, with her eyes fixed firmly on the biscuits.

Pat was plump and wore a name badge pinned to the breast pocket of her blue uniform. She gave the impression of being one of those unflustered people who does everything at a leisurely pace – perfect for the job that she was presently doing but, possibly not ideally suitable for a high-pressure environment.

Mark and Tina were hopeful of being offered refreshments as well. Sadly for them, though, hospitality at Amblemoor Residential Care Home was never extended to visitors. Once Auntie Angela had received her drink and a chocolate biscuit, Pat slowly moved on to the next resident.

For an hour or so, Mark largely sat and watched as the two women chatted. Most of the conversation was about people he didn't know or was hardly ever likely to meet during the course of his lifetime. He would have got up to leave had he not been so worried about upsetting Tina. He allowed his mind to go blank, just like almost everyone else in the lounge.

At half past twelve precisely, the lunch bell rang. As if by magic, residents who had spent most of the morning imitating zombies suddenly came to life. Quickly climbing to their feet, they headed off in the same direction. They were rather like a herd of thirsty elephants that had just spotted a water hole. Having been sitting in an armchair close to the dining room, it was actually Auntie Angela who led the stampede.

"It's so depressing," said Tina, when all the residents had eventually filed out of the lounge. "This could be us in fifty years – shut up in a miserable place like this, with nothing to look forward to except the next meal."

Mark gazed dismally out of the window. It was now raining hard, and large puddles were beginning to appear on the lawn. A flash of lightning suddenly lit up the dark sky, followed almost immediately by a deafening clap of thunder.

"I might not have to wait for fifty years," he moaned. "It could happen to me next week. I won't be shut up in a care home, though. It will either be Belmarsh or Wormwood Scrubs."

"You won't be going to prison," replied Tina reassuringly. "Providing we are both careful, you should be quite safe for several years. The problem will start when your money runs out. Sixty-five grand won't last forever."

Since the robbery, the same thought had crossed Mark's mind. He realized only too well that those precious bank notes under the mattress were his lifeline. Once they were spent, he would need to beg on the streets, starve or turn himself in at the nearest police station. Paid employment was fraught with danger as it would mean advertising his whereabouts to the tax office and possibly others. The dismal prospects for his long-term future were starting to keep him awake at night.

"Perhaps I will have to resort to burgling more houses," said Mark, who hadn't been able to come up with a better solution to his problem.

"I have a far better idea," said Tina, with a smile that suggested that she was about to reveal a master plan.

"Does it mean breaking the law?" asked Mark.

"Certainly not," laughed Tina. "There is nothing illegal about caring for an elderly relative." "I don't understand," answered Mark, with a shake of the head.

Tina gave a deep breath before launching into an explanation.

"You see, Auntie Angela is in here on a three-week trial to find out whether she likes it or not," Tina began, while brushing a speck of dust off her jeans. "If she decides to move into this place permanently, then her house will need to be sold. Of course, like most people, my aunt would prefer to stay in her own home, but knows that she is beyond caring for herself. So that is where we come in."

"But I don't know anything about looking after old people," protested Mark.

"Look, apart from being a bit confused, my aunt is reasonably healthy for her age," said Tina. "All we need to do is help around the house, do the shopping and generally keep an eye on her."

Mark looked puzzled. The previous evening's excess of wine was continuing to befuddle his brain.

He just couldn't work out why an absent-minded old dear was about to change his life.

"I can't understand what you are getting at," said Mark wearily. "How will moving in with your aunt help to solve my problems?"

"Because for a start, we will be able to live with my aunt rent free," explained Tina, a little impatiently.

"Then, because she is pretty rich, I'll make certain that she pays most of the household bills, just for the privilege of being looked after in her own home. I'm sure she'll even buy us a new car if we agree to drive her about in it."

"Which means that my money will last a lot longer," said Mark thoughtfully.

He felt that the plan was too good to be true. After turning it over in his mind for a few moments, he soon found the flaw he had been looking for.

"What are the rest of Auntie Angela's family going to say when we move in with her?" he asked. "Aren't they likely to be concerned that we are trying to rob them of their inheritance?"

A blissful smile crept over Tina's face as she gently shook her head.

"No problems there," she answered. "Auntie Angela never married or had children. In fact, she rarely sees the relatives that are still alive. My dad had an argument with her years ago and now my aunt and my parents no longer speak. I am about the only family member that she still keeps in touch with.

The mention of Tina's parents immediately sent alarm bells going off in Mark's head. Rather unfairly, he held Mrs Bailey responsible for his present predicament. He hated her for having witnessed him coming out of Mrs Fisher's house after the robbery. Had she been minding her own business, he told himself, then nobody would have been able to identify him as the probable culprit.

"So what about your mum and dad then?" said Mark, scornfully. "If they find out where I'm living, then the game is up. I'll be eating my Christmas dinner in a prison cell."

"They wouldn't dare turn you in to the police," said Tina, with total conviction. "If you get arrested, I am going to get carted off to the station as well for harbouring a criminal. There is no way my mum would allow that to happen. She wouldn't want the word to get around that her daughter had been locked up in Holloway. Anyway as my parents don't speak to Auntie Angela they are hardly likely to turn up on the doorstep one day. Nobody in Brockleby will know where you are unless I say something, which isn't going to happen".

One by one, the residents began to emerge from the dining room. This time, they walked back to their armchairs rather more sedately than they had left them after the lunch bell had rung. Now they seemed more like elderly people in a care home rather than marauding savages on the rampage.

Once Auntie Angela had returned, Tina began to advise her of the plan. Having successfully sold her idea to Mark, she now had to convince her great aunt that the arrangement would be in everybody's best interest. By the time she had stopped talking, the old lady's watery blue eyes were beaming with delight. The thought of being cared for in her own home was an answer to a prayer.

"When will all this happen?" asked Auntie Angela, excitedly.

"Mark and I will come to fetch you on Saturday morning, so remember to have your suitcase packed," replied Tina, with a warm smile. "By the way, do you have your house key with you?"

"Right here," said Auntie Angela, tapping the brown handbag that was resting on the vacant armchair next to her.

"Give it to me, then, and I'll look after it for you," said Tina, holding out her hand.

By now, Mark and Tina were feeling quite hungry. Waving goodbye to Auntie Angela, they headed back to the high street to find something to eat. Although it was lunchtime, most of the catering establishments were only half-full. Many of those who might have been planning to spend their Sunday by the sea had obviously been put off by the wet weather.

Without waiting for Mark's approval, Tina headed for a rather superior-looking Chinese restaurant. For a while, they sat studying the menu without once bothering to glance at the prices. After all, they were rich and content in the knowledge that they had no need to worry about money for a very long time.

"I'd better drive home after this," said Tina, as she tried to choose between the chicken chop suey and the sweet and sour pork balls.

"Where did you leave your car?" asked Mark, who had already decided on the roast beef curry and had put the menu to one side.

"Oh, some little side road close by," replied Tina casually. Mark raised his eyebrows.

"Hope it didn't get nicked during the night."

"There are so many dents and scratches on my old banger, I can't believe that anyone would want to take it," laughed Tina. "Anyway, I'm looking forward to Auntie Angela forking out for a new one soon."

Mark smiled as he reflected on the new lifestyle that awaited him.

"I am looking forward to watching TV again," he said, somewhat dreamily.

Tina picked up her handbag and began to rummage through the contents. Finally, she produced the Yale key to Auntie Angela's front door that the old lady had given to her earlier.

"Here, you can take charge of this," she smiled. "If I show you where my aunt lives, you can go in and watch TV whenever you like."

CHAPTER SEVENTEEN

David knew his script off by heart. Even so, he went over it once more in his head, while changing to go out. He would be following Simon's advice. Sophie would have to be made to understand that he couldn't possibly desert his family while the children were so young. However, if she were prepared to be patient, he would one day divorce his wife and marry her.

He would call her bluff. For the present, Sophie would have to accept the situation as it was or end their relationship. If she was content to break it off, he hardly felt inclined to sacrifice so much for her – seeing his kids only once a week or perhaps even less; continuing to pay the mortgage on a property that he was no longer welcome in; moving into a tiny top floor flat and being answerable to some money-grabbing landlord.

"Going out for a drink?" asked Alison, when her husband appeared in the lounge smartly dressed.

Recognizing a hint of resentment in her voice, David tried to avoid a domestic confrontation. "I've got a PTA meeting tonight," he said, confident that this explanation for an evening out would be greeted without criticism.

"That must be the first time you've been asked to go to one of those," said Alison, in surprise. "Nobody else was available to represent the teachers," answered David, looking every bit the martyr sacrificing himself for the cause.

"Never mind, this will cheer you up," smiled Alison. "I have managed to find some interesting information about Heather Marsh on the Internet."

David immediately lowered himself into an armchair. Up until that moment, he had been in a rush to get out. Suddenly, though, he decided that Sophie could be made to wait.

"Tell me more," he said eagerly.

"Well, it seems that Miss Marsh owns a very large property in Hampstead," began Alison, with her smile growing ever wider by the minute. "Anyway, for about five years, until the MP expenses scandal hit the headlines in 2009, she had been making extravagant claims for decorating her home and garden maintenance which she wasn't entitled to."

"Did she refund the money?" asked David.

Alison nodded as she fiddled with her wedding ring.

"Yes, and of course Heather Marsh apologized profusely," she replied, with a note of cynicism in her voice. "According to her, there had been some sort of misunderstanding."

David could picture the former MP in his mind's eye. When she had been a junior minister, he had frequently seen her on TV. She was beautiful, charming, brimming with confidence and adept at sidestepping a difficult question. In front of the cameras, she would deal with an interviewer like an accomplished matador with a hapless bull.

"This woman is a smooth operator," said David thoughtfully. "If we throw mud, we have to make certain that it sticks to her."

Alison had the look of somebody who had already thought the matter through. Since reading the account of

Heather Marsh's misdemeanours, her Machiavellian brain had been hard at work.

"For the time being, we say nothing," she said firmly. "We keep absolutely silent." "Why?" asked David.

"Because I am going to take that woman by surprise at the selection meeting," said Alison. "I am going to stand up and ask her why she tried to cheat the taxpayers of their hard-earned money. Why she betrayed the trust of the people that she was supposed to have represented. Then why, once her unlawful actions had been discovered, didn't she do the honourable thing and resign as a government minister?"

David gave his wife a look of admiration.

"Perhaps you should also ask her whether it is social justice for the rich to steal from the poor. I once read that Heather Marsh comes from a very rich family. Apparently, her father is a millionaire."

Alison nodded.

"I shall certainly be reminding the members of her great wealth. That will definitely alienate her from those on the left of the party and many of the more moderate ones, as well."

David glanced at his watch. He was worried about keeping Sophie waiting around for too long.

Had he not been in such a rush, he would have asked his wife whether she had plans to discredit another of his rivals, Kenny Simpson. He wondered whether she had managed to come up with a bucketful of mud to chuck at the local councillor.

The roads between Brockleby and Musselworth seemed to be busier than usual. David cursed under his breath when he had to queue up behind a long line of traffic at a roundabout. He had the urge to hoot frantically at the motorists ahead, like drivers in certain mainland European countries did to express their frustrations. Instead, though, like a true Englishman, he just sat still and suffered in silence.

Sophie was standing at the front door when he arrived. Expecting to be rebuked for being twenty minutes late, David felt like a naughty schoolboy as he hurried down the garden path. He was ready to apologize profusely and then give a lengthy account of the circumstances that had delayed his journey.

Much to his relief, Sophie didn't look in the least annoyed. In fact, she was smiling quite sweetly.

As soon as they were close enough, she flung her arms around David's neck. Then, for a few moments they stood on the doorstep hugging one another without a word being spoken.

"I've missed you," whispered Sophie at last.

David could feel his heart pounding. As their bodies clung tightly together, he kissed Sophie gently on the neck. As he did so, her soft fragrant hair fell against his cheek.

"I haven't stopped thinking about you," he replied.

"Do you really want to go out to a restaurant tonight?" asked Sophie, as she finally began to extricate herself from the embrace. "I thought that we could stay in and order a take-away over the phone instead."

David felt more than happy with this alternative arrangement. He had booked a table for two at a restaurant that had been recommended to him. However, as the proprietor had only taken his mobile number, he had no concerns about being visited by the heavy mob for having failed to turn up for a meal.

"What sort of take-away do you fancy?" asked David, as he followed Sophie through the front door of her top-floor flat.

"How about a pizza?" suggested Sophie. "Sounds fine," replied David.

Sophie opened a drawer and pulled out a pile of leaflets. Those that interested her most had been dropped through the letterbox downstairs by local fast food outlets. Nearly all seemed to advertise a free delivery service. She was often too exhausted to cook just for herself, after a day trying to control classes of unruly young people, so take-aways had become a lifeline.

"How about a Super Supremo with spicy pork sausages, pepperoni, ham, onions and just about anything else you can think of?" said Sophie, reading from a large red and brown glossy brochure.

"Sounds great," answered David.

"And how about some barbecue chicken wings and a few slices of garlic bread?" smiled Sophie. "Perfect," replied David, with an approving nod.

Having placed the order over the phone, Sophie sat down alongside her guest on the settee. "The man told me that our pizza should arrive in forty minutes," she said.

"Good, because I'm famished," said David, who was used to sitting down to his evening meal much sooner. "Anyway, tell me how you are getting on in the classroom. Are the kids still giving you trouble?"

Sophie nodded gloomily.

"I feel I am wasting my time trying to teach pupils at Brookway Manor. They show no interest at all in learning."

"So are you going to leave the profession and do something else?" asked David, as he studied the young English teacher's pretty but forlorn profile.

"I have decided to apply for a post in another school first," answered Sophie. "I want to teach children who work hard and know how to behave properly in the classroom."

"In other words, you're looking for an easy life", laughed David. "I regard those difficult kids as a challenge. Unlike many of those from better homes, they don't receive a great deal of intellectual stimulus from their parents. Probably there isn't a book in the whole house and because their mothers and fathers have been poorly educated, they aren't much help to their children with homework."

"But those kids are a lost cause," Sophie insisted. "Having fallen way behind the average child, they have no desire to catch up. They're devoid of any ambition, so they view education as irrelevant to their lives. School is like a social club where they arrive each day to meet their friends."

David shook his head firmly.

"In their own way, these kids can be as bright as any of those who end up at Oxford and Cambridge. It's our job as teachers to ignite their enthusiasm for knowledge. Demonstrate to them what it is possible to achieve if they are prepared to put their minds to it."

Sophie gave him a look of admiration.

"You really would make a fantastic MP. I could see you standing up in the House of Commons and making a passionate speech on behalf of education."

The challenges of the classroom began to recede in David's mind. Slipping his arm around Sophie's shoulders, he gently drew her closer. For a time, they kissed tenderly while locked in a warm embrace. Being so absorbed in each other, the sudden shrill sound of a bell, which was wired to the flat from the front door, rather took them by surprise.

Sophie hurried out of the room and returned in a few minutes carrying several red cardboard boxes. Soon she and David were both holding a thick wedge of pizza in one hand, while dunking chicken wings into a small white pot of barbeque sauce with the other. Focused on filling their stomachs, they remained silent for about five minutes or so.

"So have you made your decision yet?" asked Sophie, as she briefly stopped eating.

"What decision is that?" asked David, after helping himself to another chicken wing. "Whether you are going to leave your wife for me?" answered Sophie, a little impatiently. David hesitated. He had dreaded this moment. Having rehearsed his lines many times in his head, he knew them so well. How the children were too young to desert, but if she were prepared to be patient, he would marry her in the end. Yet as he gazed fondly into Sophie's eyes, his well-chosen words refused to come out. The risk of losing her was just too much to even contemplate.

It was the thought of the terrible void that she would leave in his life.

"Yes", said David, barely able to recognize his own voice. "Yes what?" asked Sophie.

"I will divorce Alison and marry you," replied David.

He could hardly believe what he had just said. It felt rather as though an evil spirit was suddenly speaking through him. There was nothing in the world that would make him walk away from his family. They were too precious to him. Even Amanda, his stepdaughter, with whom he was forever having confrontations.

"That's wonderful", cried Sophie, immediately flinging her arms around him. "Have you told Alison yet?"

"No," answered David. "I'm waiting for the right moment."

"Do it this week," begged Sophie. "You can move in here until we find a place of our own." David was alarmed that he was being pressurized into acting so quickly. He now wished he had followed his script, rather than having raised Sophie's hopes. The situation was clearly getting out of control and he seemed to be digging himself even deeper into the hole he was in.

"We'll see," said David, using an expression his mother always used when she didn't want to be committed to a promise.

"It will only make it harder if you put it off," persisted Sophie. "Tell her right away."

"I'll leave it a couple of weeks. Alison has got rather a lot of problems right now and I don't want to upset her even more," answered David, desperately trying to buy himself more time.

At that precise moment, they were interrupted by the ring tones of a mobile phone. Having scurried across the room to pick up a small pink metallic object from the sideboard, Sophie instantly disappeared out of the door. Quite obviously, the conversation she was about to have was not for the ears of her guest.

David was halfway through his fourth slice of pizza and decided he had eaten enough. Stretching right back on the settee, he took a closer look around him. Sophie kept the lounge neat and tidy, but there was hardly the space to swing a cat. Having said that, it was the biggest of the five rooms in the flat. The very idea of giving up his beautiful, spacious home to live in such cramped conditions made him shudder.

"That was my mum," announced Sophie, as she wandered back into the lounge ten minutes later. "I've just being telling her about you."

Immediately, alarm bells went off in David's head. Sophie had agreed to keep their relationship a secret and now she was going back on her word. Although her parents lived in Portsmouth, some considerable distance away, he had no idea who they happened to know in the Brockleby area.

"What did you say about me?" asked David, trying hard to stay calm.

"Only that we are thinking of getting engaged and I wanted her and my dad to meet you," replied Sophie, with a contented smile.

Suddenly the hole that David was in seemed to have grown into a bottomless pit. Had he not cared so much, he might have confessed to her right then that he was deceiving her; that their relationship had no long-term future. He couldn't bring himself to say the words, though. Gazing at Sophie as she sat down beside him on the settee, he had never seen her looking so radiant with happiness.

"Did you tell your mum that I'm married?" asked David.

"Not yet, but I will", answered Sophie cheerfully, as she picked up another slice of pizza, which by now had gone cold.

At that moment, David wished he belonged to one of those religious sects that allowed men to have more than one wife. Then it occurred to him that as Sophie didn't believe in sharing her lovers, even that wouldn't provide a solution.

"When do you want to introduce me to your parents then?" asked David, while knowing that a meeting could never take place.

"As soon as you leave your wife, if you like. We could spend a whole week with them during the Summer holidays," said Sophie excitedly.

"Look, don't tell anyone else about us," said David anxiously. "At least, not until I've had an opportunity to ask Alison for a divorce."

"Of course not", laughed Sophie. "But once we are together, I shall announce it to the whole world."

"That's fine then", said David, managing a half smile.

"Right!" said Sophie, as she finished her last mouthful of pizza. "Once I have cleared all these boxes away, we are heading straight for the bedroom. I can't wait to get under the duvet with you."

On Saturday morning, the Chambers called on Mrs Fisher again. Wearing a dark suit and a perfectly knotted tie, David looked as though he was dressed for a wedding. He wasn't the only one who had taken trouble over their appearance. The old lady was looking quite presentable in a matching grey jacket and skirt outfit, and for once, she had put a brush to her hair.

"By the way," began Alison, as Mrs Fisher ushered her guests into the drab lounge. "The *Brockleby Times* are sending two of their people to see us, a photographer and a reporter."

"Sounds very exciting," giggled Mrs Fisher. "How soon will they be here?" Alison glanced at her watch.

"Probably another quarter of an hour. I was told they would be here about ten o'clock."

David was feeling slightly edgy. For the third time since leaving home, he placed his hand inside his jacket pocket to make sure that his cheque was still there. It was to be the first contribution towards Mrs Fisher's appeal.

The *Brockleby Times*, like David, were keen to use the appeal as a means of promoting their image. They had promised to donate two thousand pounds, five hundred of which would be paid directly to Mrs Fisher in cash to cover the old lady's short-term needs.

Just after ten, Mrs Fisher opened the door to let two further visitors in. They were a pair of smartly dressed ladies, both in their mid-twenties. The slightly taller one had a square leather case that hung from her shoulder by a strap. On entering the lounge, she unfastened the buckle and produced a rather elaborate-looking camera.

After introducing herself as Jess, she charmingly suggested that everyone should briefly move into the hall. Then, with the little cramped lounge all to herself, she began to stand in different parts of the room. When she had made up her mind which was the best position to take photographs, she turned her attention to David and Mrs Fisher.

"Now if you could come back in, I want you both to stand by that wall over there," she smiled, pointing her finger. "I want you facing each other with the cheque about to change hands."

David and Mrs Fisher did as they were told. At that point, Jess took about half a dozen shots, while directing them to pose in slightly different positions.

"I will choose the best photo and you will see it on the front page next week," she smiled.

As Jess put her camera back in the leather case, her colleague emerged from the hall. David recalled that she had introduced herself at the front door as Rachel. She was dark haired, blue-eyed and particularly pretty.

"I would like to ask each of you for a few comments that will be included in my article," she began. "Perhaps I could begin with you, Mrs Fisher."

"Go ahead, dear," replied the old lady cheerfully.

Rachel quickly glanced down at the notes she had carefully prepared.

"What were your thoughts when Mr and Mrs Chambers suggested to you that they would like to start an appeal?" she began.

"I was very excited," beamed Mrs Fisher.

"I heard that you were very depressed after your money was stolen. Are you feeling any happier now?" continued Rachel.

"Oh, definitely, dear," answered Mrs Fisher, with a firm nod of the head. "I'm back to my old self again."

"My newspaper will be sending you cheques at regular intervals as the donations start coming in. So what will you do with them?" asked Rachel.

Suddenly, Mrs Fisher stopped smiling.

"They will go straight into the bank. The Chambers are going to help me to set up an account." David was delighted with the old lady's replies. Everything seemed to be going to plan. Standing next to Mrs Fisher, Jess was holding a small silver tape recorder to ensure that not a single word would be missed.

"That's all, then," smiled Rachel, after she had put several more questions to the old lady. "Now, perhaps I could turn to you, Mr Chambers."

David immediately straightened up. He was anxious not to spoil the whole thing. Certainly, he needed to avoid giving any hint of his political ambitions. Glancing across the room, he received an encouraging smile from Alison.

"What made you decide to help Mrs Fisher?" enquired Rachel, after having referred to her notes once more.

"It was just that having read about the robbery in your newspaper, I wanted to help," began David, with a rather pious expression on his face. "I hoped that if I were seen to be making a donation, then others would be encouraged to do likewise. Perhaps it would spark off a spirit of philanthropy in the town."

"Well, you've certainly succeeded in getting the *Brockleby Times* to part with some of their money," laughed Rachel, as she produced a wad of notes fastened together by an elastic band.

David and Alison watched on with pride as the reporter counted out five hundred pounds in cash on the table.

"There you are, Mrs Fisher," said Rachel, once the job was finished. "That is your first instalment. We will be making regular interim payments to you once the donations start to arrive. Remember, though, you will be receiving cheques, so get that bank account open as soon as possible."

The moment that Jess and Rachel left the house, Alison threw her arms around Mrs Fisher. At the same time, David bent down and placed his hand inside a white plastic bag that he had brought with him. Then in the next minute, he held a bottle in the air.

"Champagne, anyone?" he smiled. "I think this calls for a celebration."

CHAPTER EIGHTEEN

On Monday evening, David drove down to the Brockleby Labour Party headquarters. Having marked a stack of essays after dinner, it was well after nine o'clock when he entered the bar. Feeling exhausted after a particularly hard day, he had merely popped in for a nightcap.

The place was quieter than usual. Most of the noise was coming from the far corner, where a group of young men were enjoying a game of pool. The occasional thud of balls landing in a pocket was immediately followed by animated shouts. The remaining dozen or so members seemed content to just sit and talk, while occasionally taking a sip of their drinks.

David strolled over to the counter and waited to be served. While the barman attended to the needs of another customer, he glanced up at the large photograph on the wall. Hung up above a long line of spirit bottles was the beaming face of the Leader of the Opposition, the Right Honourable Andre Brooks MP – the man who had been elected by the membership to head the party roughly a year ago.

After Labour had lost power in the 2010 general election, Bruce Shaw had stood down as leader. Having taken more than his fair share of blame for the banking crisis, he had retired to the backbenches for a well-earned rest. He was content to sit on the opposite side of the House of Commons and see how the Tories and Liberal Democrats would fare together in a coalition government – looking on while the two parties tried to solve the country's debt problems that they were accusing him of creating.

Andre Brooks was in his mid-forties, good-looking and highly intelligent. However, after a year as the Leader of the Opposition, he had still to make any marked impression on the voters. If truth be told, though, neither had the new Prime Minister or his deputy. Not that the people either loved or loathed any one of the three. Generally speaking, they were just indifferent.

"What can I get you, David?" asked the barman, once he had served his last customer.

"Pint of bitter, please, Jerry," replied David, as he rested his elbows on the counter.

"Heather Marsh is upstairs with Tony and Bert Vine," said Jerry, as he pulled down the pump lever to allow the bitter to flow out.

"What's all that about, then?" asked David, with a frown.

"Got no idea," answered Jerry with a shrug. "Earlier though, Bert took her around here to meet some of the members. I actually got introduced myself."

"And were you impressed?" asked David.

"Yes, I was," admitted Jerry. "A very attractive lady and has a lot of the old charm to go with it."

"So if she stands for election, will you be voting for her at the selection meeting?" asked David, giving the barman a searching look.

Jerry hesitated as he gave the matter some thought.

"Possibly," he replied, after a few moments. "But I would want to see what her rivals had to say before I made my final decision."

The conversation was suddenly interrupted. Having handed David his drink, Jerry took a few steps to his left to serve another customer. It happened to be Kenny Simpson, who had just come through the door and had headed straight to the counter for a pint.

As usual, all his clothing looked as though it might well have been acquired at a jumble sale. Tonight, his unkempt appearance seemed to have taken a turn for the worse. A thick light brown growth around parts of his lower face suggested that he was well on the way to adorning himself with a beard.

"Just come back from a council meeting," he announced, after having ordered a pint of best bitter.

"Wasn't that the full one that all councillors are expected to attend every six weeks?" asked David, who vaguely remembered seeing an announcement in the Brockleby Times.

Kenny nodded. "Anyway, some of the Tories are talking about shutting down that little library in Gladstone Road. Just another of their plans to cut local services in this borough."

"I suppose the council have to find savings from somewhere," sighed Jerry, as he took the money for Kenny's drink.

Before the councillor had a chance to answer, he received a nudge in the ribs.

"Look who's here," whispered David.

Kenny turned around to see three people walking towards him. The two men were well known to him, but he had never met the woman before. However, her face was familiar enough. He had seen it often on TV.

"Good evening, gentlemen", began Bert Vine cordially. "I would like you to meet Heather Marsh. You will recall, of course, that she was a junior minister in the last government."

"Hello," mumbled Kenny, as he shook hands with the illustrious lady.

"Kenny Simpson has been a councillor in this borough for many years. Everybody respects him for the hard work he puts in. Even the Tories," said Bert, with the proud look of a father who has just seen his son win a prize.

"I understand that you may be putting your name forward to become our next parliamentary candidate," said Kenny, with a watery smile.

"I already have," smiled Heather. "Bert and Tony have just been showing me Jacqui Dunn's old office where she used to hold her weekly surgeries."

"Then we are rivals," said Kenny, with the smile now gone from his face. "I'm in the running for the job, as well."

David watched the two contenders with interest. They were so different in manner and appearance, yet both had the same ambition. Beside him stood Kenny with his far left beliefs and with the dishevelled look of a man who has slept the night in his clothes. With very little income other than his modest councillor's allowance, he could hardly be described as rich. Probably his greatest worldly asset was the old relic of a car that he drove, which was barely roadworthy. There were many classier vehicles sitting around in scrap yards awaiting the crusher.

Then in stark contrast was Heather Marsh: smooth-talking, smartly dressed and very much the professional. Unlike Kenny, who spoke like a Cockney, she possessed a plummy accent, common amongst those of noble birth.

It was the sort of voice that was always likely to be received more favourably in Parliament than on some of the run-down estates. She had never felt at ease while canvassing on the doorsteps. As a wealthy woman who had never wanted for anything, she found it difficult to empathize with those who struggle to pay their household bills.

"Well, I hope it will be friendly rivalry," laughed Bert, a little awkwardly. "We don't want any bad feeling to start creeping in."

"Will we be seeing a lot more of you before the selection meeting?" asked Kenny, who was sure he already knew the answer.

"Oh yes," replied Heather, with a firm nod. "I would like to know you all a little better and also find out more about Brockleby and some of the problems that are effecting the town."

"And what if the members select one of us locals as the candidate?" asked Kenny, with a sly grin. "Will we see you delivering leaflets down here during the general election campaign?"

There was an uneasy silence. Then, as Heather was finally about to answer, Bert suddenly came to her rescue.

"Now let me introduce you to David Chambers," he beamed. "He is a secondary school teacher and has been one of our keenest activists for many years."

Unlike Kenny, David shook Heather warmly by the hand. He admired her for what she had managed to achieve in her political career. Yet because she had been so successful, it gave him even more incentive to beat her in the contest. He wanted Andre Brooks and the rest of the top brass in the Labour Party to know that their rising star had imploded. She had been turned into a black hole by a young history teacher who would one day be shining himself.

"David has also put his name forward to be the candidate," explained Tony.

"And are you another councillor?" asked Heather, relieved to be able to switch her attention to somebody who seemed less hostile.

David shook his head.

"With my work and three young children, I simply don't have the time."

"An MP spends many hours away from home", said Heather, with a warning look. "If you are ever elected to Parliament, I hope it won't have a damaging effect on your family life."

"I have a very supportive wife," smiled David, who was trying hard to disguise his dislike for the former junior minister. "Alison knows how much I want to do my bit to help improve education in this country."

"So does everyone else in the Labour Party. That's why we provided a record amount of funding for our schools when we were in office," said Heather, proudly.

"But why impose tuition fees?", asked David, who was starting to get hot under the collar. "Why are we trying to discourage young people from going into higher education? If Britain is to prosper, we need a well-trained work force."

Heather shook her head. Having often heard similar complaints from her constituents, she made her usual response – the one that she had used on countless occasions before.

"But too many people have been going to university in the past," she began. "The problem is that when they leave, there aren't enough jobs to go around. So instead, we should be encouraging some of them to take apprenticeships. They could then train to become plumbers, electricians and carpenters."

"I see," said David, with a sardonic smile. "So the kids of rich parents become lawyers, while those from poorer backgrounds stick their hands down drains."

"Ever thought of taking up a trade yourself, Heather?" joined in Kenny, while giving David a mischievous wink.

At that point, Bert began to shepherd Heather towards the pool table. He was keen to introduce his guest to four young men who could be expected to be more deferential – members of the association who had never taken their education seriously and probably couldn't care less about tuition fees.

On his way home from school on Wednesday evening, David stopped off at a newsagent. For a moment or two, he gazed down at the photograph he had had taken with Mrs Fisher, before picking up the top copy of the *Brockleby Times* from a deep pile. He had absolutely no complaints with Jess's camera work. In his opinion, with his caring smile and dressed immaculately in a dark suit, he looked every bit like the kindly philanthropist helping a poor and needy old soul.

As he waited for his turn to be served by the shop assistant, he began to read the article. Under the heading 'Teacher makes first donation to pensioner's appeal,' he read the truly heartwarming story of how a certain Mr David Chambers, and of course, the *Brockleby Times*, had managed to put the smile back on the face of a depressed old lady. In the very last paragraph, the paper had made an appeal for the readers to make a generous donation themselves.

David arrived home to find that Alison was entertaining a guest. Looking as radiant as ever, Jacqui Dunn stood up and threw her arms around him as soon as he entered the lounge. After having been selected as the parliamentary candidate for the Cumbrian seat, the former junior Foreign Office minister and Brockleby MP, was hunting for somewhere to live in the district. For the time being, though, she was dividing her time between her new constituency and her old one.

"Congratulations on getting your picture on the front page of the *Brockleby Times*," she beamed. "I thought it was a beautiful gesture to contribute towards that poor old lady's appeal."

David felt his cheeks burning.

"It was nothing really," he replied modestly.

For a while, the three of them talked about matters in general. It was just a cosy little chat in which the world of politics wasn't even mentioned. Then Jacqui finally revealed the main purpose of her visit.

"Look, Tony, Bert Vine and myself had a meeting last night," she began, a little hesitantly. "As you know, we are the three panellists who will decide who is to be shortlisted to fight the Brockleby seat for Labour."

"Has David's name been included?" asked Alison anxiously.

Jacqui nodded her head firmly.

"I have insisted that both David and Kenny are put on the shortlist. They worked their socks off to help me win in the 2003 by-election and again in the 2005 general election."

"I suppose one good turn deserves another," beamed David with delight.

Alison smiled as she recalled that night in 2003, as they stood in the town hall alongside five other Labour Party activists, all with their hearts in their mouths, just waiting for the returning officer to announce the result. Desperate for victory. Dreading defeat. Then the euphoria. The tears of joy and the ecstatic celebrations as Jacqui was declared the winner. The realization that she had actually achieved her greatest ambition – becoming a Member of Parliament.

Jacqui suddenly looked serious.

"Once the shortlist is officially announced, Tony and Bert will be campaigning for Heather Marsh. They feel that her reputation will win her votes in the general election."

"In what way will they campaign?" asked David suspiciously.

"By getting in touch will all the members," answered Jacqui. "Tony is producing an updated list of the names and addresses of everybody. I have insisted on having two copies of the printout myself so that I can pass them on to you and Kenny. We need a level playing field in this contest."

"And will you be campaigning for anyone?" asked Alison.

Jacqui shook her head.

"My loyalties are divided between Kenny and David. However, I shall cast my vote at the selection meeting for the one who impresses me most."

Suddenly, there was a break in the conversation. A loud crash, which seemed to come from the next room, followed by a wail, suggested that one of the children had come to grief. Immediately, Alison rushed off to investigate. A few moments later, she returned cradling a small sobbing boy in her arms.

"Joshua just slipped over," she explained, while hugging the boy to her breast.

"I'm surprised that you aren't supporting Heather Marsh as well, seeing as you were both in government together," said David, once he was satisfied that his son hadn't suffered a life-threatening injury.

Jacqui turned her nose up contemptuously.

"Heather only climbed the ladder so quickly because she kept in with the right people. Before the last election, she just happened to share an office with Andre Brooks, of all people."

"Do you think they were having an affair?" asked Alison, eagerly hoping for a juicy bit of gossip.

Jacqui shrugged.

"Not sure. What I do know is that Andre is desperate for Heather to return to the Commons."

Joshua stopped sobbing. Having climbed off Alison's knee, he was now trying to haul his mother towards the door. When the heavier family member refused to be shifted, he sank down on the floor and began to whine. In a small, plaintive voice, he demanded to be fed, played with and be given money for an ice cream from a van outside. It had just announced its arrival with a shortened and not particularly melodic version of "The Teddy Bears Picnic".

Jacqui glanced at her watch.

"Must be going," she said, while getting to her feet. "I will drop that membership list in to you as soon as I get it."

Jacqui wasn't the only one who had been keeping a close eye on the time. David had arranged another evening with Sophie. It was to be a re-run of what they had done the previous week: a take-away for two, followed by a half-hour or so under the duvet together.

"I won't be needing a meal tonight," said David, as soon as Jacqui had gone. "I'm going down the pub with a few of my colleagues."

"Not again," said Alison, with exasperation. "Why is it that you never take me out?"

"We'll arrange something for next week," said David, as he hurried upstairs to get changed. "If you choose the restaurant, I'll book up a table for two."

"No, I shall make the booking myself", said Alison firmly. "Next Wednesday evening, we are going to that nice Chinese restaurant in the high street. So you had better warn your colleagues that you won't be joining them for once."

Sophie seemed in a particularly good mood. Once they had eaten their take-away – a medium-size pepperoni pizza on this occasion – David was hurried off to the bedroom with even more urgency than usual. Then, in a frenzy of passion, two naked bodies, one on top of the other, made love. When the storm had finally abated, the lovers lay peacefully in each other's arms.

"Have you said anything to your wife yet?" asked Sophie, after a while.

It was that dreaded question again; the one to which David could never give Sophie the answer that she wanted to hear, and the one that she would only stop asking once their steamy affair had come to a sad and bitter end.

"I will as soon as the selection meeting is over," answered David. "If I do it sooner, it could damage my chances of becoming the Labour candidate for Brockleby."

With her head resting on the pillow, Sophie gave him a long, hard stare.

"And why exactly will it damage your chances?"

"Because it will go in my favour if the members think I am a happily married family man. It's just what people like to see in their politicians," said David, who felt rather pleased with this explanation as to why he hadn't had that conversation with Alison.

"OK then," said Sophie, having given the matter a few moments thought. "So when exactly is this selection meeting?"

"A date hasn't been set yet, but I understand it could be about a month," replied David. "The chairman of the association will wish to give the members ample notice of the meeting."

"So when exactly will you be leaving your wife then?" asked Sophie, with more than a hint of impatience in her voice. "I am not prepared to wait forever."

"The weekend after the meeting, I shall move in with you," smiled David, reassuringly.

Sophie buried her head in David's chest.

"Promise?" she murmured.

David hesitated for just a split second.

"Promise," he replied, knowing that his miserable lies would weigh heavily on his conscience for many years to come.

⊘⎯ ⎯⊘

"Have you seen this?", said Maureen angrily, thrusting a copy of the *Brockleby Times* in front of her husband's face. "They are making an appeal for that silly old bag who had her money stolen by Mark Wright."

Harvey Lucas swore out loud as soon as he began to read the article. It was his firm belief that those people who knew Mark Wright wanted him caught for one main reason. It was out of sympathy for Mrs Fisher. They wanted to see the poor old lady get her money back.

The last thing he wanted to hear was that the local do-gooders were sticking their noses in. If Mrs Fisher got all her savings back in full, then close friends of the thief might even be wishing him good luck. They might hold back information that could help to track him down. Ultimately, the only losers in the whole affair would be rich philanthropists, stupid interfering schoolteachers and himself who was owed money.

"And I see that if the police ever recover any of the stolen money from Mark Wright, it could end up going to charity," fumed Harvey, as he threw down the paper in disgust.

Maureen nodded.

"Assuming that the old bag should end up with more money than she started with."

Harvey glared hard at his wife. It was not that his anger was directed towards her. He was just livid with the injustice of it all – the thought that all that beautiful loot could be dished out to so-called 'good causes'; beneficiaries who were often people who were too shift-less to even get up in the morning to do a day's work. In any case, that is what the leader writers in his daily newspaper were always saying.

"I'll catch up with him long before the cops get a chance to," he snarled. "Our tracing agents are bound to come up with something before too long. As soon as our young Mr Wright starts splashing all his cash about, we'll have him."

"I'm beginning to think it would be better if you don't catch him," said Maureen. "If you murder that young man, you could spend the rest of your days in a prison cell."

"Look, this guy has gone missing and I will make absolutely certain that he never gets found," answered Harvey, smiling for the first time. "Don't forget, the cops are out there looking for a fit and healthy person, not a corpse."

"And where exactly are you going to leave his remains?" asked Maureen, looking rather uneasy.

"Leo MacDonald will take young Wright up to the Scottish Highlands, tied up in his van before putting a bullet in his head," explained Harvey, after drawing hard on his cigarette and blowing out a great billow of spoke. "Leo was brought up in those parts by his grandparents, who were crofters, so he knows a few very remote areas. They are so far off the beaten track that hardly anyone ever goes there. A grave could lie in one of those places for decades without ever being discovered."

Maureen shook her head.

"I still don't like it."

"Don't worry," grinned Harvey. "Old Leo will make certain that the young man gets a good send-off. As a good Presbyterian, he intends to say a little prayer and sing a hymn or two over the grave. Such a beautiful occasion, I may even attend the funeral myself. Tears come into my eyes just thinking about it."

CHAPTER NINETEEN

Ian Porter brought the service to a close. The worshippers filed out of the church and formed into little groups on the grass. It was a warm summer evening and nobody was in a rush to get home. Being amongst friends they had known all their lives, they were content to stand and talk for a while.

The Eternal Fellowship held church meetings once a day except Sundays, when there were four or five. Worship was simple, with no ritual or liturgy and participation was encouraged from male members. Women were supposed to remain silent in accordance with the teachings from the first book of Corinthians.

Fellowship churches were different from those of other Christian denominations. There were no pews, pulpits, religious icons or stained glass windows. In fact, as far as the latter was concerned, there were no windows at all; just a plain, square table serving as an altar and rows of wooden stackable chairs.

Followers had a very simple faith. They were taught to believe exactly what the Bible prescribed: that the world was made in six days, homosexuality was an abomination and the vast majority of the human race, living, dead and yet to be born, were doomed. After the Day of Judgement, those that didn't share their beliefs would be packed off to hell.

Ian Porter was the last to leave the church. After having locked the heavy wooden door, he cast his eye around for John and Hilary Chambers. In his hand, he carried a rolled up newspaper, which he gently tapped against his thigh.

Ian was now in his early forties. He could best be described as an unordained priest who acted as one of the spiritual leaders of the Brockleby Fellowship. Ideally suited for his role, he possessed a friendly authority and provided a guiding light for other followers. A rock who remained steadfast to his religious beliefs, he tried to ensure that those who were more fallible did likewise.

"Have you seen this?" asked Ian, excitedly, after he had managed to track down the couple that he had been looking for.

The Chambers were rather taken aback. They found themselves staring at a photograph of their wayward son – the one that had rejected the word of the Lord in order to serve the Devil. John took the copy of the *Brockleby Times* from Ian and began to read the article.

Generally speaking, the Eternal Fellowship disapproved of newspapers. The spiritual leadership didn't like their followers to read sordid accounts of what the godless masses are getting up to. However, they were happy for the rules to be bent when something of real importance was published. This just happened to be one of those occasions.

"I suppose it was generous of him to donate so much money," said John, somewhat grudgingly, before passing on the newspaper to Hilary.

"Very kind indeed," said Ian, who was prepared to be more fulsome in his praise. "You know, I think it's about time I had a little chat with David. It has been eight years since he parted company with the Fellowship. Perhaps he might just be thinking of repenting."

John shook his head.

"Highly unlikely," he said. "First we might need to separate him from his wife. It was she who was responsible for tempting him away from the Lord in the first place."

A look of pride appeared on Hilary's face as she finished the article. As soon as she glanced up, she was confronted with the outstretched arms of other people in her group, who had now formed into a circle. They seemed almost as anxious as she was to see exactly what her worldly son had been up to.

"He was a lovely boy, but too easily led astray," remarked Hilary, as she passed on the newspaper to the elderly lady standing next to her.

"Look, go ahead and speak to David if you like, Ian, but I fear you will be wasting your time," said John. "I fear my son will never escape the clutches of the Devil."

"Perhaps I should remind you of what Luke had to say in chapter fifteen, verse four," said Ian, who had a remarkable ability for quoting from the Bible. "What man of you, having a hundred sheep, if he lose one of them, does not leave the ninety and nine in the wilderness and go after that which is lost until he has found it."

John and the rest of the little group nodded submissively. After all, who amongst them could possibly argue with a parable from the Gospels, particularly when they had been reminded of it by Ian Porter, of all people – a senior figure in the Fellowship, whom they regarded as being far wiser than themselves.

RICHARD GARDNER

On Friday night, the shortlist was confirmed. David received a telephone call from Tony in the evening informing him that his name had been included. He would be one of the four people to stand up and face the members at the selection meeting, to try and make his case as to why he was the person to represent the Labour Party in Brockleby at the next general election.

"Six people finally put their names forward and we choose the best four," explained Tony.

"And who were the other three?" asked David, reasonably confident that he knew the answer already.

"Heather Marsh, Kenny and Carol," replied Tony, confirming David's suspicions. "As Carol is pregnant, she is just there to make up an equal number of male and female candidates. She is not a serious contender and won't make any attempt to encourage the membership to vote for her other than at the selection meeting."

"Should be an interesting contest," said David.

"By the way, congratulations on getting your photograph on the front page of the *Brockleby Times*," said Tony cheerfully. "Can I assume that you were after the publicity in order to further your political ambitions?"

David smiled to himself. He could hardly believe the number of people who had seen the local paper that week. His donation had even become a major talking point at school. Much to his surprise, he had become a bit of a hero. Many of the toughest kids in the playground had been displaying their softer side. Over the last day or so, he was being continually asked how they could make their own meagre contribution to the appeal.

"Yes, you can," he replied, with passion in his voice. "I want to further both my ambitions and those of many young people in this country. I am tired of hearing about

242

politicians who tamper around with the education system, when they haven't been in a classroom since the day they left school."

"Education is very important, but at the selection meeting you will need to talk about other matters as well," warned Tony, "Law and order, health, defence and the economy, to name but a few. That is where Heather Marsh may score over everybody else."

"Don't worry," answered David reassuringly. "I shall arrive at the meeting well prepared."

Saturday afternoon was a scorcher. The sky would have been entirely deep blue, but for the odd fluffy white cloud in the distance. Alison had taken the three children swimming at the local lido, leaving David to relax in the back garden with a book. He had planned to mow the lawn but had quickly gone off the idea. It was simply too hot.

Everything was quiet and still. Even the dog next door, which had been barking earlier, had probably decided that it wasn't worth the effort and had fallen asleep. Only the bees seemed to have any energy; circling around in the air, hovering around the lavender bush, then landing on one pinkish violet flower after another, before flying off again.

The patio door was wide open. Had it been shut, David would never have heard the front door bell ring. Almost reluctantly he hauled himself out of his deck-chair and went back into the house to find out who was calling. He was hoping that it was somebody that he could get rid of very quickly – perhaps a door-to-door salesman or the fellow who came to read the gas meter from time to time.

He wasn't in luck. The tall figure who stood on the doorstep was somebody that he hadn't seen in a very long time; somebody that he would have to invite in and probably wouldn't be in a hurry to leave, and somebody that he would be very polite to initially, but might well end up arguing with.

"Good to see you again," said Ian Porter, as the two men shook hands. "It must have been eight years since I last saw you. The time has just flown by."

"Come in," said David, putting on a false smile and attempting to sound more welcoming than he was actually feeling.

He directed his visitor into the back garden. Then, after vanishing into the shed, he reappeared carrying another deckchair. Had he invited anyone else into his home, David would have automatically offered them refreshments. Such a gesture would have been pointless in Ian Porter's case, of course. Being a follower of the Eternal Fellowship meant that he could neither eat nor drink with non-believers.

"I noticed your photograph on the front page of the *Brockleby Times*," smiled Ian, as he sunk down in his deckchair. "I was very impressed with your generosity. You appear to have made an old lady very happy again."

"Perhaps others might be encouraged to contribute to the appeal, as well," replied David, hopeful that his wealthy visitor would take the hint.

Ian laughed.

"I shall drop a cheque in the post."

David gave Ian an appreciative nod. He was actually surprised to see how little the priest had changed since they had last met. Perhaps the belly had swelled out a bit more and the thick bushy hair was beginning to turn grey at the sides. Other than that, he looked quite a youthful forty-year-old.

"So how is everybody in the Fellowship?", asked David.

For the next twenty minutes, Ian filled him in with all the latest gossip. Some of it David had already heard from Simon Broadbent, but there were little tidbits of which he wasn't aware, such as Mrs Dyer having been carted off to A & E after being hit by a cricket ball in the park.

"And how about Mum and Dad?" asked David, as the priest had made no mention of any of his family members.

"Still missing your grandfather, but other than that, they are both fine," answered Ian. "That's good," smiled David.

For a few minutes, Ian sat staring ahead of him as though deep in thought. David felt reasonably confident that the priest hadn't just dropped by on a social visit. Almost certainly, he must have had an ulterior motive.

"As well as your grandfather, your parents miss you also," said Ian suddenly. "I wonder, do you ever get bored with the ways of the world and think of returning to the Lord?"

David smiled to himself. He rather suspected that his visitor would come up with a remark like that. Ian was obviously trying to catch the lost sheep and carry it back to the fold. The Good Shepherd wanted to reunite it with the other fleecy specimens who hadn't strayed from the flock.

David shook his head.

"I have lost the faith I once had. I no longer believe in the same things as you," he replied. "That is because you have let Satan take control of your life. You have allowed him to put doubts into your head," said Ian, with the look of a father who has been disappointed by his son's school report.

"It has nothing to do with Satan's influence," said David, who was trying to remain calm. "It is me, thinking for myself, and deciding that it is madness to interpret the Bible literally. It's a book that was written two thousand years ago by people who didn't have the benefit of knowing what we do today – people who thought that the sun revolved around the earth, that God was angry every time it thundered and who believed that the world was manufactured in six days."

"I believe that the Book of Genesis is absolutely correct," said Ian, looking rather shocked at what he had just heard. "God did build the world in six days and on the seventh, he rested,"

David smiled with amusement.

"And do you honestly think that the first *homo sapiens* and the whole animal kingdom were all created in the same week?"

"Of course," replied Ian, with total conviction in his voice. "That is what it tells us in the Bible." David felt as though he was back in the classroom. Like the priest, many of the pupils that he taught believed exactly what they read, but in their case, it was the tabloid press. If their daily newspaper reported that the moon was made of Cheddar cheese, then it had to be right. It was that inability to question; not having the wit to think for oneself.

"But the world has been around for four and a half billion years. Man is merely a newcomer. Dinosaurs roamed the earth long before we humans started to inhabited it," protested David, feeling as though he wanted to give his backward student a textbook to read on the subject.

"Dinosaurs never existed," answered Ian. "The Devil scattered some monstrous bones about the place just to confuse scientists. It was a cunning ploy to stop people like you from believing in the true message of the Bible."

David felt that it was too hot to argue. Anyway, it seemed pointless to try and explain to the priest about the scientific process of carbon dating. He would only reply that such an invention was merely a tool of the Devil to deceive mankind into rejecting the word of the Lord.

"I suppose we will never agree," said David, with a resigned smile. "Look, can I offer you a beer?" Ian shook his head.

"You should know by now that followers of the Eternal Fellowship cannot eat and drink with non-believers."

David could feel another argument coming on. Even though part of him was trying to avoid confrontation. When he was a follower of the Fellowship himself, he had always hated the idea of not being able to eat with the infidel. He didn't want others to feel that somehow he thought himself to be morally superior to them.

"Perhaps I should refer you to the first book of the New Testament, Matthew, chapter nine, verse ten to thirteen", said David, who still remembered much of what he had learnt from the Bible, even though he hadn't read much of it in recent times. "The Pharisees asked the disciples of Jesus Christ why their master ate with publicans and sinners, to which Christ replied that he had not come to call the righteous, but the sinners to repentance."

"But we in the Fellowship do not claim to be the Son of God. Jesus Christ was a very special person. A one-off, you might say," explained Ian.

"Don't you think that you should follow his example, then?" asked David. "Isn't that what those who believe in his teachings should do?"

Ian shook his head. For once, though, he seemed stuck for a response. Perhaps nobody had put that question to him before. He would probably speak to the spiritual leadership at the earliest opportunity to see whether they had an answer. There had to be some passage in the Bible to which the wise ones would refer him.

Ian Porter left soon after that. He was convinced that the lost sheep could never be recovered. Almost certainly, the Devil had claimed him for his own. Doubtless, he would be sent to that other place on Judgment Day, to burn in the hellfire for eternity with all the rest of the heretics.

***

Tuesday was sports day. It was an occasion David always looked forward to. He enjoyed seeing some of the less academically gifted pupils coming into their own; winning trophies instead of trailing behind the rest of the pack as they normally did with their regular schoolwork, and basking in glory instead of being dismissed as one of life's failures.

David had been chosen to officiate some of the events. Like most of the pupils, he had prayed for fine weather. Sports day was invariably cancelled when it rained. It was always a great disappointment for everyone. Instead of competing out there in the fresh air, the whole school was just made to get on with their lessons.

The school competed in an outdoor sports centre that had excellent facilities. A four hundred metre synthetic running track surrounded an oblong area of well-cut grass for the field events. To one side was a covered wooden grandstand for spectators to cheer on the athletes.

Fortunately, David's prayers were answered. The recent warm spell continued into yet another day and there was barely a cloud in the sky. There was even a gentle refreshing breeze in the air, so that the atmosphere wasn't too oppressive for the competitors.

A number of family members had turned up to watch – parents who looked and talked like older versions of the offspring that they had turned up to support, as well as younger brothers and sisters who seemed like miniature editions of their older siblings and would soon be taking the place of some of today's pupils. There were also grandparents, great aunts and uncles who might themselves have once been taught at Brookway Manor Secondary School.

David was kept quite busy trying to make sure that the competitors were ready and waiting to participate in their events when the time came. He carried a bright orange Bisley starting revolver in preparation for the track events, and made absolutely certain that nobody jumped the gun in the sprint races. He assisted various absent-minded boys to find lost trainers and other equipment in the changing rooms, and was on hand to answer questions from not only the pupils, but many of the relatives, as well.

Sophie also had her part to play. One of her roles was to judge the girl's long jump. Once a competitor had landed in a great heap of sand, it was her job to measure the distance of the leap. It was something that she seemed more comfortable in handling than attempting to maintain control in the classroom.

All the trophies were awarded at the end. David was assigned with the task of calling out the names of the athletes. Mr Cheeseman, the headmaster, then shook their hand and presented them with a cup. A procession of proud young people, some swaggering, others blushing, walked away to warm applause from the large crowd of spectators.

Once the awards ceremony ended, most people began to disperse. David was about to make his way to the car when he was waylaid by one of the mothers. She was vaguely familiar to him, but he couldn't quite place her. The woman was in her early thirties, excessively overweight with tattoos on her flabby arms and wore a silver stud pierced to her chin.

"I want to have a word with you about our Craig," she began.

David looked blank. There were at least a dozen boys in the school that came to mind. Craig had been a very popular name in the nineties for newborn male babies. Had the woman called her son Jeremiah or Gustav, then the history teacher might not have needed any further assistance in establishing the boy's identity.

"What is the surname?" asked David patiently.

"Radley," replied the woman, with just a note of exasperation in her voice.

The name sent a shiver down David's spine. Craig Radley, the biggest troublemaker in Year Eight. This was the boy who had a habit of occupying the teacher's chair whenever the figure of authority left the room; the little pest who was always distracting everybody's attention during lessons. The irritating little sod who needed to be taken to a desert island and left there to rot.

"How can I help?" asked David, with a smile.

"Our Craig tells me that he has to learn all this Shakespeare stuff. That ain't going to get him nowhere", complained Mrs Radley indignantly. "I want him to have proper lessons. Stuff that is going to be useful to him when he leaves school."

"I don't actually take Year Eight for English, but I will pass your comments on," replied David.

"Anyway, our Craig says that all that Shakespeare stuff is a load of old rubbish," said Mrs Radley scornfully. "He reckons that it don't make no sense."

Much to David's relief, rescue was at hand. Mrs Radley spotted her husband and Craig walking away and hurried off to try and catch them up, her oversized buttocks wobbling like two great jellies as she moved.

David quickly made his way to the car park before anyone else had a chance to delay him. He wasn't in the mood to listen to complaints concerning a curriculum over which he had no control. As he was about to drive away, he saw Sophie waving to him. She had just appeared from behind the changing rooms.

"Hello," he called out, after rolling down the window.

"You'll never guess what," said Sophie excitedly, when she got close enough. "Last night, I joined the Labour Party. A lady called Carol came around to my flat and I signed the forms."

David looked at her in alarm. "But why?" he gasped.

"Because I want to be able to vote for you at the selection meeting. I want to be there when they announce that you will be our candidate at the next general election," she said proudly.

David could feel his stomach churning over. He was horrified at the prospect of having to make the speech of his life, in front of a large audience, with both Alison and

Sophie in the same room. Not that they were necessarily going to get to know each other, but it was still unnerving, all the same.

"My wife will be at the meeting, you know," warned David.

"Why are you so concerned?" laughed Sophie. "Aren't you supposed to be leaving her shortly after the meeting is over?"

"Of course," said David, with a half-smile. "Thanks for reminding me."

CHAPTER TWENTY

Mrs Fisher's appeal was going extremely well. After only one week, the *Brockleby Times* was reporting that over twenty thousand pound had already been received. The newspaper had begun to publish the names of all those who had made donations, along with the actual amount. For many of the local businesses, it was good advertising.

David was delighted with the response. Having been instrumental in launching the appeal, he sensed that he had greatly enhanced his chances of becoming the next Labour parliamentary candidate for Brockleby. Many of the members who were likely to be at the selection meeting were saying how impressed they were, not only by his generosity, but also his ingenuity. By helping to raise money for a poor old lady who had been robbed, he had managed to create a spirit of philanthropy in the area.

"Actions speak louder than words," said Alec Stokes, one night in the bar. "Unlike some of these socialists who just talk about helping the poor and needy, you have actually put your hand in your pocket. Not only that, but you have managed to get others to do the same."

"Can I count on your support then?" asked David, with a sly smile.

"I've yet to decide on who I'm going to vote for, but it certainly won't be Heather Marsh," replied Alec, with a look of distaste. "Some of the national newspapers seem to think that it's a foregone conclusion that she will get the nomination, just because she was a junior minister in the last government."

"What have you got against Heather Marsh, then?" asked David.

"She is rich, snooty and doesn't come from these parts", answered Alec contemptuously. "Mark my words. If she doesn't get the nomination, she will never set foot in Brockleby again."

It was a sentiment being expressed by other members in the association. However, Heather Marsh wasn't the only candidate who had critics. There were those who were deriding David for never having stood for a council seat. Behind his back, they were saying that he was only interested in a well-paid position as an MP. He had never shown any desire to represent the Labour Party at a local level.

Alison was trying her best to get her husband selected. During the day, she went out visiting retired party members in order to win their support. Very skilfully, she would talk up David's attributes, while being scornful of both Heather Marsh and Kenny Simpson. She would also remind everyone that Carol, the fourth contender, was only standing to make up the required number of women candidates. She had no wish to be an MP after the next general election.

In the evening, it was David's turn. He would call on some of those party members who had been out at work all day. Like Alison, he was scathing about his opponents, while at the same time promoting his own credentials. It also gave him an opportunity to address the area where he was most vulnerable – the fact that he had never put himself forward to be a councillor.

"Unlike Kenny Simpson and Heather Marsh, you have no real experience of how politics actually works," said one man, who had been in the Labour Party for many years. "You don't know what it is like to sit on a council or parliamentary committee. Why should I vote for you?"

"Because with my background as a school teacher, I have the kind of experience that is of far greater value. If we are to improve the education system in this country, we need people in government who have worked in it and recognize the problems," explained David, who repeated this answer every time the question was put to him.

"But Government isn't all about education," protested the man. "What about the economy, for example?"

Again, David was well prepared. The answer was on the tip of his tongue. He appreciated how important it was to avoid any hesitation. It was almost fatal to dither. Others might conclude that he hadn't already thought of the question himself.

"The Government needs to invest more money in the right areas if it is serious about regenerating the economy," replied David, as he looked the man straight in the eye. "Increased spending on education just happens to be one of those areas. A well-trained work force is essential if we are to get out of this recession. In order to have growth, Britain must have people who can help to provide the goods and services that are required both home and abroad."

The supporter seemed impressed by this response. However, he didn't say whether he would be voting for David at the selection meeting. He said only that he would wait and see what the other contenders had to say. He was not untypical. Others were also making it clear that they would wait and hear what was said on the night before deciding on which way they were going to vote.

David had been so busy trying to win over party supporters that he had given little thought to Sophie. He knew that sometime in the very near future, he would have to end their relationship. Deciding when and how to do it, though, was another matter.

Sophie had sent him a number of text messages, but he had ignored every one. Whenever they passed each other fleetingly in the school corridor, David tried to avoid eye contact. Sometimes he would pretend to be deep in thought. On other occasions, he would turn his head around and make some remark to any pupil who just happened to be following him.

One evening he arrived at Labour headquarters about nine thirty. He was worn out after a day in the classroom, followed by several hours of campaigning in the homes of party members. There were probably less than a dozen people in the bar. David recognized the four young men gathered around the pool table. They seemed to spend most of their leisure time in the same spot, clutching their cues in one hand and holding a pint glass in the other. From time to time, a cheer would ring out from their direction as a ball dropped down into a pocket with a thud.

David gave the pool players little more than a glance. He was more concerned about the three people who were on the far side of the room. Tony and Bert Vine were sitting talking to a young woman in a blue blouse. The party organizer and the chairman of the association were in the process of introducing themselves to a new member.

David almost froze as he made his way to the counter to order a drink. He had no need to make himself known to one of the latest recruits to the party, although he could hardly ignore her. To say that he knew her intimately would have been putting it mildly. After all, they were not only colleagues, but lovers, as well.

Having bought a beer, he strolled over to join the threesome. After the initial shock of seeing Sophie in unfamiliar surroundings, he had just about managed to compose himself. David knew he had to take great care in what he said and how he conducted himself. A word out of place could be disastrous. If his infidelity was discovered, then his marriage would be in jeopardy and after that, his whole life could start falling to bits. Both Tony and Bert had known Alison for many years. It was therefore possible that they would report back to her if they even suspected that her husband was being unfaithful.

"I've come to join you," announced David, as he prepared himself to sit down in the vacant chair alongside Sophie.

"Good to see you," answered Bert, in his usual jovial way. "I understand that you and Sophie are teachers at the same school."

"Yes, we have worked together for a while," replied David, managing a watery smile.

"I was just telling these gentlemen how good you are at your job and what a wonderful MP you would make", said Sophie, turning her head sideways and giving David a look of admiration.

"Well, it seems that you have got yourself another vote," laughed Bert.

David felt compelled to acknowledge Sophie's complimentary remarks with an appreciative smile.

However, her vote was one that he really could have done without. He dreaded the idea that both she and Alison would both be at the selection meeting. In fact, he was really annoyed that she had decided to join the Labour Party. This was a part of his life that he wanted to keep her away from.

"Will you gentlemen be voting for David as well?" asked Sophie.

Tony was about to answer the question, but Bert stepped in first. Not wishing to offend a new member, he decided that tact and diplomacy was required on this occasion.

"I intend to cast my vote for the candidate who is most likely to defeat the Tories at the next general election," said the local party chairman.

"In that case, you should support this man sitting here," answered Sophie, giving David an adoring smile. "I'm sure that many parents of pupils at Brookway Manor would vote for him. He is one of the most respected teachers in the school."

Tony gave David a searching look. He was never one to jump to conclusions, but he had just a hint of a suspicion that something other than a good working relationship was going on between the two teachers. There was something in Sophie's manner that wasn't quite right. He was no expert in these matters, but there seemed to be a dreamy look in those beautiful blue eyes every time she turned to face the gentleman sitting next to her.

"Have you been thinking of joining the Labour Party for a while?" asked Bert.

"No," answered Sophie, with a gentle shake of the head. "It was only when I heard that David was a member that I decided to join myself."

Tony's curiosity was growing by the minute. Having just glanced down at Sophie's left hand, he noted that she wasn't wearing a ring. He appreciated that men have affairs with married women as well as single ones, but probably not so frequently. After all, it wasn't so convenient for those with families to escape for any length of time.

"But you were saying earlier that you live in Musselworth," he said, suddenly fancying himself as a sleuth. "I'm surprised that you didn't join the association over there."

"I just decided to join this one instead," answered Sophie with a shrug.

David was beginning to feel physically sick. Tony and his wife Carol had been friends with Alison for many years. It was clear to him now that he would have to finish with Sophie as soon as possible. He couldn't afford to allow her to be part of his life for any longer. Otherwise, not only his marriage, but his whole world would be in ruins.

He was desperate to turn the spotlight away from Sophie. She had probably done enough damage already, but he still wanted to shut her up. This woman that he was in love with had now become a nuisance. She had provided him with a great deal of happiness while their relationship had lasted, but the time had come to get rid of her.

"Being a teacher herself, Sophie is keen to help me to try and transform the education system in this country," explained David. "Like me, she believes that it is important to invest heavily in our young people's future. After all, having a well-trained work force has to be of benefit to Britain in the long run."

"Quite right," said Sophie, with a firm nod of the head.

Like Tony, Bert was quietly observing the two teachers. He, too, had the distinct impression that something was going on between them. If that was in fact the case, it could be very good news. It might just prove to be a stumbling block in David's bid to become the parliamentary candidate.

The local party chairman was still having pressure applied to him from on high. The leader of the opposition, the Right Honourable Andre Brooks himself, had actually rung Bert earlier in the day to find out how things were going. The great man had made it very clear that he expected everything to be done to ensure that Heather Brooks was selected to fight the Brockleby seat for Labour at the next general election.

Although he had assured the party leader that the lady was on course for victory, Bert was worried. He was well aware that Heather Brooks was not turning out to be as popular with the members as he had hoped. Many complained to him that they found the ex-government minister to be rather haughty and too full of her own self-importance for their liking. Although she had probably started as the frontrunner, it seemed certain that the other candidates were catching her up.

"So how are Alison and the kids, by the way?" asked the party chairman, with just the faintest of smiles. "Everything going well at home?"

"Fine," replied David.

"Joshua, Abigail and Amanda looking forward to their summer holidays?" asked Tony. "Very much," replied David.

In fact he very much resented these questions. It was clear to him what the pair of them were trying to achieve. They wanted to make certain that Sophie was aware that he was a married man with responsibilities. In a less than subtle way, she was being warned off from messing around with somebody else's husband.

Of course, Bert didn't exactly have the best interests of David and his family at heart. He was still intent on making sure that the school teacher's immediate political ambitions were scuppered. However, he was a kindly man and didn't want to see Alison get hurt. She was a lady he had known for many years and greatly respected. So he would just have a quiet little word in her husband's ear and hope that it would do the trick.

Much to David's relief, the subject quickly changed to political matters. At that moment, they were joined by Alec Stokes, who had just returned from a council meeting. He had brought away with him a pile of papers, which he would have to find the time to read at home.

Alec was suddenly the centre of attention. Everybody looked horrified when he announced to the group that the council was proposing to shut down the local indoor sports centre. Were the idea to go ahead, it would mean that the good people of Brockleby would have to travel three miles or more to enjoy their swim or use the gymnasium.

"We need to get a leaflet out quickly," said Bert, as he turned to Tony. "Labour will fight this proposal tooth and nail."

"Whoever becomes the parliamentary candidate in a few weeks will have to lead the campaign," said Tony. "He or she needs to let it be known that they are somebody who is prepared to fight for this town. That person should tell the council in no uncertain terms, that they are not prepared to stand back and see cuts made to local services."

"I'm sure that David wouldn't be afraid to speak out," chipped in Sophie proudly.

"So would Heather Marsh," said Bert, "I can assure you that she is no shrinking violet." In a while, the group began to break up. Bert was the first to leave, and the others quickly followed. It was a warm evening and the stars shone brightly in a cloudless sky.

"Just wait for a few moments," said David, as he walked Sophie to her car.

Like the others, she had left it in one of the parking spaces in front of the party premises. For a few moments, they stood and waved to the others as they drove away. Then, once Sophie felt sure that nobody was about, she reached for David's hand. Had she looked up, though, she would have noticed the severe look in his eyes.

"Are you OK?" she murmured. "You didn't seem like your usual self tonight."

"You embarrassed me in there," snapped David. "Now probably it will start getting around that we are having an affair. Why couldn't you have been more discreet? Why did you have to come here tonight and spoil everything?"

"So what if they did suspect that something is going on between us?" asked Sophie, with a note of surprise in her voice. "Before very long, we will be together permanently."

"That isn't going to happen," snapped David. "I am not going to abandon my family just like that. As far as I'm concerned, it's all over between us."

"But what has made you change your mind?" gasped Sophie.

David hesitated for a moment. The truth was, of course, that he had never really intended to desert his family for her. Their relationship had been a beautiful experience, but now it had to end. Sophie's behaviour that evening had suddenly brought everything to a head. It would mean that they would have to go their separate ways sooner rather than later. He was anxious, though, not to be portrayed as a philandering cad.

"I just can't bring myself to walk away and leave Alison to bring up three children by herself. It just wouldn't be fair," he replied.

"You never intended to leave your wife did you?" sobbed Sophie. "It was just a game to you. I was just a little bit on the side, as far as you were concerned."

Suddenly, David's anger began to melt away. Sophie's tears made him feel guilty and now he desperately wanted to take her in his arms. He cursed himself for being married and wished that he were free to start a new life with her. But he couldn't turn back the clock. What was done was done.

"You weren't just a bit on the side," answered David, as tears began to fill his eyes. "I love you, but I just can't leave my family to fend for themselves. I am so sorry."

Sophie was sobbing hard now and took a small white handkerchief out of her shoulder bag to blow her nose. David tried hard to comfort her by putting his hand on her arm, but she immediately pulled herself away. Then, having climbed into her car, she slammed the door and quickly drove off.

David felt partly relieved as he watched the car disappear around the corner. He had finally summoned up the courage to break off the relationship and now he could concentrate fully on other things. No more slipping off for a rendezvous in Musselworth. From now on, he would give his full attention to his family and fulfilling his ambition of becoming an MP.

He felt anything but happy, though, as he wandered slowly over to his own car. The loss of Sophie would leave a large gap in his life. He only wished he could have made her understand why it had to be all over between them. Perhaps then she could forgive him.

❧ ☙

The following day, Bert Vine arranged an emergency meeting with Heather Marsh for that evening. Just after eight, the pair took their drinks from the bar and headed upstairs in the direction of Jacqui Dunn's old office. The former MP had removed all her belongings, and now the room looked quite bare. Only the large desk that covered much of the room, four padded back armless chairs, and the two grey filing cabinets and several wire in-trays remained.

Heather had already decided that the room needed brightening up. Once she was selected as the candidate and the office became her own, she would order a new carpet and make arrangements to have the walls decorated. In addition, the antiquated wooden desk, which had marks and stains all over the surface, would have to go. Dipping into local party funds, she would buy a new one from that nice little furniture shop in Hampstead. Expensive, of course, but exceptionally good value.

"So what do you want to see me about?" she asked, having first brushed down the chair she was about to sit on.

Bert hesitated briefly. He appreciated that Heather Marsh was the type of person who didn't take kindly to criticism. Therefore, he would need to use tact and diplomacy.

"As you are aware, I am supporting your bid to become our candidate at the next general election," he began, fidgeting slightly in his padded back chair as he spoke. "However, I am concerned that one of your rivals appears, at the moment, to be a more popular choice with our members. In fact, it is likely that he could end up beating you, unless we do something about it."

"I shall wipe the floor with the lot of them at the selection meeting," replied Heather scornfully. "I am a former government minister taking on Carol, a pregnant woman who doesn't want to win by her own admission; Kenny, the Marxist hippy and David, who has never even thought to put himself forward in a council election."

Bert was irritated by her haughty egotism, but managed to control his feelings.

"Actually, David is the one you need to watch. It is true that he has never shown any interest in becoming a councillor. However, he has devoted a number of years of his life to teaching. Now he wishes to use his experience to help improve the education system in this country. Many people might consider that to be very commendable."

"But I have been a government minister," protested Heather. "Surely people will see that a few years in the classroom can't compare with the reputation that I have managed to acquire."

"Look!" snapped Bert, who could feel his blood pressure rising. "For whatever reason, Andre Brooks wants you back in Parliament and I've been told to make it happen. So shut up for a few minutes and listen to me."

Heather was taken aback. However, she managed to resist the urge to stand up and strut out of that shabby little office. It occurred to her that she might need the backing of this silly old fool. After all, it would be pretty humiliating if she was beaten by a mere schoolteacher. Her political future might be in ruins.

Bert handed her a slip of paper. On it was just a name and address. The chairman of the association explained that Heather was to go and see a certain Sophie Duncan without any prior warning. The pretext of the visit would purely be to ask for the lady's vote at the selection meeting. After that, Heather was to try and broaden the conversation.

"It is a delicate matter so your questions mustn't be too direct," said Bert. "However, the bottom line is that I want to know whether Miss Duncan and David Chambers are having some sort of affair. Find out what you can and report back to me. I will do the rest."

"So do you think that David is cheating on his wife, then?" asked Heather hopefully.

"Possibly," answered Bert. "But if that is the case, I think that David could be persuaded to drop out of the selection race all together."

CHAPTER TWENTY-ONE

Life couldn't have been better for Auntie Angela. After her short stay in Amblemore Residential Care Home, she was now back in more familiar surroundings, living in the house that had been her home for many years and sharing it with two young people who were looking after her. She had nothing to worry about now. Between them, Tina and Mark were doing the cleaning, cooking and going out shopping. They were also providing her with constant companionship.

Mark had adapted surprisingly well to his role. Doing the housework was a new experience for him, as his mother had always taken care of that side of things at home. Tina had allocated him a set of chores and he quickly got into a routine. Soon, he was taking pride in performing his duties; polishing this, cleaning that, while making caustic remarks to anyone who happened to step on a floor that he had just swabbed.

He was growing quite fond of Auntie Angela. Her absent-mindedness always amused him, but the old lady never seemed to take offence when she saw the smile on his face. She was always ready to laugh at herself.

"Now, where are my glasses?" Auntie Angela would say as she rummaged around the lounge. "I know I put them down somewhere."

"You're wearing them," might reply someone who just happened to be in the room at the time. "What a silly old fool I am," Auntie Angela would answer before bursting out with laughter.

Mark now had his own TV, which was kept in the dining room. It allowed him to watch football or some action movie, while the two women enjoyed their soap operas and costume dramas in the lounge. The arrangement suited everyone and meant that there were no arguments as to which channel to have on.

Sexual relations with Tina had also improved. He had found a way of ignoring her ugliness while making love. It wasn't a case of laying on his back and thinking of England as women in days gone by were supposed to have done. Rather, it was a matter of operating in the dark and imagining that the woman beneath him was a glamour model.

The days passed happily enough. When the weather was warm and sunny, Mark and the two women would usually spend the afternoon on the beach. Auntie Angela was happy to sit in a deck chair while the two younger ones went for a swim.

Tina, as ever, was fearful that Mark would be recognized and his whereabouts reported to the police. Therefore, they always avoided the main beach, which attracted the crowds. Instead, they would drive along the coastal road and end up in a small, secluded bay. On either side, there were high chalky cliffs and rarely were there more than a scattering of people about.

Tina's old car had now been scrapped. Accompanied by Mark, she had gone to a nearby showroom and chosen a new Vauxhall Corsa. Of course, it was registered in her name alone, as she wasn't the one who needed to conceal her whereabouts. Auntie Angela had agreed to pay the full cost on the understanding that she was chauffeured around. It was a satisfactory arrangement for all concerned.

When out shopping, Mark would often buy large packs of beer from the supermarket. Of an evening, he would then sit in front of the TV and drink four cans or more. He sometimes wished that he were able to share them with some of his old friends. Of course, he knew deep down that most of them would now disown him. They would despise him for having stolen the life savings from a poor old woman. He suspected that some might even hate his guts.

He often wondered what Amanda would think of him now. After all, Alison and probably others, too, would have told her about the robbery. She might well have read a full account of it in the *Brockleby Times*. It was hard to imagine that a girl of eleven wouldn't have found out either one way or another.

Seven years without seeing his beautiful daughter seemed like an eternity. She had been like a miniature version of her mother, with the same flaxen hair and those dark blue eyes shaded by long lashes. How often he had yearned to be part of her young life again – listen to her problems, help with homework and do all those other things that fathers are supposed to do for their children.

Of course, he had made that agreement. After breaking up with Alison, he promised never to go near Amanda again. Were he to do so, then his ex-partner would immediately claim maintenance from him for the child. Being the shiftless, work-shy individual that he was, Mark had decided to keep to his side of the bargain.

At the time, broke and jobless, as he normally was, losing permanent contact with his daughter seemed like a price he would have to inevitably pay.

Now, Mark was having a rethink. His circumstances had changed dramatically over the past few weeks. The threat of claims for maintenance payments hardly came into the equation. The authorities would have to locate him, for a start. In any case, he was already being pursued for a far more serious offence in the eyes of the law.

Gradually, the idea of seeing Amanda again was turning into an obsession. He now knew the name of the school that his daughter attended. Ross Young's mother had provided him with it that day in the car. Having done some research on the Internet, which Tina had just had installed in the lounge, he had managed to find the whereabouts of Collingwood Secondary. As he might have expected, Alison had ensured that it was located in one of the posher neighbourhoods of Brockleby, where some of the better-off parents sent their children.

The plan that Mark was conjuring up was audacious. It would mean taking the risk of being recognized and putting his freedom in jeopardy. He was thinking of hanging around outside the school and waiting for the pupils to come out for their break. Then he would call to anyone who just happened to be near the fence, to point out his daughter. He just wanted a glimpse of her. Perhaps even take a photograph or two and then go.

Of course, he would need to hide his appearance as best he could. There was no point in being too reckless. A pair of dark glasses and a cap to cover the top of his head would help. He also decided that it would be safer to travel by train. Although he could drive the Corsa whenever he wanted to, there was always a chance that somebody might recognize him and jot down the registration number.

Mark said nothing to Tina about his idea. He knew only too well that she would be horrified to learn that he was thinking of setting foot in Brockleby again. Almost certainly, she would do her very upmost to stop him going. Not that he could really blame her. Should things go wrong and he was arrested, she would have some very awkward questions to answer. She would need to explain why she was harbouring a criminal, for a start. It was even possible that the police would suspect her of being an accomplice in the robbery.

In order to put his plan into operation, Mark needed to be away from the two women for the afternoon. The morning was always set aside for the chores around the house. He needed to think of a good excuse for wanting to be alone, though. Tina always liked them to do everything together. He rarely had an opportunity to be by himself for more than five minutes.

"Do you fancy going for a long hike this afternoon?" he asked casually, as Tina was mopping the kitchen floor.

Tina gave him a surprised look. It was almost as though Mark suggested that they throw themselves under a bus together. She was the type of person who tried to avoid any form of strenuous exercise. In her opinion, it was rather pointless to walk any distance when she was the owner of a lovely new car.

"I thought we were taking Auntie Angela down to the beach," she answered.

"But we do that every day," protested Mark. "I thought it would be nice to do something else for a change."

"It's going to be too hot for walking," objected Tina, as she turned to look out of the kitchen window. "Today is going to be another scorcher like yesterday."

"The heat doesn't bother me too much," said Mark. "If you don't want to come, would you mind if I went off by myself this afternoon? It would be nice to explore the surrounding countryside."

"If you want to, I suppose I can't stop you," answered Tina, looking rather disgruntled. "Look, I just fancy a change," said Mark, as he kissed Tina on the cheek. "Tomorrow we'll all go down to the beach together as usual."

Generally, Mark sat down to lunch with the two women. On this occasion, though, he just made himself a sandwich a little after midday before setting off for the station. Tina seemed to be sulking as he left the house, but made no attempt in persuading him to stay. She had obviously made up her mind that it would be a waste of time and effort.

Mark was feeling tense as the train set off. He had bought a newspaper for the journey and tried to read for a while. Taking an interest in world events for more than two minutes became almost an impossibility. He was too concerned about what was soon to happen in his own life. The likelihood of seeing his daughter. The possibility of being arrested and ending up in a prison cell.

As soon as he got off the train at Brockleby, he put on his dark glasses and a black baseball cap.

He knew that these articles wouldn't totally disguise his appearance, but they might help. It occurred to him after he had been walking for a few minutes that he should have been growing a beard over the past few weeks.

Mark reached into his pocket and pulled out a map. It had been one that he had printed out earlier from the Internet. He wanted to know exactly where the school was located and which was the best route to follow. At all costs, he wanted to avoid the main roads, where traffic was likely to be heaviest. It was possible that at least in one of the vehicles that would pass him by, someone would just happen to recognize him.

After a brisk half-hour walk, he finally found himself outside the heavy iron gates of Collingwood Secondary School. The two-storied red brick building was about one hundred and fifty metres away from the road. Through the railings, Mark noted the cricket pitch on his right, with nets alongside the boundary, where several boys were practising their batting strokes. At that moment, though, there wasn't a match in progress.

Of far greater interest to him was what was happening to his left. Well away from the cricket pitch, twenty or more girls in white blouses and grey skirts were involved in a game of rounders. Mark was no expert on these matters, but he guessed the players were about eleven or possible twelve. It was probably their first year at secondary school. If that was correct, he wondered whether any of these young ladies, only a short distance away, could actually be his daughter.

Although Mark hadn't seen Amanda for seven years, he knew that his daughter couldn't have undergone a total transformation. Were she to be one of the players, it had to be one of those with flaxen hair. That being the case, it was either the chubby little girl fielding at first base, the tall one queuing up to bat or the backstop who wore a red hair band.

For a time, Mark stood and watched the game. He wasn't deterred at all by the teacher in charge who kept glancing over her shoulder at him. She seemed the bossy sort, who was capable of keeping a class of children under control – an overweight, stern-looking woman who never missed the opportunity to raise her voice whenever the players failed to do something right. Those who dropped a catch or failed to run whenever the opportunity presented itself were promptly made aware of her displeasure.

Suddenly, the ball was struck high into the air before being caught by the fielder at second base.

There was a ripple of applause as it meant that the team wearing an orange sash had finished their innings. Then, having told the girls to take a break, the teacher marched menacingly towards the point where Mark was standing behind the railings.

"Can I help you?" she asked, rather disapprovingly.

Mark felt sure that she suspected him of being a pervert – the sort of unsavoury character that takes an unhealthy interest in under-aged girls. However, he wasn't prepared to be driven away just yet. Not at least, until he had established whether any of the rounders players just happened to be his daughter.

"I am a friend of Mrs Chambers," he began, trying to sound a little more certain of himself than he was actually feeling. "She asked me to give a message to her daughter Amanda."

The teacher stood perfectly still for a moment while she considered the matter. Then, without a word, she turned and strode back to her young charges. Mark watched on with bated breath as this rather imposing figure approached the backstop with the red hair band, before pointing in his direction.

Much to Mark's delight, the child began to walk towards him. Thankfully, the teacher didn't consider it necessary to accompany her, but nevertheless was keeping a close eye on the situation. At the first sight of any funny business, she intended to be over like a shot. She had read about these predatory men in the Sunday newspapers.

"Are you Amanda Wright?" asked Mark when the child came close.

"Yes," came the meek reply. "Miss Lane said that you had a message for me from my mum."

Mark felt a warm glow inside. Although much older now, Amanda was still as beautiful as ever.

She was even more like her mother than she had been seven years ago. The soft, flaxen hair, those tantalizing dark blue eyes and the delicate silky white skin. He desperately wanted to throw his arms around his daughter and give her an almighty hug.

"Oh, it was nothing, really," he smiled. "It was just that your mum wanted to know whether you would be home for tea at the usual time."

"Of course not," answered Amanda, with a look of annoyance. "She knows perfectly well that I am going round to Amy's house for tea. Mum and I actually spoke about it before I set off for school this morning."

"I will remind her for you then," said Mark, making a promise he would never keep.

Amanda gave the man behind the railings a long, hard stare. She wondered whether she had seen him before, but in those dark glasses, it was difficult for her to tell. It struck her as odd, though, that her mother should use him as a messenger. Normally she would have phoned her on the mobile or sent a text message.

"Who are you?" she asked suspiciously.

"Somebody that loves you very much," answered Mark, as he took off his dark glasses in order to see his daughter more clearly.

"But I've never met you before," said Amanda, who seemed taken aback.

"You have seen me many times in the past, but you probably don't remember. It was many years ago," said Mark.

At that precise moment, the conversation was brought to an abrupt halt. In a voice far louder than was really necessary, Miss Lane made it known to the girls that the break between the two innings was over. It was time to stop talking and get the game started again. Amanda immediately turned and ran back to join the other players before she received a harsh rebuke.

Mark decided to watch the rounders match for a little longer. He wanted to see how his daughter performed with that truncheon-shaped bat; to be the proud dad as she swiped the ball into the distance and scored the winning run for her team. For Amanda to be the hero of the hour and to bask in glory as the other players cheered on in admiration.

Of course, it was only wishful thinking. Amanda didn't even manage to connect with the ball when it was her turn to bat. She even got run out when trying to scamper to the first base. But Mark didn't feel in the least bit disappointed. He had a beautiful daughter and that was the only thing that mattered. She shone in his eyes, even if she wasn't the greatest rounders player that had ever lived.

At last, Mark put on his dark glasses and made his way home – not the house in Brockleby where he had lived for practically all of his life, but the new one down by the sea; the place where he felt safe with Tina and Auntie Angela. It was somewhere where he had no need to hide his appearance in any shape or form.

He felt rather pleased with himself as he boarded the train. After the publicity he had received in the local paper, he assumed that there must be plenty of people in Brockleby on the lookout for him. Yet he had achieved what he had set out to do and appeared to have got away undetected. As he sat back in the carriage and shut his eyes, he was starting to get that feeling of invincibility. He had the idea that he was too smart for the lot of them.

It was clear from the expression on Amanda's face that somebody had annoyed her. After climbing into the car, she slammed the door behind her. Amanda had been to tea with her friend Amy, and Alison was just about to drive her home.

"Who was that man who came to my school today?" demanded Amanda angrily. "He was standing on the pavement outside, as the girls in our class were playing rounders."

"Which man are you talking about?" asked Alison.

"Oh for goodness sake", snapped Amanda. "The one you sent along to come and speak to me. You told him to ask me whether I was coming home for tea at the usual time. Why couldn't you have just sent me a text message?"

Alison was dumbfounded. Had Amanda been in a better mood, she would have suspected that her daughter was trying to wind her up. She felt convinced that on this occasion, though, that this was no joke. Something sinister might be happening and she needed to get to the bottom of it.

"I promise that I didn't send anyone to your school to give you a message," she answered. "Did this man tell you what his name was?"

Amanda's anger immediately turned to dismay. She was frightened that perhaps she was being stalked by one of those paedophiles who the teachers were always warning everyone about. If so, she realized that she could be in great danger.

"No, he didn't tell me his name," she answered with a slight tremor in her voice. "But he did say that he used to see me a lot many years ago."

"And did he say anything else?" asked Alison.

"I know it sounds creepy, but he said he loves me very much," answered Amanda. "Would you have any idea who he might be?"

"Possibly," said Alison thoughtfully. "When we get home, I will show you a photograph which was probably taken very recently. You can tell me whether it is the same person."

Once indoors, she immediately went to a drawer in the dining room. After a brief search amongst a pile of papers, she pulled out a copy of the *Brockleby Times*, now several weeks old. It was the edition that reported the robbery that had taken place at Mrs Fisher's home. Then, with the front page facing upwards, she laid it on the table in front of Amanda.

"Is this the man you saw today?" she asked, pointing at Mark's photograph.

"That's him," answered Amanda excitedly. "To start with, he had his shades on, but then he took them off. Yes, that is him all right."

"I thought so," said Alison with a scowl. "That guy just happens to be your dad."

Amanda looked shocked. She had only been four when she had last seen her father and just had vague memories of him. Also, when her parents had split up, Alison had destroyed all the photographs of the ex-partner she now hated. Until now, even the edition of the *Brockleby Times* which lay on the table, had been kept from her, just in case she found it too upsetting.

"Why do you think he wanted to see me after all this time?" she asked.

"I have absolutely no idea," replied Alison. "What I do know is that he is a very bad man and is in serious trouble."

As Amanda wandered upstairs to her bedroom, Alison picked up the phone. Her first thought had been to ring the police, but then she changed her mind. Instead of speaking to an officer down at the station, who might be unfamiliar with the case, she decided to call Maureen Lucas instead. The woman appeared to be taking a keen interest in tracking Mark down. Alison was now desperate to see him caught before he got it into his head to try and abduct her daughter.

"I told you that he could be lurking around the school," said Maureen triumphantly, once she had been given the news.

"But why did he want to see her?" asked Alison in bewilderment. "As far as I am aware, he has never tried to make contact with Amanda since the day we broke up.

I am certain that finding out the name of her school wouldn't have posed much of a problem for him."

"Because he doesn't want his daughter to think too badly of him for committing the crime," explained Maureen. "It is likely that he values her opinion of him above all others. Once he has formed a relationship with her, he will start to justify his actions."

Alison wasn't convinced that Mark cared what anyone thought of him. Had he done so, she felt, he would have tried to change his ways years ago in order to earn other people's respect. However, it hardly seemed worth arguing the point.

"I don't want him anywhere near Amanda," she said vehemently.

"In that case, please tell your daughter to ring me straight away if he tries to approach her again. I will have a car around there in less than five minutes."

"Have there been any other sightings of Mark that you are aware of?" asked Alison.

"Not as yet," answered Maureen. "But it could be that things might be about to change. Perhaps our fugitive is starting to take a few risks. It might be that he's tired of remaining in hiding and may be prepared to come out into the open from time to time."

"Please do your best to make certain that he never bothers my daughter again," begged Alison. "Rest assured, Mrs Chambers, once we find him, he won't be causing you or your family any more trouble," replied Maureen with venom in her voice.

CHAPTER TWENTY-TWO

Finally, Tony had set a date for the selection meeting. As it was the second Friday evening in July, it didn't give the candidates a great deal of time to prepare. However, David, with Alison's help, was probably putting in more effort than any of his rivals. Together, the couple had canvassed dozens of local Labour Party members for their vote. Then, with only five days remaining they decided it was time to change course.

David began to focus on presentation. With Alison and her mother as an audience, he spoke for half an hour at a time about his political beliefs and why he wanted to be an MP. The two women would fire questions at him for twenty minutes or more. Afterwards, the three of them would sit down and discuss how well it had gone – in particular, what the candidate needed to do in order to improve his performance.

David spent hours on the Internet researching information. Although he was well informed on matters relating to education, he was aware that he needed to be better prepared when he was questioned on health, law and order, green issues and the economy. He appreciated, too, that it wasn't only important to get his facts straight. When asked for his opinion on a subject, he needed to answer with fluency. Fumbling around for an answer might give the impression that he hadn't prepared himself properly for the occasion.

"What are your views concerning the Coalition's health reforms?" asked Alison one evening. David looked blank. He was well aware that his party opposed the reforms, but he had very little background knowledge on the subject. He had to admit to being stumped, and spent an hour or so doing some research on the Internet. Then, when Alison asked the question at the next session, he was able to reply with confidence.

"It is madness", began David scornfully. "The Coalition plan to abolish primary care trusts wholly by the end of March 2013, after which, the role of commissioning hospital treatments will fall entirely on general practitioners. Surely we want our doctors to spend their time caring for patients, rather than dealing with yet more paperwork."

"But we are told by the Prime Minister that this reorganization will save money. As the economy is in such a mess, don't you think it is wise to cut costs wherever possible?" asked Alison, trying to play devil's advocate.

"I am happy to see savings provided that patient care isn't compromised in any way," answered David. "What worries me also is that the Government is moving ever closer towards the privatization of the NHS."

"The Government would accuse you of talking rubbish," joined in Alison's mother. "They claim to support the NHS and say they have no intention of trying to dismantle it."

David shook his head firmly.

"The reforms the Government are making allows the GP to commission services from what they refer to as any willing provider. Therefore, it is likely to mean the closure of some hospitals and other facilities in order to make way for private companies to step in."

"Good answer," answered Alison with a smile of approval. "You seem to be a little tense, though. Try to relax more as you speak."

"I'll try my best," answered David, grateful for any advice he could get.

Gradually, he was growing in confidence. With the two women's support, he felt instinctively that his overall performance was improving. His answers were becoming more informed and his opinions better thought out. Of course, he had no knowledge of which questions might be put to him at the selection meeting. On the other hand, he appreciated that the same applied to his rivals.

David was still concerned about the threat that Heather March posed. Clearly, as a former government minister, she would have the edge over him when it came to national and international affairs. On the other hand, it was a different matter when it came to local issues. The three candidates who had lived in Brockleby all their lives had the advantage over a relative stranger.

＊＊＊

David hadn't spoken to Sophie since the evening that he had terminated their relationship.

Several times when their paths had crossed in school hours, the two teachers had exchanged cursory nods, but that had been the only contact between them. It was as though they had gone back to being just colleagues again, and no more than that.

Although sad, David was relieved that the affair was over. He was now able to give his full attention to the family and his political ambitions. He had been concerned that Sophie might try to become difficult and somehow try to put pressure on him to continue their relationship. However, so far she had been keeping her distance.

Then one afternoon, he was sitting alone in the staff room. Busy marking a pile of essays, he was unaware that somebody had pushed open the door and was now standing alongside him. It was the gentle cough that suddenly made him look up.

"I had a visit last night from a lady called Heather Marsh," said Sophie, her face expressionless. "She had come to ask me whether I would vote for her at the selection meeting."

"That is hardly surprising," answered David, with a hollow laugh. "That woman must be trying to drum up all the support she can get."

"I believe the reason for her visit may have been more devious than that," replied Sophie. "At one point, she actually had the nerve to ask me whether you and I were a little more than good friends. She was obviously trying to damage your reputation in order to enhance her own prospects of becoming the Brockleby candidate."

David could feel his heart beating quickly. He was sure that Sophie was spot on. That being the case, he couldn't believe that Heather Marsh could stoop to such a level. It seemed that his worst nightmare might be about to come true. He feared that both his marriage and any hope of becoming an MP were about to come to an end.

"So what did you tell her?", he asked anxiously.

"I told her the truth," said Sophie contemptuously. "I said we weren't having an affair and as well as that, I couldn't stand the sight of you."

David let out a sigh of relief. At a later date, he would feel wounded at Sophie's feelings towards him. For the moment, though, he felt grateful to her for not taking out her revenge on him, as she could well have done under the circumstances.

"Thank you," he said humbly.

"I wasn't trying to avoid wrecking your life," answered Sophie scornfully. "I was more concerned about my own reputation. The other day, I applied for a post at another school. It is one in a nicer neighbourhood, where the kids are likely to be better behaved. Anyway, as I will need a good reference from Brookway Manor, I didn't want it to get around that I was having it off with another member of staff."

David nodded.

"I guess it wouldn't have looked too good."

"I have to be off now," said Sophie, quickly glancing at her watch. "I have a lesson in a few minutes."

David was relieved that their conversation was about to end without confrontation. He had feared that another member of staff would enter the room at any moment and witness a heated argument. In fact, having treated Sophie so badly, he admired her for acting with so much dignity.

"Good luck on getting that new post you are after," he smiled. Suddenly Sophie's expression began to soften.

"Good luck in becoming the next Labour Party candidate for Brockleby," she answered. "Make sure you beat Heather Marsh. I didn't take to her at all."

David managed to resist the temptation to stand up and kiss Sophie on the cheek. A large part of him was still in love with her, and he wished that circumstances could have been so much different.

Nonetheless, he was a married man with responsibilities, and nothing was going to change that. Gone was the starry-eyed teenager who had started to take him over in recent weeks. Once again, he would try and be the adult who tried to command respect from the rest of the world.

Life was becoming mundane. Mark's only companions now were Tina and her senile old aunt. He was growing tired of their drab conversation and longed to go out with the lads now and then. Have a few pints down the pub and talk football.

He was also giving more thought to Amanda. More than ever, he regretted all those lost years when he had not been at hand to watch her growing up. He had missed so much, and he knew he had only himself to blame. Having been a selfish, inadequate father when she had been a small child meant that he was now having to pay the price.

Mark wanted to make amends. The idea suddenly occurred to him to give his daughter a present – perhaps put a twenty pound note into an envelope and post it to her. He would enclose a letter just to explain who had sent the money; even add that he loved her very much and hoped that she might be able to forgive him for having been absent from her life for so long.

There was one major obstacle to his plan, though. Mark hadn't got Amanda's address to put on the envelope. He had once heard the name of the road, but had long forgotten it. He was reasonably sure it began with the letter 'B'. Berkshire, Buckinghamshire and

Bedfordshire all came to mind. It was definitely the name of a county, or so he thought. On the other hand, he also appreciated that the Chambers might have moved home. Having spent some time on the Internet looking for road names in the town that might jog his memory, he was forced to admit defeat. Then he began to search online for anybody in the area by the name of David Chambers. There happened to be two, but in neither case did the address look familiar. Nor was there a telephone number to ring which suggested that both were ex-directory.

It was at this point that he decided on a change of plan. Instead of sending the money, he would deliver it personally to Amanda. Then he would know beyond a shadow of doubt that she had received it.

The following afternoon Tina took Aunt Angela out to buy a pair of shoes. Excused for once from having to accompany them to the beach, Mark caught a train to Brockleby. Of course, he said nothing to the two women about where he intended to go. He just mentioned that he was off on another of his long walks.

As soon as Mark arrived at Brockleby station, he put on his dark glasses. As on the previous occasion, he chose to walk along the quieter roads, where there was less chance of being spotted by somebody who knew him. Finally, he turned the corner, and there was Amanda's school ahead of him. He was feeling tense, but also excited at the prospect of seeing his daughter once more.

It was now ten past two. Today, the playing fields were deserted. Mark wondered whether he might have to wait until the pupils came out of school before he could give Amanda her present. The problem was that he had no idea when that might be. He resigned himself to the fact that he could be hanging around for some time.

At a quarter past three, parents began to congregate around the school gates. They appeared to pay little attention to the figure in dark glasses, with a baseball cap pulled down over his eyes, standing some distance away. Most were too preoccupied with talking to one another as they waited for their offspring to appear.

Mark was on the lookout for Alison. He had no idea whether she came to pick up Amanda or not.

If she were to appear, he knew his plans would have to be aborted. He was reasonably confident that were she to spot her ex-partner, the police would be notified straight away. She had doubtless heard about the robbery and would have no qualms in seeing him arrested.

Finally, the front doors swung open and a stream of pupils of varying sizes began to emerge. A sea of blue blazers were soon heading towards the iron gates. Mark gave a quick glance to the face of any girl with flaxen hair. There were far more than he had imagined, but finally he spotted his daughter. Amanda was busy chatting to a group of friends as they strolled leisurely along the gravel path.

Mark had satisfied himself that Alison wasn't among the parents awaiting their offspring, so as soon as Amanda had passed through the school gates, Mark immediately approached her with the envelope. Once more, his heart swelled with pride as he was reminded how pretty she was.

"This is your birthday present," he smiled. "Sorry it's a few months overdue."

Amanda seemed stunned to see him again. Hesitantly, she reached out and took the envelope, as if expecting it to explode at any moment. Because Mark had stopped her in her tracks, her friends had already begun to walk on.

"Thank you," she replied, a little nervously.

"I'm your real dad," said Mark, feeling the emotion boiling up inside him. "I'm sorry I haven't been there for you over the years."

"I have to be going home," answered Amanda, as she began to back away. "Mum will be wondering where I am."

"Please stay and talk for a while," pleaded Mark.

"I can't," replied Amanda, as she turned her back and began to hurry off.

Mark felt depressed as he started to head back towards the station. His short meeting with Amanda hadn't gone anywhere near as well as he had hoped. It was almost as though his daughter was afraid of him. He doubted now whether it would be worth taking the risk of trying to see her again, knowing only too well that Brockleby had now become a very dangerous place for him to show his face.

Mark had no idea he was being watched. While following him at a safe distance of about sixty metres, Amanda was on the phone. From her mobile, she was providing Maureen Lucas with her father's movements. Very soon Harvey and 'Mad Dog' MacDonald were on their way.

In less than ten minutes, the Porsche screeched to a halt beside the kerb. Mark's blood ran cold to see the towering figure of Leo MacDonald scramble out of the car and rush towards him. Sitting at the wheel was

Harvey Lucas with a gloating grin plastered all over his face.

Mark was too nimble for Mad Dog. As the giant Scotsman attempted to grab him, he quickly darted out of reach. Harvey Lucas had already prepared himself for such an outcome. Immediately the Porsche sped off and came to a halt at the end of the road, and Harvey climbed out of the car. The fugitive appeared to be trapped, with one loan shark ahead of him and the other behind.

Mark tried to stay calm. The one clear advantage he had over his pursuers was his agility.

Although powerfully built, both Harvey and Mad Dog were considerably overweight, whereas he was slim and took regular exercise. Apart from the last few weeks, he had rarely had access to a car and travelled mainly on foot. Although he no longer played for a team, he would also keep fit by joining in a game of football with local kids in the park. There was never a referee, of course, and coats on the ground served as goal posts.

Avoiding Mad Dog's outstretched arms with little difficulty, Mark immediately sped off. He was now moving in the opposite direction from where he originally intended to go. The least of his problems was that he was getting further away from the station. His major concern was to escape from the two heavies.

Mark sprinted to the top of the road and quickly turned the corner. He had absolutely no idea where he was or where he was heading for. Having lived for most of his life on the other side of Brockleby, this was a district that he was far from familiar with.

Soon the Porsche caught up with him. Having then slowed down, the driver tried to keep pace with the runner on the pavement. Suddenly the window on the passenger side began to roll down before Mad Dog's shaven head popped out. Mark merely gave him a quick glance before increasing his speed even more.

"Look, laddie," shouted Mad Dog, in his strong Scottish accent. "Just jump in the car and show us where you keep the money. Once you pay us back the debt, we'll leave you alone."

Mark kept his eyes fixed on the way ahead. There was no way in the world that he was going to be persuaded to climb into the Porsche. The loan sharks were violent men and took a dim view of people who disappeared while owing them money. He was also aware of their dubious accounting methods in respect of calculating interest. Almost certainly, they would claim every penny that had been taken in the robbery – all sixty five grand. Having passed a long line of houses, Mark glanced around and noticed a large wooded area to his left. There were a number of oak trees with thick trunks surrounded by bracken. He had absolutely no idea whether it would provide a suitable escape route, but it seemed worth a try. He was in no doubt that the Porsche would have great difficulty in pursuing him through the undergrowth, so Harvey Lucas and Mad Dog would have to continue the chase on foot.

Although almost completely out of breath, Mark made one last frantic dash through the wood.

In a few minutes, he spotted a red brick wall ahead. It was about eight foot in height and it seemed to stretch for quite a distance both to his left and right. Close to exhaustion, he didn't feel he had the energy for climbing over the obstacle that now barred his way. It quickly dawned on him that he had been cornered and would soon face the consequences.

Mark glanced over his shoulder. He was beginning to slow down and the two bullies were steadily closing in on him. They were probably less than fifty metres away and were looking fresh having just emerged from the Porsche.

At that moment he cursed himself for his stupidity. Why, he wondered had he taken the risk of coming back to Brockleby again? It was apparent to him that Amanda seemed less than impressed about seeing her long-lost father. In fact, his sudden appearance had made her quite anxious.

Out of the corner of his eye, he noticed a sudden movement. Turning to his right, he saw an old man with a dog on a leash. He had just emerged from a gap in the wall that a second ago had been obscured from Mark's view by a cluster of trees.

Instantly, he hurried over to investigate. He found himself at the beginning of a long alleyway with a wooden fence on either side. At the sight of a car passing by at the opposite end, his heart leapt. He had found a means of escape and just needed to ensure that the bullies didn't gain any further ground on him. The problem was that he was now desperate to stop for a rest.

Before he was halfway down the alleyway, he could hear heavy footsteps on the gravel path behind him. They seemed to be getting louder by the second and Mark tried to run faster, but his legs were incapable of obeying his brain's instructions. At school, he had always been one of the best sprinters. He specialized in the hundred metres, rather than the longer distances. For some reason, he had never possessed the stamina for even the mile, let alone cross-country.

Now, panting as though his lungs were about to burst, he finally managed to get to the end of the alleyway without being caught. By this time though, he could hear somebody breathing down his neck. All seemed to be lost and it was as though he was just trying to avoid the inevitable. At any second he expected a hand to wrench hard on his tee shirt.

Then he noticed a bike leaning against a fence on the opposite side of the road. Quickly, he rushed over and narrowly avoided being struck down by a car. It gave Mark precious time, as Mad Dog was made to wait a while for a long line of traffic to pass by.

Mark didn't waste a second. Jumping on the bicycle, he began riding along the pavement.

Fortunately, there were no pedestrians around to impede his progress. Only when it was clear of vehicles did he then take to the road. Even though he was too weary to pedal fast, he was beginning to widen the gap between himself and his pursuers. Having at last given up the chase, Harvey and Mad Dog stood and glared angrily at the back of the fugitive as he got away.

It was another very warm day. Sweat poured from Mark's face and his body felt hot and clammy beneath his clothes. Now suddenly familiar with his surroundings he estimated that he was about two miles from the centre of town. He was desperate to get away from Brockleby and return to the coast, where he felt safe.

In half an hour, Mark was propping the bike up against a wall outside the station. He was hopeful that it would soon be reunited with the owner. It occurred to him to leave a note of apology in the saddlebag for having borrowed it without permission. As he had neither pen nor paper, though, the idea had to be abandoned.

Having boarded the train, Mark sat back and shut his eyes. He still couldn't understand how Harvey and

Leo MacDonald had managed to track him down. Had they just spotted him by chance or had he been recognized by somebody else? Who had then got in touch with the two heavies, he wondered. Finally, he gave up trying to solve the mystery. What really mattered to him was that he was still free. From now on, he would settle down to a quiet life with Tina and Auntie Angela and stay well clear of Brockleby.

CHAPTER TWENTY-THREE

David didn't even have a chance to change into his slippers. No sooner had he opened the front door than Amanda bounded down the hall to break the news to him. She couldn't wait to provide him with a full account of the dramatic events that she had just witnessed.

"What a pity he got away," said David, once Amanda had recounted the details in full.

"When I rang Maureen, she told me that Mark had only managed to escape by a whisker," said Alison, as she emerged from the kitchen with an apron tied around her waist. "She is confident that her guys will catch him next time he shows up."

"You should have called the police," said David, as he turned to Amanda. "It's their job to chase criminals."

A look of indignation immediately appeared on Amanda's face. It hardly seemed fair to her that she should be criticized for following her mother's instructions. However, having seen that her daughter was upset, Alison quickly intervened.

"Like me, Maureen is concerned about Amanda's safety," she explained. "She promised me faithfully to be on the spot were Mark ever to show up outside the school again. Today she was as good as her word. If the police take longer to respond, Amanda could end up being abducted by her father. I just cannot afford to take that risk."

David was happy to concede that his wife had a point. However, he had a nagging doubt about the situation as a whole. In his opinion, the matter needed to be dealt with by the appropriate authorities. In fact, he was curious to know exactly who this mysterious woman called Maureen was. Right now, though, he was too tied up with other things to make further enquiries. Every available minute he had was spent preparing for the selection meeting, particularly now, when there was little time left before the big night.

Suddenly Amanda waved a twenty pound note in front of David's face. "My dad gave me this," she cried excitedly.

David managed a smile. He didn't feel like explaining to her that it was stolen money. It was only likely to prompt another heated exchange with Alison, and he really wasn't in the mood.

"Have the police at least been informed about what took place today?" he asked, while finally getting around to taking off his shoes.

"You have no need to worry yourself on that front," replied Alison, as she was about to return to the kitchen. "Maureen has given them every little detail. In fact you are very unfair to be so suspicious of her. She told me that with their numbers being cut, the police are only too grateful for any outside assistance. It helps them to try and contain crime in Brockleby."

❦

Harvey Lucas and 'Mad Dog' MacDonald stood fuming by the roadside. They felt helpless as they watched Mark Wright gradually disappear into the distance on a pushbike. Both uttered the sort of expletives that would be frowned upon in polite society.

Feeling demoralized at their failure to catch the runaway, they trudged back through the wood.

Angrily, Mad Dog swung his foot at a stone and narrowly avoided serious injury to a squirrel that had been darting around in the undergrowth. The creature immediately turned and scampered up the nearest tree before disappearing into a hollow close to the top.

"His luck is going to run out before long," snarled Harvey. "Next time he shows his face around here, we'll have his guts for garters."

"I can't wait to kill the bastard", vowed Mad Dog, as he clenched his enormous fists.

As the pair hadn't managed to lay their hands on Mark, they were determined to vent their anger on someone. Once they returned to the Porsche, Harvey referred to a printed list of debtors. They were all clients who were due a visit – people who had defaulted on their repayments recently and needed a sharp reminder.

Harvey's eyes settled on the name of Peter Norton. Being underlined in red ink meant that the debtor was an extreme priority; a person who might well have received a solicitor's letter had he have borrowed from a bank or a legitimate loan company.

Harvey checked the address that was scrawled beneath the name. Then, having entered the postcode into the SAT NAV, the Porsche sped off and soon arrived on a run-down housing estate. Boarded-up windows and an assortment of rubbish dumped by the roadside seemed to advertise the fact that it was home to a number of problem families.

The Porsche stopped outside a block of flats. Several young men were kicking a ball around on the grass outside as Harvey and Mad Dog made their way towards the entrance. The Nortons lived on the fourth floor, which meant that the loan sharks had a bit of a climb ahead of them. Much to their annoyance, a large notice stuck to the door stated that the lift was out of order.

As they made their ascent, the two men were greeted by the pungent smell of urine. They smartly sidestepped several puddles on the ground, which possibly contributed to the stench. The walls were covered in graffiti that was mainly of an obscene nature. However, there were also political slogans, which suggested that the contributors were largely of a far-right persuasion.

Finally, the pair arrived outside the door of number forty six. Slightly out of breath after his climb, Mad Dog pressed the bell before glancing around at his partner. The look in both men's eyes suggested that they were in no mood to be merciful. If the Nortons couldn't produce the money that they owed, then someone was going to be made to suffer.

After a few moments, the front door swung open. Wearing a red dressing gown with polka dot pyjamas partly visible underneath stood a young woman with dark frizzy hair. As it was now late afternoon, her attire seemed rather inappropriate for the time of day.

"What do you want?" she asked in a surly voice.

It was hardly the sort of greeting that was likely to soften Mad Dog's anger. When clients owed money, he expected them to behave rather submissively. Having taken an instant dislike to the woman, he was ready to vent his feelings. He was going to teach her to be more respectful to him in the future.

Having pushed the woman to one side, he forced his way into the flat. With Harvey following closely behind, he marched several steps down a hall and into a sitting room. It was occupied by a baby in a high chair drinking from a plastic beaker and two small boys who were wrestling on the floor. In the middle stood an ironing board, while an assortment of clothes were draped over a well-worn grey settee.

"Get out or I'll call the police," shrieked the woman.

"Where is Peter Norton?" demanded Mad Dog with a threatening glare.

"He's gone down the shops," answered the woman, who was now shaking with fear. "Are you his wife?" asked Harvey.

"Yes," replied the woman, now sounding less assured than she had at the door. "What do you want with Peter?"

"We were promised two hundred quid from him this week. Therefore my partner and I are here to collect our money," explained Harvey in a gruff voice.

"We don't have it," sobbed Mrs Norton. "Neither of us are working right now."

Mad Dog shoved her up against the wall. With one hand around the terrified woman's throat he raised his arm, threatening to slap her across the face. The baby suddenly screamed, while the two boys who had stopped wrestling watched on helplessly.

Harvey spotted a black handbag on the windowsill. Strolling across the room, he lifted it up, unfastened the catch and emptied the contents on the table. A smile spread over his face as he noted a pink purse with a white rabbit embroidered on the side. Having unzipped it, he pulled out several bank notes and quickly counted them.

"Forty-five quid here, Leo," said Harvey. "Guess that will have to do for today. We'll have to call back next week for the rest."

"Please don't take that," pleaded Mrs Norton. "It's all we have to live on for the next few days. I can't sit and watch the kids go hungry."

"Not our problem," answered Mad Dog, as he took his hand away from Mrs Norton's throat. "Your husband shouldn't borrow money if he isn't able to pay it back."

Leaving Mrs Norton whimpering on the floor, the loan sharks headed back to the car. Once inside, Harvey referred to the high priority list once more. Of course, Mark Wright had been placed at the very top. Amongst the twenty or so other names, one stuck out in particular. It was only because the debtor in question just happened to live around the corner.

Tom Desmond was somebody who hadn't received a visit for over a week. He was an elderly man in a wheelchair who had lost contact with his family many years earlier. With no savings and having only the state pension to live on, he had fallen behind with the rent. Fearful of being evicted from his one bedroom flat, he had sought advice from a neighbour.

Mary Higgins, who often went out and did his shopping, suggested that he should apply to the bank for a loan. However, when his request was refused, Mary then recommended that he should speak with Harvey Lucas – a gentleman, she had heard, who could always be relied upon to help out in tight situations.

"OK, let's call on the old boy," grinned Harvey as he started up the car. "As he lives by himself, I'm sure he would appreciate a little company."

"Quite right", sniggered Mad Dog. "Let's bring a little excitement into his life."

⁙ ⁙

Mark mentioned nothing to Tina about his latest trip to Brockleby. Were she to find out, she would demand to know why he had allowed himself to be put in danger of being caught. She would doubtless accuse him of not only putting his own future at risk, but hers, as well. After all, were he to end up in a prison cell for burglary, she was likely to be charged for harbouring a crook.

The following afternoon, Mark and the two women were prevented from taking their regular drive to the beach. In fact they were all ready to set off when the doorbell rang. Having gone to see who was calling, Tina was confronted by an old lady in a floral dress. Immediately, her heart sank. Miss Davidson was one of the most tiresome people she had ever met – the type of person who talks non-stop, yet never has anything interesting to say.

"Is Angela there?" she enquired.

Tina's immediate reaction was to say that she wasn't. Unfortunately, it was pointless to lie. Aunt Angela had appeared in the hall and was standing right behind her.

"Hello Vera. Do come in," smiled Auntie Angela,

Vera was already wittering away even before she sat down in the lounge. Mark, who had been looking forward to a swim, was almost forced into becoming part of her audience. Having never met the old lady before, he was unprepared for what was about to come. Very soon he, like Tina, was desperately trying to think of a means of escaping without appearing to be rude.

At first, Mark tried to take a polite interest in what Vera had to say. Like others who had attempted to do it in the past, though, he was soon forced to give up. Even in mid-sentence, Vera would flit from subject to subject, so that it was virtually impossible for the listener to follow.

"I blame the Government for the state the country is in," said the old lady as she continued to prattle on relentlessly. "And of course, you know that the couple next door to me aren't married. Three children they have right now, and another on the way."

Auntie Angela looked bemused.

"Surely the Government aren't trying to prevent your neighbours from getting married, are they?" she asked. Vera merely ignored the intervention, as she normally did. Instead, she went on to inform her audience about an incident concerning a dog across the road. Apparently, the animal had ventured into her front garden and left something rather nasty on the lawn.

"Talking about gardens," said Tina, as she suddenly had a stroke of inspiration. "I think it's time that Mark and I did something about ours."

"Good point," said Mark, as he exchanged a knowing look with Tina.

However, neither of them was in the mood for gardening. The weather was far too hot for any strenuous work. Instead, having taken two colourful deck chairs from the shed, they sat out on the patio. Both felt a sense of relief that at last they had managed to distance themselves from the monotonous voice that had been ringing in their ears.

"Auntie Angela and I have arranged to see a solicitor tomorrow," began Tina, as she smeared a thick layer of sun cream over his face. "My aunt has agreed that I should have the power of attorney over her financial affairs."

"Fine," replied Mark, as he put on dark glasses to protect his eyes against the glare of the sun.

They were the same ones that he had worn the previous day in an attempt to disguise his appearance in Brockleby.

"I am also getting her to change her will at the same time," continued Tina, as she swatted away a fly that had just landed on her knee. "I was going through a drawer the other day and I just happened to come across a copy of her current one. Apparently, she was intending to leave her entire estate to various animal charities."

"So on Auntie Angela's death, you wouldn't have received a penny," said Mark thoughtfully. "Exactly," replied Tina. "And not only that, but the two of us would have been looking around for a new home. The charities would have been eager to sell this house in order to raise funds." "Let's hope that your aunt doesn't die tonight then," smiled Mark.

Tina didn't reply. Now in the mood for tidying up those affairs that had been bothering her for a while, she wanted to bring up a rather delicate subject with Mark. She was determined to make their future as secure as possible.

"I think it is time that you put your money in a safe place. It's crazy to keep all that cash in a suitcase," she began, a little apprehensively. "You need to look at bonds or starting an ISA. Get a return on your capital, otherwise inflation will start to erode its value."

As it happened, Mark had also felt uncomfortable about keeping his entire worldly wealth in the house. He had scoffed at Mrs Fisher for having kept her money in a shoebox. Now, other than storing it in a different type of container, he was doing precisely the same thing himself. The irony wasn't lost on him that one day a burglar might break in and take the whole lot.

"It's the same old problem," explained Mark patiently. "The moment I show my face in a bank, someone will be wanting all my details. Name, address and what I had for breakfast. My whereabouts will then start circulating around the world and before you know it, the Old Bill will be knocking on the door."

Tina was already one step ahead. Having anticipated Mark's concerns, she had already come up with a solution.

"Then any account could be opened up in my name," she said triumphantly. "I will then draw money out as and when you need it."

The idea seemed to make sense. However, Mark could see a major flaw. The arrangement would allow Tina to have an even greater hold over him. Should he ever want to break free of her, she would be in control of his money.

"Let me think it over," he answered.

"You need to," said Tina. "It's so dangerous to keep all that money in the bedroom."

Mark smiled to himself. The truth was that he was more uneasy about the prospect of being tied down to a woman with whom he wasn't particularly enamoured. Although dependent on her at the moment, he hoped that before long things would change. He was already considering the idea of adopting a new identity and moving to another part of the country – somewhere far away, like Cornwall or Cumbria, where nobody knew him, and hopefully beyond the grasp of Harvey Lucas. Under those circumstances, he appreciated that the money was best left where it was for the foreseeable future.

Time was running out. In less than 24 hours, members of the Brockleby Labour Party would start to assemble in the main hall to select their candidate to take on the Tories at the next general election.

Bert Vine glanced down yet again at his watch. For the past half hour, he and Tony had been kept waiting in Jacqui Dunn's old office. Not for the first time, Heather Marsh was running late and couldn't be bothered to ring up to apologize. Contacting the lady in question had been impossible, as her mobile had been switched off.

"Perhaps she isn't coming," suggested Tony.

"You could be right," replied Bert, who was clearly running out of patience. "Let's go down to the bar for a drink. There is no point in hanging around up here all night."

At that very moment, the door swung open and Heather Marsh breezed in. Without any attempt to explain what it was that had delayed her, she immediately crossed the room and threw open both of the top windows. Then, having turned around, she dragged a chair from beneath the desk and sat down to face the two men.

"This meeting was supposed to have started at seven," said Bert as he resumed his seat. "The traffic was heavy on the M25," answered Heather, with a look of indifference.

"Perhaps another time you would be kind enough to phone us if you have been held up for any reason," said

Bert irritably. "Anyway, you're here now, so let's get on. There is no point in wasting yet more time."

"Right, so what do you want to see me about?" asked Heather, clearly showing no remorse for having upset the chairman of the association.

Bert looked thoughtful as he tried to choose his words carefully.

"Tony and I want to know how confident you are of winning tomorrow night." "Very confident," replied Heather. "The competition are all rubbish."

Tony felt indignant. As his wife was one of the candidates, it angered him to hear her described in such a disrespectful fashion. He even felt an urge to defend both Kenny and David, who both worked tirelessly for the party. However, he managed to keep himself in check.

"Don't be too complacent," he warned. "Your three opponents should know more about local issues than you do."

"Look, I've been in Government," replied Heather scornfully. "Because of my reputation, everyone knows I have a far better chance of beating the Tories than the other candidates. Few people in their right mind would want to turn out and vote for any of them."

"As I told you before, don't be so quick to discount the teacher", said Bert. "He and his wife have worked hard over the last few weeks in order to try and get him selected. Between them, they must have canvassed a good many members in the association. It is just possible that their efforts might be rewarded."

"Precisely why we sent you over to Musselworth to speak with Sophie Duncan," joined in Tony. "Had she confided in you that she was having an affair with David

Chambers, we could have blackmailed him into dropping out of the race."

"Pretty dumb idea, really," replied Heather disdain-fully. "Why would Miss Duncan admit to a total stranger that she was having an affair with a married man?"

Bert shrugged. "It was worth a try, I suppose."

At that moment, the meeting was interrupted by the ring tones of a phone. Heather immediately dipped into her black leather bag before withdrawing a bright pink mobile. Then, much to the men's exasperation, she started on what was to become one of those prolonged female to female conversations.

Of course, Tony and Bert were only able to listen to approximately half of the dialogue. However, even allowing for that, they quickly concluded that the call was hardly urgent. In their opinion, a discussion on a future dinner party or a visit to the hairdresser could have waited for a more convenient moment.

"See you at the weekend," said Heather finally, before she switched off the mobile.

"Look, if you want to get selected tomorrow night you are going to have to give it your very best shot", said Bert, trying his level best to remain patient. "I warn you that you are facing some very stiff competition."

"Right, well if that is all, I shall be off, then," answered Heather, as she picked up her bag and headed for the door. "I really will have to get something done about this office when it becomes mine."

Once Heather had left the room, Bert kicked the table leg. However, he listened for the patter of her feet to fade away as she descended the stairs before verbally expressing his feelings. Then he let out a string of expletives all in quick succession.

CHAPTER TWENTY-FOUR

The school had granted David permission to take the day off. The time spent at home would be invaluable, as it allowed him to prepare for his speech. Having written down exactly what he wanted to say, it was now a matter of memorizing as much as possible. He was keen to try and maintain eye contact with the audience, rather than having to keep referring to notes.

Body language was something of which he was very conscious. Standing in front of a full-length mirror, he observed his movements and facial expressions carefully as he addressed his reflection. While appreciating the need to appear both warm and friendly for much of the time, he had to be ready to show passion on certain occasions.

As the day wore on, David became increasingly nervous. When it was actually time to set off for the meeting, he was beginning to feel like a man about to face a firing squad. Panic set in as he tried to remember the speech, but discovered that his mind had gone blank. Nothing came to him until he quickly referred to his notes. Only then did the words start flooding back into his head.

"By the way, we are stopping off to pick somebody up," said Alison, as she climbed into the front passenger seat. "Mrs Fisher has requested a lift."

"Where to?" asked David in surprise.

"Same place as us," answered Alison. "She is very keen to vote for you."

"But Mrs Fisher can't attend the meeting", objected David. "She isn't a member."

"That is where you are wrong", laughed Alison. "Carol signed her up last week and now she has become a card holder."

"Great," answered David, as he started up the engine. "Every vote counts."

"My next objective is to try and take a few votes off Heather Marsh," said Alison, as she fastened her seat belt. "I can't wait to see that woman's face when I ask her to explain why she fiddled her parliamentary expenses."

"Make certain that you get your question in," said David anxiously. "Don't forget that it has now been decided that the audience are permitted only fifteen minutes to interrogate each candidate."

"I will be the very first to raise my hand," Alison promised.

The members had turned out in force for the meeting. Having arrived in the bar, David had to stand in a long queue to buy drinks for himself, Alison and Mrs Fisher. By now, he was desperate for a double Scotch in order to settle his nerves.

While waiting to be served, David looked around for familiar faces. He spotted Kenny and Alec Stokes sitting at a nearby table and appearing to be in earnest conversation, while Carol, who had just emerged from the ladies room, looked as white as a sheet. Almost immediately Tony, who had been hidden from view by the crowds, came over to put an arm around her shoulders.

David felt certain that Carol was suffering every bit as much as him. Even though she had no wish to be selected as the party candidate to fight the next general election, the anxiety had probably got to her all the same. There was still the dread of standing up in front of so many people and making an utter fool of oneself.

Having comforted his wife, Tony then stood on a chair. After he had called out for attention, the sound of a multitude of voices gradually died down.

"Right, will those attending the meeting tonight please make your way into the main hall, the only exception being the four candidates, who should come and join me in the little room next door," he announced.

David felt dismayed that he hadn't been able to buy drinks. Ahead of him, there were still a number of people waiting to be served. Reluctantly, he trudged after Tony, hoping that he wouldn't be called upon to address the audience first. That being the case, it would probably be possible to nip out and grab a drink before having to speak himself.

The room set aside for the candidates to be briefed was generally used for storage. Tonight, however, the piles of political leaflets and dusty old files that were usually stacked up on the floor had gone. Possibly the same person who had tidied up was also responsible for having vacuumed the threadbare darkish brown carpet.

"Has anyone seen Heather Marsh yet?" enquired Tony, once the other three candidates had taken a seat.

Everyone looked blank.

"Have you tried her mobile?" asked Carol.

"It's switched off, as usual", replied Tony scornfully. Kenny glanced down at his watch.

"The meeting starts in less than ten minutes. If she isn't here by then, you should disqualify her."

Tony shook his head.

"I can't see Bert Vine agreeing with you. The problem is that Central Office would go absolutely mad if we did that. All the party top dogs want her to win to-night."

"And isn't that what you want, as well?" asked David.

"Not any more", replied the party organizer. "I've come to the conclusion that Heather Marsh would upset too many people in the association. If we are to win back Brockleby at the next general election, we need a candidate to whom the activists are happy to give their support; somebody who can inspire them to deliver leaflets and go out canvassing on a cold winter night."

"But if this woman puts up an impressive performance this evening, I can see her winning the ballot," said Kenny. "People can be so easily persuaded by fine words."

Tony grinned as he stroked his beard.

"Having made a few enquiries about Miss Marsh, I have come up with something of interest. All will be revealed when I state the facts in the form of a question."

"Does it have anything to do with the fiddling of her expenses?" asked David, concerned that he was intending to bring up the same subject as Alison.

"No," replied Tony. "Other people are likely to be probing Miss Marsh on that. I am well aware that certain members have been researching details of her financial impropriety on the Internet. This is something entirely different."

Having already been given all the facts by her husband, Carol just smiled knowingly. However, David and Kenny were both intrigued and would have pressed for further information had there been time. But Tony was in a hurry and keen to press on.

"Right now, about this meeting," he began. "Each of you will be permitted ten minutes to address the members and then there will be fifteen minutes to answer questions from them."

"Seems a long time to be interrogated," complained Kenny.

"Moving on," continued Tony, deliberately ignoring the interruption. "We have taken all your names out of a hat and this is the order in which you will present yourselves. Carol will begin, followed by Kenny, then David and finally Heather. Assuming, of course, that the good lady actually chooses to turn up this evening."

Having briefed three of the four candidates, the party organizer left the room. The main hall was filling up quickly now, and he was anxious to claim a seat near the front. Relieved that he wouldn't be first to address the members, David immediately headed in the direction of the bar for that double Scotch to steady the nerves.

At precisely seven-thirty, Bert Vine opened the meeting with an introductory speech. To begin with he paid tribute to Jacqui Dunn, who had until 2010, been an MP for the constituency. He praised her for winning the Brockleby seat in two elections before going on to become a junior minister at the Foreign Office.

The chairman of the association then turned to the present. He stressed the importance of choosing the right person who would be able to follow in Jacqui's footsteps – a candidate able to not only appeal to the membership, but also the voters in the constituency; someone who would work tirelessly for the party and motivate other supporters to do the same. In short, a person capable of turning the political complexion of Brockleby from blue back to red.

Bert Vine was not a man to make lengthy speeches. Having finished his introduction, he was anxious to get the selection process underway. With a beaming smile, he called for Carol to come and join him on the stage. The warm applause that followed demonstrated just how much she was admired by the rest of the membership.

At the beginning, Carol seemed nervous and slightly hesitant. Soon, though, sensing so much goodwill towards her in the hall, she began to gain in confidence. She found herself discussing politics with a passion that she had always tried to disguise, speaking about issues that really mattered to her, like the state of the NHS and global warming. It felt as though some mysterious being had suddenly taken control of her. It occurred to her that in spite of being pregnant, perhaps subconsciously, she really did want to be selected.

"Why do you want to be an MP?" asked an elderly gentleman in the back row.

Bert Vine had only just advised the audience that this was the very last question they could put to her. Having never really given much thought to the idea of sitting on the green benches in the House of Commons, Carol couldn't manage to conjure up an instant response.

"Don't we all want to change the world?" she replied after a long pause.

Tony was shocked as Carol returned to her seat amid thunderous applause. He had to admit that it had been an impressive performance by his wife. In spite of warning certain people not to vote for her, he wondered whether the message might be ignored by some. He shuddered at the prospect of having to take care of a small baby while being married to an MP who spent sixteen hours a day at work.

It was now Kenny who was centre stage. Having remembered to brush his hair and put on a clean shirt, he was looking more presentable than usual. As a borough councillor, he was used to speaking in public and didn't appear in the least daunted by the occasion. Looking calm and relaxed, he seemed to relish the attention being given to him.

David felt sure that Kenny had been taking advice from someone. For once, he wasn't speaking like an angry left-wing extremist. Tonight, he seemed rather more conciliatory. Instead of advocating the need for wholesale nationalization, as he might normally have done, he spoke of the need for the government to support small businesses in the private sector. These were words that would have gone down well in Upper Oakham and other affluent districts of Brockleby. Then, having appeared to please the audience with the answers that he gave to their questions, he, too, left the stage to generous applause.

Finally, the moment had arrived for David. Because the two previous candidates had been outstanding, he felt under even more pressure than before. It felt as though weights had been attached to the soles of his shoes as he made his way to the front. At that precise moment, he didn't care whether the members selected him or not. He just wanted to get the ordeal over and done with.

When he turned to face the audience his fears began to vanish. He imagined himself back in the classroom taking a History lesson. Suddenly he felt strong and powerful. He was in control as usual. It was his job to teach and those sitting out there to listen.

"Why should you vote for me?" David began, as he glanced around at the sea of faces looking up at him. "What do I have that the other candidates don't?"

He paused for effect. Had he been back at school, he might well have expected a witty response from at least one of the pupils, if not many more. It would never happen at a meeting like this, though, he was able to assure himself. People were far too respectful.

"What I have is a very valuable asset," he continued with a gentle smile. "It is my wonderful wife, Alison, somebody who has been in the Labour Party even longer than me and shares my beliefs and values. She will be there to support me when times are difficult and offer advice when I need it. By voting for me, you are getting one of those two for the price of one deals."

At that moment, a door at the back of the hall swung open. As everybody in the audience turned around, Heather Marsh breezed in and stood still for a few moments, looking for somewhere to sit. Then, after spotting a vacant chair in the middle of a row towards the back, a dozen or so members were made to stand as she jostled her way past them to get to it.

"I believe that there are too many people from the legal profession in Parliament today", David continued, the criticism being partly aimed at Heather's own background. "It is crazy for barristers and solicitors to be appointed as government ministers for Education, Health and the Environment. We need specialists in those particular fields. As a teacher, I want to see your children and mine getting the best start in life; training them to learn the skills employers need when they leave school. I don't want to be a minister at the Home Office because I wouldn't know what I was talking about. My expertise is in education and nothing else."

RICHARD GARDNER

David was given a generous round of applause. Heather Marsh, though, wasn't one of those expressing her appreciation. Instead, she was desperately ferreting through her brief case for something. Then, having pulled out a note pad she began noisily flicking over the pages. Once the clapping had died, it was the only sound in the room.

"If everyone could be quiet, please, while the candidate is speaking," called out Bert sternly. David didn't allow himself to be distracted by the interruption. He was beginning to enjoy himself and was thankful for all the preparation he had put in beforehand. When the audience put questions to him, he had no difficulty in providing them with answers. Having done so much research on the Internet, his head was now crammed with information.

Like Carol and Kenny, he too left the stage to an enthusiastic ovation. Although trying his hardest not to show outward signs of it, David was feeling rather proud of himself. Even if he failed to get selected, he was content in the knowledge that he had performed well.

"Please would you give a warm welcome to our final candidate, Heather Marsh," called out Bert, once the applause for David had died down.

A long line of people were forced to stand up again as Heather pushed her way towards the aisle. At one point, she stumbled over a bag left on the floor. Although she regained her balance, the expression on her face suggested that the incident had left her feeling rather disgruntled. However, after managing to put on a watery smile, she started to make her speech.

Heather had decided to play her trump card for all it was worth. She was not backward in reminding the audience of her role as a junior Home Office minister in

316

the last Labour Government, nor that Andre Brooks, the leader of the opposition, was a very close friend. She informed everyone that she had once shared an office with this gentleman at the House of Commons.

A number of those listening to her were less than impressed with what they considered to be bragging. One of those was Alison, who couldn't wait to put her question to the former junior minister. Tony was another who was impatient for her to stop advertising the fact that she had managed to build up a reputation. He was eager to find out how she would respond to the accusation with which he was soon to confront her.

Heather attempted to talk on beyond the ten minutes that each candidate was permitted.

Having cut her short in mid-sentence, though, Bert Vine immediately got to his feet and called for the questioning to begin. As an experienced chairman, he was always keen to ensure that meetings didn't drag on for too long.

Alison's arm shot up, along with a forest of others. Before Bert pointed a finger at her though, he had already given an opportunity to five fellow members to address the candidate. Their questions however, were put more politely than a couple that were soon to follow.

"In 2009, you were found guilty of robbing the taxpayer," began Alison, in a voice loud enough to be heard throughout the hall. "In your role as an MP, for five years you had been making extravagant claims for decorating your home and garden maintenance. This was not money to which you were entitled, and could have been spent on the NHS, on educating our young people or helping the poor. For the life of me, I can't understand why a wealthy woman who owns a large property in Hampstead could do such a thing."

Heather seemed taken aback. Alison had spoken with anger, and a number of people in the audience clapped. Sitting only several rows ahead of his wife, David was tempted to cheer. Being a fellow candidate, though, he decided it might be more appropriate to show some restraint.

"Until 2009, it wasn't made clear as to which expenses an MP was entitled to claim for and which ones they weren't," explained Heather, slightly sheepishly. "Anyway, I have since apologized for my error and have repaid the money in full."

"But as someone with a legal background, you should know that ignorance is no defence in law," countered Alison. "Also, if a burglar broke into your home, stole some of your most valued possessions and then returned them five years later, he would still be charged with theft. That being the case, what makes you any better than a common criminal?"

"I hardly think you can compare burglary with an MP making a simple mistake," replied Heather with a superior smile.

The jeers that greeted her latest reply suggested that a number of members disagreed.

Tony sensed from this reaction that Heather's political prospects for the immediate future had been badly damaged. Keen to get another dagger into her as quickly as possible, he was delighted to see Bert's finger now pointing his way. Having been warned that the party organizer had something of great importance to ask the candidate currently on stage, both Kenny and David were suddenly on the edge of their seats.

"I don't understand why you are trying to become the Labour candidate for Brockleby," began Tony, giving

Heather an enquiring stare. "Surely you would be better off attempting to win back the Stormfield seat that you lost at the general election. After having served there as an MP, you would have the advantage of being well known to the constituents."

Heather gave a casual shrug.

"I just thought Brockleby would be more winnable."

"According to a friend who is a keen party activist in Stormfield, most of the members didn't want you to stand again," said Tony, raising his voice so that all could hear. "In fact, the chairman of the association told you to bugger off before you were deselected."

"Only because I didn't get on with him and a few others there," replied Heather indignantly.

"I understand from my friend that practically the whole membership hated your guts," said Tony, giving the candidate an icy glare. "You were rude to everyone, and either late for meetings or couldn't be bothered to turn up at all. Then you were never to be seen at fund-raising events when help was needed. Furthermore, while busily fiddling your parliamentary expenses, you were voting in the House of Commons for welfare cuts to the poor. I believe you are a disgrace to this party."

Many of the members were clearly shocked by Tony's revelation. As jeers rang out, Alec Stokes, who had put his hand up at the beginning, was finally given the green light. It was to be the last question of the night.

"What are your future intentions if you are defeated tonight?" asked the councillor with a sly grin. "Abandon us down here in Brockleby, or go out canvassing for the winning candidate during the next general election campaign?"

"I prefer not to think of outcomes that may never arise," replied Heather, adept as ever in managing to evade a straightforward question.

The time had now come to vote. A row at a time were asked to stand up and form a queue on the far side of the room. As each member arrived at a table, they were given a ballot form. Then, having marked a cross against their favoured candidate, they folded up the sheet of paper and dropped it into a large cardboard box.

The candidates were left with an agonizing wait. It seemed like an age before everyone had taken part in the ballot. Then more time was needed to count the votes. Finally, it was Tony who marched up to the stage and handed a sheet of paper to Bert Vine.

The chairman looked taken aback as he studied the figures in front of him. For a few moments, he and Tony seemed to be in earnest conversation. Then, as the party organizer returned to his seat on the front row, Bert Vine called for silence.

"Right, well as it is late, I won't keep you any longer," he began. "Here are the results of the ballot in the order that each candidate spoke tonight. Carol Harper ... thirteen votes."

Carol looked relieved as the audience applauded enthusiastically. It couldn't have gone better, as far as she was concerned. Clearly, she wasn't going to win with so few votes. On the other hand, she had hardly disgraced herself.

"Kenny Simpson .... forty votes," boomed out Bert, to even greater cheers.

David held his breath as the chairman opened his mouth to speak again. He could feel the blood pumping through his veins. "David Chambers ... forty one votes," shouted Bert, to gasps and then even louder cheers. "And finally," began Bert, before pausing briefly. "Heather Marsh … twelve votes."

Ecstatic cheers followed after Bert announced that David had been chosen to fight the Brockleby seat for the Labour Party at the next general election. Kenny and Carol were among the very first to congratulate the winner and promised to give him their full support. However, hardly anyone noticed as Heather Marsh stormed out of the hall looking poker faced. She was sure, though, that Andre Brooks would look for another seat for her where there was a vacancy. After all, it was much more convenient to continue their affair when both of them were in Parliament together.

David was called on to the stage to give his acceptance speech. It felt strange to him that he was being treated like a hero while having done so little to deserve such a status. Cheered and hugged, it was as though he was a football star who had just scored the winning goal in a cup final.

"First I would like to commiserate with the losing candidates," he began to loud clapping. "Kenny in partic-ular was desperately unlucky to be just one vote behind. In many ways, as a Labour councillor for so many years, I feel that he deserves to be up here more than anyone. However, as you have chosen me to try and win back this seat for the party, I promise faithfully to do my best.

"It isn't just for you and myself that I want to succeed in beating the Tories at the next general election. I want the opportunity to help young people in this country to receive the education that they deserve. The chance to stand up in the House of Commons and argue that the Treasury should be spending money on schools and hospitals, rather than wars that we are never going to win in the long term. I want to fight for the poor and make sure that the rich pay their fair share in taxation. So if you believe in the same values as I do, then please support me in the battle ahead."

There were further cheers as David left the stage. Everybody, it seemed wanted to come up and congratulate him. He felt like staying all night and basking in the glory. However, Alison reminded him that it was late and they had to take Mrs Fisher home.

"So how is the appeal going?" asked David, as he started up the car.

"Wonderful," replied Mrs Fisher enthusiastically. "I've not only received all my money back but there is a surplus now that the *Brocklebv Times* are sending to charity. People are so generous".

"Fantastic", said Alison. "I'm so pleased".

"Of course it is all thanks to you, Mr Chambers for getting the appeal going in the first place. I shall always be grateful to you."

David smiled to himself.

"Perhaps you have already returned the favour. Without your vote tonight, it would have been a dead heat between myself and Kenny Simpson. Under such circumstances, there is no guarantee that I would have gone on to win in a second ballot."

Mrs Fisher seemed overjoyed.

"So you don't think I am such a silly old fool after all, then?"

"Far from it," laughed David. "In fact, I think you are a real diamond."

CHAPTER TWENTY-FIVE

David was surrounded by newspapers. The numerous weekend supplements and glossy magazines had been tossed to one side. His quest was to search for reports on the previous evening's meeting. As the entire press had assumed that Heather Marsh would be selected, he was keen to discover how the political pundits had reacted to the result.

As expected, the tabloids had come up with the snappier headlines. David smiled to himself as he read 'History teacher condemns Marsh to the past' and 'Ex-minister given a lesson by school teacher'. The more serious newspapers, though, provided more detailed articles. Every report referred almost entirely to the defeated candidate, rather than the victorious one – a man the media knew little about.

Just after nine, he was wanted on the telephone. It was the first of many calls he would receive that day. The *Brockleby Times* wanted to conduct an interview. They enquired as to whether it would be convenient to send around both a reporter and photographer in the afternoon. Of course, eager for the publicity, he readily agreed.

The next call was entirely unexpected. It was Andre Brooks, the Leader of the Labour Party. The great man rang to congratulate him on his success. If he was disappointed that Heather Marsh hadn't been chosen as the candidate, he managed to disguise it in his voice.

"I look forward to visiting Brockleby before too long and meeting everyone down there," said Andre cheerfully. "Most importantly though, you and I need to sit down and get to know each other."

"Sounds good," answered David, hardly able to believe he was addressing such a well-known public figure.

"Brockleby is high on our target list for the next election," said Andre. "Labour have won it in the past, so there is no reason why we can't regain it. All that is required is the right candidate and a good team of willing party workers to support that person."

"Everybody down here is ready for the challenge," replied David confidently.

"Just remember that, although most people believe that there won't be a general election until 2015, it could be called a lot sooner," warned Andre. "I am far from convinced that the Coalition will serve a full five-year term. Long before that, the Tories and Lib Dems might decide that they are finding it too difficult to go on working with one another."

"I can't wait for the battle to begin," answered David enthusiastically.

"Well, good luck and I look forward to meeting up with you soon," said the great man before putting down the phone.

David felt as though he was on the crest of a wave. Everyone wanted to congratulate him on his success. It wasn't just party members, but also friends and neighbours. While some rang, others came knocking on the door wanting to shake him by the hand.

At school on Monday, adulation continued to be heaped on him. Both fellow teachers and pupils alike were eager to praise him on his achievement. However, he was soon to learn that he wasn't the only member of staff being talked about. During his absence on Friday, while he had been preparing for the selection meeting, it seemed that Sophie Duncan had caused a bit of a stir.

Various sources had given him a rough account of what had transpired, but David had to wait until lunch-time before Laura Nixon, who taught music, filled him in with all the missing details. Sitting down with their sandwiches, they were alone together in the staff room.

"Year Eight were playing Sophie up as usual," began Laura sadly. "She was trying to give the class an English lesson, but those brats started to make fun of her. When finally she screamed at them to be quiet, they just laughed at her. It was then that poor Sophie rushed out of the room in tears."

"Did she make any attempt to go back?" asked David. Laura shook her head.

"After spending about fifteen minutes in the ladies' loo, she went straight up to the headmaster's office. Apparently, Sophie told Mr Cheeseman that she wanted to resign with immediate effect."

"What did the big white chief have to say about that?" asked David, as he sipped his tea from a plastic cup.

"As you can imagine, he wasn't best pleased," replied Laura. "Brookway Manor is already understaffed as it is. Anyway, Mr Cheeseman told Sophie that if she left on the spot, he would ensure that her teaching career was finished."

"Of course he has the power to do that", said David thoughtfully. "If Sophie ever applies for another post, she will need a reference from this school. Under the circumstances, Cheeseman isn't likely to give her a glowing endorsement."

"That's for sure," answered Laura, with a slight nod of the head.

"So I take it that Sophie wasn't persuaded to stay, then," said David, "I didn't see her car parked in the usual spot this morning."

"She isn't coming back," replied Laura, as she took another nibble out of her ham sandwich. "Last night, I had a long telephone conversation with her. When I called, she was in the middle of packing. Apparently, she has finally decided to spend time with her parents in Portsmouth, while trying to decide her future."

"I remember she was talking about doing that some time ago," said David. "Personally, I think she would be far happier taking up another profession. Sophie is too fragile for teaching."

"By the way," smiled Laura. "She was delighted about your victory on Friday night. She wishes you luck in your quest to become an MP."

"Sophie was a sweet person," said David, as he gazed down forlornly at the floor. "I just hope that she finds happiness one of these days."

"Why don't you give her a ring?" suggested Laura. "I have her parents number if you want it." David merely smiled as he shook his head. He had no wish to open old wounds again. His relationship with Sophie had been one of those precious episodes in his life that he would always treasure. He had been in love with her and still was. But having a family meant having to face up to his responsibilities. It was all about doing the right thing.

Bible Studies were held regularly on a Wednesday evening. Ian Porter stood up to say a closing prayer. A small child at the back suddenly let out a shrill cry. An embarrassed mother quickly escorted the distressed toddler out of the nearest door. The rest of the congregation remained motionless with their eyes tightly shut.

As soon as the service was over, the worshippers began streaming out into the sunlight. Once in the open air, everyone began to gather in groups for a chat. It was an opportunity for the followers to socialize a little before making their way home.

As soon as Ian Porter had locked the church door, he hurried over to join a small group that included John and Hilary Chambers. By chance, the priest had been passing a newsagent in the high street that day and had seen the front page of the *Brockleby Times* through the window. Much to his amazement, he recognized the face that was smiling back at him. Eagerly, he entered the shop and purchased a copy of the local paper.

"I see that you son could soon be an MP," said Ian, as he brandished the newspaper in front of John Chambers.

John looked stunned as he read the article. He was aware that David had become involved in politics, but had no idea that his son could one day be in a position of such power. Unable to think of anything appropriate to say on the spur of the moment, he passed the newspaper on to his wife.

"Knowing the local MP could be very useful to us," said Ian, who had already considered the implications of the situation. "He could use his influence in helping the Fellowship to purchase that spare piece of land next to the church. The council won't sell, for some reason and we desperately need it for parking during our meetings.

At present, most of us are having to leave our cars out on the road."

John looked shocked. As far as he was concerned, an irreconcilable rift had formed between himself and his son. Unless David was prepared to repent, he could never be forgiven and welcomed back into the family. However, after eight years of following in the ways of Satan, it seemed that the sinner was highly unlikely to ever change his ways.

"Surely you can't be serious?" he answered, with a look of horror.

Hilary stopped reading the article and looked hopefully at Ian. If he was willing to start building bridges between the Fellowship and her son, then it was very likely to happen. Nobody ever challenged the authority of the priest. Many years ago, those at the top in the sect had put him in charge of the Brockleby division of the church. Therefore, what he said tended to go.

"No need to worry just yet," smiled Ian. "The next general election isn't likely to be for another three and a half years. In addition to that, there is no guarantee that he will win the seat. The Tories are quite capable of holding on to Brockleby."

"But our motives may look too obvious if we try to bury the hatchet the moment David becomes an MP," protested Hilary. "Perhaps we should do it much sooner." Ian looked thoughtful. He was prepared to concede that Hilary was probably right in wanting to patch things up with David sooner rather than later. Then he was struck by an idea. Although the Fellowship were forbidden to involve themselves in the political process, he was wondering whether he could bend the rules just a little bit.

"Perhaps we should strike a deal," said Ian, with a crafty smile. "The Fellowship could make a generous donation to the Brockleby Labour Party. In return, should David get elected to Parliament, he would help us to purchase that piece of land."

"It would be nice to have more parking space," said Hilary longingly.

John had never been known to argue with Ian Porter. Today was to be no exception. He just stood and sulked like a schoolboy who had been scolded for stealing apples.

⁂

Mark woke up late. As it was Sunday, he was excused from performing household chores.

Instead, he was sent out by Tina to buy a few groceries. As the weather was warm and sunny, he had no objection to taking a short walk. The high street was less than a quarter of a mile away.

His journey took him past the recreation ground. Through the green iron railings, he could see young parents pushing prams, people of all ages walking dogs and a group of footballers taking part in a training session. At that moment, standing in a long line, the players were waiting their turn to take a penalty kick.

Mark noticed an older man looking on. Suddenly, the man shouted out an instruction to the goalkeeper, suggesting that he was almost certainly the coach. Wearing a bright red cap, he was short and round with a flabby stomach that hung over his belt. Clearly not the fittest of men, it was likely that any guidance he had to offer would be done verbally, rather than actively on the pitch.

Keen to join a team himself, Mark thought that he would make a few enquiries. After passing through the main gate, he slowly made his way towards the tubby man whom he assumed to be the coach. As he strolled along by the touchline, the ball suddenly came bouncing in his direction. Skilfully, he trapped it beneath his right foot before kicking the ball back to the nearest player.

"Are you in a league?" asked Mark, once he had stopped beside the tubby man.

"We are in a local pub league," said the man. "Nothing serious, but it gets us out of bed on a Sunday morning. Also helps to clear the head after a night on the booze."

"Sounds OK to me," laughed Mark. "Any vacancies at the moment?"

"I need a couple of people before the new season starts in September," said the man, turning to give Mark a closer look. "Before signing anyone on, though, I need to see how good they are first."

"That sounds fair," replied Mark.

"Look, we'll be starting a match between ourselves in about ten minutes, so you are welcome to join in", said the man. "Fifteen players have turned up today, so you can even up the numbers."

While he was waiting, Mark began to limber up. Having done a few stretching exercises, he started to jog up and down the touchline. It had been a while since he had last played football, and he was suddenly concerned about his fitness. He was now almost thirty two, and hadn't done any serious training for years. Some of the players on the pitch looked much younger, and he wondered whether they might run circles around him.

Mark was not properly dressed for a game. He felt out of place in a T-shirt, jeans and trainers.

The regular players were fully kitted out with football shirts, shorts, shin pads and boots. However, the coach, who introduced himself as Barry, seemed happy to overlook the matter.

Barry was carrying a large leather bag. Among the contents were a number of red and white striped shirts. They were part of an away kit that the team had discarded several seasons ago.

Although too shabby now for proper league matches, they were considered to be good enough for training purposes.

Having overseen a few stretching exercises, the coach called for the match to start. The players had sorted themselves into two teams of eight. Mark had been selected for the side instructed to change into the old striped shirts, while the opposition were to remain in their present attire.

Mark was told to play up front. The position suited him perfectly, as he had always been chosen as a striker at school. He had the ability to score goals both with his feet and head, an achievement that had won him admiration from fellow pupils and teachers alike.

Barry blew the whistle to get the game underway. For the first five minutes, the striped team were defending and Mark was finding it difficult to get involved. Then suddenly, his right full back hoofed the ball up the field. It sailed high into the sky before landing just beyond the centre circle.

It was the opportunity that the player making his debut had been waiting for. With the ball at his feet, he sped down the centre of the pitch just as he had done as a teenager. Feeling exhilarated, he dribbled passed two defenders before firing a shot into the top corner of the net. Having tried in vain to make a save, the goalkeeper now lay flat on his stomach. At the same time, Mark had begun to celebrate with his teammates.

Later on in the first half, Mark scored a second goal. From a corner, he leapt high above a tall centre back and headed the ball beyond the outstretched hand of the goalie. Even before completing his hat trick ten minutes from the end, he had done more than enough to impress the coach.

"Great performance," said Barry, as Mark handed back the red and white striped shirt. "How do you feel about signing up for us then?"

"Fine by me," replied Mark.

"I'm afraid there is one condition", said Barry with a half-smile. "We are a pub team and the Kings Arms down the road sponsor us. As they buy all our kits, they expect our players to go and drink there."

"No problem," answered Mark.

He had often passed the Kings Arms, but had never ventured inside. As he had yet to make any friends since moving away from Brockleby, he did all his drinking at home. In his opinion though, nothing compared with enjoying a pint of beer with a few mates in the pub. The sheer pleasure of sharing dirty jokes, perhaps a bag of cheese and onion crisps and that comforting feeling of a warm fire on a cold frosty winter evening was like a little piece of heaven on earth.

As the players left the pitch, they headed towards a one-storied brick building. Before following the rest, though, a tall man with a shaven head came over to speak with Mark. The two of them had been on the same side.

"I'm Ash, by the way", said the player as he extended a large hand. "You did well today."

"I was lucky to have received such good support from the rest of my team," answered Mark modestly.

"If you are feeling hot and sweaty, there are showers in the changing room," said Ash. "Then once we are back in our normal clothes, the lads are off to the pub for a few pints. Feel welcome to come and join us."

The invitation was readily accepted. When they arrived in the Kings Arms, the landlord provided the team with a free round of drinks. Very soon, Mark was seated around a long table accompanied by many of his newfound friends. As scorer of a hat trick, he was very much the centre of attention.

Barry collected ten pounds from each player for the kitty. It was money intended for future rounds of drinks. Mark hesitated before making his contribution. He knew he should be heading off to the shops. It was now nearly one o'clock and Tina would be wondering where he was. It occurred to him that she and Auntie Angela were probably waiting for his return before sitting down to lunch. That is what they had always done in the past.

Mark no longer possessed a mobile phone in order to ring home. On the day of the robbery, he had dropped his last one down a drain by the side of the road. He had quickly come to the conclusion that most of the calls he received from that moment on would be unwelcome ones. Also, were he to use it to get in touch with somebody, the signal could assist the police to trace his whereabouts.

Having briefly considered the situation, Mark handed Barry a crisp ten pound note. He had money now and he wanted to enjoy himself. Knocking back pints of beer in all male company while discussing football was a delight that he had been starved of in recent times. He decided to stay in the pub for as long as he liked and leave the women by themselves for once.

"So what do you do for a living?" asked a dark curly-haired man, who had been answering to the name of Dobbo.

Mark was well prepared for such questions. He had invented not only a career but also a past for himself. The replies that he had carefully devised were intended to create as little further interest as possible.

"Civil servant," he answered in a flat voice. "I work mostly on the computer at home. Financial reports and all that kind of thing. All pretty boring stuff, really."

Clearly the ploy worked. Dobbo had no follow up questions and began to talk about his own job as a plumber. After less than five minutes or so, Mark felt he had heard enough about blocked drains and was relieved when Barry came to the rescue.

"What are you drinking?" asked the coach.

"Make it another pint of best bitter," replied Mark, before switching his attention away from Dobbo and listening in on a conversation that was taking place on the opposite side of the table.

Soon he was beginning to feel light-headed. It had been ages since he had drunk so much alcohol. He had only been vaguely aware of handing Barry another ten pound note as the coach went around collecting for the kitty again. Almost everyone by now had lost count of the number of drinks they had consumed. Bladders were starting to work overtime as players made frequent visits to the loo to relieve themselves.

Finally, somebody decided it was time to be on his way. By now the group had been in the Kings Arms for more than two and a half hours. As always happens in such social gatherings, one departure triggered off a few more. When at last Barry stood up to go, Mark and the rest who were still there decided to leave, as well.

Most of the players were unsteady on their feet as they headed for the door. Then once outside, they began to hug one another like long-lost relatives before they parted company. Thankfully all lived close by, so there was no need for any of them to drive. Had somebody in that condition attempted to get behind the wheel, there might well have been a fatality.

"Don't forget that the next training session is at six o'clock on Tuesday night," said Barry, giving his new striker a third reminder in as many minutes.

"I'll be there," promised Mark, before turning around and starting to make his short journey home.

Tina was standing at the front door as Mark staggered down the garden path. Meanwhile, Auntie Angela was looking down anxiously from her bedroom window. With no tea bags, milk, sugar or bread in the house, both women had been waiting for several hours for fresh supplies to arrive. Now it suddenly occurred to them that they were likely to be in for a big disappointment.

"Where is the bloody shopping?" cried Tina.

Mark seemed not to have heard. Instead, he barged past Tina before making his way along the hall and then up the stairs. In his drunken state he cared nothing for such trifling matters as tea bags. After all, he was a soccer star who had scored a hat trick and there would be many more goals to come from him in the future. Then he remembered nothing else as he drifted into a deep, peaceful sleep.

CHAPTER TWENTY-SIX

The sky was clouding over again. As David and Simon were approaching Broadstairs, it started to drizzle. When arrangements were being made to visit Rebecca eight weeks earlier, there were hopes that part of the day could be spent on the beach. Because of the gloomy weather, though, the idea of sitting on wet sand gazing out at the grey sea had little appeal.

Rebecca had spent much of the morning preparing a meal for her two guests. Generally, on a Saturday she would have been cooking for more. On this occasion, though, Graham her husband had taken the four children up to Yorkshire for the weekend to stay with his parents. Had he not have done so, David would never have received an invite.

The Eternal Fellowship were not supposed to entertain non-believers in their homes. Actually eating with so-called 'worldlies' was strictly forbidden. As David's lifelong friends, however, Rebecca and Simon had always been willing to breach the rules in his case, even though such disobedience might well lead to their expulsion from the sect.

The school holidays had finally arrived and David was looking forward to a few stress-free weeks away from the classroom. It meant that he had no need to spend his evenings and weekends marking homework.

Until the next term began in September, his time would be his own. He would have the opportunity to relax and recharge the batteries.

"Congratulations on your recent success," smiled Rebecca warmly, as she greeted David at the front door.

"He hasn't started yet," Simon grinned. "Before long, he'll be moving into Ten Downing Street."

"Heaven help Britain if that were ever to happen," answered David modestly.

Rebecca turned and led the way into the lounge. As the guests followed in her footsteps, they were greeted by a delicious aroma. It had been a number of hours since the two men had last eaten and suddenly they were beginning to feel ravenous.

"What time is lunch?" asked Simon.

"Another twenty minutes," answered Rebecca. "Do you two want an aperitif while we're waiting?" The offer was eagerly taken up. Once the guests had stated their preferences, Rebecca soon returned from the drinks cabinet carrying three glasses – a sherry for herself and scotch for the two men.

"I got a call from Ian Porter yesterday," began David, once the hostess had sat down.

"Apparently he wants to meet up with me next week. Do either of you know what it might be about?"

Simon nodded.

"As you know, the Fellowship are desperate to get their hands on that piece of land next to the church. They want to use it for parking space during their meetings, rather than having to leave their cars on the road. So, as you could be heading for a position of power, Ian thought you may be able to help."

"Why should I?" answered David indignantly. "The Fellowship haven't exactly treated me well in the past. Eight years ago, they sacked me from my job, threw me out of my home and cut me off from my family and friends. Ian Porter can get bloody stuffed."

"Don't be too hasty," warned Simon as he sipped his drink. "I'm told that Ian has a proposition for you. As a form of peace offering, he is prepared to allow you to have some contact with your family and Fellowship friends again. In addition to that, he is willing to make a handsome donation to your local party."

"So he is trying to bribe me," said David, with a look of disgust. "What if he is?" replied Simon. "Ian only wants you to put pressure on the council to sell a strip of wasteland."

"And just think what you have to gain," joined in Rebecca enthusiastically. "You could take your kids to meet their grandparents. Also introduce them to some of their uncles and aunts."

"And don't forget the donation," said Simon. "Producing a few more leaflets might help get you elected to Parliament."

"I will have to speak with Alison before agreeing to anything," replied David thoughtfully. "I am not certain that she would welcome the Fellowship interfering in our lives."

At that moment, Rebecca disappeared into the kitchen to check on the meal. She was smaller than Simon, her twin brother, but possessed the same high forehead and dark, sparkling eyes. She was quite stunning, even without any make-up to enhance her beauty. Like all Fellowship women, she was forbidden to wear cosmetics. As a part of the sisterhood, she was also not permitted to cut her thick, shining hair, which, as a result, hung loosely down to her waist.

Rebecca did her best to conform. However, she had grave doubts as to the beliefs of the Eternal Fellowship. In secret, she read books that the sect would have regarded as being both heretical and subversive. Apart from making a study of many other religions, she was also interested to know what atheists had to say. Then, having been fascinated by Darwin's *The Origin Of Species*, she was forced to admit to herself that evolutionists were able to make a very convincing argument.

Of course, Rebecca would never leave the Fellowship. Unlike David, she couldn't face the thought of being rejected by her friends and family. It would probably mean the break-up of her marriage. The sect would put pressure on her husband to start divorce proceedings. There would then be uncertainty regarding the future of the four children. She couldn't be absolutely certain of being granted custody.

"So are you still having an affair with that teacher?" asked Simon, as his sister was about to set the table.

"It's all over between us," replied David. "I decided to break off our relationship before it went any further."

"You did the right thing," said Rebecca with an approving smile. "She wasn't worth ruining your life for."

"Sophie was very special to me," said David sadly. "I was tempted to sacrifice everything for her, but in the end I decided to do the right thing."

"You'll get over it," said Simon, giving his friend a comforting pat on the back.

"So what is the latest news from the Fellowship?" asked David, keen to change the subject. "Plenty of gossip as usual," grinned Simon, as he took his place at the table.

Over lunch, David was entertained with some amusing little stories, like the one about Mr Harris, who got his tie stuck in the front door. Having left his key in the house, he needed to call out to a neighbour to cut him loose. Then there was Miss Stapleton, who fell asleep on the bus after a Bible study meeting. Later that evening, the elderly lady had a nasty shock when she woke up and saw Trafalgar Square coming into view.

Rebecca insisted on doing the washing up alone. As she was busy at work, her two guests were stood by the bay window in the lounge gazing up at the sky. There was still drizzle in the air and the banks of clouds gathering overhead looked threatening. They both dismissed any slight hope of enjoying a pleasant afternoon on the beach.

Outside, a postman went from door to door delivering letters. On the opposite side of the road, a woman passed by holding up a bright red umbrella. Meanwhile, a puddle in Rebecca's front garden continued to get bigger as the light rain went on falling.

"This chap looks as though he may have had a little too much to drink," said Simon with a smile. "From the state of him, I should think that he must be smashed out of his mind," grinned David. The person they were referring to had just appeared around the corner. He was staggering from side to side on the pavement, while frequently stopping and clinging to a garden wall for support. Tall, with an athletic physique, he looked to be in his early thirties.

Rebecca's guests continued to watch the drunk in amusement. However, David's jaw suddenly dropped as the swaying figure got ever closer. He saw the face, and immediately his heart started pounding. If it wasn't the same man, he told himself, then the character outside trying to stay on his feet bore an uncanny resemblance.

"Rebecca, could you spare me a moment? I need your help," he called out.

Immediately, the clatter of pans ceased. Seconds later, Rebecca emerged from the kitchen in a floral apron. Looking somewhat taken aback by the urgency in David's voice, she was still holding a dripping sponge in her hand.

"What is it?" she asked.

"Do you recognise that drunk coming along the road?" asked David, as he pointed his finger. "Of course," answered Rebecca, as she crossed the room to join her guests at the window.

"That guy and his girlfriend moved in with my next-door neighbour a few weeks ago. From what I have heard, they are acting as carers for the old lady."

"Any idea what that chap's name is?" asked David. Rebecca looked thoughtful.

"When I was in the garden the other day, I overheard his girlfriend shout out to him. I think she called him either Matthew or Martin."

"How about Mark?" suggested David.

"That was it," said Rebecca. "Do you know him, then?"

"Let's say that our paths crossed a few years ago," answered David, reluctant to reveal too much at that particular moment.

"He certainly looks in a state," laughed Simon.

The inebriated neighbour was now directly outside. Suddenly he stumbled and needed to hold on to Rebecca's waist-high brick wall to support himself. Having taken a brief rest, he staggered on another ten yards before coming to a halt in front of next door's wooden gate. After struggling with the catch for another minute or so, he almost fell into a rose bush while making unsteady progress down the garden path.

"Would it seem extremely rude if I were to drop in and say hello to him?" asked David, now totally convinced that he had just seen Alison's ex-partner. "I shouldn't be away for too long."

"Please feel free to do as you wish", smiled Rebecca. "But at the moment, I hardly think that my new neighbour looks in a fit condition to be receiving visitors."

David knew that she was right. He also doubted that he would receive a warm welcome after presenting himself on the doorstep – not that the thought of a cool reception discouraged him in any way. Of course, he appreciated that he had the option of allowing the police to handle the situation. However, something was prompting him to speak with Mark first.

Like Rebecca, Auntie Angela lived in a large detached house. The passer-by would have noticed that each property had four bay windows at the front; two up and two down. These residences were not popular with postmen. Because of the long gardens, they were expected to walk over twenty metres from the gate to the letterbox with the post. Then there was the same distance back again.

Rebecca had lived in Broadstairs for many years. To begin with, she and her first husband had bought a bungalow. However, after her second marriage to Graham, it was decided that something much bigger was required. Now that the couple had grown into a family of six, it was obvious that the move had been a sensible piece of forward planning.

David could hear raised voices as he pressed the doorbell. It sounded as though a man and a woman were trying to discover who could shout the loudest. Then a much older female seemed to want to enter the contest. The heated exchanges seemed to get noisier by the minute.

Frustrated at having to stand out in the rain while the commotion continued inside, David gave a double ring on the bell this time. Suddenly, the shouting stopped. Then through the frosted glass he could see somebody advancing towards him. In the next few seconds the door swung open and there stood a woman in her late twenties or early thirties. The angry scowl on her face obviously reflected the way she was currently feeling.

"I have come to speak to Mark Wright," David announced.

"Are you from the football team?" asked the woman suspiciously.

"No, I'm not", replied David. "I want to come in and talk to Mark about a robbery that took place in Brockleby a few weeks ago. An old lady had all her life savings stolen."

"He isn't here," answered the woman, nervously wringing her hands together.

"Look, I saw him coming down your garden path less than five minutes ago," said David. "If you don't let me in, I will be left with no alternative but to call the police."

Briefly, the woman looked undecided. Then, standing aside, she beckoned David in. "Down the hall and through the door on the left," she said.

David found himself in a lounge the same size and shape as Rebecca's. Looking around the room, he noticed a number of plants growing out of vases of various dimensions; while on the mantelpiece and windowsill were several foot high figurines, all elegantly dressed ladies and gentlemen in Georgian costume.

Until David's arrival, there had been two occupants in the room. Mark was sprawled out on a three-seater sofa with his eyes shut. While his head rested on a red velvet cushion, at the other end, a pair of muddy shoes perched on top of the arm. Sitting facing him was an elderly lady with a look of disapproval written all over her face.

"Look," said the younger woman who had opened the front door. "It won't be possible to get any sense out of Mark at the moment. Perhaps you and I could go into the kitchen and talk."

"Seems like a good idea," answered David, as he stared down at the heap on the sofa.

"I'm Tina Bailey by the way", said the woman as she lead the way into the next room. "Mark and I have known each other for a long time, but it is only recently that we have got together".

As they sat down with cups of tea, David introduced himself. Tina was interested to learn that he was the step-father of Mark's daughter. She was also surprised to discover that her next-door neighbour was one of his closest friends. Soon the pair of them were getting on very well together.

"So when you saw Mark, why didn't you go straight to the police?" asked Tina. "You've already told me that you know about the robbery."

David sipped his tea for a few moments before replying. He could see that Tina was still quite nervous, even though the atmosphere was quite convivial.

"I want to find out why Mark burgled that old lady's home," explained David, "You see, my wife was Mark's partner for several years. Alison knew he had many faults, but stealing wasn't one of those that she recognised. Also, I understand that until that day several weeks ago, Mark didn't have a criminal record. So I'm interested to know why that suddenly changed."

"Those bloody loan sharks forced him into it," answered Tina bitterly. "Two big brutes who prey on vulnerable people who just happen to have fallen on hard times. As the banks have now stopped lending, those bastards have been getting plenty of business in the Brockleby area."

"So have these two been putting pressure on their clients?" asked David.

"That is putting it mildly," replied Tina with a look of disgust. "I have heard that those monsters often use physical violence if they don't get their money back on time. Men, women and even the children of clients are liable to get beaten up."

David looked horrified. He couldn't understand why he had never heard about this kind of thing before. Why, he wondered, weren't the police doing something to stop such abuse? There had been nothing reported in the local press, as far as he could recall. Then the answer came to him in a flash. It was because the poor victims were too terrified to speak out.

"What can you tell me about these moneylenders?" he asked. "Not a lot," replied Tina. "You would really need to speak to Mark."

David checked his watch. He knew he should be getting back to Simon and Rebecca. They might think that he was being extremely rude if he were to spend the whole afternoon chatting with the neighbours. On the other hand, he wanted to do something that was effecting the lives of many residents in Brockleby – people whom one day he hoped to be representing in Parliament.

"I'll be back at six o'clock," he said, getting to his feet. "Can you make sure that Mark sobers up in the meantime? Get some black coffee down him or something."

Tina nodded. She decided to say nothing to Mark about David's visit when he woke up, just in case he got into a panic and went on the run.

As promised, David returned at six. He said nothing to Rebecca or Simon about what had been discussed with Tina. As far as the twins were concerned, he was just paying another quick social call before travelling back to Brockleby.

When Tina showed him into the lounge for the second time that day, Mark was sitting watching TV.

Auntie Angela, though, was no longer there to keep him company. Instead, she could be seen from the patio window watering plants in a greenhouse at the bottom of the garden. Being a creature of habit, it was a job that she did each evening at roughly the same time.

"You have somebody to see you, Mark," announced Tina, as she indicated to the visitor to take a seat. "This is David Chambers, somebody that you have met before, I'm told."

Mark froze. A little voice inside his head told him to run, but his body refused to move. He couldn't understand why Tina looked so calm. The thought suddenly flashed across his mind that perhaps she had betrayed him. Like Judas Iscariot, she had revealed his whereabouts. Not for thirty pieces of silver, of course, but whatever reward had been placed on his head.

"What do you want?" he demanded brusquely, in order to disguise his alarm.

"I need to talk to you," answered David, as he made himself comfortable in the armchair that Auntie Angela had occupied earlier.

"About what?" asked Mark, with a look of hostility.

"About these two thugs who are chasing you for money," said Tina. "This man is anxious to put a stop to their activities."

"What does it matter to him?" asked Mark suspiciously.

"Because it seems that these two are hurting a lot of people in Brockleby," replied David, with a steely look in his eye. "In several years, I aim to be the constituency MP, so let us stop wasting time. Tell me everything you know about these two moneylenders, starting with their names."

Prompted by a dig in the ribs from Tina, who was now seated on the sofa beside him, Mark began to talk. He not only divulged details of his own experiences with the thugs, but also stories that had been related to him by others. David sat facing him with paper and pen, taking down notes. He was barely able to believe what he was hearing.

"And you say that they punch and kick women as well as men?" gasped David in disbelief. "Those two don't believe in sexual discrimination," said Mark. "They are happy to assault anyone. People who can't keep up their repayments are made to live in fear. Some will actually resort to crime in order to raise the money like I did."

"So now you've discovered where Mark is living, do you intend to go to the police?", asked Tina anxiously.

As David had now stopped writing, he was able to glance out of the window. Auntie Angela was still pottering around in the greenhouse carrying a watering can.

She looked a picture of contentment. Tina had told him earlier that she and Mark had rescued the old lady from a residential home to care for her themselves. It seemed a shame to disturb such a successful arrangement.

"Look, I have a proposition for you, Mark," he said thoughtfully. "Help me to gather together names of people who owe money to Harvey Lucas and his partner – perhaps twenty or so. Secondly I want you to stay away from Amanda as you are causing her and her mother a great deal of distress. Alison is concerned that you are trying to abduct Amanda. In return, I promise never to reveal to anyone where you are living."

"You've got a deal," said Mark with a look of relief. "But will you also be expecting me to return Mrs Fisher's money to her?"

David shook his head.

"If you help me, I am happy for you to keep the money. You see, I asked the *Brockleby Times* to start an appeal for Mrs Fisher. There was such a big response from some of the local firms that the old lady got all her savings back. In fact, so much money was raised from donations that there was a surplus, which went to charity. So everyone ended up happy."

"What about those companies that sent donations?" asked Tina. "They lost out, didn't they?" "Not really," smiled David. "It was good publicity for them. They all got a mention in the *Brockleby Times*."

"This calls for a drink," said Mark cheerfully.

"Sounds good," said David. "And while we are drinking, you can write down a few names of Harvey Lucas's clients for me."

CHAPTER TWENTY-SEVEN

David remained true to his word. He said nothing about his encounter with Mark, not even to Alison, whom he felt certain would wish to do the right thing in the eyes of the law. Doubtless, she would also relish the prospect of knowing that her ex-partner could be put behind bars; no longer able to hang around her daughter's school.

There was, though, another subject that David was happy to mention to his wife. It was the little matter of the Fellowship's wish to buy the piece of land next to the church. Alison's negative reaction to the idea hardly surprised him. In fact, she shuddered at the prospect of having any dealings whatsoever with members of the sect.

"But I see no reason why I shouldn't try and help them to get more space to park their cars," said David, having now had time to give the matter a little more thought. "After all, it is only a bit of waste ground that nobody else wants."

"In fact, somebody else does want it," replied Alison, "you should pay closer attention to the *Brockleby Times*. Apparently, a local action group want the council to turn that land into a kids' playground. So if it gets reported that you are supporting the Fellowship to purchase it, you are liable to upset a number of parents in that area."

"But don't forget that Ian Porter has offered to make a donation to the Brockleby Labour Party", said David. "Could come in very useful in helping us produce a few more leaflets before the general election comes around."

"We don't need to accept bribes," replied Alison scornfully. "You can win this seat off the Tories by campaigning on issues that really matter to people."

David said no more. It hardly seemed the ideal moment to admit to his wife that he had invited Ian Porter around on Thursday evening. As there were still four days to go before the meeting, he decided to drop the subject for the time being. In any case, at present he had more important things to occupy his mind. His main concern was the moneylenders and trying to stop their reign of terror.

It was Monday morning when David got down to work. Now the school holidays had arrived, he had all the time in the world on his hands. He was anxious to track down as many of Harvey Lucas's clients as possible. Mark had provided him with six names. Of these, however, he had only been able to remember the addresses of three.

The first name on the list lived on the other side of Brockleby. It was one of those deprived areas where the crime rate was well above the national average. The results of vandalism were manifested in the boarded-up windows, graffiti on walls and the occasional burnt-out car.

The sun shone brightly in a cloudless sky as David pulled up outside a small terraced house. As the road was narrow, he followed the example of other residents and parked partly on the pavement. Without such consideration for other road users, the constant flow of traffic would have been caught in a perpetual jam.

The person that David had come to visit was a Mr Harold Sutton. According to Mark, he was an elderly gentleman who had recently lost his wife and had gone to Harvey Lucas for a loan to cover the funeral costs. Having borrowed only a thousand pounds, due to an exorbitant rate of interest, he now owed three times as much. On his meagre state pension, he was now struggling to keep up the repayments.

Having rung the doorbell, David was made to wait for a while. Looking towards the downstairs window, he saw the grey curtains move a few inches. Then in a flash, the pale blue eyes that had been watching him disappeared. Very soon, he could hear slow heavy footsteps approaching from within the house.

"I'm David Chambers," he smiled cheerfully, as soon as the door swung open. "I wonder if I might come in for a moment. I won't keep you long."

The old gentleman nodded before leading the way down a dark, dingy hall. Soon David found himself in a small room and immediately felt slightly guilty. On the dining table that covered most of the space, he saw a plate with a half-eaten piece of toast on it, a milk jug, a bowl and a cereal packet. He realised that he had come at an inconvenient moment.

"Sorry to disturb your breakfast," he said.

"It isn't a problem," replied Mr Sutton, as he resumed his place at the table. "Anyway, how can I help you?"

"I understand that you, along with many others are having problems with a couple of money lenders", said David.

"Are you a policeman?" asked Mr Sutton.

"No," answered David. "I'm from the Labour Party. Somebody told me that you and many other people are being bullied by two very nasty individuals, so I thought I would make a few enquiries. I want to check out all the facts first before involving the police".

"Harvey Lucas and his partner are evil," said Mr Sutton bitterly. "They don't care who they hurt." "Have they ever been violent with you?" asked David.

Mr Sutton stood up and began unbuttoning his shirt. Having taken the garment off, he turned around. David was horrified to see four bruises on the old gentleman's back. The brown ugly marks were approximately the size of cricket balls.

"When did they do that?" gasped David.

"Three days ago," answered Mr Sutton. "And Harvey Lucas says that I will feel his fist next week if I don't find the money to pay him back."

David was incensed. Quickly, he jotted down a note in an exercise book he had brought with him.

Having always been taught to respect the elderly, he couldn't believe anyone could do such a thing to a frail old gentleman. It was simply beyond contempt.

"Look, would you be prepared to repeat all this to the police?," asked David. "Then I'll get these bastards arrested and put behind bars".

Mr Sutton shook his head firmly.

"There is no way that I'm going to stand up in court and give evidence. Knowing the British justice system, Harvey Lucas and his partner will serve a few months in prison at the most. Then they will be free to come after me."

David could hardly blame him for being afraid. It would be unfair to describe Mr Sutton as a coward. When confronted with two great bullies, he had little chance of defending himself. With little confidence that the police could protect him in the future, it was a matter of self-preservation.

"Do you happen to know anyone else who might be suffering at the hands of these villains?" asked David.

"Please don't ask me anymore questions", pleaded Mr Sutton. "It makes me feel quite ill just thinking about those vicious brutes."

David decided to respect the elderly gentleman's wishes. He was hopeful that the second name on Mark's list might be more willing to co-operate. Once again though he was in for another disappointment. Miss Welch, an unmarried mother of two, was equally reluctant to speak to the police.

"I've got my kids to consider," she explained. "If I gave evidence against those men, I would expect around the clock protection for the rest of my life. With all these cuts, I can't see the police agreeing to that."

Having left Miss Welch to get on with her housework, David set off to make another visit. Oliver Hughes was the final name on the list with an address. Mark had said that he was a personal friend who spent most of his money gambling. His addiction had got so bad that he had been forced to seek a loan from Harvey Lucas, after everybody else had turned him down. It was a move he was soon to regret.

David soon found himself in one of the better parts of Brockleby. His SAT NAV guided him into a road of large, mainly well-maintained semi-detached properties. Number twelve very much resembled most of the other houses, with a garage attached at the side, a newish Ford Focus parked on the drive and a shoulder-high privet hedge serving as a front garden wall.

David rang the bell and waited. For once, he didn't feel concerned about returning to his car and finding that it had been vandalised. Unlike at the two previous addresses he had just visited, there were no youths playing football out in the road. In fact, although it was the school holidays, there were no sign of children whatsoever. Everything was quiet and peaceful.

After a few moments, a woman in a plastic apron opened the front door. She was probably in her early seventies, with white, neatly permed hair. At her side was a brown boxer dog with black liquid eyes. The animal made a sudden attempt to go outside before the woman swiftly grabbed it by the collar.

"I'm looking for Oliver Hughes," said David.

"He doesn't live here anymore," answered the woman, in one of those rather refined voices common to certain people who believe themselves to be a cut above ordinary folk. "Oliver was one of my lodgers for a short while, but I had to tell him to leave a few weeks ago. At first, he got behind with the rent. Then two nasty individuals came to the house and started causing a disturbance. They claimed that Oliver owed them money."

"Do you have any idea where Oliver is now?" asked David.

"Haven't a clue," replied the woman with a casual shake of the head. "What I do know is that he has plenty of debts. Does he owe you money as well?"

"No, it was just a social call," smiled David. "Sorry to have bothered you."

David was feeling frustrated as he strolled back down the garden path. Without addresses for the other three people on Mark's list, he held out little hope of tracing them. None of the names even appeared in the local telephone directory. Even if any one of them had been listed, he would have been reluctant to ring the number. He would have found it extremely difficult to have given a reason for his call. More than likely, the person on the other end of the phone would have never heard of Harvey Lucas.

That evening, while the rest of the family were watching TV, David went into the garden to make a phone call. He was anxious that Alison didn't hear his conversation. Were she to discover that he was conspiring with her ex-partner, she would doubtless try to put a stop to it. Probably she would be putting her friend Maureen on the case.

"How are you getting on with those names I gave you?" asked Mark, after Tina had passed the phone over to him.

"Hopeless," answered David wearily. "They either won't talk or have disappeared without a trace." "Look, I've been doing some thinking since we met up on Saturday", said Mark. "I know where we can get a complete list of Harvey's debtors, with names, addresses and even phone numbers."

"Where?" asked David, eagerly.

"They are mostly sitting on the back seat of his Porsche," said Mark. "He keeps that and all the rest of his paperwork in two large brown envelopes."

"So are you suggesting that we break into his car?" asked David.

"Nothing so crude," laughed Mark. "Just listen to my plan and tell me what you think."

David opened a can of beer as he sank back in his deckchair. The patio door was wide open and he could just make out the familiar theme tune of one of the TV soap operas blaring out from the front room. He had no idea whether the programme was just starting or coming to an end and cared even less. What Mark was saying interested him far more.

"Sounds a bit risky, but I'm prepared to give it a go," said David, once Mark had revealed his plan.

"And are you certain that these brown envelopes contain all the information that we need?"

"Absolutely," replied Mark. "You'll have enough evidence to put an end to this sordid little business venture. Don't forget that as one of Harvey's so-called clients, I have sat in his car while he has been scribbling down notes. Everything is recorded – all the threats and even the violence that he dishes out. It's just so that he remembers what has happened when he next has a meeting with that person."

"So when and where shall we meet?" asked David.

"I could be in Brockleby at eleven tomorrow morning," answered Mark. "Could you meet me at the station? I think it would be unwise of me to be seen walking along the high street in broad daylight."

At eleven o'clock the next day, the two men met as arranged. As David drove along, Mark outlined his plan once more. The details were simple enough, but he was determined that nothing should go wrong. He kept reminding himself that it wasn't just the loan sharks who were after him. The local constabulary were also interested in locating his whereabouts.

"Right, stop here," said Mark, as they were about to pass a cemetery on their left hand side. "If you turn the next corner, you should see a Porsche parked at the side of the lane. It's a silver Cayenne. Harvey Lucas always conducts meetings with his clients in his car at this time of the day. If he has one right now you will have to wait until he is free."

David could feel his stomach churning over as he stepped out of the car. His role seemed simple enough, but he was concerned that something would go wrong. It was too late to back out now, though, after Mark had made the long journey up from Broadstairs.

"See you soon," he said, as his partner was just about to set off for the woods ahead.

"Good luck," replied Mark, as he slipped on a black baseball cap and dark glasses. "And make sure you are waiting for me just beyond the traffic lights."

David took a deep breath as he turned the corner. Sure enough, a silver Cayenne was parked in the lane, but facing the opposite direction. With the sun shining through the car window, it was just possible to make out the back of a head. It was hairless and slightly pink in colour. There were no other occupants though.

The lane was narrow, with woods on one side and the cemetery on the other. As David approached the Porsche, he happened to glance briefly to his left. Through the iron railings, he saw a hearse draw up outside the little chapel. In slow pursuit was a cortege of cars all carrying people dressed in black attire. It seemed a timely reminder of his own mortality and the danger he was just about to face.

David stepped out into the road and stopped beside the Porsche. Looking in through the open window, he was able to have a closer look at the person in the driver's seat. The man was reading a newspaper that was partly spread out over the wheel, while a cigarette smouldered between his thick lips.

"I need a loan and was told that you could help," said David.

"Get in," answered the man, as he casually pointed towards the passenger seat in the front. David's pulse quickened as he walked around to the other side of the car. As he opened the door, he noticed the two brown envelopes on the back seat. Each well worn from constant handling, they had notes scrawled all over them; some in pencil, but most in black ink.

"I need five hundred quid," said David, once he had sat down and shut the door. "I take it that you are Harvey Lucas."

"That's me," replied the man. "I'll start by asking you if you have any form of collateral. For example, do you own a property that could be sold in order to pay off your loan to me should the need arise?"

"No," replied David.

He appreciated that under the circumstances, it was necessary to lie. After all, people with assets rarely went to a loan shark to borrow money. Most reputable financial institutions were prepared to do that, even with the economy in the state that it was in.

"Without collateral, I would be taking a risk in providing you with a loan. Therefore the interest I charge you will have to be quite high," explained Harvey.

"Very well, then," replied David. "Because I'm desperate, I have no choice but to accept your terms."

"Actually, your face looks familiar," said Harvey, taking a closer look at the man in the passenger seat. "I'm sure that I've seen you somewhere before."

David froze. If Harvey had spotted him on the front page of the *Brockleby Times*, then he would have some difficult questions to answer. A teacher and an aspiring

Member of Parliament would hardly be a likely candidate to be borrowing money off back street money lenders.

"You've probably seen me in the high street," he suggested, with a shrug of the shoulders. "I remember now," said Harvey with a broad grin. "It was in The Crown. I often see you drinking in there."

"Of course," replied David, with a sense of relief. "Nice pub, that."

It was a case of mistaken identity. David had no idea where The Crown was. However, he had absolutely no reason to point that out to the loan shark. He wasn't exactly sitting in the car to discuss his social life. There were far more important things on his mind.

At that moment, he saw Mark emerge from the woods. Wishing now to be recognized, he had taken off the baseball cap and sun glasses. Swiftly crossing the road, he walked straight up to the Porsche and kicked the front door on the driver's side. Then he stood back two paces.

"Come and get me, you ugly bastard," he shouted through the open window.

Harvey looked aghast. The Porsche was his pride and joy. He would have acted angrily had anyone have dared to kick the car. The fact that it was Mark Wright who had committed the offence made him even more furious.

Quickly Harvey scrambled out of the car before lunging at Mark. The younger man, though, adeptly swayed out of reach. Then he turned and headed back into the woods, closely followed by the loan shark. Very quickly, the pair of them had disappeared behind the trees and bushes.

Everything was going to plan. Left in the car by himself, David grabbed the two envelopes off the back seat, along with a lever arch file that had been left beside them. Soon he was striding back to his car with the precious evidence he hoped would destroy Harvey Lucas and his nasty little business.

David shouted for joy as he set off in his car. As arranged with his accomplice in crime, he drove for a quarter of a mile before stopping just beyond the first set of traffic lights. Then he sat back and kept his eye on the rear mirror. He couldn't wait to start examining Harvey's business records, but knew that he needed to be patient for just a little bit longer.

Mark had never been in danger of being caught. The star striker recently signed by the King's Arms in Broadstairs simply sprinted away from the overweight money lender. In fact, as he climbed into David's car, Harvey was still back in the woods. Out of breath, he had just flopped down on a wooden bench to rest. Then, picking up a stone, he hurled it at a tree in frustration.

Having exchanged high fives, David drove Mark back to the station. They were in high spirits at having achieved their goal together. A bond was starting to grow between them, even though their lives were so different. One was a pillar of society. The other was a thief on the run from the law.

"So what will you do with Harvey's records?" asked Mark, as the car was approaching the station.

"Have a good read myself, to begin with," answered David. "I need to make certain that I have got the evidence to incriminate Harvey Lucas and his partner. If I have, then the whole lot will be handed over to the police."

"And what about me?" asked Mark. "Will you be giving the Old Bill my latest address?"

"Not possible," replied David with a broad grin. "I've forgotten where you live. However, should the police ever catch up with you, then let me know. I will vouch that because you were under severe duress, you had little choice but to steal that money."

"Cheers, mate," said Mark, as the car stopped and he began to unfasten his seat belt.

"You take care of yourself and those two ladies that you are living with," smiled David, as the two men shook hands. "I'll ring and let you know what has happened to Harvey Lucas and Leo MacDonald. Hopefully, you won't have those two on your trail for very much longer. Remember though, to keep away from Amanda. If you are seen around her school ever again then I shall have no hesitation in going to the police and telling them where you are living".

Suddenly Mark's face dropped.

"Amanda seems to be frightened of me so there seems little point in me causing her anymore distress. You have my word that I will stay away from her in future".

That afternoon, David got down to work. Sitting down at the dining room table, he emptied out the contents of the two brown envelopes. Inside each one was a bulky computer printout. One was a list of client addresses and the other a debtors' list. The latter displayed the borrower's name, amount of the loan, repayments made and the balance outstanding. It was the type of report regularly produced by many perfectly respectable and worthy companies.

Then David turned his attention to the lever arch file. He discovered that it contained mostly information relating to the meetings conducted with clients, with paperwork being filed alphabetically according to the borrower's surname. However, it didn't make for pleasant reading.

"Tenth of January. Punched Atkins in the stomach twice for failing to make his weekly instalment. Threatened more of the same to follow unless overall situation improved."

"Seventeenth of January. Smacked Atkins around the face three times for failing again to pay amount agreed upon last week. Threatened to hit his pregnant wife next time."

There was page after page of similar comments. Although heartily sickened by what he read, David was consoled by the fact that he had found the incriminating evidence that he needed. In what was almost certainly Harvey's own handwriting, he had found what amounted to dozens of confessions concerning not only his own violent and callous behaviour, but also that of his business partner.

Before David finished with the file, he was interested to find out what had been written about Mark Wright. Of course, much had been recorded about his disappearance and the attempts to track him down. However, there was one entry that was of particular interest to him.

"Sixth of July. Sent Maureen round to visit Alison Chambers, Wright's ex-partner. It was possible that she may have known where he is hiding out. AC unable to help, but promised to get in touch if she learns anything."

"Right," muttered David angrily, as he closed the file. "I think there is a third person that the police will be keen to interview. And to think that Alison actually trusted that bloody woman."

CHAPTER TWENTY-EIGHT

At last the train slowed down as it approached Broadstairs station. Mark felt a sense of relief to be back again. Unlike Brockleby, it was where he felt safe. There was no need to walk around wearing dark glasses, unless they were intended to protect his eyes from the sun. Other than Tina, nobody living in the seaside town knew he was in trouble with the law.

There was still a slight nagging doubt that was floating around in his head, though. First he had been spotted on the beach by Tina. Then David Chambers had seen him coming home from the pub. Mark was aware that even Broadstairs wasn't entirely a safe haven for him. Were somebody else to recognize him, he could still be spending a Christmas or two in a prison cell.

Realizing that Mark would be late for lunch, Tina had left a salad out for him. Then, as the hero was eating, he provided her with a full account of the mornings events. He spoke with great pride at what he and David Chambers had managed to accomplish.

"I can't believe you kicked the door of his car," said Tina with a look of amazement. "I bet that Harvey Lucas was livid."

"You should have seen his face," laughed Mark. "I wish I had taken a photograph."

"So do you think that David Chambers will have the necessary evidence to get those two arrested?" asked Tina. "I hope so,", said Mark, as he took a sip of water. "It will be a great weight off my mind if I know Harvey Lucas will no longer be hunting me down."

"So will David let you know what is happening, then?" asked Tina.

Mark nodded.

"He promised to ring me with any news."

"David seems like a really top bloke," said Tina with a fond smile.

That evening, Mark made his way down to the recreation ground. The King's Arms had arranged to take on the White Swan in a friendly match, and he had been invited to play. It was a local derby, as the pubs were in the same street and there was keen rivalry between the two teams.

The evening was perfect for football. It was cooler than it had been during the day, with a gentle breeze in the air. A few spectators were watching as the game kicked off. Some were just passers-by, but most were wives and girlfriends of the players.

Mark knew that he had a lot to live up to. Having acquired a reputation in the Kings Arms as the new goal scoring sensation, he was desperate not to let his team mates down. Little that he had done during his life-time had earned him much respect. Playing football was the exception. He was good and others looked up to him because of it.

Soon after the match kicked off, Mark had a feeling that luck was on his side. The centre back who had been instructed to mark him was small, slow and overweight. With little effort he was able to slip by the defender.

Within ten minutes, he had put the Kings Arms ahead after placing the ball beyond the reach of the lethargic goalkeeper. By the time the referee had blown the full-time whistle, the star striker had gone on to score a hat trick.

During the team talk after the game, the coach was full of praise for Mark. The King's Arms had won by four goals to two and Barry appeared to give his latest signing most of the credit for the victory. Then it was down to the pub to celebrate.

Once more, Mark was the centre of attention. As the hero of the hour, everybody wanted to buy him a drink. Before long he was back and forward to the toilet to relieve himself. It was after making one of these visits that a woman stepped in front of him wearing a big smile.

"I see you haven't lost any of your old magic, then," she said.

"When did you see me play before?" asked Mark, experiencing a sudden panic attack. "When we were at school together," laughed the woman. "I was Lindsey Hook before I got married. You used to sit behind me in class."

"I remember," answered Mark, trying his best to appear calm. "So what are you doing down here in Broadstairs?"

"This is where I live now," explained Lindsey. "About a year ago, Dean and I bought a house just around the corner."

Mark had already assumed that Lindsey was either Dean's wife or girlfriend. For much of the evening, she and the King's Arms goalkeeper had been sitting together with two other couples.

Because the bar was so crowded, the team and their followers had been left with no alternative but to split up into groups.

"Do you ever see any of our old classmates?" asked Mark, hopeful that all might not be lost. "I still stay in touch with a few," replied Lindsey. "Janice Morgan, Pat Cummings and Debbie Hudson. You remember those three, don't you?"

"Yes," said Mark, suddenly feeling as though the bottom was just about to drop out of his world. "Of course, they aren't called those names anymore," smiled Lindsey. "All three are married now. Next time I speak to one of them on the phone, I'll mention that I've met up with you again."

"Do they all still live in Brockleby?" asked Mark, in the faint hope that these ladies might be residing in some foreign country – if not abroad, then some place in Britain where people didn't read the *Brockleby Times*.

"Yes," answered Lindsey, with a nod. "It is only me who has moved away from the town. So are you living down here too, then?"

Mark nodded. "My girlfriend and I have got a place a few streets away."

"I must be getting back to my husband, I suppose," said Lindsey. "It's good to see you again."

By the time Mark returned to his seat, his teammates had bought him two more pints of best bitter. For the moment, he decided to forget his conversation with Lindsey and just enjoy himself. For this evening, he would bask in the glory that was being showered on him. Tomorrow would be soon enough to start looking for somewhere safer to live – a place far away, where his past life was less likely to catch up with him. Perhaps a seaside town in Cornwall, with a beach covered in golden sand.

David had spent well over an hour at the police station. When he finally drove away, he was feeling slightly uneasy. The version of events that he had given hadn't been entirely accurate. In order to conceal Mark's whereabouts, it had been necessary to tell Detective Inspector Mitchell a lie. He had said that his accomplice had initially got in touch with him.

"And why would Mark Wright have done that, Sir?" the detective inspector had asked with a look of surprise.

"Because he had heard that I was making enquiries about Harvey Lucas," had been David's reply. "So why did you decide to become a sleuth, Sir?" the detective inspector had then gone on to ask. "Surely if you had grounds to believe that Harvey Lucas was acting improperly, you should have come to us first. That is why we are here."

David had made no attempt to defend his actions. However, having put himself at risk in trying to help many vulnerable people, he felt that he deserved some credit, as well as criticism. Alison saw no reason to praise him, either. After he had repeated to her the slightly distorted version of events that he had given to Detective Inspector Mitchell, she looked furious.

"Mark is a thief," she snapped. "You should have had him arrested."

"But Mark was one of the victims," David protested. "He committed robbery because Harvey Lucas and his partner were terrorising him. Others will be driven to crime or even suicide unless those evil buggers are put behind bars."

"And there's another thing," said Alison with a look of horror. "You shouldn't have got involved. If those men are violent, then they might inflict harm on somebody in this family. It could be you, me or even one of the children. Did you consider that before you decided to play Sir Galahad?"

"But they don't know where we live," replied David, while appreciating at the same time that his answer sounded pretty lame.

"But just suppose that they do happen to find our address," said Alison. "Just make certain that your picture doesn't appear in the *Brockleby Times* in the next few weeks. I know you are looking for recognition in order to win votes at the next general election, but perhaps you should stay out of the limelight for a while."

"I didn't do it to win votes," objected David. "I did it because it was the right thing to do. I wanted to rescue many people from a life of bullying."

"Well, you should have consulted me first before you went ahead with your little plan," answered Alison bitterly, before storming out of the room.

David gave his wife time to calm down. After reading a newspaper for ten minutes, he stood up and made his way into the hall. From the kitchen, he could hear the clatter of pans. Having taken a deep breath, he gently pushed open the door. A rather apologetic smile appeared on his face as he cautiously entered the room.

"If it's any consolation to you," he began before clearing his throat. "Mark has promised that after to-day he will never set foot in Brockleby again. In any case, he feels that the risk of being recognized is too great. So you needn't worry anymore about him hanging around outside Amanda's school."

"And how do you know you can trust him?", asked Alison.

"Because I've made him aware, that I shall disclose his whereabouts to the police if he breaks his promise", replied David.

Alison didn't reply. Instead, she reached across and switched on the radio, before continuing to prepare the evening meal. David noticed, however, that her facial muscles relaxed ever so slightly. Then he decided it was time to give his wife news that would shock her even more.

"By the way, your friend Maureen is a fraud. She is Harvey's wife and probably couldn't give a damn about Mrs Fisher," he said, with a look of disgust. "She was looking for Mark in order to get the money back that was owed to the loan sharks."

For a moment Alison looked stunned.

"How do you know?", she asked at last.

"Because it is all there in Harvey's files," answered David. "You were just being used to help track Mark down. I always knew there was something suspicious about that woman."

Alison picked up a disk cloth and flung it in the sink.

"I'll kill that bitch if I ever lay my eyes on her.", she shouted.

❧ ❧

Harvey sat on the wooden bench for five minutes or so while trying to catch his breath. Having lost Mark Wright in the woods, he had given up any hope of catching up with him. Frustrated and angry, the moneylender trudged back towards the road. He was anxious to see what damage had been inflicted on his car door. Although it was beautifully designed, the manufacturers had probably never considered that it might have to withstand a good kicking someday.

A shock awaited him when he returned to the car: not the dent in the door, which he had rather expected to find anyway. It was that his new client had gone and more worrying, so had the brown envelopes and file on the back seat. Desperately, he searched the Porsche. It was a task that lasted only a few seconds. Satisfied that the records hadn't slipped under one of the seats, it was blatantly obvious to him that he had been robbed.

His first inclination was to go looking for the culprits – drive around the nearby roads and see whether he could spot one or even both of them. Then the red mist began to clear. With clients to meet and money to collect, he hadn't got time to waste. In any case, it suddenly dawned on him that all might not be lost after all.

Immediately, he rang Maureen on his mobile. As always, he expected her to drop everything and come to his assistance. "Print off a debtors' list and bring it down here as quickly as you can," he ordered brusquely. "I can't meet with clients without knowing how much they owe and when it is due."

"But I got you one off the computer this morning," Maureen protested. "What have you done with it?"

"It got nicked by Mark Wright and one of his mates," snapped Harvey. "But how?" gasped Maureen.

"I haven't got time to go into the details right now," replied Harvey impatiently. "All I will say is that Mark Wright will wish he had never been born. Unfortunately for him, I recognized his friend and know where he can be found. So once Leo and I get hold of that little creep who took my records, we'll have him squealing like a pig."

"Who is this friend of Mark Wright's, then?" asked Maureen.

"Tell you later," answered Harvey. "Just bring me down that printout and be sharp about it. There's a client coming down the lane now, and I need to check his details before my meeting with him can go ahead."

※ ※

David was suddenly reluctant to go out. Alison had managed to convince him that he needed to stay at home in order to try and protect his family. He was praying that Harvey Lucas hadn't been able to place him. Having had so much publicity in recent weeks and with his connections with the Labour Party so well known, he realized that he would be easy to track down. So when the doorbell rang at ten o'clock in the evening, he almost jumped out of his skin.

It was only two days since he had taken the file and brown envelopes. The children were up in bed, while both he and Alison were falling asleep in front of the TV. The Chambers weren't expecting any visitors and it was rare for late-night callers to descend on them unannounced.

David tried to put on a brave face for Alison's sake. After pulling himself up from the settee, he crossed the room and stepped out into the hall. Through the glass in the front door, he saw a shape, but it was too dark outside for it to be distinct.

"Who is it?" he asked in a hoarse whisper.

"Alec Stokes," came the reply from outside.

David heaved a sigh of relief as he opened the front door. It was unlikely that any visitor to the house had ever received a more welcoming smile.

"Just passing, so I thought I would give you the news," said Alec, trying with some difficulty to contain his excitement. "Tony was telling me in the bar this evening that Andre Brooks is coming down to Brockleby in two weeks. He is keen to meet all the members, but especially you, as the Labour Party candidate."

"Great," beamed David.

"Tony wants a photograph of you and Andre standing side by side," continued Alec. "He thinks that it would look impressive on the front page of the *Brockleby Times* and help raise your image in the town. He wants to make sure that as many people as possible get to know who you are."

With some difficulty, David managed to keep on smiling. The last thing he wanted at the moment was to see his face plastered all over the front page of the local paper – not, that is, while the loan sharks were free to hunt him down.

The following morning, he rang Detective Inspector Mitchell. It had been three days since he had handed over Harvey's records, and he was desperate for a progress report. He wanted to be reassured that the police weren't dragging their feet. The sleepless nights were beginning to grind him down.

"We are working on the case," said the detective inspector. "I can't release any further information at the moment, I'm afraid"

Alison was frustrated with the response. Concerned about her own safety and that of the children, she decided that the four of them should move in with her mother for the time being. David, though, refused to join the rest of the family. He wanted to be on hand to protect the house if the need arose. As he had taken Harvey's property, he was concerned that the two bullies might take their revenge by breaking in and smashing the place to pieces. Not that he had any intention of standing up to them but, rather to alert the police on his mobile.

That evening, David had company in the form of Ian Porter. As arranged, the Fellowship priest had come around for their little meeting. It was the second time the two had sat down together in just a few weeks. On the first occasion, they had ended up having a heated theological argument.

As the weather was warm, they sat out on the lawn in deckchairs. While David wore only shorts, Ian was more formally dressed in a dark suit, having just led a church service.

To begin with, the conversation was cordial enough. They discussed the weather before going on to enquire about each other's family. Finally, Ian got around to bringing up the subject that had prompted his visit.

"Look, we feel that in the past, the Fellowship may have treated you rather harshly," he began, with an apologetic smile. "Perhaps it is about time that bridges were mended between us."

"So what has changed?" asked David, with mock surprise. "I am less sympathetic towards your beliefs than I was eight years ago. That was surely clear to both of us when last we met."

"It is a matter of forgiveness," replied Ian, with that pious look common to saints on stained glass windows.

David wasn't to be fooled. Simon had already given him an advance warning of Ian's motives. They had nothing to do with Christian teachings. The priest was merely acting in the best interests of the Fellowship. It had always been that way. He seemed to care little for those who weren't followers of the sect.

"What exactly am I being forgiven for?" enquired David with raised eyebrows.

Ian ran his fingers through his thick, greying hair. He was reluctant to offend anyone who might be of use to him in the future, particularly a person with influence who could assist the Fellowship in purchasing that piece of land next to the church. So the priest decided against informing his host that he was being pardoned for upsetting his parents eight years ago by rejecting the word of the Lord.

"Just a slip of the tongue," he explained, a little uneasily. "Actually, your parents have invited you and your family to come and visit them."

"So why didn't they make contact with me themselves, instead of sending you along with a message?" asked David.

"I think they were too embarrassed to ask you themselves," explained Ian. "Anyway, can I tell them that you are happy to accept their invitation to visit?"

Before David had a chance to reply, the telephone rang. After apologising to his guest for the interruption, he disappeared through the open patio doors and into the hall. As Alison was away with the children, he had been expecting her to call.

"This is Detective Inspector Mitchell," said the voice on the other end of the line. "I'm ringing to let you know that Harvey Lucas and Leo MacDonald have just been arrested and charged with grievous bodily harm."

"What a relief," sighed David.

"I suggest you thank your lucky stars," said the detective inspector. "There is a gentleman fitting your description who has just been admitted to the General Hospital with severe head injuries. Those two thugs set on him earlier this evening in The Crown. The poor bloke went to the loo and came out a little later on a stretcher. According to Harvey Lucas, he mistook the victim for you."

David froze as the information sunk in. He realised that he was partly responsible for the vicious assault on a perfectly innocent man – somebody who had taken a good hiding just because he happened to have a similar appearance.

"Is this man likely to die?" he asked anxiously.

"Too early to say," replied the detective inspector.

"When we sat in the car together, Harvey Lucas mentioned that he thought that he had seen me in The Crown," said David, as he recalled the conversation. "Of course it wasn't me, because I have never been in that pub. However, I didn't correct him because I was happy for that animal to confuse me with somebody else."

"And no doubt as those two were battering the living daylights out of that poor devil, they kept asking him where Mark Wright was hiding," said the detective inspector. "We won't know that for sure until the victim regains consciousness. Assuming, of course, that he does."

"How are your investigations going into the money-lending racket?" asked David.

"Extremely well," answered the detective inspector. "Soon we should have enough on that pair to put them inside for a very long time."

"And are you going to question Maureen Lucas about her role in her husband's nasty little business?" asked David.

"As it happens, Mrs Lucas is down here at the station this very moment answering questions", replied the detective inspector.

Once the call was finished, David immediately rang Alison with the good news. Naturally, she was greatly relieved and agreed to come home with the children the following day. At present, the two youngest ones were fast asleep in bed, so it seemed only sensible to keep them at Grandma's just a little bit longer.

David briefly considered ringing Mark Wright and telling him of the two arrests, but then decided that the call could wait. In any case, he felt that it would be impolite to leave his visitor for too long. However, when he went back into the garden, he saw that Ian Porter was preparing to go. He was standing up, brushing down his jacket with his hand.

"So will you be accepting your parents invitation to visit them?" asked the priest.

"I will need to discuss it with my wife first," replied David. "Alison has never liked the idea of our children having anything to do with the Fellowship." Ian immediately stopped brushing.

"I can't see why she should object."

"Because she thinks that some of your beliefs are quite obnoxious. For example, like me, she detests the way the Fellowship demonise homosexuals. Surely gay people are just part of the rich tapestry of life," said David.

"Thou shalt not lie with mankind as with womankind. It is an abomination. Leviticus, chapter 18, verse 22," quoted Ian.

"And how about Matthew, chapter nineteen, verse twenty one. If thou wilt be perfect go and sell all that thou hast and give to the poor," replied David with a twinkle in his eye. "When are you going to start putting all your possessions up for sale, then?"

"I shall see myself out," said Ian, as he headed towards the patio door. "I will ask the Fellowship to pray for you."

"You might also ask them to say a prayer for a car park," smiled David. "Personally, I think that the land next to your church would be ideal for a children's playground."

CHAPTER TWENTY-NINE

The last few days had been lonely by himself. Without the sound of children racing around and screaming, the house had seemed like a morgue without the bodies. David was relieved that his period of isolation was about to come to an end. Before setting off to collect the family, he decided to ring Mark Wright. He was anxious to pass on the good news that Detective Inspector Mitchell had given him the previous evening.

It was Tina who picked up the phone. After hearing her speak, David immediately suspected that something was wrong. Having been told that the moneylenders had been arrested, she seemed hardly ecstatic. Of course, she said that she was pleased, but her voice sounded rather flat. It was almost as though she didn't care in the slightest.

"Mark has gone," she said. "Gone where?" asked David.

"All I know is that it is far from here," replied Tina with a sob. "He left early yesterday morning without as much as a word to either me or Auntie Angela. He just left a note on the kitchen table."

"What did it say?" asked David gently.

"Just that people were beginning to recognize him in this town and he needed to move much further away from Brockleby," said Tina, with a few more sobs.

David wanted to comfort her as best he could. There were few words of consolation that he was able to think of at that moment, though. After Tina had read out Mark's note in full over the phone, he was surprised that the brief message had lacked any warmth or tenderness. It just ended with a thank you for having helped him out during a very difficult period.

"So what will you do now?" he asked. "Continue to stay and look after your aunt or return to Brockleby?"

"I don't know," answered Tina, with a weary sigh. "At the moment, I can't decide what to do." David was reluctant to offer any advice. He just wished her luck as they said goodbye. Quite obviously, Tina had been treated shabbily. However, he hoped that in time, she would come to see that things had probably worked out for the best. Sharing a life with a wanted criminal was hardly ideal. Mark would be constantly looking over his shoulder unless the long arm of the law was on the point of arresting him. If they were to be torn apart, then it might as well be now rather than later.

On the way to picking up the family, David stopped off in the high street. Feeling guilty that those he lived with had felt the need to leave home for a few days because of his actions, he decided to buy presents for everyone. Then, as a further treat for the children, he would take them swimming in the afternoon. The Cavendish was a large sports complex just outside the town. Its two heated swimming pools were always popular during the summer holidays.

David was about to step into a florist to buy Alison a plant when he heard somebody calling his name. Turning around, he saw one of his fellow teachers from Brookway Manor coming towards him. It was Laura Nixon. Since the end of term, she had developed a healthy tan, but the expression on her face was rather serious.

"I've heard some distressing news about Sophie Duncan," she began. "Apparently a few days ago, she took an overdose of sleeping pills."

"Oh no," cried David in horror. "How is she?"

Laura shook her head sadly.

"I'm afraid she managed to kill herself."

David froze. After breaking up with Sophie, he had done his best to put her out of his mind. Now, suddenly, he could feel those pent-up emotions rising to the surface. Even so, he was aware of the need to keep himself in check. On no account did he want to give Laura Nixon any hint that he had been anything other than a colleague and friend of the young English teacher.

"How did you manage to find out?" he asked, trying hard to steady his voice.

"I just happened to ring her number down in Portsmouth to have a little chat. As you know, after leaving Brookway Manor, she went down there to stay with her parents for a while. Anyway, it was her mother who answered the phone and gave me the terrible news. Poor woman could hardly speak for crying. It was absolutely awful," said Laura, who seemed very close to tears herself.

"Are you going to the funeral?" asked David.

"Unfortunately, it's next week, when I'll be on holiday in Turkey," replied Laura. "Actually, I was just about to follow you into the florists to buy a wreath. I have all the details if you would like to send one, too."

David readily agreed to the suggestion. However, seeing that Laura had copied down the time, date and the crematorium where the funeral was to take place, he decided to attend. It was something that he felt compelled to do. Although it was too late to apologize to Sophie for the heartless way he had treated her, at least he would have the opportunity to pay his last respects. In the unlikely event that the deceased was looking down on him from above, she might just be prepared to forgive him.

"I'll go," he said as he searched through the catalogue for a suitable wreath. "It would be nice if somebody were to go along to the crematorium to represent Brookway Manor."

"That is kind of you," answered Laura with a warm smile. "I'm sure that everyone at the school would be most grateful."

David left Laura to finish her shopping and went for a walk. The news of Sophie's death had left him in shock. He was concerned that she had taken her life because of their break-up. Had there been a suicide note, he wondered. Perhaps all might be revealed at the funeral, he decided.

For a time, David walked without any clear idea where he was heading. He wandered along back streets that were unfamiliar to him. Pedestrians passed him by but all were strangers. He saw shops, pubs and other landmarks that he never knew existed. In a district of mainly terraced houses without garages, cars were often parked with two wheels on the pavement.

Today though, David had little interest in his surroundings. In his head he was reliving those happy times shared with Sophie: intimate moments in the bedroom or just sitting in her flat with a take-away. He thought of those occasions when he had tried to help the young English teacher overcome her fears in the classroom. Having been in love, such memories now seemed precious, and he savoured each and every one of them.

He tried hard not to dwell on the way he had ended the relationship. It was just too painful. That night when he had told her that he wouldn't be leaving Alison would haunt him for evermore. Telling her that they would be spending the rest of their lives together had all been a wicked deception. Of course, it had been easy enough to justify his behaviour to himself at the time. He had done the right thing in respect of his family and his career. Poor Sophie, though, had been made to suffer.

Suddenly, David's thoughts returned to the present. Hearing familiar ring tones he immediately grabbed his mobile from out of his pocket. A quick glance at the screen advised him that his wife was calling.

"Where are you?" asked Alison. "The kids and I are waiting for you to come and pick us up." David looked down at his watch. It came as a complete shock to him that he had been walking aimlessly for over two hours. Where the time had gone was a complete mystery to him.

"Sorry, I've been delayed," he answered, before immediately turning on his heels and heading in the general direction of the car. "Be with you as soon as possible."

That evening, David appreciated having his family home again. Once the children were in bed, he was able to have a long conversation with Alison about the events that had taken place over the past few days. He told her about Sophie but managed to hide the real extent of his feelings concerning her suicide.

They also discussed Ian Porter's proposal to build bridges with the family. As David had expected, Alison was vehemently opposed to the idea. She had always been suspicious of the Fellowship and feared that they might try to interfere in the lives of the children. She didn't want her offspring to develop strange beliefs that could turn them into social outcasts.

However, the conversation was dominated by the arrest of the moneylenders. Alison was relieved that the two men were no longer at large, but she was also keen that Maureen Lucas should receive her just desserts. This was a woman she now hated with a vengeance.

"I hope they lock her up and throw away the key," she said bitterly. "To think that the bitch fooled me into thinking that she was trying to get Mrs Fisher's money back for her. Then I discover that she was just using me as a tool of her nasty little business."

"I believe you should speak to Detective Inspector Mitchell," said David thoughtfully. "What Maureen was doing was fraudulent, and you are a first-hand witness to that. Of course, the police will hopefully charge her with other offences, but just in case they don't...."

"You're right," said Alison with a firm nod. "I'll ring the detective inspector in the morning."

The following day, Andre Brooks arrived in Brockleby as planned. It was to be a very brief visit, because as leader of the opposition he had a number of engagements to fulfil. However he was keen to meet up with the membership, particularly, the man who had just been selected as the new parliamentary candidate for the constituency.

Andre Brooks looked every bit like a prime minister in waiting, with a charming smile, well groomed and smartly dressed in a dark suit, probably a recent purchase from Savile Row. In his late forties, he was married to an attractive wife who often appeared in glossy women's magazines and had three children. Although not considered to possess the greatest mind in his party, he looked good on TV, which more than compensated for any intellectual deficiency.

Bert Vine and David were waiting to greet their illustrious guest on the forecourt as his chauffeur parked the car. Neither had met Andre Brooks before, although they had both spoken to him on the phone. After the introductions were over, the party leader was taken inside to meet some of the other local members. As it was a weekday morning, though, there was only a scattering of people about. Those of employment age were mostly at work.

David led Andre around and introduced him to those that were present. With his engaging smile, the party leader shook hands and said a few words to each one. Unused to speaking with famous people, some appeared overawed, but others took the occasion in their stride.

As usual, the bar was cluttered up with boxes of political leaflets. They were either lying on the floor or on top of tables. Nobody had bothered to tidy up for the benefit of Andre Brooks. In fact, many of the members thought that the party leader would be impressed with what he saw. They felt that the mess was a reflection of the activity that was taking place in the association.

Andre was offered an alcoholic drink, but asked for black coffee instead. He wasn't concerned about being caught drunk at the wheel because he had his chauffeur waiting outside for him. It was more a matter of keeping a clear head, he explained.

Amongst those present, only one wasn't a member. A photographer from the *Brockleby Times* had been invited along to take pictures. One was to appear the following week on the front page of the local newspaper. Readers would have the opportunity to see Andre Brooks and David Chambers standing side by side with broad smiles on their faces.

Finally, the Labour Party leader glanced down at his watch. As usual, Andre Brooks needed to be somewhere else shortly, but he wanted to have a brief chat with the newly selected parliamentary candidate before heading off. That, after all, had been the main purpose of his visit.

David led the way up to his new office. The thought of a private meeting with the great man made him feel apprehensive. He was aware that behind the charming smile, Andre Brooks had been studying him very carefully.

"Right," began Andre breezily, when the two men were sitting facing one another across David's wide desk. "Brockleby is one of Labour's biggest target seats for the next general election, so it's essential that every effort is made to take it off the Tories."

"Of course," said David, with a firm nod.

"The Coalition don't have to call the election for another three years. However, with the tensions mounting between the Tories and Lib Dems, we may not have to wait until 2015. That means you and your team of activists should be campaigning on both national and local issues now. Make certain that you get plenty of publicity in the local press and produce lots of leaflets to drop through those letterboxes."

Andre Brooks seemed to like to talk, so David needed to do little more than sit back and listen.

He was aware that the Labour Party leader had wanted another candidate to fight the seat. Unfortunately for him, though, members of the association had rejected Heather Marsh and had selected a little-known schoolteacher instead.

"A word of advice," said Andre, after taking yet another quick glance at his watch. "If you want to succeed as an MP, it is as well to support party policy. I understand from Bert Vine that you are not happy with some of the things that Labour stand for at the moment. Tuition fees, for example."

"I believe that education should be free for all," replied David.

"But the country faces a debt crisis. To be perceived as a creditable party, Labour needs to be seen to be supporting measures to reduce public expenditure. Tuition fees are one means to show that we are serious," explained Andre.

"But in the long term, spending less on education is a false economy," David protested. "There will be fewer young people qualified to fill the jobs of the future when they become available. We will just end up paying out more in unemployment benefits."

Andre shook his head.

"Too many have been going to university. We need more young people to take up apprenticeships, and learn the skills that will help them to become builders, plumbers and electricians."

"So before very long, all our doctors and lawyers will be coming from wealthy backgrounds. It sounds to me as though you want to take Britain back to the past," said David scornfully.

"Whatever the rights and wrongs of the case, tuition fees are here to stay," answered Andre, with a shrug of the shoulders. "Anyone who ends up serving in my cabinet will have to accept that fact. Unless you wish to spend the whole of your time at Westminster sitting on the back benches, you'd do well to remember that."

"What is power if it means sacrificing your principles?" said David moodily.

"And what good are principles without the power to implement them?" countered Andre with one of his engaging smiles.

David allowed the great man to have the last word on the subject. Having checked his watch yet again, Andre rose to his feet. It was his way of announcing that the meeting had come to a close. Being on a very tight schedule, he was anxious to get away.

David, alongside other members of the association, stood and watched as Andre's chauffeur-driven car disappeared into the distance. He had been disappointed with the man who was considered to be a prime minister-in-waiting. Of course he ticked all the right boxes that seemed to be expected of a politician in modern times: white, male, in his forties, upper middle class, looked good on TV and adept at sidestepping difficult questions.

David had always held the opinion that the Labour Party leader lacked conviction. His brief meeting with the man had done little to change his mind on the matter. Andre Brooks didn't seem to possess a radical vision for Britain's future; a zeal, perhaps, for creating a fairer, more equal society. In fact, if elected to power, it seemed highly unlikely that his government would act very differently from the Coalition.

After having consumed a pint of best bitter in the bar, David went home to lunch. It was another warm and sunny day, and he planned to spend the afternoon in the garden with a book. As soon as he opened the front door,

Alison immediately emerged from the kitchen. The look on her face suggested that she had some important news to give him.

"I rang Detective Inspector Mitchell this morning about Maureen, as you suggested. Anyway, during our conversation he told me that Harvey Lucas and his partner are now on a murder charge. That man in the pub that they assaulted died late last night," she announced rather dramatically.

David stared at her in disbelief. As the intended victim, he had thanked his lucky stars that somebody else had been beaten up rather than him. The death of the man, though, now made the moneylenders' mistake even more scary.

"I feel partly responsible," he said as the news gradually sunk in. "I allowed Harvey Lucas to think that it was me who he had seen drinking in The Crown. Perhaps I should try to make it up to the victim's family in some way."

"You'll do nothing of the kind", warned Alison, with a threatening look in her eye. "According to the detective inspector, The Crown has a reputation for attracting criminal types. He told me that the victim was actually a member of a drug trafficking ring that the police have been closely monitoring. Maureen Lucas is so scared about reprisals that she has asked for police protection."

"Now that police numbers have been cut, I can't see her getting that," replied David.

"Unless she ends up in a police cell, of course," replied Alison, with a sardonic smile. "The detective inspector took a keen interest when I told him that Maureen was using deceptive means in order to get hold of Mrs Fisher's money. He has also started making enquiries into the part she played in her husband's shady little money-lending business."

As planned, David spent the afternoon in a deckchair on the lawn. For the first time in a while, he had the opportunity to sit and read a novel without interruption. Alison had taken the two younger children down to the park, while Amanda had gone to visit a friend. Because he was at work, even the next-door neighbour, who had a habit of popping his head over the fence for a chat, wouldn't be disturbing him.

However, David found it difficult to concentrate on reading. His mind just kept wandering. The book that he had borrowed from the local library was unable to hold his attention for too long. He had to keep reading paragraphs over and over again to try and make any sense of them.

The memory of Sophie was beginning to haunt him again. The idea that he might be responsible for her death was weighing heavily on his conscience. He cursed himself for the callous way he had treated her – pretending that they were going to spend the rest of their lives together and then suddenly just dumping her without warning. The timing couldn't have been worse, either. The poor little angel had probably felt that she had failed as a teacher. Then, without pity, he had come along and kicked her while she was down.

After a while, he fell asleep. He dreamt that he was back in Sophie's old flat. Together, they sat on the sofa eating pizza and laughing happily. Then four men in black appeared in the lounge carrying a coffin and he pleaded with them to go away. They didn't seem to take any notice of him, though. It was as though he was invisible.

Sophie had changed. Having been wearing a red jumper and jeans, she was now dressed in a silk shroud. Her face, which had shone with happiness, was blank and deathly white, while her body had become stiff and lifeless as the men lifted it up and placed it into the mahogany box before nailing down the lid.

Suddenly, he woke up with a start. It took him a few moments to appreciate that Amanda was standing by his side. Next to her was a girl roughly the same size and age. David recognised her as Gemma Bickle, his stepdaughter's closest friend.

"You know that we are going to Spain the week after next," began Amanda, rather sheepishly. "Is it possible that Gemma could come, too?"

David smiled to himself. His relationship with Amanda had been poor of late. They always seemed to be getting on each other's nerves. It was something that was beginning to bother him. The tension between them had also been upsetting Alison. There was a strong likelihood that arguments could break out between him and his stepdaughter in Spain which would spoil the holiday for everyone.

The idea of taking Gemma Bickle appealed to him. Amanda was less likely to get bored and irritable if she had somebody of the same age to keep her company. Hopefully, she wouldn't be moping around and upsetting the rest of the family by making caustic remarks. The girls would be taking themselves off and doing their own thing.

"I'm agreeable," smiled David. "However, I will need to speak with the travel agent. It may be too late to get Gemma a seat on the plane or to squeeze her in at the hotel."

"Mum has already checked and everything is fine," said Amanda excitedly. "She just wanted to make sure that you are happy about taking another young person."

"Tell mum to make an extra booking, then," answered David with a warm smile.

"Thanks, Dad," said Amanda, as she bent down to give her stepfather a hug. "I promise we won't cause you any problems while we are away."

David was taken by surprise. It was the first time for a while that Amanda had showed any sign of affection towards him. He hoped that it might be the start of better things to come between them. For his part, he was happy to make the effort.

CHAPTER THIRTY

The funeral service was due to start at two o'clock in the afternoon. David arrived fifteen minutes early and was directed into a large reception room by a member of staff at the crematorium. Inside, strangers in dark clothing with sombre faces were gathered together in small groups. Those that spoke did so in hushed voices, as though they feared offending the dead.

The room was steadily filling up. Having found a suitable space in the far corner, David stood with his back to the wall studying some of the other mourners. After only a few minutes, he was confident that he had identified Sophie's parents. Looking slightly uneasy, various people were wondering over to the couple and appeared to be offering them their condolences.

David considered introducing himself, but decided to leave it until after the service. He was anxious to express his deepest sympathy to the family, like everyone else. A part of him wanted to tell them that he shared their grief. Like them, he had loved Sophie, but in a way, perhaps his pain was even worse. Having treated her so despicably in the last few weeks of her young life, he was now suffering from remorse.

The mourners were eventually shepherded into a small chapel. As they took their places on the rows of pews, all eyes gazed on the coffin at the front. It had been placed on a plinth with rollers, known as a catafalque. A recording of Bach's 'Jesu Joy Of Mans Desiring' brought tears to the eyes of many who were now assembled.

The reverend leading the service wore a black cassock. He was short and tubby, with rosy cheeks.

After welcoming the congregation, he invited them to say a prayer with him before announcing the first hymn. Like others present, David would have struggled to remember the words had it not been for the order of service. It was printed on two A4-sized sheets of paper, which had been folded in half and then stapled together.

Later, the reverend left the pulpit and his place was taken by the man David had earlier assumed to be Sophie's father. Tall and lean, with thick white hair, he was probably in his late fifties. For several minutes, he gazed upon the eulogy that was written down in front of him. Clearly unable to trust himself to speak, he needed a little time to steady himself. Then, having brushed a tear from the corner of his eye with a handkerchief, he finally began.

Mr Duncan painted a glowing picture of his daughter as a child: sweet, gentle, loving and always full of fun. He told how she had loved dancing, horse riding and swimming, and how Sophie had excelled in her schoolwork before going on to university, where she was awarded with a degree. Then, how she had finally achieved her lifetime ambition of becoming a qualified teacher.

So far, Mr Duncan had managed to speak without any outward sign of distress. Suddenly though, he began to struggle as he tried to overcome his emotions. It seemed that in the very last few weeks of her life, Sophie had begun to lose weight and started to complain of abdominal pains. For some time, she had been passing blood during her visits to the toilet, but had failed to seek medical advice. When at last, she underwent an examination, the consultant confirmed the worst. The cancer in her bowels had reached an advanced state and was beginning to spread to other parts of the body.

Sophie's suicide note provided the rest of the story. Concerned about having to be dependent on others, a loss of dignity and the pain that was to get progressively worse, she had taken an overdose of sleeping pills. It wasn't until the following morning that her body was discovered.

Mrs Duncan had screamed when she had entered her bedroom. The cup of tea that she had brought for her daughter just dropped from her hand.

David felt a tear trickling down his cheek. He had no idea that Sophie was anything other than a healthy woman. However, he had read enough about bowel cancer to know that those afflicted can go on leading a normal active life, while being completely unaware as to what is happening to them. He also knew that cancer often spreads much more quickly in younger people than in older sufferers.

With an amazing amount of self-control, Mr Duncan managed to complete his eulogy. His wife patted him affectionately on the arm as he returned to his seat. The grief that they had both suffered since their daughter's death would have probably brought them even closer together.

Suddenly, the coffin started moving backwards along the catafalque. Then, having reached a certain point, it disappeared behind the two curtains once they had come together. The time had come when the wooden box and the body inside were about to be incinerated. The beautiful Sophie would be no more than a pile of smouldering ashes. Memories would forever live on, though, in the minds of those who had come to mourn her.

Once the service had been brought to a close, those that were present made their way into the next room. Upon a long oak table by the wall were laid the wreaths that had been sent. They provided a splash of colour on such a gloomy occasion. David spotted his own after casting his eye up and down the line several times. It was a beautiful array of Anthuriums, Calla lilies, Gerbera and Carnations in mango, lemon, white and green.

David waited his turn in order to pass on his condolences to Sophie's parents. Finally when others had drifted away he got his opportunity to speak with Mrs Duncan. Under her wide brimmed black hat with lace, her eyes were red from weeping. However she managed a smile for all those expressing their sympathy.

"Sorry to hear of your sad loss," said David, as he shook Mrs Duncan by the hand. "I'm a teacher at Brookway Manor. Sophie and I were friends."

"Sophie mentioned some of the other teachers at her school," replied Mrs Duncan. "She may have mentioned you. Could I ask your name?"

"David Chambers," came the slightly mumbled reply.

Mrs Duncan nodded. She was finally able to put a face to the name. Sophie had talked a great deal about Mr Chambers. She had spoken about bringing him down to Portsmouth for the weekend and even sharing the same bedroom.

"Sophie seemed to regard you as a little more than just a friend," said Mrs Duncan somewhat disdainfully.

"She was under the impression that you intended to leave your wife and children for her."

David stared down at the floor. He felt like a naughty schoolboy standing in front of the headmaster. Suddenly, he regretted his decision to come over and introduce himself. As a bereaved mother, Mrs Duncan was suffering enough without having something else to cause her grief he thought to himself.

"I admit to acting shamefully," said David, wishing that the floor would swallow him up. "Oh, you aren't entirely to blame," said Mrs Duncan, suddenly sounding less reproachful. "Sophie was always chasing married men. I used to tell her to set her sights on single ones, but she wouldn't listen."

David was relieved that somebody standing behind him had caught Mrs Duncan's attention.

Stepping aside, he allowed a short gentleman with a grey beard to come forward and express his condolences. Meanwhile, Mr Duncan was now surrounded by three elderly ladies who were nodding gravely, while appearing to be hanging on to his every word.

David began to edge his way towards the door. If his presence was causing distress, then there seemed little point in him hanging around. He had accomplished what he had set out to do. He had paid his last respects to Sophie while finding out why she had taken her life – not because he had treated her badly. She had wanted to die peacefully and avoid the horrors of cancer that were gradually taking over her body.

When David arrived home he found a letter waiting for him. He didn't need to open the envelope to know who it was from. His father's untidy scrawl was the worst example of handwriting he had ever come across. At first, he was concerned that something had happened to his mother or some other family member. However, he smiled once he had read John Chambers' brief letter.

Dear David,

I am writing to invite you and your family to visit us. Perhaps you would be so kind as to ring me, in order that we can set a date that is convenient for everyone.

The Fellowship have come to the conclusion that they may have been too harsh on those members who have left our church in the past. Perhaps we should have been more understanding and helped them as they struggled to accept the word of the Lord. Instead, we abandoned them to follow in the ways of the world – a path that will ultimately lead them to eternal damnation.

Your mother will be preparing a meal for the occasion. Unfortunately, because you no longer share our Christian beliefs, we will have to sit down to eat separately. It can easily be arranged, as we have tables both in the dining room and in the lounge.

Love and best wishes,

Dad.

David passed the letter to Alison. Then he watched in amusement as his wife's face turned almost crimson. She looked as though she might be about to explode at any moment.

"They think they just need to snap their fingers and we will come running," she said angrily. "You go if you wish, but the kids and I are staying well clear. That lot aren't right in the head."

David took the letter back and began tearing it up into tiny pieces. He had suffered greatly after having been expelled from the Eternal Fellowship eight years earlier. Having been cut adrift, he had longed for the companionship of the family and friends with whom he had suddenly lost touch. Now, though, the wounds had healed. He had built a new life for himself, and the old one was little more than a distant memory.

"There is little point in me going, either," he said, with a shake of the head. "It would only lead to arguments. What is the point of trying to repair bridges between us if they are just going to crumble and fall apart again? I agree even less with the Fellowship's beliefs and view on the world than I did when we parted company. Now I even question the existence of God."

"So will you write back to your father and tell him exactly what you feel?" asked Alison. David shook his head. "I'll just ignore his letter and hope that he gets the message. There seems little point in writing things that are likely to upset him and my mother."

"You are too kind," smiled Alison.

David got up from his armchair before taking his place next to Alison on the settee. As a result of his affair with Sophie, his marital relations had deteriorated over the past few months. His constant arguments with Amanda hadn't helped the situation, either. Now, though, he was determined to put matters right.

"I'm looking forward to our holiday in Spain," he said dreamily, as he put his arm around Alison. "It will be great to go away with you and the kids."

"Amanda is delighted that we are taking her friend Gemma with us," said Alison, as she stroked David's hand. "You know, I finally think she is beginning to look on you as her real father. She is starting to see Mark for what he really is: a no-good thief who cares for nobody but himself."

"I must learn to be more tolerant when she plays music in her bedroom," said David.

"But I need to tell her to keep the sound down when you are trying to mark homework," replied Alison with a smile. "Then I will be the big baddie sometimes, rather than you."

They kissed tenderly. Mr and Mrs Chambers were back in love again. David began to wonder why he had ever wanted anyone else. Alison was the perfect wife for him. Beautiful, gentle and she believed in the very ideals that he did: a free NHS at the point of need, world peace, social justice and a first-class education system for all.

"You know, I was thinking that we could drop the kids off at my mum's for a couple of hours", said Alison, with a seductive look in her eye. "Then perhaps we could get up to some mischief while we have the place to ourselves."

"Sounds good to me," smiled David. "I'll go and get the car out of the garage."

Lightning Source UK Ltd.
Milton Keynes UK
UKOW02f1828050516

273641UK00001B/3/P